THE JUST BEYOND

MARK TUCKER

a 48fourteen Publishing Trade Paperback

The Just Beyond. Copyright © 2013 by Mark Tucker.

Edited by Matthew Brennan. Cover by www.ravven.com.

Library of Congress Control Number: 2013957176

ISBN-13: 978-1-937546-22-9
ISBN-10: 1-937546-22-5

For Valerie, the love of my life
... and after

Love is a door.

PROLOGUE
Spring

IF A WATCHED POT NEVER boils, then love is much, much worse. Everybody knows that if you watch a cooking pot long enough, it will, in fact, eventually boil. But it is quite possible to exhaust an entire lifetime looking for love and never find it. If you're holding out for *true* love – the kind children dream about, that teenagers think they see everywhere, and that couples who don't have it eventually decide never existed in the first place – the odds are even longer.

But it *does* exist, this magical love, this romantic enchantment everlasting.

Oh, yes.

THEY WERE KIDS ON THE cusp of adulthood, poised at that singular point in life where the indentured servitude of childhood is finally behind and a vista of limitless possibilities lies ahead unspoiled. They had noticed each other, though neither knew it at the time. Michael had looked away quickly – it was never a good idea to stare at a girl who didn't know you, especially if you intended to introduce yourself properly when the opportunity arose. Vicki, frustrated at having wound up in a seat toward the rear of the classroom that limited her view to the back of his head, got up and left the lecture on pretense of using the ladies' room just so she could steal a look on her way back in and determine if he could really, *possibly* have been as teen-crush cute as the memory of her first glimpse claimed. A discrete glance on her way back confirmed that he was.

It started to rain. It was the last period of the day for the University of California at Santa Cruz, and as the storm grew heavier there were audible groans from freshmen and sophomores who were banned from purchasing campus parking permits. Off-site parking was precious, and this particular lecture hall was about as far from the nearest offsite space as any building on campus. Looking back, this combination of circumstances would seem downright conspiratorial, as though the stars themselves had aligned to herd these two lives into collision. And maybe they had. Because of course it would be this way. It *had* to be.

Against his better judgment, Michael manufactured a glance behind him while stretching his arms for the momentary pleasure of one more look. She was breathtaking. When the rain began, he pressed his luck with another go, as though the window behind her would give him the best view of the storm. Their eyes met, and he was *sure* she was on to him. But she didn't scowl, didn't turn up her nose, didn't roll her eyes. She held his gaze a second longer than necessary – at least that's how it felt to him. Then, with a look of embarrassment, she returned to the book on her desk. Or maybe her expression was fear; it could have been interpreted a number of ways. But Michael was young and full of optimism. He smiled.

By the time class ended, the rain had become a downpour. Michael was first to his feet and out the door like The Flash. He flew down three flights of stairs and raced through the storm to the student union building and the little kiosk store inside.

Among the items for sale were cheap collapsible umbrellas, stocked for exactly this purpose: life-savers for students caught off guard by the weather. Michael knew they were there because he had one himself, black with a dark wood handle, bought on a similar occasion his freshman year. He hadn't brought it today because the morning's amiable sky had given not a hint that it might be needed.

He settled on a sky blue model with a blond maple handle, threw a twenty-dollar bill at the bewildered cashier to cover the fifteen dollars on the price tag, and dashed back into the storm toward the lecture hall. He opened the umbrella on the run, hoping she wouldn't wonder how a man equipped with such protection could have gotten so drenched. If he could have seen himself, he would have realized that was a futile wish.

He burst into the building and was overjoyed to find her just coming down the stairs to the first floor. He made a silly attempt to blend into the bone-dry crowd, braced himself against his pounding heart, and approached as she reached the doors.

He had expected, even hoped, that she would eye the storm with distaste. She didn't. In fact, she appeared poised to march out into the rain with Zen-like nonchalance.

"Where'd you park?" Michael hoped the line would seem casual, the sight of his umbrella confirming it as nothing but common chivalry.

Vicki was mildly startled, but as soon as she saw who he was, her eyes went wide and a beautiful smile spread across her face. "Other side of High Street, over by the theater. Why?"

"Me, too. That seems like the closest you can get and count on finding a spot."

"Yes."

He tipped the umbrella toward her in a genteel gesture and smiled. "Want to share?"

It was only there for a fleeting second, that look in her

eyes – surprise, delight, hope, and trepidation all at the same time. But Michael recognized it at once. It was exactly how *he* felt.

"I guess I'd better." Vicki regained herself. "It looks like you bought that thing just for me."

"Huh?"

Vicki pointed to the price tag still dangling prominently from the umbrella handle.

"Aw, *shit*," Michael exclaimed, then cringed in horror at having let out an expletive in his first conversation with a woman he was feeling more infatuated with by the minute.

Vicki giggled. It was the easy, heart-warming laugh of the rarest of souls: a true free spirit.

Michael was falling hard. *Is this what they mean by love at first sight? he thought. Can that really happen?*

And there it was again, his romantic thoughts and feelings mirrored in her eyes. She was looking at the umbrella now, not with playful disparagement but with appreciation, with awe and humility that this handsome gentleman may have *actually* run out and bought an umbrella just so he could escort her to her car. *Dear God*, she thought, shaking her head in protest at the rapid pace at which she seemed to be losing herself. *Be careful, Vicki. Don't read more into this than it is.* But *God, oh God*, she thought, if he really was doing it, if this dreamy, adorable guy was trying to pick her up …

Vicki swallowed. Her mind cried for caution, but her heart was already gone.

THEIR RELATIONSHIP WENT ON FOR two years. Vicki Valentine, the talented art student whose whimsical paintings seemed to come from some rich metaphysical Wonderland, and Michael Chandler, the heartbreakingly compassionate philosophy major and pilgrim of Truth, were never long apart. His gentle thoughtfulness felt to her like a precious gem, and her fairy-like spirit never ceased to surprise and delight him. They were the perfect couple, soul-deep lovers, mutually smitten and complementary in every meaningful way. They had Thanksgiving with Michael's parents, where Vicki was grateful for the way they welcomed her like a daughter, making sure she knew that they saw in her the very image of a perfect mate for their son. Christmas they spent with her father, sharp-minded and funny but in failing health, and Vicki's heart melted at the sight of Michael openly flirting with the elderly ladies at the convalescent home.

Toward the end of that idyllic time, he slept at her apartment more than his own, and it became more and more apparent where their relationship was heading. Marriage seemed inevitable, and soon, provided nothing unexpected occurred. Of course nothing would. Plane crashes and lightning strikes only happened to other people. Cancer never overtook the young.

Graduation was coming, and with it the promise of a blissful life where they would pursue their dreams and grow old together in comfort and grace. The notion that fate might intervene with a different agenda was inconceivable.

They planned the years, unaware that only weeks remained. They knew nothing at all of the impending fire that would leave one of them broken and the other dead.

CHAPTER 1
The One-Way Door

IT WAS DARK BY THE time Michael Chandler pulled in to the carport in front of his lonely San Mateo townhouse on the last normal day of his life.

It was a Friday in late August, a sensuous breeze scenting the San Francisco suburb with a nostalgia of mown grass, sun-warmed honeysuckle, and the distant ocean. A corona of indigo clung tenuously to the western horizon, a last glimmer of sun surrendering to a starry summer night. It was the kind of evening, inherently romantic, that always reawakened the crippling ache he felt over Vicki's death. These sights and smells and the warm air on his skin recalled carefree picnics in Golden Gate Park, intimate dinners at Neptune's looking out over the Bay, sunsets lazily enjoyed from the bluffs above Seacliff Beach. Even now, ten years after her passing, the memories could crush him.

As he rolled to a stop and shut off the headlights, his peripheral vision caught a flicker of motion. Though he couldn't place it, as he climbed out of the car with his two containers of Chinese food from the grocery deli, he was gripped by a prickly feeling that something was not right.

There it was. An unfamiliar glow was faintly visible through his upstairs bedroom window. Not a house light or the power indicator of some electronic device; it was too diffuse for that, the color was wrong. And it was moving.

He wasn't in the habit of leaving things on when he left the townhouse. In fact, he was habitually careful to see that everything but the air conditioner was off. The first explanation that occurred to him was the bedroom television. His morning routine included watching the news while shaving, so it wasn't out of the question. A more sinister notion occurred to him, the possibility that a burglar might be ransacking the place; the twitching glow might be the cold blue shine of a xenon flashlight. The thought stopped him for a beat, but he reasoned that an intruder surely would have heard the car, seen the headlights, and be flying downstairs, out a window or through the back door, not still poking around up there. It must be the TV.

He turned his key and cracked the door open, listening. *Nothing amiss.* He went inside and switched on some lights and the little electric waterfall on the kitchen counter. With some cheer in the place, his apprehension waned. *It's the TV for sure,* he comforted himself. *You're just edgy from missing the flight.*

Dropping his keys and the food near the microwave, he grabbed a beer from the refrigerator and cracked it open on his way upstairs.

He took one step through his bedroom doorway and stiffened, shivers of fear rippling the hair on the back of his neck.

The TV was off. But there, cut into the floor – which he knew to be directly above the kitchen – was a jagged hole about the size of a door. Wisps of dark flame licked its edges as though it had burned its way through, and black mists swirled low over the carpet like a swarm of ghostly cats. Within the cavity, a rough stone stairway descended down and down, seemingly to infinity, the steps themselves faintly illuminated but flanked on either side by utter darkness.

And the steps were not empty. Ascending from the crevice, drifting toward Michael like steam out of a bog, was a translucent female figure. An overpowering beauty made her all the more terrifying, a lithe apparition whose colors seemed inverted like a photo negative, dark skin contrasting against a glowing, light-colored gown, a mane of long hair billowing back over her shoulders. She rippled in unnatural slow motion while leaf-like fragments of her tore away as if blown from a tree, twisting strips of garment, hair, and dark flesh swirling behind her down the stairwell. Yet somehow her form never diminished, as if the torn-off bits regenerated the instant they left her. She was staring directly at him with cold, dark eyes, ascending the last few steps with an aura of condemnation so enveloping that it felt like a physical force.

Michael was completely unaware that his beer had dropped to the carpet and was spreading in a foamy amber pool. He did not believe in ghosts, zombies, or anything of the kind, at least not as portrayed in popular culture. He had always held a firm conviction that if such phenomena existed, they would have long since been documented by serious investigators using unassailable scientific means. But now that very conviction robbed him of any sane context for what he was seeing just six feet away.

THE TIME WOULD COME WHEN Michael, looking back on that fateful day and the events that followed, would wonder whether it could have all started with a seemingly innocuous, almost forgotten gesture he had made ten years before.

The Wal-Mart in San Mateo, California was hiring. Michael Chandler, owner of a fresh bachelor's degree in Philosophy from the University of California at Santa Cruz, sat in the Customer Service lobby outside the manager's office, waiting for an interview. A menial, minimum wage job wasn't what he'd planned when choosing his field in school, but no one had told him that the market for Philosophy majors without a post-graduate degree was virtually nil. His father, who had never been to college, was proud that Michael had gone at all, though a bit perplexed and disappointed that he hadn't majored in something more practical. His mother, whose education had peaked with a community college certificate in Event Planning, tended to block out any perspective that involved worrying about the future.

His professors, counselors, and fellow students had been infected with the blinkered optimism that persists only within academia, expecting every graduate to toss a cap at the end of Commencement and walk straight into a career that made good use of their degree. But nine months of searching had turned up no calls for a Philosophy B.A. outside the clergy. Even of those, none paid enough to live on without a second job, and he didn't meet some of the requirements anyway. Not that it mattered. Michael was not impious, but he was no fan of organized religion, having sought fervently but unsuccessfully throughout his youth for a denomination whose message seemed both coherent and genuine. Career-wise that frustration now proved fatal, because his fundamental earnestness would defeat any hope of prospering in an environment toward which he held such misgivings.

And so it was that Michael Chandler, twenty-three years old with mounting disillusion, found himself frostbitten by reality and applying for anything, anything at all, that could pay for canned food, store brand necessities, and his one-room apartment's rent. The remains of his student loan would run out soon, along with the short lease his parents had helped fund as a bridge between graduation and employment.

A commotion erupted in front of a stuffed animal display at the end of a nearby aisle, the kind of intentionally misplaced set-up designed to inspire impulse buying in mothers who had no intention of going near the actual toy section. Attention drawn, Michael looked up from the travel magazine he had been flipping through to see what was going on.

A young woman was engaged in an animated exchange with her son. She was homespun pretty, the kind of girl a seedy club crawler would probably pass up but whose type of unvarnished genuineness Michael had always found appealing. She looked roughly his age, younger with the exception of her life-worn eyes, and at first Michael thought she might be the boy's aunt. But aunts can afford to spoil. Mothers must be practical, responsible, a model of long-term values like discipline and thrift. Aunts could treat every encounter as a special occasion, whereas motherhood was a career, a joy when viewed from well-rested detachment, but at the minute-to-minute level a physical and emotional grind that could wear down even the most doting. All the more so for a struggling single mom; Michael's bachelor eyes had registered the absence of a wedding ring, and the fray of her jeans looked the result of honest wear and not the pretentious factory-inscribed damage that had inexplicably become *haute couture*.

"*One*," she rasped tightly to the boy, who looked to be six or seven years old. He was holding a pair of stuffed animals: a cushy, football-sized turtle with a pink and blue checkerboard shell and a small blue cow of the dubious quality found in coin-op crane machines. "Just pick one so we can pay for this stuff and get back home."

The boy was crying, not the kind of incessant wail that could drive patrons to the other side of the store but rather a soft whimper of agonized helplessness. "I can't decide." His little voice quivered. "The turtle's my favorite, but the cow is *sad*. She *needs* me."

"Sad? Why is she sad?" the mother inquired, choosing not to question how he could tell the cow's gender, let alone its state of mind.

"She thinks no one will pick her."

"Oh, honey, someone will pick her. She's sweet and pretty and I'm sure some little girl or boy will give her a nice home. She won't sit there for long."

"They won't," the boy lamented. "Nobody wants cows. She's been waiting a long time, she's all dusty!" He used one free finger to stroke the cow's head with motherly tenderness. "I just want her to feel loved."

"Then put the turtle back." His mother sighed in frustration. "We can't afford both. We've talked about this."

The boy said nothing. For a moment, his lips trembled, then he dropped his gaze to the floor and began shaking with a quiet sob that wrenched Michael to the core. Interview or not, he could no longer stand by.

"Hi," Michael greeted her as he approached. "Sorry, I couldn't help noticing." The mother bristled at this intrusion, but Michael sank to one knee, eye-level with the boy, and continued. "I had that same turtle when I was a kid. Cool, isn't it?"

The boy sniffed, nodding weakly. "You wanna pet him?"

"Sure!" Michael cradled the toy close to his chest and combed his fingers through the lush, improbably-colored fur. "So soft," he admired. "Smart, too. I called mine Simon, you know, like the Chipmunk."

The boy smiled, then sobered as he eyed the cheaply made, nondescript little cow. "But *she* needs a family, too."

Michael regarded the two stuffed animals. He had to admit that the boy was probably right. On a Christmas list scale that included furry pastel turtles, cheap featureless cows were just about off the chart at the opposite end. It was blue, that was something, but not nearly enough to overcome its basic lack of appeal.

Michael returned the turtle and stood back up, addressing the young mother quietly.

"That is one thoughtful little feller you have there. How about I spring for the cow? If it's all right with you, of course."

"No," she replied with conviction. "He has to learn that you can't have everything in life."

"Yeah, I know." Michael leaned even closer and did his best to keep the boy from hearing. "Look, I can see you're a wonderful mother and I know it's none of my business. But that heartfelt compassion your son has – especially at his age

– that's precious, and it seems worth nurturing. The world could use more of it, that's for sure." He smiled warmly. "Let me help just this once. It'll make me feel like I did my good deed for the day."

"I appreciate the kindness." The woman softened. "You're very sweet. But we have rules, and I don't want him expecting some generous stranger to pop up every time he wants something we can't afford."

Michael pursed his lips for a moment, casting about for a way to reward the little trooper without appearing to challenge the young mother's authority or judgment. *I could buy it myself*, he pondered. *Promise to take it home, feed it ice cream every day and leave the TV on so it can watch cartoons while I'm at work. No, scratch that. I'll say I'm going to take it by the hospital or an orphanage and make sure it goes to some kid who's absolutely thrilled to have it.*

That wasn't right either. It might mollify the boy in the short run, but Michael had been serious about wanting to reinforce the little guy's priceless magnanimity. The best way to do that was to send him home with a durable, tangible reminder. And suddenly, an approach occurred to him that felt like just the right touch.

Shielding the boy's view, he pried open his wallet without removing it from his pocket and fished out the lone twenty-dollar bill.

"All right," he said. "You're his mom and you know best. But take it anyway." He pressed the money gently into her hand, so unexpectedly that she closed her fingers around it by reflex.

As their hands touched, Michael felt an unexpected jolt. It had been almost a year since the loss of Vicki, and his romantic faculties had lain so dormant that their reawakening startled him. He thought he saw something similar flash across the woman's face, and his clasp lingered a moment longer than necessary. *Should I just ask her out now? At least get her phone number?*

But he wasn't ready. His fingers released, and the spell

was broken.

"If you change your mind," he continued, "you can explain however you think best. If not, just use it for something else. Like school supplies. Or maybe caramel apples at the park."

"I can't ..." She shook her head, motioning to give the money back, but Michael was already ten steps away. "Sorry — appointment," he called pleasantly over his shoulder. "It was nice meeting you." And with that he ducked into the men's room to seal the transaction beyond her reach.

He gave his empty wallet a wistful look. He hadn't eaten all day, having planned to grab something at the store's lunch counter after his interview. But it wasn't worth dwelling on; he had simply done what he had felt compelled to do.

After what seemed a safe length of time, Michael emerged back into the lobby and returned to his seat. The woman and her son were now in the checkout line. The turtle was nowhere to be seen; the boy hovered at his mother's side clutching only the cow. *She didn't do it*, he thought and pursed his lips. *And that little bugger took the high road anyway*. He buried his gaze in a magazine to stifle the tickle in his tear ducts.

A minute later, his peripheral vision caught something that made him look up. With only one customer in front of them, the young mother suddenly broke out from the checkout line with her son in tow. They hurried back to the toy display, both grinning. The boy reached for the turtle and rocked it tightly with the little cow against his chest.

"Thank you, Mama!" he cried excitedly.

"I love you." She smiled.

MICHAEL WAS THE LAST OF three people Wal-Mart hired that day for shelf-stocking positions, despite concerns that a college graduate might leave for a better job before the company's training investment was recouped. Such worries were needless. He was a loyal employee and a good stocker right from the start, impeccable in attendance and efficient in his work.

But he proved extraordinary in a role only peripheral to his position: helping customers who approached him in the aisles. Michael took this duty seriously, going so far as to study Spanish on his own initiative so he could serve native speakers better. It took only six months for management to note the pattern of glowing feedback from patrons so appreciative that they were inspired to inform his superiors. Recognizing his potential, the regional manager created a special "Customer Advocate" position just for Michael, freeing him to roam the store with the sole responsibility of seeking opportunities to create goodwill.

Two years later, they gave him supervisory duties over the stocking crew on his shifts, mostly to facilitate a salary and benefits package with occasional business travel that the company's policies could not otherwise support. From a practical standpoint, that hadn't worked out so well. He won his subordinates' adoration by showering them with praise and encouragement, but he was no good at managing poor performance. Michael's empathy ran deep, and he was pathologically accommodating of excuses for substandard work, whether due to personal problems, frequent illness, or even innate incompetence. He always gave people the benefit of the doubt, assuming they were doing the best they could under the circumstances, and he believed it was pointless or even "wrong" to demand more.

Inevitably, his humanistic style sometimes ran afoul of company standards, and there were times when Michael's supervisory conduct seemed incompatible with a long term Wal-Mart career. But no one doubted his good intentions, and as a person he was as highly regarded by company officials as by his co-workers and customers. In the end, with some quiet dilution of his management responsibilities and staunch advocacy by those who felt his value justified some flexibility, Michael kept his job.

And for the remainder of his post-college decade, so things stayed.

IT WAS JUST AFTER 6:00 P.M. on that August Friday, a mere two hours before Michael Chandler would encounter an apparition in his rented townhouse that would disrupt his life forever. With a sole exception, the Wal-Mart night staff had taken the store over from the day crew. Michael alone had stayed past the end of his shift to put his workload in order ahead of a week's vacation. He hadn't fully succeeded – there were two customer calls and a report for Corporate he had run out of time for – but if he didn't leave soon he would risk missing his 7:55 flight.

He was feeding bills into the break room vending machine when he heard heavy footsteps and then the voice of Carl Adams, his first real friend at the store. Carl was the night produce manager, but they had been hired the same day and come up together through the shelf stocking ranks. They seemed nothing alike. Carl was a large, coarse high school football star whose climb to management was remarkable for a senior-year dropout. His keenness toward money and the material couldn't have been further from Michael's view of the world. What linked them was a shared optimistic gentleness at heart, and they had hit it off immediately, establishing a friendship that had persisted through the years. But like all of Michael's "friendships," in fact all of his relationships since Vicki, it had never reached the level of intimacy required to call it "close." As well-liked as he was, no one in the world truly understood Michael Chandler. He never let them near enough.

"Can I have some?" Carl was saying, leering at the wad

of bills protruding obscenely from Michael's wallet, five or six hundred dollars by the look.

"Vacation stash," Michael explained, stuffing a can of Coke and pack of chewing gum into a knapsack already crammed tight with clothing and travel necessities. "I'm flying down to see that Beatles Reunion thing at the Hollywood Bowl."

"Beatles Reunion? Didn't that just run for two nights at the Graham Auditorium right in San Fran? Why go all the way to L.A.?"

"Ever been there?" Michael zipped and shouldered the pack. "The Beatles' 1964 gig at the Hollywood Bowl was one of the greatest concerts of all time, and to me, it's the perfect place. It's going to be *electric*. Both of the living Beatles up there with Julian Lennon and Ralph Castelli, right under the night sky, movie stars in the audience ... *and* it's the last show of the tour. Even the band will be stoked." Michael beamed. "It's the concert of a lifetime, man. I paid fifty bucks to join a fan club just so I could buy tickets on pre-sale. It worked, too. I was able to get two seats right in the middle, just five rows back from the stage. I figure that if you're going to do something like this at all, you might as well go all the way."

"Pffft," Carl dismissed, the logic seeming to escape him. Coming from Michael Chandler, it shouldn't have surprised him at all.

MICHAEL WAS MAKING HIS WAY through the employee parking area at a brisk pace when he noticed someone from the day shift fretting under the hood of his car. It wasn't a friend – Michael didn't know the man's name – but the face was familiar, belonging to a cashier he recalled waving to in passing from time to time.

"Michael! Thank God," the man called in a strained voice. "Do you know anything about cars?"

"Not really," Michael replied, approaching. "What's the problem? Oh, and," he stretched out his hand and clasped the other's briefly, "I've seen you around, but I apologize for not knowing your name."

"Steve Shelby," the man replied. "This goddamn thing won't start, and I've got to pick up my kids!" The man's anguish was palpable. "It's not the battery, it's turning over fine. It just won't start. Could you just take a look and see if you see anything?"

Michael obeyed just to be courteous, but his untrained eye was no better than Shelby's. "Nothing obvious, but that doesn't mean anything. I'm not much of a car guy."

"Damnit." Shelby threw up his hands. "My wife is going to kill me. She's on graveyard as a police dispatcher so I have to pick up the kids from daycare, and they close at seven o'clock. The thing is ..." Shelby made a face like a dog that knows it's peed on the carpet. "I've been late a few times, totally my fault. Once in a while, when I could get out of here a little early, I used to try and squeeze in nine holes of pitch-and-putt at McInnis Park on the way home. The last time I was late, the daycare lady said if it happened again, no matter what the reason, she would kick us out. I've gone hell-for-leather to be on time every day since then. And now this crap." Shelby shook his head bitterly. "I know it's no picnic running a daycare – that lady has the patience of a saint. But she's never going to believe me and I don't think it would make any difference if she did." His eyes moistened. "It took us so long to find a place good enough to leave them in good conscience. My wife is going to be absolutely furious."

"It's not your fault your car won't start," Michael comforted. "I'm sure she'll understand that."

"It won't matter. I know my wife. She'll say today may not have been my fault, but if I hadn't golfed all those times, we wouldn't be at the end of the rope in the first place. She'll say I should have taken better care of the car. She'll say I don't give a damn about the kids." Shelby looked down, utterly dejected. "I am *so friggin' stupid*!"

"How far is the daycare?" Michael asked softly.

"San Rafael. That's where we live. Clear on the other side of San Francisco."

Michael stood silent for one full minute, the joy that had buffeted him all week now draining like sand from a punctured bag. He could suggest a taxi, but with less than an hour to get to San Rafael, a cab's transit time from the point of dispatch might be enough to put a timely arrival out of reach. He looked around them. The shift change was complete and the employee section of the lot was devoid of human activity. The distraught father's options for salvation were down to exactly one.

"I'll take you," Michael said.

Shelby gasped. "You will?"

"Sure," Michael confirmed, trying to smile through his grief at the realization that he was putting his attendance at the "concert of a lifetime" in jeopardy. "Let's go. I think we can make seven, but we'll have to hurry."

THE SHELBY CHILDREN, A SEVEN-YEAR-OLD girl and five-year-old boy, fell upon their father as though it were Christmas and they hadn't seen him in a year. Even the daycare matron smiled and waved from the doorway as they piled into Michael's old blue Saturn sedan. Traffic had crawled across the Golden Gate Bridge, and for a while their prospects of beating the clock had looked dim. But things had cleared up around Sausalito, and they pulled in to the daycare with eight minutes to spare. *Crisis defused.*

Steve Shelby's exuberance at having avoided catastrophe was palpable, and the glow of simple family affection put a wide smile even on Michael's face. This seemed to embolden Shelby to voice a further request.

"I hate to ask, man, but … do you think it would be okay to make a quick stop at the Safeway? It's on the way to our house. We do our shopping on Saturdays, and it's kind of a tradition to get that deli Chinese on Friday nights."

"Happy to," Michael replied. "Maybe I'll get some for me." He was getting hungry now that Shelby mentioned it, but he would have obliged anyway; a fifteen-minute detour wasn't going to worsen his concert situation. In any event, by this time he was feeling more positive about his travel dilemma. He had rationalized that since the show wouldn't start until around nine o'clock the following evening, there should be plenty of time for the airline to squeeze him onto another flight. If it meant taking a taxi straight from LAX to the venue and possibly losing his rental car, hotel reservation, or both, he would deal with it. This was just the sort of contingency his travel cash was meant to insure against. For that matter, if push came to shove, he could simply drive the six hours to Los Angeles, leaving the Bay as late as tomorrow afternoon. He would be all right.

The Safeway parking lot was almost full to capacity, but as they wove through the aisles looking for an opening, the rear lights suddenly lit up on an SUV occupying an end space near the store entrance right in front of them. Michael braked and the vehicle slowly backed out, two large dogs panting through the window.

"Perfect!" Shelby exclaimed, then frowned in puzzlement as Michael drove past the parking space, trailing the SUV as it headed away.

"Hey! There was a spot right where this guy pulled out, didn't you see?"

"Yeah, I leave those for people who need them. I'm in perfectly good health, I'm not going to take a spot from some eighty-year-old woman who really needs it."

"That's what those handicapped spaces are for." Shelby pointed to three empty slots in the next row over painted with the blue and white wheelchair icon.

"Not everybody who has trouble walking has a handi-capped sticker. It's not just old ladies, it could be somebody with the flu. Or some ex-jock with bad knees and a macho complex. Or someone who's down here picking up Advil because they overdid it in the garden and their back is killing them."

"What are the chances," Shelby challenged incredu-lously, "that out of all the possibilities, one of those people is going to be the very next car to pass that spot?"

"Not high, but that's not the point. It's not going to kill me to walk an extra fifty feet on the off-chance." He glanced at the back seat. "But you guys don't have to. Here, I'll stop at the curb and you three can jump out while I park."

"No, no, no," Shelby protested. "We'll walk. I was just saying."

On their next pass, a car toward the end of the aisle vacated its spot and drove off as Michael slipped in.

"Okay, kids," Shelby prompted cheerily as they unfas-tened their seat belts. "What are we having tonight?"

AS MICHAEL CHANDLER STOOD PATIENTLY near the Safeway deli holding two warm boxes of Chinese takeout and waiting for the Shelbys, back in San Francisco a dark drama was unfolding in an office suite on the 39th floor of a deserted high-rise.

"All right, son. You asked for this meeting. What have you got?" Eldridge Raymore sat behind his desk in a high-backed leather chair and poured himself a shot of Southern Comfort. His posture was relaxed, dark eyes boring through the gloom illuminated by a single Tiffany desk lamp. He was a handsome and imposing figure despite his sixty-two years, with a full head of neatly-cropped brown hair graying at the temples and deep, rapturous facial features complimented by an athletic frame in a tailored Italian suit. His demeanor was calm, measured, and charming. Yet there was a subtle undercurrent of menace, the manner of a man skilled at influencing through graciousness but unhesitant to employ less savory methods should the circumstance arise.

"A lot of things." Eldridge Raymore Jr., best known by his truncated middle name, Sid, chose to stand even though his father gestured toward a stylish guest chair at the front of the desk. Aside from the pair of cultivated "campaign aides" with vaguely defined responsibilities standing silent and disinterested near the office door, they were alone.

He consulted the file folder he was carrying with a grim look. "For starters, the campaign account is missing almost $2 million. The rules are clear on this, we won't be able to skirt around it at filing time. Can you tell me where that went?"

"Your role does not extend to auditing the finances," the older man said. "Leave that to Bernie. He's good at it." He sipped his drink.

"My role is giving legal advice," his son returned. "Failure to document the lawful expenditure of campaign contributions accepted under tax-favored conditions is a federal offense. And two million is way too much to explain away as carelessness or ignorance."

"That is Bernie's business," the elder Raymore repeated sharply. "By the time filings are due, it will all be neatened up and accounted for. There's nothing to worry about."

"Do you know where that money went?" Sid pressed.

"I can't personally keep track of every little expense. Running for governor bleeds cash. Ad collateral, facilities, staff pay, including your rather generous retainer, I might add," the father stabbed pointedly. "You have to be nimble and hit opportunities on the spur of the moment. You can't always get receipts and make ledger entries as you go. You hesitate in this game, you lose." He smiled. "It will be clean and perfectly documented when the time comes. That's what

Bernie is for. He takes good care of things."

Sid Raymore pursed his lips. "Bernie Blenheim is a convicted felon who spent three years in the Ohio state pen for corporate tax fraud. I suppose you knew nothing about that."

"I *do* know. I also know that that was fifteen years ago and that he hasn't had so much as a parking ticket since." The father's countenance furrowed and his words came out carefully measured. "What I want to know is what the hell nonsense you've been wasting staff time on to scrape up something as obscure and irrelevant as that."

"It's not going to seem irrelevant if the media gets it." Sid returned his father's bloodless smile. "It probably wouldn't make or break you by itself. But it's not by itself. Not by a long shot."

Candidate Raymore leaned forward darkly. "I think it's time you told me exactly what you're getting at."

Sid Raymore sucked in a galvanizing breath. "I found one ledger, at least, that seems to have been kept meticulously up to date. Not a paper file, just an Excel spreadsheet with a nearly bulletproof password, which I arranged for a discreet forensic expert to crack. Over the past few weeks, I've had a very intimate relationship with that file. I couldn't decipher all of it, but I did figure out a few of the entries. One of them associates a ten thousand dollar figure with Norman Tuggs, who happens to be the Assistant Chief of the San Mateo Police. No doubt his support helps to make sure the PD plays nice with your 'creative' business affairs. But just to be sure, I checked your bank records courtesy of the Power of Attorney I had you sign when I joined the campaign. Sure enough, a ten thousand dollar debit has been fed into some unidentified account every month for years. Is that the kind of thing the missing funds are paying for?"

"You have no right getting into my private records," the elder fumed. "For your information, Norm Tuggs is a close friend of mine. And that payment is a contribution to the police charity that provides juveniles with alternatives to incarceration."

"Really?" His son could barely restrain a smirk. "Then why not make it public? Wouldn't a generous contribution to a noble charity enhance your image?"

"I don't answer to you." Eldridge Raymore leaned forward and pierced his son with an icy glare. His tone was methodical and deliberate. "Now, I have patiently addressed every issue you have raised. Is there anything else? If so, spill it in a hurry. I've got better things to do."

"Here's another entry." Sid quickly consulted his file. "This one appears to mention the AFL-CIO and Proposition 2, which happens to be the ballot measure banning mandatory union membership. I interpret it as 'support me and I will make sure Prop 2 never sees the light of day.' As if you had personal control over the vote. What a coup! You didn't even have to buy them, just make promises you'll have no power to keep even if you win."

This time the older man made no attempt to explain the allegation away. "Anything else?" he said in a low, even tone, his features inscrutable in the dimness.

Sid took a deep breath. "Nine years ago, you were brought in by the police for questioning in connection with racketeering activities down at the port. Same thing two years later. Both times, you were released very quickly for lack of evidence, much to the consternation of the investigating officers. It's not public record because you were never subpoenaed or charged. But if it were ever disclosed, especially with all this other stuff, it would paint a rather unflattering picture."

"All right, Sid." The father's tone was quiet, deliberate, and paralyzing. "You are off the campaign staff as of midnight tonight. We'll tell the press you had some private life issues, which is not untrue." He smiled dimly. "But you had best remember – and I mean, you had god damned well better remember – that this conversation, and everything in that folder, is protected by attorney-client privilege. You are going to lay that thing down on my desk, you are going to walk away and go back to your practice, and you are going to respect the confidence under which you have been employed as my election counsel."

"No." Sid Raymore shook his head, but his tone was conciliatory and his face had lost its defiant affect. "I don't want to ruin your life, Dad. We've never seen things the same way and we never will. But ..." The beginnings of tears started to pool at the corners of his eyes. "You're my *dad*. You're the only father I have." Sid sniffed and straightened himself. "I didn't come here tonight to destroy you. I just want you to leave the race. I can't countenance you getting into public office knowing what I know. It's been eating me so bad I've barely been able to sleep. But if you drop out – I'll wait till Monday so you have time to think it over – I will turn my back on this and never mention these issues again."

"That," his father said testily, "is not going to happen. And you are going to stay out of it regardless. If you breathe one word of this outside this room, you will be in violation of your fiduciary oath. Hell, I could have you arrested right now for accessing my accounts using a false pretense. You're going to get smart about this, or I'll have you disbarred in a heartbeat. Your charmed life will be over."

Did his father really have that kind of influence with the State Bar? Sid shuddered. He couldn't rule it out. But having come this far, he wasn't about to drop the matter.

"I believe I could make a case that there's no privilege violation under the crime-fraud exception," he challenged wryly. "And I doubt I'd be prosecuted for any of this once the scandal was revealed. But it doesn't matter. I'm prepared to lose my license or even serve time. I don't think it would happen, I don't believe a jury would treat me too harshly under the circumstances. But it doesn't matter, like I said." Sid's eyes were pleading now. "*Please*, Dad. Just drop out of the race and go back to your ... your ... whatever your business is."

"And what do you think you can do about it if I don't?"

"If you don't," Sid said, his voice beginning to crack and his legs to shake. "If you do not decide by Monday to call things off, then on Tuesday morning I will deliver copies of this file to the Attorney General, the state Party Chair, and the publisher of the *San Francisco Chronicle*."

Ridge Raymore's face became a nuclear mushroom cloud. "This talk is over." He shot a commanding glance toward the two men that had been lurking all this time in silence.

Sid panicked. "What, now you're going to have your goons work me over like some junk dealer skimming off the take?"

There was no reply. His father's glare was so terrifying now that it drained Sid of all courage and noble intent. He made for the door but the enforcers blocked him, the shorter one leering like a dog about to be thrown a raw steak.

"No!" Sid screamed. "Dad, no!!"

The file folder flew, its contents scattering like bird feathers in a shotgun blast. Eldridge Raymore drained his shot glass and poured again.

MICHAEL STOOD FROZEN BEFORE THE manifestation in his bedroom: the entity that could not exist standing on stairs that couldn't be there. Though Michael could feel himself mentally unraveling and was shocked to the core, he never had the slightest doubt that the apparition – this horrifying, impossible being coming at him from a hellish hole in his bedroom floor – was real. Dreams could seem very real, leaving residual elation or, more commonly, trauma, that persisted well past waking. But the reverse was not true. Pinch-test cliché aside, no mentally-sound person ever mistook reality for a dream. And it was a clear, terrifying reality that gripped Michael now, so powerfully that he was afraid his pounding heart might literally burst and kill him.

As the figure topped the steps, she raised her arm and pointed a finger at Michael's chest, fixing him with a black gaze so terrible that it, too, threatened to kill him outright.

Her voice threatened his sanity, a chorus of dark, female tones out of phase with each other like a stadium echo, some clear and commanding, others obscure and distorted as though passing through water or reverberating off canyon walls, a cacophony of shifting, overlapping words that seemed to come from the figure, the stairwell, the hall behind him, the rooms downstairs, the night beyond his windows, the private, fear-soaked chambers inside his head.

"Michael Chandler," declared the hideous choir: "BY THE TIMELESS ARE YOU BOUND THIS NIGHT TO LAURIA."

Michael ran.

CHAPTER 2
The Rabbit Run

"DAMN YOU, BURKO!" ELDRIDGE RAYMORE bellowed at the man sitting beside him in the black, tinted-window Lincoln Navigator. "If he dies, I swear to God ..."

The driver looked ashen. His voice shook. "We didn't mean to, you gotta believe that! We didn't do nothing worse than usual, I swear!"

"Well this is the first time it caused a heart attack, you shit for brains! How do you explain that?"

For a long moment, John Burko stared silently at the road ahead, terrified. Finally he said, quiet but tense, "I dunno, Mr. Raymore. He must have had a weak heart or something. I'm telling you, we just smacked him around like you said. No way he should be like this."

Raymore shot a glance toward the back seat. "How is he?"

The man in the back, stoic but grim, looked back into the cargo area. "The same. Well, breathing, but kinda shallow now."

Raymore glared back at the driver. "Step on it, you moron! If he dies before we get to Dr. Firello, there won't be enough of you left for your wife to bury!"

"It ain't my fault!" Burko pleaded. "And anyway, why me? Why you laying this all on me? What about Chaz?"

"Shut up, Burk!" the man in the back seat yelled. "All I

did was hold him. You're the one that messed him up."

"Fuck you!" Burko squealed.

"Just … get … there," Raymore said with a tone whose vitriol was giving way to worried desperation.

The pale driver laid on the gas.

MICHAEL FLEW DOWN THE STEPS virtually without touching them. He grabbed his keys off the kitchen counter, yanked open the front door without bothering to close it and bolted to his car. For what seemed like forever, he fumbled his keys frantically against the car door lock. When at last he got inside, he again jammed his key repeatedly against the ignition, unable to slow down or overcome the shaking that made aiming impossible, glancing reflexively at the townhouse's front door just steps away, afraid both to look and not to, gripped with terror that the horrible dark thing was going to emerge any second now, shatter the car window glass, and bore its dead black finger right through his breastbone.

Then suddenly the key was in, and Michael jerked the car to life, screeched back out of his carport space, and tore out of the parking lot, heading he did not know where, caring only that it was away.

His mind raced. What could he do? Call the police? Somehow he felt certain that if he called the authorities, when they inspected his bedroom the stair-hole would be gone, the mist dissipated, no shimmering specter waiting patiently for a handcuffed ride to jail. On those ghost-hunter shows, you never saw the police called in, let alone coming away with evidence bags full of ectoplasm, disembodied audio that could be spectrally analyzed against the human voice, photographs of apparitions to be compared with living pictures of the deceased, or corroboration of anything else that could not be naturally explained. It didn't work that way.

His parents ... He punched their number into his cell phone down to the last two digits, then snapped it shut, grateful for once for his persistent procrastination against setting up speed dial. The futility of involving them, he realized, was clear. His mother would panic, devastated, running about uselessly and on the verge of a nervous breakdown at the prospect of losing another son. With his father it would be straightforward, but no more helpful. George Chandler would simply not believe him. He would demand to know what drugs Michael was on, or at least an explanation of how he may have injured his head, and no matter what Michael said, his dad would maintain the conviction that these were the only possible causes. It wouldn't make things better; all it would do was inject heartache and trouble into their deservedly comfortable lives.

Briefly, he entertained the thought of not telling them, just showing up and asking if he could stay with them for a few days. But that wouldn't solve anything either. They would want to know why, they would speculate worriedly about all manner of catastrophic scenarios, and ultimately, since he could not live there forever, it would amount to nothing more than a temporary postponement of the inevitable. In any event, what Michael needed now was not just a safe resting place but an objective and reliable ear, someone to whom he could unburden himself without creating turmoil, or being patronized, or thought insane.

Friends? In his mind, Michael ran methodically through the names of those he considered close enough to approach with this. Carl Adams, his best friend at Wal-Mart? Carl would never take this seriously and, even if he was supportive, Michael couldn't imagine him offering any useful counsel. His boss, Gene Faraday? That thought forced a grim chuckle. It didn't take genius to predict the impact on his career if he admitted to management that he had fled from some ghoul coming out of a hole in his bedroom floor.

As he flipped through his mental Rolodex, it became clear that all of his friends – none of whom, he reflected sadly, were all that intimate – were either coworkers, too practical to take him at his word, or too socially distant to risk confiding in, at least with something as mad and incendiary as this.

He suddenly wondered, surprised as always by the sharp pang in his stomach whenever his thoughts turned in this direction, whether it would have been appropriate to call Max if he had been alive. It was a hard question to answer because, when his younger brother was alive, they had not been particularly close. Two years apart was close enough in age to fuel competition, and from the day Max took his first steps until he was senselessly murdered sixteen years later, sibling rivalry had indeed coalesced into a defining core of their relationship.

It wasn't just age, either. Max and Michael were different in ways so fundamental that each of them had come to view the other as constitutionally inferior. Michael was gentle, bookish, good-natured, openly and unabashedly emotional. Max was a fighter. He was no less cerebral or sensitive than his brother, but he held his feelings very close to the vest, with the result that, periodically and inevitably, they escaped in brief bursts of resentment and rage, and this caused him trouble with both teachers and classmates. His grades suffered from bouts of half effort due to disdain toward a teacher or contempt for a particular piece of work, invariably traceable to some specific incident in which Max felt he had been wronged. As for schoolmates, it was a narrow thing that he never managed to get expelled for any of the physical confrontations in which he was involved, often leaving him visibly battered. But never as severely as his opponent. No one who crossed Max ever did so twice.

And yet, Michael recalled clearly, he had never for a minute doubted that Max would eventually grow out of it, come to terms with himself and his potential, and channel that formidable energy and resolve into an accomplished life. There were signs all along. Max was brilliant when he chose to be, protective of animals, respectful of girls, and an undisputed athletic star, making the varsity football team as a sophomore where, according to the sports beat writer for the local newspaper, he played linebacker "like a tactical nuke".

Then all of a sudden, in the spring of that year, just months after helping the school win the state football tournament, he was gone. Killed by a stranger for no reason except being in the wrong place at the wrong time, a life of promise snapped off at the base, leaving Michael Chandler an only child, his mother in the hospital as a pitiful wreck, and his stolid, practical father welling up with the only tears Michael would ever see him cry.

He knew the answer. A mature, adult Max would have been a staunch ally, bound to Michael by shared experience and a unique mutual understanding. He would have been strong, defiant, fearless.

Michael could see that Max in his mind's eye, the man his brother would have grown into, could feel his fiery gaze and hear his boldly comforting voice: "Get the car, Mikey. Let's go shove that thing right back down the stairs."

But Max was not there. He was gone forever, his last vestige the gaping wound his mother could only block out and echoes of that same wound in his dad and brother. It did what almost nothing else could: it made Michael angry. For a moment, the bitterness was so intense that it threatened to consume him, narrowing his vision, tightening his grip on the steering wheel so powerfully that his hands began to go numb. Then he stopped, let out his breath, blinked the tears out of his eyes, and willed the unbidden monster back to its quiet cell in the dungeons of his memory, the dark place where he kept it locked away so its grief and rage would not incapacitate him. After another minute it stirred no more, and the world was returned – not to normal, but to the brooding surreality this night had taken on.

And with that separation, taking some comfort in the fact that nothing seemed to be following him and nothing threatening had occurred since he had bolted from the scene, Michael was at last free to ponder analytically what had happened. The stairway, extending downward past the edge of perception, had struck him at the time as a passage from Hell. That, he knew, was nothing but a knee-jerk impression; it might just as well lead to another dimension, if they existed, or to another part of the universe through a cosmic wrinkle, or to some other terminus the nature of which he was totally ignorant. For that matter, it may literally have stretched to infinity. He tried to recall its features and thought it had appeared to be made of rough-hewn stone. That might or might not be an indication of ancient origin. What of the dark mists? For this he had no insight except that they had seemed to emanate from the vacant blackness on both sides of the stairs. And what were those voids, anyway? Dimensional barriers? Patches of outer space so remote they were beyond even a flicker of starlight? The very boundaries of reality?

And then it dawned on him, not merely who he needed to talk to, but why. And he realized with surprise that he had not been driving aimlessly. Guided by his subconscious, he had all along been taking the most expeditious route toward the one person who truly might be able to help him, a one-of-a-kind font of understanding, insight, and hope.

Danny Hendrick.

DAN HENDRICK WAS A TENURED professor of theoretical physics at Boston University, well known and respected within his field, and the author of two books that had been equally well received by his peers and by the lay public toward whom they were aimed. But in a previous life, specifically his adolescence in San Mateo, California, he had been Michael Chandler's best friend.

They had parted ways after high school, Michael to Santa Cruz and Danny to Stanford. Michael might have joined him there – though Michael's SAT scores were borderline – except that his parents could not afford tuition at a world-renowned private college. Scholarships had relieved Danny of that obstacle. They had kept up with each other, albeit less as time went by, until Danny had earned his doctorate and accepted a position with the highest bidder on the other side of the country.

Dan was a certified genius, whose insights into string theory and quantum mechanics inspired both admiration and envy in his colleagues. Even in high school, Michael and Dan had spent many an evening circling San Francisco on the Embarcadero expressway, discussing the latest in physics from the professional journals Dan was reading even then.

Notably, for all his academic prowess and analytical proficiency, Dan was an unwavering Christian. His mother had been raised a Southern Baptist in Tuscaloosa, Alabama, and his father's parents had moved west bearing the same tradition from Mississippi. Inheriting their faith, he had nonetheless never felt nor understood evangelical objections to modern science. He found it absurd to interpret the Bible as contradictory to principles like natural selection, the genetic basis of homosexuality, and the Big Bang. To Dan Hendrick, science was nothing less than a revelation of the exhilarating magnificence of God. And clerical authorities opposed to this view were guilty of the same blind hubris as their ideological forebears who had burned Giordano Bruno at the stake and forced Galileo, under threat of torture, to renounce his preposterous assertion that the earth orbits around the sun.

Yet Dan was equally defensive of religion. "Science can say a lot about the universe, the nature of it, the way it physically started, how it might end, and maybe even what came before," he liked to say. "It can explain almost everything that exists. But it can't answer the most fundamental question: *why should there be anything at all?"*

Nor could Michael. But this kind of dialogue, he realized with the first glimmer of hope he had felt since fleeing the house, was exactly what he needed. Dan was firmly grounded in both the empirical and the metaphysical, with a clear and confident vision of their intersection, of what was real and what was possible, what was established by unassailable evidence and what could be rationally speculated despite its absence. What was more, perhaps more important than anything else, he knew that Dan would listen. He might have an answer – Michael believed he could, desperately hoped he did – or he might be just as perplexed as Michael. But he could count on Dan Hendrick sitting down, focusing his full, sharp attention on Michael, and taking every word at face value. And the comfort of that prospect washed through Michael like the first warm wave of intoxication from a stiff drink, and he was beyond thankful that if nothing else in the world right now, at least he had someone like Dan to go to with this overwhelming and shatteringly lonely quandary.

There was just one problem. Boston University was about as far away as you could get from the California coast, and Michael did not know Dan's telephone number. Their correspondence had degenerated to sporadic emails over the past few years, and he could not recall the number, even if it hadn't changed by now. So he was heading for the home of Dan's parents, the house Dan had grown up in and where they had gathered once a week with the dozen other boys that made up the Cub Scout troop Mrs. Hendrick had led as Den Mother. He knew it was late, and he hated to bother them, but Michael was sure Dan's mom would be only too happy to reconnect Dan with the friend she had sometimes referred to as "my other son."

With this destination resolved, Michael's thoughts returned to analysis of the townhouse incident, specifically to what the apparition could have possibly been. But he hadn't gotten far along these lines when suddenly the familiarity of the surroundings jolted him alert. He had been driving on autopilot, daydreaming behind the wheel, and now all of a sudden he was coming right up on the quiet street that ran along one side of the Hendricks' corner lot. This realization snapped him back to the objective at hand.

The neighborhood had changed some but not dramatically, a bit of landscaping here, a new color of paint there. As he drew up to the cross street that ran in front of the Hendrick house, the old Thackeray place directly across from it looking exactly as it had all those years ago, his mood brightened. In just a few minutes he would have some relief. He could picture his Den Mother's warm smile, could hear in his head Dan's indefatigable voice on the phone, sympathetic, encouraging, offering rational feedback and practical advice.

But it wasn't there. Dan's old house was gone. No, not gone, gone was not the word, because no house could ever have been there in the first place.

Dominating the lot, squarely in the middle of the otherwise vacant parcel and right where the Hendricks' living room should be, stood an enormous Monterey Cypress tree that could not possibly have been less than a hundred years old.

Oh my God, dear God, please help me, Michael trembled. *Have I gone insane?* But before that line of thought could go any further, an even more acute and alarming circumstance snapped his attention away.

In the opposing lane, just short of the intersection, a tiny one-year-old boy in just a diaper and T-shirt was toddling erratically, elbows bent like chicken wings and his little hands flopping to help keep his balance, taking a step this way, another that way, then spinning in a half circle. And in that same lane ahead, still distant but closing the gap in a hurry, a dark SUV was barreling toward the intersection at twice the speed limit, with absolutely no chance of braking fast enough to avoid the child.

Michael didn't think; there wasn't time. His reaction was as automatic as breathing. The whole world seemed to slow down so Michael could see with utter clarity, perceiving every key factor in the situation, knowing exactly what he must do, the precise angle, the timing, the speed. He jammed on the accelerator with just enough restraint to maintain traction, his eyes trained on the SUV like a sniper. An instant before the Lincoln entered the intersection, Michael jerked his steering wheel to the left and floored the gas.

His grille smashed into the left front corner of the black Navigator, shoving it violently sideways in an explosion of sparks and glass. His airbag popped and the scene vanished, his extremities numb, all sensation blocked except for the shriek of tires and the acrid smells of engine fluids and hot rubber.

The airbag deflated, exposing the results of Michael's brash gambit. His own car was destroyed, its windows obliterated, its body crumpled, pungent smoke steaming from the engine compartment. The SUV had been shoved hard off of its trajectory toward the child, but its momentum had kept it moving even after the collision, scraping its left side along Michael's front end and skidding it into the side street. Its hood was buckled, smoke or steam jetting up from the motor, and now the mangled left front door was opening with a harsh grating as the dazed driver clambered out.

Two more men exited from the passenger side, conversing heatedly in words Michael couldn't make out. They headed toward the rear of the vehicle, the older man making a cell phone call. *Thank God they're okay*, Michael thought, and then added, checking himself briefly, *and the same for me.*

"Get back here and help!" one of the passengers barked, and the driver made his way around to join the two at the rear hatch, the man with the cell phone ranting unintelligibly.

Michael was about to push his way out of his own car to assess matters and explain about the little boy when they did something very strange, something that made him stop, giving him a grisly, prickly feeling for the second time that night.

They were momentarily obscured as they opened the hatch door, and then the driver and the man that had called to him came around on the car's near side, dragging between them what Michael first took to be an awkward piece of soft luggage but which he quickly realized, to his bewilderment and horror, was the limp figure of a fourth man. They maneuvered the body – whether dead or just nearly so, Michael couldn't tell – up and into the driver's seat. One of the men wiped the steering wheel with a Kleenex, then proceeded to force the slumped man's hands onto it, closing the limp fingers around it several times with his own. Finally they lowered the figure gently down onto the street surface on its back, where it lay motionless with eyes closed, clothes disheveled, face and head swollen and bruised.

Michael was still puzzling numbly over this, unsure what to think or feel, when an unmarked police car rolled up with blue lights flashing, but no siren. A single plain-clothes officer stepped out and, after a quick glance at Michael, approached the man with the cell phone immediately. At once relieved and stunned at his own absent-mindedness, Michael realized that it had never occurred to him to call 911, the obvious first thing that should have been done. He was glad the man in the other car had maintained a better presence of mind.

The policeman knelt over the man on the ground and checked him thoroughly, then returned to his cruiser and made a radio call. Again he consulted with the man who had placed the cell call, this time both of them shooting intermittent glances in Michael's direction. Though he couldn't hear them, they appeared to be arguing. Abruptly, the officer turned, the other still talking to him, and strode briskly over to Michael's car.

"License and registration," he demanded dourly. To Michael he seemed more irritated than even these circumstances called for. It also struck him as odd that a plainclothesman had been dispatched instead of a uniformed patrol. But he was quite addled enough without wasting concern on such trivial points and handed his documents through the glass-less window without a word, deciding it would behoove him to wait and tell his story only when duly asked.

A minute later the policeman re-emerged from his car and started toward Michael with a clipboard in hand and a new bulge in his blazer pocket. Handcuffs? A gun?

"Tuggs!" shouted the man the policeman had been arguing with before. The cop ignored him.

"*Tuggs!*"

The officer stopped and turned to the other with an ominous glare. The man's return gaze was even more ominous and threatening. Time seemed suspended while the two men stared at each other in palpable mutual defiance.

To Michael's amazement and growing alarm, the civilian won.

Now he approached Michael himself, leaving the police officer standing at a sullen distance with his arms folded but his lips in check, his poisonous scowl no longer aimed at anyone in particular.

"We're annoying the chief there, son, so I'll make this brief. Do you know who I am?"

And incredibly, now that they were face to face under the street light, Michael did.

"Are you Ridge Raymore?"

"Indeed." The campaign smile showed briefly, but under these circumstances even Raymore couldn't maintain it for long. "Now, we are about to have a conversation that never happened. Do you understand?"

Michael was speechless. He had no idea where this was going, but all of a sudden it was starting to look like a very bad place.

Raymore frowned at the non-response. "That boy waiting for the ambulance over there is my son. Now, I don't know why you hit me, maybe you don't like my politics, or maybe it was just an accident. I don't—" He chopped the air emphatically to squelch Michael's attempted reply. "I don't give a shit. I'm going to give you the big picture, and you are going to embrace it, because no matter how much trouble you think you're in here, believe me, it can be much, much worse." Raymore paused to assess the effect, and this time, after a wrenching pause, Michael nodded.

"Good. Now, we won't say you planned this ill-advised stunt, and that's going to help you considerably. Assuming you play well." Raymore moved his face closer, blotting out the street light. "So here's how it went down. My son was driving my attendants and I to the home of a doctor friend to talk through some health care matters. You recognized me from TV, your convictions got the best of you, and you decided to shove us off the road to make your point. You didn't mean to kill anyone, you just wanted to scare us, maybe hurt us a little. You feel disenfranchised and this was your chance to make a difference. Unfortunately—" Raymore cut him off again. "—my son wasn't wearing his seat belt, and he got hurt bad. Real bad."

"But I saw—"

Raymore reached in with his fist and cinched Michael's collar under his throat. He checked over his shoulder to make sure the policeman was staying put. When he faced Michael again, his voice rasped and his eyes were filled with fury.

"There's no time for bullshit, just shut up and listen. That officer waiting over there to arrest you is the Assistant Chief of Police. He is also a campaign supporter and one of my closest friends. We have a long history together. He knows what happened, and his investigation is going to back it up. Tight. Do you get it now?"

Michael just shook. Raymore maintained his grip on the shirt. "Listen, bud. There are lots of ways to die in jail. You don't even want to hear about them. Shut up and take what's coming and you won't have to worry. You'll be out in three or four years, no worse for wear." Now Raymore pressed his face so close that Michael could feel the heat and smell the whiskey. "But you say one word, you make one move to cross me, and the trustees will find you hanging from your bed sheet before your public defender even gets your file. It happens, you know. All the time. People sick in the head, can't live with their guilt, or just can't face being locked in a box. Oh, they watch for it down there, the SMPD does a damn good job. But they can't catch all of them. Nobody can." Raymore leered. "You know what it's like strangling from a bed sheet? It doesn't snap your neck like a gallows. The chair drops out and all of a sudden it's worse than you ever imagined and you change your mind, you just want to get down, but your hands are tied behind your legs and there's nothing you can do, not one goddamn thing you can do but hang there in agony, waiting to die."

Raymore turned to see Norm Tuggs marching in their direction. He released Michael and trotted toward Tuggs, gesturing for a word. Tuggs shook him off, but Raymore persisted, barking some threat that once more caused the officer to halt. They huddled near the police car, bickering in hushed, animated tones.

Michael imagined that this whole situation was testing Tuggs' moral tolerance, that no matter what rash choices and unforeseen entanglements Raymore had maneuvered him into, Tuggs was at heart a decent cop, wishing against hope that he could cut their ties cleanly and doing everything he could to limit the injustice Raymore was working to engineer. But Michael had seen enough to know how it would end. Raymore would win when the chips were down. Harsh regrets and noble wishes aside, Norman Tuggs was not going to save him.

Broken, rudderless, and losing his composure now along with his sanity, Michael thought suddenly of the toddler, the whole reason he was in this mess, at least this part of it, and he turned to look back through the rear window and saw that the boy was not there. Not clinging to his mother's breast like a monkey barnacle as Michael would have hoped, not sitting between his father's legs on one of the doorsteps, but also not a splotch in the roadway or still careening in the traffic path. There was this, at least: he had saved the boy. The price of this sacrifice was yet to be tallied, and it was looking unspeakably high. But it had been the right thing.

And then he saw something else, an old metal spike screwed down into the yard next to the Thackeray house. All at once, there was starlight again, one thin but bright gleam of hope reaching out to Michael where a second before there had been absolutely none.

Hollis Thackeray hadn't liked it when the young couple who bought the place adjoining his backyard put up a fence with the ugly side facing his. So he built his own fence, eighteen inches taller so his neighbors would have something to look at, and clear enough of the property line so there could never be any dispute about his right to have it there. Clear enough, in fact, for roguish young boys to file between the fences unseen. On the near side, the entry gap was obscured by the old stucco home next to Thackeray's, whose unfenced yard was patrolled in daytime by a mastiff on a tether. At the far end, the two fences let out into a patch of wood with a creek running through it that had been left as a green belt by the developer of the more upscale properties on the other side. Thus, guarded by the light-sleeping dog and wary tennis club mothers, not many boys knew of this expedient route. But among those who did were Danny Hendrick and Michael Chandler.

And expedient it was, sometimes a life-saver. Michael and Danny had used it more than once to lose Billy Tuggs, a school bully two years their senior. It was well known that Billy was regularly thrashed by his father the beat cop, the selfsame officer currently contesting with Eldridge Raymore only yards away, who went to no great lengths to hide it. But that was slim comfort to the hapless unfortunates who accidentally incurred his ire, or who just happened to be within reach when Billy went victim hunting.

Michael hadn't used the fence path since his school days. Now, he realized, it once more offered him his best chance of escape, his briar patch for a rabbit run whose stakes vastly overshadowed any he had ever faced in youth.

Eldridge Raymore and Norman Tuggs were still rapt in

their power struggle, but Michael knew that it wouldn't last long. The man who had been driving the SUV was smoking a cigarette and staring absently at the ground. The other, however, the back seat passenger, had not lost his bearings and remained vigilant, continually shifting his wary gaze about the scene. And now there were sirens, distant but getting closer, and he knew that the real police would arrive any minute, along with the ambulance, and his window of opportunity would slam shut.

Slowly, Michael inched his way through fragments of safety glass to the passenger seat and undid the door latch, clutching one strap of his knapsack and mouthing a silent litany. Calm down ... breathe deep ... wait ...

The wary man turned halfway in the opposite direction. It was the best shot he was going to get. Michael slipped out of the car, bent as low as he could, and dashed for the fences.

CHAPTER 3
Flight Change

ALL AT ONCE THERE WAS an explosion of voices. He thought he heard Ridge Raymore cursing at the top of his lungs, and a snarl from Norm Tuggs, just as loud and angry. Others joined in, and Michael knew it was now a race.

He glanced back as he neared the end of the fence line and saw the red and blue flashes of the arriving first responder vehicles reflecting like lightning off the house behind. A flashlight beam swept across the dog yard entrance.

He kicked into high gear and spilled out into the green belt. The wood was dark, the trees visible only as black silhouettes against fragments of sky where starlight broke through the canopy. But he was so familiar with these surroundings that he could navigate by the sound of the stream.

There was only one spot where it was possible to jump across, a short waterfall where a chunk of volcanic basalt had resisted erosion. It was the creek's loudest feature, and Michael homed in on it as he had done many times before. He was sure the police wouldn't turn back at the prospect of getting wet up to their calves, but it might slow them down to look for a better option. Every second counted.

He cleared the waterfall with inches to spare. It had seemed much easier in his younger days. It didn't matter; he would have gladly soaked his legs and ruined his shoes if it had come to that. Still, he was glad it hadn't.

A minute later he was in Mrs. Carey's yard, flying across the grass using her lemon trees as cover. He reached the tall wooden gate separating the front and back yards and flipped up the familiar latch. He pulled the gate shut on the other side and heard the latch slip back into place, one more obstacle for his pursuers.

And then he was free, emerging onto the sidewalk and forcing himself down to a leisurely pace less likely to draw attention, free to … to …

To what?

Michael swore, realizing that he was far from out of trouble.

There was no sign of further pursuit and the sirens had shut off; the dispatched units were all on scene. Any minute, he knew, as soon as they were sure they'd lost him, the patrol cars would start to fan out in search. For that matter, with Tuggs involved, probably every cop the force could spare would be out for him. He had to get out of here, pronto, the further and faster the better. But he had no car, which might have made running easier except for the inconvenient fact that he had nowhere to go.

He couldn't go home, and it dawned on Michael that, in all likelihood, he would never be able to go there again. His cherished books, his framed movie posters, the music that defined him. The mahogany desk his woodworking grandfather had lovingly built him from scratch. His last bottle of Gabbiano Chianti Riserva, the plasma TV that had cost half a month's salary even with the employee discount. His clothes, every shoe, sock, jeans, black Jockey briefs, and his collection of tavern T-shirts from around the world, except for what he was wearing and what he had packed. Every earthly good that evidenced his life or meant anything to him – gone, and irretrievable.

What would become of it? The police would no doubt tear through it none too carefully. Would whatever survived be sold off by his landlord to make good on his lease? What about the little lockbox that contained his most cherished mementos: his Scout rank badges, Max's coin collection and, most of all, the envelope of photographs and emails from Vicki Valentine. Would those things precious only to him end up in a dumpster among the rat droppings, cigarette butts and moldy orange peels?

And he thought of the tickets, the two unused tickets tucked in his wallet behind his driver's license, to see the Beatles at the Hollywood Bowl. He had expected one stub to be the next treasure to go into that box. He'd bought two tickets on the chance that by the time the concert rolled around six months later he would have a girl in his life to share it with. When not one slim prospect for that had occurred and the date was approaching, he had worked up the nerve to ask the sparkly Marketing Director at work. She had very tenderly but with a clear message turned him down and left him hoping to scalp the extra pass before the show. Now even that wouldn't be possible. Ironically, he was going to wind up with two tickets in pristine condition that, under normal circumstances, he could have salted away until they could fetch a premium on the collector's market. Could have, that is, if he had had a lockbox to put them in and the expectation of some semblance of a normal life, which now seemed an eminently reasonable and yet utterly unobtainable desire.

On the other hand … did he really have a better option than L.A.? Zipped into the outer pocket of his knapsack was a boarding pass that he had printed just before leaving work. It was a long walk to the San Francisco International Airport, but what alternative did he have for putting distance between himself and Ridge Raymore's dragnet? He did a rough calculation and figured that he could get there, if the dictates of caution didn't hamper him too much, in about two hours. If he managed to squeeze onto one of the next few flights, before the police obtained a search warrant and found his travel plans on the computer, he should be able to lose himself in the labyrinth of Los Angeles. That would at least buy him a little time to figure things out in an environment where, while they might be looking for him, he doubted they would apply the level of focus and urgency that Raymore and his cronies would be marshaling here.

He had been walking for about twenty minutes, keeping to shadow and twice ducking from view as a police cruiser whizzed around the corner, pondering with increasing concern how he was going to traverse the exposed grounds surrounding the SFO terminal without being seen, when the solution literally appeared before him in the form of the San Mateo Marriott Hotel.

A smile spread across his face as he marveled at his good luck. He would have to be poised, convincing, and purposeful, but if it worked, it would get him inside the terminal and to the ticket counter without being apprehended en route.

Using vehicles and groups of people as camouflage, he made his way to the back of the hotel building. He milled about for a tense ten minutes before a lone twenty-something with a scraggly beard and two earrings through an eyebrow parked nearby and approached a rear door with card key in hand. Ambling naturally toward the door, smiling genially and reaching toward his own pocket as they neared each other, Michael paused with an "after you" gesture, waited for the young man to unlock the door, and followed him inside.

He strode up the hallway past the guest rooms to the lobby, crossing the southwest-themed tile floor to the men's restroom. He latched himself inside a vacant stall and set about changing his clothes. In three minutes, he was a new man; his tan khakis, navy polo shirt, and polished loafers had been replaced by jeans, closed-toe sandals, and a black T-shirt from the Hollywood Hard Rock Café. He flushed the john, washed his hands and face, and made his way out through the lobby doors to the check-in portico.

"Airport van running?" he inquired of the uniformed attendant behind the sidewalk podium.

"Should be back any minute, sir," the bellman smiled. "Heading home?"

"Yes," Michael returned. "But I'll be back." How ironic, he thought, that both of these statements were probably lies.

The green and white courtesy van showed up as promised, and Michael climbed in behind the driver while the bellman helped a middle-aged couple and a teenage girl traveling alone with their bags.

"Which airline?" the driver asked as he made a right turn out of the hotel lot onto the thoroughfare.

"Horizon," Michael replied.

"Alaska/Horizon first stop," the driver intoned. "How about you folks?"

MICHAEL ROSE AS THE SHUTTLE pulled to the curb outside the Alaska Airlines ticket area, straining not to look anxious. The door scissored open and he started down the steps. As he reached the last step he thought better, paused and reversed, pulled his wallet out of the zippered knapsack flap, and handed the driver a ten-dollar bill.

"Much obliged, Boss." The driver grinned toothily. "You have a nice and safe trip."

"Thank you," Michael replied more curtly than he wanted to sound.

As the van pulled away, he sucked in a deep breath. This part had been easy. Now came the dice roll. Now came the part he could only pray would go well.

A dozen travelers were stacked into the cordon maze leading to Alaska's check-in counter, shuffling luggage at their feet. Michael was disheartened. He had gotten here in pretty good time, but every minute that went by drew the inevitable police invasion nearer. Normally, he would have avoided this altogether, making straight for the gate with his preprinted boarding pass, but that flight had gone without him. It would probably make no difference since there was no telling how soon they could squeeze him onto a flight, but it was one more crank of tension. He wanted to be through this, sitting at the designated gate with an assigned seat for a specific plane, where he could at least stop running and could rest in the knowledge that for now, he had done all he could. Even as he thought this, he realized how ludicrous it was to think of the gate area as a haven. If anything, he would be easier to apprehend once he was past the security screen and into the controlled confines of the boarding zone.

He had almost reached the check-in line when he heard a voice that made his heart jump, speaking the last words in the world he wanted to hear.

"Mr. Chandler?"

He turned instinctively before realizing that he shouldn't. Twenty feet away and closing rapidly was a young woman in a blue and white uniform, *Alaska Airlines* emblazoned on the lapel. "Michael Chandler?"

He could not mask his alarm. Desperately, he began casting about for a way to extricate himself once again. In this facility dense with security staff, checkpoints, and surveillance cameras, it was impossible. Did Ridge Raymore's influence know no bounds?

"No. Sorry." He forced an unconvincing smile. "I'm, uh, my name is … Steve Shelby."

As soon as it came out, he felt like an idiot. He wasn't concerned that Shelby might help the police find him if this woman gave them his name. Steve Shelby had no useful information to divulge, not even about the concert trip, which had not been mentioned during their drive because it risked making Steve feel badly about Michael missing his plane. But if she did talk to the authorities, even if Michael managed to escape the airport somehow, that foolish mention of his co-worker's name would help to confirm Michael's own identity and movements, Because once they talked to Shelby and learned about the daycare drive earlier in the evening, it would be logical to suppose that the man calling himself Shelby at the airport might be Michael. And once they knew when and what to look for, it would be easy to find him on airport security video. They would even see the clothes he had changed into. How different this night could have been, he thought bitterly, if he had simply left Shelby to his predicament.

"I know who you are," the woman said quietly. "You're in big trouble, Michael, and I'm here to help you. You need to trust me."

"How do—"

And all of a sudden, now that she was just two feet away and he could really see her, smell the subtle but powerfully feminine bouquet of her perfume, her allure hit him like a bombshell.

To Michael, she was beyond beautiful. Lush auburn hair spilled over her shoulders in sensuous waves, full, round lips beckoned with a soft, faint luster, her doe-like eyes ravishing and formidable, penetrating. Her smooth, full breasts perched like fruits at the peak of ripeness, and the rest of her was composed of curves so brazen they made her conservative uniform blush.

And she seemed somehow familiar. How could that be? Her appearance had struck him so dramatically that he was positive he would remember if he had ever seen her before. Then he recognized the feeling for what it was. It had nothing to do with this woman pre se. Her attractiveness was simply waking a memory long dormant, of the way he had felt around Vicki, the only woman he had unreservedly loved, senselessly torn away, leaving a wound in him that all these years had failed to heal.

"Come with me," she commanded. "Quickly, and don't look at anyone or say anything."

She's trapping me, Michael thought with absolute certainty. *She's delivering me to Ridge Raymore's guys, and this time they won't bother with the police. They'll just take me somewhere safe to toss the body and spare the jail a bed sheet.*

It made no difference. Though a case could be made that he had no choice, that to run would ensure disaster while to comply preserved a small chance of salvation, logic played no part in his decision. It was the most primal force, the indomitable power of pure sexual attraction, the same intoxicant that bled the treasure of a nation to raise the Taj Mahal and mustered the combined armies of Greece against Troy. She was out of his league, an exponent above anyone he had ever dated, so radiant with female aura that she was hard to look at. Under normal circumstances, he could never have found the courage to approach her, let alone to ask her for a date. And yet, fully aware of how utterly irrational and even dangerous it was, he felt compelled to present the most accommodating and appealing impression possible, just in case there was a ghost of a sliver of a chance. His protest dissolved into a weak nod.

She led him to a door behind the ticket counter, past looks of mild concern from the two staffers checking customers in, swiped her pass card, and pointed Michael though.

She ushered him down a short corridor and into a small break room containing little more than two air pots of coffee, a water cooler, and a microwave, and gestured for him to take one of the four seats around the functional table. She ducked out without a word, and Michael was convinced that this was it, that Raymore's muscle would appear any minute, kill him with one silenced shot, and cram him into a box or some luggage that could be carried from the terminal without drawing attention. But a minute later she returned alone with her purse, sitting opposite him and methodically fishing things out.

"This is a parking voucher, prepaid." She handed Michael a small laminated card the size of a lottery ticket. "I've written the space number here, see? Fifth floor, Section J, spot 12. You put that into the meter as you head out. Are you familiar with the airport parking?"

"Yes," Michael said through his trance.

"Good. Now here are some credit cards." She dropped a Visa credit card and a Shell gas card near the parking slip. "Get rid of your cards and use these, so they can't trace you.

Charge whatever you need - food, gas, motels. Just take care of yourself, and don't worry about the money. I've got it covered no matter what you spend."

"I don't understand. How do you know me? Why are you doing this?"

"You don't need to understand. All you need to do is follow my instructions." Once more she fished around in her purse. "And here is the key. Take the car and get out of here as fast as you can. And not to L.A. You can't go where they might expect you. You've got to leave California altogether."

Michael took it all in, shocked. Of all the things he had imagined might happen, this was not one.

"Now go," the woman said, standing. "Time is the enemy."

Suppose the police or Raymore's men are camped near the car, waiting to pounce and stuff me into the trunk. It was possible. Probable, even. It was the only explanation he could think of for what the woman had done. Maybe he could approach cautiously and spot them before they saw him, and then, having confirmed the conspiracy, get out of the airport some other way. But it made no sense. Raymore had no inkling of Michael's concert plans, and yet the woman seemed to know everything. Could the police have dissected his computer already?

A thought occurred to him, and for a few seconds he relived that awful moment in his bedroom as clearly as watching a video. "Are you Lauria?"

"What?" She twisted her head as though to hear better, and he thought he caught a flash of alarm.

"Are you Lauria? Is your name Lauria?"

She regained herself. "No, sweetie." She picked up the Visa card and handed it to him, pointing to the name embossed on it.

"Barbara Jordan." Michael read it aloud, disappointed. And that very disappointment, magnified by his overpowering attraction to her, caused him to babble in spite of himself.

"I know I have to go. But I'll be fine in L.A. I know

my way around down there and I can keep a low profile. You want to help me, how about you pull some strings and get us both on the next flight out? You can get the rental car and stuff so we don't have to use my cards. I'll pay it back to you as soon as it's safe. I don't want you sacrificing for me." He smiled. "Besides, I won't have to waste my extra ticket to the Beatles Reunion."

"Michael." She took his hands in hers and spoke in a tone soft, warm, reassuring. She looked deep into his eyes, and what he saw in her scared him to death. There was a tension, an urgency, maybe exasperation. But overlying it all was a desperate passion, a vulnerability, a pleading hope that felt for all the world like genuine love.

"You can't go to the concert. You can't fly to L.A. When the police ran your license they picked up your flight schedule through Homeland Security. TSA is already deployed at the departure gate. For all we know, you've already been recognized. We can't sit here talking about it. You've got to go *now*." She gathered the remaining items up from the table and handed them to him. "The gas tank is full. Head east. Go to your friend."

"What friend?" The glow in him was degenerating back into sick apprehension.

"The friend who is going to help you understand."

"*What friend?*"

"Drive east," she repeated. "My part in this is done. Please don't let it have been in vain."

"Come with me?" Michael felt limp.

"I ... *can't*." And there was that longing again, that human frailty in her eyes. He felt physically ill at the unfairness of it, that at *this* inopportune moment he should finally, all this time after Vicki, meet someone that seemed so perfect to him and who seemed sincerely, even passionately to want him, too. To be taunted with this possibility only to have it crushed before it could even start, crushed by the barbarism of a criminal power monger whose path Michael had never set out to cross, seemed despicably cruel. *Why, God?* Michael beseeched. *What am I being punished for?* He ached almost badly enough – almost – to wish he had never met her.

He had no strength to fight. "Can I at least have your phone number?" he begged miserably, digging the cell phone out of his pack and setting up to take a picture to remember her by.

"You can't take that," she declared, and before he knew what was happening, she had snatched his phone and smashed it to pieces under the heel of her shoe.

"What are you doing?" he cried.

"They'll trace you," she replied tersely, scooping the phone fragments into a trash bin and covering them with a crumpled lunch sack. "They'd track your location from the towers."

And that was that. Michael realized that if this woman was telling the truth, she was dead right on every point. And if she wasn't, he was already cooked. There was no sane alternative except to do as she said, let himself believe, if not wholeheartedly then at least with sufficient faith to march like a good soldier, and defer for the time being to providence.

He got up from his chair, put the key and cards in his pocket, and shouldered his backpack. She stood aside to let him through the door.

"I wish ..." he started.

"Me, too. Oh, Michael, Michael ... you have no idea."

He started down the hallway. "Thanks for helping me," he said earnestly over his shoulder. "I don't understand it, but thank you."

Then she flung herself around his neck, pulled him in to her, and gave him a long, deep kiss that left him tottering, euphoric as a heroin blast.

"Godspeed, Michael Chandler." She squeezed him one more time, tears on her cheeks, and then she turned and darted into a side room, closing the door behind her, leaving him as she had found him, alone.

CHAPTER 4
The Hitcher

NO THUGS AMBUSHED MICHAEL IN the parking garage. The fifth floor was completely deserted, the only sounds coming from his own footsteps and the whoosh of traffic on the ground transport loop below. He reached the Mitsubishi Eclipse unscathed and regarded it, forest green and a recent model by the look of it, with approval.

The key fit. He chucked his pack onto the passenger's seat and climbed in, taking the time to adjust the driver's seat and steering column. He backed out gingerly, aware from his rental car days that it was important to be careful until he had a feel for the car's braking sensitivity, turning radius, and other unique features. It responded nimbly, felt natural, just 40,000 miles on the odometer and in excellent shape. It looked like the car would serve him admirably, unless Barbara Jordan was just setting him up. If she was, the vehicle's apparent suitability would mean nothing.

He fed the parking stub into the machine at one of the unattended exit kiosks. The bar gate retracted and he was out, heading for Interstate 80, the fastest and easiest route out of the state.

They may still have me, he thought as he picked up speed. *They may have planted a tracking beacon. Or they could just follow till I let my guard down.* But this scenario seemed feeble and, unlike the fleeting glimmers of hope he had experienced intermittently throughout the ordeal, this time a true and lasting relief began to set in. In this car, he realized, which no one could possibly trace to him, anonymous and in the dark of night, he could drive right past a police cruiser with no risk of suspicion or discovery.

He was still tense, but the paranoia had eased by the time he reached the Bay Bridge. As he crossed Treasure Island, beholding the shimmer of downtown lights off the placid bay with a sense of calmness he had not felt for hours, he realized, now that he was leaving it behind him, just how much he loved San Francisco. The bridges – megalithic marvels that, in his mind, dwarfed and emasculated the proud water crossings of other cities. The frenzy of Chinatown, the bark of sea lions sunning themselves at Fisherman's Wharf, the timeless serenity of the Palace of Fine Arts. But it wasn't just the icons. It was the orphaned parrots at Telegraph Hill, the tiny bistros of Haight-Ashbury where the populism of the 1960s lived on, the sheer audacity of a city unafraid to defy the federal government in matters of compassion and human dignity. It was his town. There was no other like it, and he had never for a minute wanted to live anywhere else. Now his future was a fog of abject uncertainty save for one point: that he could not remain in the one place in the world he wanted to be.

A half hour later, he crossed the bridge out of Contra Costa County and reached Vallejo on the northeast edge of the interlocking bays. In minutes he was through it, climbing into the hills past Sulphur Springs Mountain, the lights winking out in his rearview mirror, and the Bay Area was at last truly behind him.

The acute tension began dwindling away, and he was surprised at how much he had been holding in. At last, alone with his thoughts and for the moment safe, with a definite if not ultimate destination before him, he felt the breathing space to resume his attempts at making sense of what had happened that night.

He thought first of the apparition in his townhouse.

What exactly was that thing? He ticked off what he knew. It was female, no doubt about that. It had been rippling slowly, the whole figure and not just her clothing, and seemed to be shedding its very being as though torn by unnatural wind or some other unseen force. Not really wind-like, he realized; it was not just its clothing but the figure itself that had been undulating, as though seen through disturbed water. Was that why its billowing had seemed supernaturally slow?

The finger pointing at him had been the darkest black, not like human pigment but rather the color of coal. The voice had come from so many directions and in such variation that it was possible the figure was not even its source. Had its lips moved? He couldn't recall. What did it all mean?

At first, it hadn't seemed like any ghost or demon he had seen in fiction. But then, how accurate could you expect pop culture depictions of such things to be? He had the gnawing feeling of having seen its like *somewhere* before, but the memory lurked just beyond reach. And then it hit him – *banshee*, an ill spirit of Irish lore: the terrifying harbinger of death in the movie *Darby O'Gill and the Little People,* so frightening it had evoked nightmares in little kids everywhere and ire in parents who had thought taking them to a Disney film was safe.

Except that figure had been complete, not vapor from the waist down. So what was it? Maybe not a banshee, but it certainly had been the terrifying harbinger of *something*. Michael's own death? Had the figure come to him for the same reason the banshee had manifested to Darby O'Gill, to command him, willing or not, into a black carriage drawn by ghastly steeds that would transport his forfeited soul to its hideous fate beyond the grave? Was the Death Coach even now hovering in the twilight with eternal patience, biding its time until the appointed hour? If so, how long did he have?

And who was Lauria? More than that, what did it mean to be "bound"? It might mean marriage, but that seemed unlikely in the context. It might mean that his fate and the fate of this "Lauria" were somehow entwined – through in what way, he couldn't imagine. There were darker possibilities – like physical restraint, or slavery, or to stretch things, maybe even the connection between an assassin and its target. Was Lauria some woman assigned to kill him? If so, why? It made no sense. Then he had an even more troubling thought. Though its words had been phrased in the third person, could Lauria be the figure on the stairs itself?

With these thoughts running in fruitless circles, he turned his ruminations to the tree. It had been the right lot; there was no doubt about that. Aside from the Hendrick property, every house and feature of the neighborhood was still there. Could it have been transplanted? Could he be wrong about its age? He thought not. It had been enormous, the trunk as thick as a small car, its canopy shielding the entire parcel like an umbrella. So what did it mean? Outside the possibility of hallucination – which Michael had to admit could not be ruled out – he could think of no rational explanation.

Then there was the crash. What were the chances that he would be drawn by freak circumstances to a familiar place he had not visited in years, and once there, encounter a lone little boy toddling in the street, in the path of a car bearing down at just the right moment for Michael to save him? Or that this car would carry a man with both the temperament and the power to frame an innocent stranger, sparking Michael's desperate run for the airport? And once he got there, having wound up at the terminal as he had been planning for months, but hours behind schedule – how could this woman, a complete stranger yet an employee of the very airline he needed to engage, not only know anything about him? How could she not only know of his predicament but have planned and set up, brilliantly, his way out of the danger? Beyond that, why had she seemed so connected with him? She had said her "part" was done, and sent him on to "the friend who is going to help you understand," but then refused to name the friend or explain anything further. What the hell was going on?

Yet on that last point at least, Michael felt a measure of solace. By "friend", the woman could only have meant Dan Hendrick. He had sought Dan out himself, precisely because he was a "friend" Michael believed could help him "understand". Besides, he had no other friends east of California. He had relatives in various parts of the country, a few casual acquaintances, a handful of Wal-Mart colleagues – but not friends. "Friend" was the exact term she had used, and that could mean only one thing: monster cypress aside, Dr. Dan Hendrick was real.

So that much was clear, and perhaps, Michael mused with a confidence rising from the ring of truth it had, was all he really needed to know just now. It gave him a plan, a clear direction, a source of hope to occupy him for the immediate future. It laid down for him a yellow brick road to follow. He was going to Boston.

As he pondered these things, the answers eluding him, the miles and minutes melted quietly under the rolling tires. Gradually, a glow materialized in the sky ahead, stronger by the minute. The time had flown by; he was already approaching Sacramento.

He looked at the car clock, to which he had been oblivious up to now. It was almost midnight. Suddenly, he became aware of how hungry he was, his dinner still sitting uneaten on the kitchen counter back home.

He checked the gas gauge. Less than a quarter of the fuel was gone. Still, if he was going to stop anyway, he might as well fill up, and it would be a good test of whether the Shell card raised suspicion. And there was another reason: he needed a map. He had no idea how to get to Boston, and didn't want to risk precious time trying to figure it out as he went.

He pulled into a mini-mart on the outskirts of town. There were no other customers in sight. The card swiped without incident. He filled up the tank and walked into the convenience store where the cashier, its sole occupant, barely looked up from her novel as the tinkling bells announced his entry.

Ordinarily, he would have regarded with aversion the cheap, greasy fare that had been aging in the food warmer for who knew how long. But at this moment, warm, rich, and filling were just what he craved. He reached for the warmer's door but stopped himself, moving to the map display near the store entrance. Not finding what he was looking for, he approached the woman behind the counter and waited patiently for her to finish the paragraph she was reading. She looked up.

"Excuse me," Michael said. "I can't find a map of the United States. Do you have anything like that?"

"Sacramento, San Francisco, West Coast, and State of California," the woman ticked off. "That's all we have."

Damn. "All right, thank you." He returned to the food warmer and took out two crusty corn dogs and a serving of thick-cut french fries as dry and shriveled as mummy toes, setting them in a paper tray while he poured and lidded a sixteen-ounce coffee.

When he was finished, he laid on the counter all the sustenance he had gathered in a brief but methodical patrol of the store, including besides the hot goods a bottled water, a bag of trail mix, a tube of Pringles, two each of Almond Snickers and Salted Nut Rolls, and a large box of preservative-filled shortbread cookies topped with dollops of fruit goop that were sure to have the consistency and nutritional value of petroleum jelly. It was probably overkill, but the weakness he was starting to feel from an empty stomach made everything look good, and besides, he thought it prudent to collect some supplies early before an all-points manhunt reached critical mass.

"You know," the cashier said as she rang him up, "there's a bookstore around the corner that might have maps. The owner is some ex-hippie night owl who keeps it open until midnight."

"Really?"

"Yeah, just head toward town and take the first left. I

forget what it's called but it's right next to Walgreens."

"Great! Thanks!"

It wasn't hard to find. And it wasn't the hole in the wall he had expected. It was the size of a Hallmark store, with at least a dozen large, well-organized shelves. Nor was it deserted. Several college-age patrons perused the various sections for whatever purposes impelled them to seek reading material deep into a Friday night, and an elderly woman with a well-behaved Pomeranian on a yellow leash was poring raptly over the Science Fiction and Fantasy section.

Seeing that label on the shelf near the woman and dog gave Michael a sudden inspiration. He rushed through the aisles until he found it: Science and Natural History. Excited, he fingered his way to H, and there they both were. *The Cosmic Tapestry,* with a Hubble photograph of the Pinwheel Galaxy on the cover, and *All From Nothing,* a glossy black background with iridescent blue math formulae exploding outward at all angles. Both authored, their covers boldly proclaimed, by Daniel A. Hendrick, PhD.

He picked up the latter, whose paperback release was so recent he had not yet had a chance to buy it, and started down the aisle, only to spin back a few steps later and grab *Tapestry,* too. He had read that of course, twice, and had a perfectly good copy of it on his bedroom bookshelf. But that shelf may as well have been a continent away, and he wanted the book with him so he could digest it anew, examine it page by page for clues about what had happened to him, details that may not in previous readings have made an impression but would now seem more pertinent.

With Dan's books in hand, he made another stop, at the section marked Philosophy and Religion, suspecting he might not find what he was looking for but thankful when he did: a small Revised American Standard edition of the Bible.

He found the maps, and the selection was indeed broader than the one at the mini-mart. There were maps of Nevada, Oregon, Arizona, and the United States from the Rocky Mountains west. He still, however, didn't see anything that could guide him through the unfamiliar eastern half of the country.

"Can I help you?" A tall, pleasant man in his mid sixties appeared at Michael's elbow. He bore a full head of thick white hair, chino pants the color of sand, a worn brown Cardigan sweater, and gold-rimmed spectacles.

"I'm trying to find a road map for the entire U.S. Do you carry one?"

"Hmm." The older man surveyed the map display, then moved left and took a bound volume from the shelf next to it labeled Travel. "How about this?"

Michael took the book. It was a large but not overly thick reference titled *Rand McNally Road Atlas of the United States*. He flipped through the pages. Every state was accounted for in alphabetical order with a clear, detailed map of major roads and features, labeled at the edges with the page numbers where each bordering state could be found. He thumbed his way to Massachusetts and found a satisfying depiction of the routes into Boston. After Wyoming there was a full map of the country spread across two pages, and after that came maps of major cities, Boston included, necessarily lacking enough detail to find an obscure address for which you had no frame of reference, but quite adequate for navigating the main arterials.

"Perfect!" Michael smiled. "Thanks for your help."

"Not at all." The man tipped his head in a gesture that said *at your service*. "Planning a trip?"

"Yeah, sort of. I'm on my way to see an old friend."

"Whereabouts?"

"Florida," Michael lied, a twinge of apprehension building at the old man's interest in his plans.

"Lucky you." The elder smiled, then let out a resigned sigh. "I guess you'll be going south then. I was kind of hoping it might be east."

"Why?" Michael tried to keep the alarm out of his voice.

"My daughter in Reno just had a baby," the old man

said. "My first grandchild. I was going to head over this weekend and see them, but my car broke down and it won't be out of the shop for a week."

Michael gave a sympathetic gaze. "I'm sorry to hear that."

"There were some complications with the birth. Nothing life-threatening, but she's still in the hospital. I guess they did a C-section and found something that might require more surgery. She's on her own, you know, not married, and she's kind of freaked. She's all grown up, but she's my baby girl. I really wanted to get over there and show that her dad loves her, you know? That everything is going to be all right."

Don't do it, Michael warned himself. *Don't tempt fate after how lucky you've been. It's not necessary, it's not worth the risk, they'll be perfectly fine.*

And then he did it anyway.

"I, uh … I'm not really on a time schedule. I could detour over and drop you in Reno."

"Oh, goodness no, I didn't mean that," the old man assured graciously. "I just meant if you were going through anyway …"

"I don't mind. Really." Michael smiled and waved off the protest. And it was a genuine smile. Now that he had made the offer, there was no point retaining any reluctance. It helped that the worry had also deserted. If the man wanted the ride in order to do him harm, he wouldn't have risked losing it by pretending to decline. And if the purpose of his inquiry had been merely to discover Michael's destination so he could pass it along to malefactors elsewhere, well, that had backfired, because now they would be expecting him in Florida, taking roads a thousand miles from his actual path.

"I… I really shouldn't." The old man gazed sheepishly at his shoes. "I shouldn't have said anything. It's late and I've been fretting about it, I guess. I'm truly sorry. Your offer is kind, but …"

"Look." Michael reached out and gently squeezed the

man's shoulder. "I hate I-5 anyway. From here to Los Angeles it's six hours of straight, flat asphalt full of truck exhaust and lane-skating maniacs. If the fumes and nut-balls don't get you, you could fall asleep at the wheel out of sheer boredom." He smiled confidently and gave the man a firm, direct look. "I hadn't thought of it, but now that I have, it makes perfect sense. I'm going to head through Reno whether you're with me or not. I'll take a look at the atlas later and figure the best way to ease back south. It would be senseless for you not to come. And it would make me feel bad."

"Are you positive?" The man looked doubtful.

"Dead serious. As long as you're able to go now, which I assume you are or you wouldn't have brought it up."

Michael stacked his books together and pulled his wallet out. "I haven't eaten since lunch, I just got some food at the gas station. Let's ring these up and I'll go eat while you're closing."

"Closing?"

"The store. The girl at the gas station said you close at midnight. I assume you put the money away, vacuum, lock up and whatever. About how long do you think you'll be?"

The man grinned mirthfully, sheepishness gone, and Michael could have sworn he saw one eye twinkle like a winking star.

"I don't work here," he said.

CHAPTER 5
A Fork in the Road

"CHARLIE PARIS." THE MAN FROM the bookstore introduced himself after buckling into the passenger seat of Michael's car. Michael gave the extended hand a civil but cursory shake. He did not volunteer his own name. He felt unsettled and confused. Not only had he agreed but practically manipulated this man into accompanying him to Reno, and now, after the matter was all settled, it looked like he had been tricked. He could not for the life of him figure out why, and that made it worse.

It pushed him to the border of anger, because Michael was sick to death of surprises. Especially surprises begging questions that went unanswered. And yet, there was something unexpected in the quick handshake, not at all the stuff of dark conspiracies or clever tricks. It was a stunning gentleness, a simple, disarming innocence like the smell of baby powder. On one level, it exacerbated Michael's unease because it thickened the mystery, an incongruous monkey wrench tossed on top of a heap of paradoxes and non sequiturs that had made only Alice-in-Wonderland sense to begin with. Yet at the same time, inexplicably, it had a powerfully pacifying effect.

"All right," Michael said tersely, having decided it was better to take the direct approach than to stew over it. "If you don't work there, then why did you ask me if you could help?"

"You looked frustrated." Charlie shrugged. "And lost. I'm quite familiar with the store. It just seemed like maybe you could use some guidance."

If that was it, Michael thought, there were better ways to have done it. "I couldn't help noticing ..." or "Sorry to interrupt, but ..." or even just, "What are you looking for?" Any of them might have prevented him from mistaking Charlie for the store manager.

But, Michael realized, Charlie had done nothing overt to encourage this assumption. It wouldn't have worked if he had, because he would have been unmasked as soon as Michael encountered the real manager at the cash register. But Charlie had attempted no such deception. Aside from the story about his daughter, Charlie had said nothing about himself at all.

"I know it's not customary to go around helping perfect strangers," Charlie continued. "But look what *you* offered to do for *me*."

To that, Michael had no retort.

He stole a look at Charlie as he twisted toward the rear window and backed the car out. As much as he wanted, and fully expected, he could not detect a glimmer of ill intent. Well, he thought, that doesn't prove anything. After all, the Antichrist was supposed to be the Prince of Charming, the very picture of smooth, affable, and appealing; that was how the Bible said he would be able to deceive the masses. Appearances could not be trusted when judging evil.

Nevertheless, when Michael eyed Charlie quickly again as he turned back and shifted into drive, he did draw some conclusions. Now that he was conscious of it, his passenger struck him as a cross between Jimmy Stewart and the soft-spoken children's television host Mr. Rogers. That didn't seem like the type of charisma that would serve the architect of Armageddon. Involuntarily, he giggled. Whoever he was, Charlie Paris was not the Antichrist.

Charlie, who had seemed nervously aware of Michael's

agitation, appeared somewhat relieved and smiled faintly at the giggle. Nevertheless, he exhibited the keen discretion not to risk any word or action that might unsettle things again, remaining still and studiously quiet in his seat.

Michael started in on a corn dog and held the cardboard tray in Charlie's direction. "No, thank you," the older man said.

"I have some trail mix and cookies in the sack," Michael offered.

Charlie shook his head. "I'm good."

About twenty minutes later, there was a mild shudder and the buzz of tires on the grooved asphalt that warned drivers they were drifting dangerously off the road.

"You okay?" Charlie asked.

"I think so," Michael replied. But with his stomach full and the last of the adrenaline dissipated, exhaustion was catching up with a vengeance.

"Why don't you get some rest and I'll drive," Charlie suggested. For a moment, Michael felt apprehensive and wary. But he had been awake now for twenty hours, and he was frankly so tired that he found himself unable to muster the energy or even the will to protest. He pulled the car over and slid across the seats while Charlie walked around and replaced him behind the wheel.

Michael tilted the passenger seat back as far as it would go and tried to settle in, but it was just not comfortable enough for sleep. He unfastened his seatbelt and climbed gingerly into the back, kicked off his sandals, and curled into a fetal position on the upholstered bench seat, comforted by the car's gentle motion and the faint hum of tires on the road.

In two minutes, he was sound asleep.

"WHERE ARE WE?" MICHAEL STARTED as he awoke

and sat up, aware of something out of the ordinary that he couldn't put his finger on, then realizing what it was: somehow, Charlie had removed his Cardigan sweater and carefully draped and tucked it over Michael's slumbering form.

Before Charlie could answer, a sight out the left window jerked Michael alert.

It was still dark outside and starkly so, not a trace of city lights or traffic anywhere. But Michael had no trouble seeing the enormous lake passing by right up against the road.

"Stop the car!" he shot. "Pull over. I need to drive."

"Sure thing." Charlie pulled the car to the shoulder of the deserted road, and the two of them got out and moved around the vehicle to change seats. They were utterly alone amid the chirp of crickets, baritone of bullfrogs, and occasional call of a night owl. It was windless and seemed surprisingly cool for a Nevada summer, but Michael reasoned that, far away from the ocean's mitigating effects, the desert temperature fell rapidly at night. More surprising still was the magnificent vista. Isolated from any man-made light, the stars blazed with brilliant glory, and starlight alone was enough to illuminate the lake surface and the nearby desert floor. The night sky itself seemed alive, framing in contrast the black silhouettes of distant mountains.

"You look spooked," Charlie observed. "Bad dream?"

"Water," Michael replied, pulling back onto the road and exposing his weakness before it occurred to him that it might be ill-advised. "I have a phobia of it. I need to be in control around it or I get panic attacks."

"Really?" Charlie looked concerned. "How come?"

"I've always had it, but there was an incident that made it worse." Michael sighed, gazing out the window and shaking his head. "When I was eight years old, my parents sent me for swimming lessons at the YMCA. I wasn't happy, but it was tolerable while I was in the starting group. The Crawdads, I think they called it. They stayed in the shallow end doing non-threatening things like the dog paddle. When I graduated to the Beavers, they threw in some face-under-the-water practice, and I just wasn't good at it. In fact, I hated it. Half the time I took a bunch of that stinging chlorine water up my nose. You know what I'm talking about, that violently sick feeling you get when water gets up in your sinuses? I hated it. They'd have us do the crawl stroke where your head goes up and down and you're supposed to exhale into the water. I never got the hang of that routine and I cheated as much as possible." Charlie nodded sympathetically, saying nothing.

"Then they moved me to the Sharks." Michael's features darkened. "The very first day, the kids were supposed to go off the diving board head first with our arms pointed like the prow of a ship. I was terrified. It was all I could do to pull off a cannonball into the shallow end with a life preserver and holding my nose closed with my fingers. I still got some water up there from time to time, but you popped up to the surface right away, no chance of getting in real trouble."

Sadness crept into his voice as he saw in his mind's eye the frightened little boy he had been. "Five or six kids went ahead of me and had no problems. When it was my turn, I couldn't do it. I stood out there at the end of the board and just cried. The instructor kept telling me there was nothing to worry about and that she and the lifeguard would be right there. I was terrified they were going to force me. But they didn't. When she saw I wasn't getting any better, she said I could come down.

"So I turned around, and ..." Michael's lips quivered. It had been a long time since he had confronted the awful memory, let alone shared it with anyone. "I don't know how exactly but I slipped and lost my balance. It all happened in a split second. My foot shot out from under me and I went clean off the board. I smacked the back of my head on it as I was falling and went straight in the water before I even knew what was happening.

"It was awful, Charlie. It was my big nightmare, the worst thing that ever happened. I felt like the whole ocean was on top of me. I kept screaming and screaming for my mom, screaming with my mouth closed. A bunch of water got shoved up my nose and I was flat-out hysterical. All I could think was, *I'm going to die, I'm going to die, I'm going to die! Mommy, help me!*"

Michael shuddered. "I guess the instructor dove in and pulled me out. I don't remember. They said I was only under for a matter of seconds, but it seemed a lot longer. It's all blurry after that. The next thing I remember clearly is lying on a bench in the locker room with towels wrapped all around me, shaking like hell while they called my folks. When they got there I got halfway up to hug my mom, and I seized up suddenly and threw up all over her dress. And that was the end of it. I never had swimming lessons again."

Charlie remained silent, but his eyes betrayed a deep, agonized sympathy.

"Have you ever had your worst fear come true, Charlie?"

"No."

"It changes you." Michael looked drawn and gaunt, traumatized even by the memory, shivering as he spoke. "I had always been terrified of drowning, but after that happened, it became an obsession. I thought I'd outgrow it someday, but it's only gotten worse. I get these horrible images of having that 'water-up-your-nose' feeling with no way to stop it, inhaling water right into my lungs and choking by reflex, making it even worse. I can't stand the thought – just thinking about it makes me panic even when I'm not near water. I have to consciously block it out of my mind." Michael paused to compose himself. "I couldn't stand it, I just couldn't. I think I'd rather be eaten by a tiger."

Charlie looked genuinely concerned. "But there's a whole other lane plus a guardrail. You couldn't get to the water unless you drove there on purpose."

"Sure you could," Michael countered. "The car could malfunction. You could fall asleep. Or have a heart attack. A truck could knock you across from behind."

"I wouldn't fall asleep, I guarantee that," Charlie soothed. "And there hasn't been another car for miles, let alone a truck."

"I know it's irrational. But I can't help it. I guess it's so horrifying to me that I can't stop obsessing on it. Sometimes, I even wonder if Hell is a place where the whole universe is water, and you just keep drowning in agony, with no way to get out because there's nothing else to get to."

"I'm sure it's not like that," Charlie assured. "It doesn't say anything like that in the Bible. What kind of God would create something like that?"

"What kind of God would make people burn for eternity?"

Charlie said nothing.

They drove in silence for five more minutes before Michael suddenly realized that, irrational fears and metaphysical conundrums aside, the lake they were passing shouldn't even be there. Granted, he had only driven to Reno a couple of times, but he could not recall a body of water like this along the way, and he knew he would have remembered. Was it Tahoe? No, you didn't get close enough to see Lake Tahoe from I-80, and even if you did, it would be on the other side of the road.

"Where are we?" Michael repeated.

"I believe," Charlie pondered, "I saw a sign that said something like ... Walton Lake? Walker? Yeah. Walker Lake."

"And you drove straight toward Reno? You didn't leave the freeway?"

"Well ... yes and no," Charlie blurted. "We're long past Reno. I turned off the Interstate once we got there. We're headed toward Vegas."

Michael was dumbfounded. "Vegas? You mean the Las Vegas?"

"Yeah." Charlie was squirming again. "I didn't have the heart to wake you, man. You were so exhausted. I just decided to give you as long as you needed."

"How long?" Michael blinked.

"About four hours," Charlie said, checking the radio's clock. "I kept an eye on you. You slept the whole time."

"But why?" Michael tried to get his head around how Las Vegas was on the shortest route to Boston. "Why didn't you wake me up in Reno so I could drop you off with your daughter?"

Charlie looked down, sighed, then turned to Michael with a rueful and apologetic gaze. "I guess now's the time. Please believe me Michael, I can imagine what you must think, but you've got to believe that I'm your friend and not your enemy. The fact is, I made that stuff up about my daughter. I don't have a daughter. I'm not even married. I only said that to persuade you to take me."

"Why?" Michael felt on the edge of tears. He should have been thunderstruck, mad even, but instead he only felt defeated and helpless. His life was careening out of control, and it seemed like no matter what he did, no matter how careful, rational, or well-intended, the world would not stop blindsiding him with its puppet-masterly grip.

"To help you. It's as simple as that. There's no other reason."

"You don't even know me!" Michael wailed. "God Almighty, what is happening?"

Charlie looked apologetic and genuinely concerned, benevolently so, and his expression conveyed the same wholesome gentleness as the handshake that had pacified Michael when they had first gotten into the car. "I know how you must feel— No, just let me say my piece." He cut Michael's attempted comeback short. "You need to listen to this."

Charlie paused, looking him straight in the eye, and Michael did his best to marshal an expression of focused, deferential attention. Charlie began.

"It's true we've never properly met. But I do know a thing or two about you. It's not hard knowledge to come by; it's right there to see. You're a man who's spent his whole life giving the shirt off his back to others without a second thought. In fact, you can't help it. And while many people – most people, let's be hopeful about it – do an admirable job of taking care of their friends and kin, *you* hand out that level of compassion and kindness to everyone. You draw no distinction between the people you know, the people you're related to, and a total stranger. All you care about is that they're a person in need. And a person in need fortunate enough to trip across your path is a person blessed by God."

Michael felt dazed, detached. The words were coming in, and though he barely understood them and was utterly failing to comprehend what the babble was about, he wasn't trying to resist, he wasn't apprehensive, at least not with the kind of intensity he had experienced so many times this night. What he did feel was a numbness, mental rather than physical, a dust cloud rising from the rubble remains of the scaffolding that had supported his world until now, obscuring the landscape so he couldn't get his bearings, cloaking him in a miasma of uncertainty. So he didn't challenge Charlie, nor did he accept; he felt too weak for either.

But Charlie had his "piece to say," and he went on. "Now, you know all that. You don't dwell on it, but you know the person you are, whether you'll admit it or not. But what I'm here to tell you, what you *don't* understand, is that on occasion, you yourself – *you*, Michael Chandler – can be the one in need. That doesn't seem natural to you, does it? But you *can*. Anyone can. And it would be a sorry world if karma didn't even things out once in a while for people like you." He fixed Michael with a solid gaze, the power of which Michael would have thought him incapable just hours before. "And when that happens, Michael, when someone reaches out to help you, it's okay. I'm sure to you it feels wrong and uncomfortable, but it truly is okay. You *must* accept that."

I never told you my name, Michael thought grimly.

THEY DROVE IN SILENCE AND gradually, left to itself, Michael's perspective cleared enough to ponder. He was fed up with surprises and inexplicable coincidences. But what could he do? Charlie was here, any chance to ditch him without repercussions had been lost. And when it came down to it, if he was telling the truth, jettisoning Charlie might be the worst mistake he had ever made.

THEY REACHED THE SMALL TOWN of Mina, Nevada around 5:00 a.m., a faint glow on the eastern horizon beginning to swallow the stars. Except for the pavement and a few dim street lights, it might have been a ghost town by the look of the old wooden buildings slowly disintegrating on either side of the road, their windows boarded up and paint long since stripped away. "I hope there's gas here," Michael declared, eyeing the fuel gauge which was dipping perilously toward the red.

He pulled in where a badly weathered sign said "Muletown Gas" and stopped next to the pump island without much hope. The pumps were dark and there was not a single light on anywhere, not even a security light inside the rustic convenience store.

"Damn," he said, reading the business hours by the glow of the headlights on a large wooden placard: 7am – 7pm Weekdays, 7am – 9pm Saturday, Closed Sunday.

"How far is the next town?" he asked Charlie. "Did you see any signs?"

"No," his companion replied, eyeing the gas gauge, "but let's not give up on this one just yet."

"There's not so much as a stray dog here," Michael

replied. "We may just have to wait." But Charlie had already unfastened his seat belt and was opening his door, saying, "Just give me a minute to see if I can't rustle someone up."

Michael shrugged skeptically, cutting the lights and engine but leaving the electrics on so he could fiddle with the radio while Charlie cased the store. He swept the dial through the AM band twice without finding a single intelligible signal. He caught two stations on FM, one with classical music and the other, as best he could tell, some kind of religious talk, but both were weak, fluctuating, and so compromised by clipping and distortion that trying to listen wasn't worth the annoyance. He turned the car off.

All of a sudden, catching Michael completely by surprise, the lights on the gas pump flashed to life.

Charlie came around the corner of the mini-mart and ducked his head in the passenger door. "You actually found someone?" Michael said.

"Something like that." Charlie grinned. "Go ahead and fill her up. I'm going to stretch my legs."

Michael got out, swiped Barbara Jordan's Visa card, and propped the nozzle open in the gas intake. A gentle wind smelling of dust and flowers was blowing warm air in ahead of the day. *How utterly bizarre it's been,* he mused as he marveled at the intense tequila sunrise swelling at the edge of the desert sky. This time yesterday morning he had been making coffee in his townhouse at the start of a day brimming with excitement and good cheer. Twenty-four hours later, here he was gassing up a car that didn't belong to him in a skeleton town in another state, running from some kind of death spirit and, as if that weren't harrowing enough, a vindictive crime boss with political aspirations thrown in for good measure.

And running to what? He realized that in the frenzy of the night's trials and the numb exhaustion that followed, he had never thought specifically about where his life was now going. Work was no immediate problem, technically he was on vacation now and they wouldn't expect him back for another eight days. But sooner or later he'd have to return or he would be out of a job, and how could he do that with the police and Eldridge Raymore's goon squad poised to strike? Dan would put him up for a time in Boston, he was sure, but after a few weeks he would have to convey his thanks and move on, and what then? He had his cash and the loaned credit cards. Maybe when things cooled down he could figure a way to get the rest of his money out of his Wells Fargo account, but at some point he was going to have to get a new job and his own place to live. Would that even be possible without exposing him to the police and Raymore? How could he be sure a background check by a prospective employer or landlord wouldn't lead to a knock on his door in the middle of the night, or a bullet in the head?

The nozzle latch clicked loudly as it shut off the flow of gas. Michael replaced it in its carriage and screwed on the car's gas cap. The pump went dark again, and Charlie appeared around the side of the mini-mart with impeccable timing.

"You didn't, like, just break in through a window and turn the pump on, did you?" Michael asked as they pulled back onto Route 95 and left Mina behind.

"Of course not," Charlie replied in a tone that convinced Michael there would be no point in pressing him further.

An hour later, during which neither of them spoke, Michael ruminating while Charlie gazed through the windows and occasionally out the back, they passed a sign promising Las Vegas in 220 miles. The sun was pulling itself just clear of the mountains on a fresh new day, and Michael made up his mind.

"I'm going to trust you, Charlie," he began. "But the deal is you've got to be straight with me. No more cryptic answers or unexplained miracles. Okay?"

Charlie nodded. "I'll tell you everything I can."

CHAPTER 6
The Dice Roll

"DEAL." MICHAEL SHOOK CHARLIE'S HAND. "Now, let's start with how you knew my name."

Charlie took a long time to think about this. *Is he trying to remember*, Michael wondered, *or stalling while he makes something up?*

"I've been watching you," Charlie said at last.

"Watching me?"

"For some time now. Not all the time, but enough to feel like I know you. Watching from a distance, or tailing you from time to time as circumstance allowed."

"Why?" Michael was perplexed.

"I know you're thinking there must be some deep and hostile conspiracy at work. But the truth is nothing more than that our lives intersected by chance. Not in the bookstore—" Charlie cut off Michael's interjection. "Not in the bookstore last night, a long time before."

Charlie smiled. "The first time I saw you, I was shopping along at Wal-Mart, minding my own business, when I saw you helping a customer in tears. They didn't ask for it, you just walked over and introduced yourself. And they went away smiling. You know, most store clerks are plenty busy between their normal tasks and customers who approach *them*. It made me curious about what sort of person you were, and I started looking for you every time I was at

Wal-Mart. And I was pleasantly surprised to find that you did stuff like that all the time.

"I thought maybe it was just your job, or an act to get you a pay raise or something, so I started watching outside of work. And I saw that you were no different in private. In fact, your life seemed like an endless parade of arbitrary kindnesses. So I had my answer, but I kept watching. Because with all my heart I believed that someone like you, someone who did those things not just as an occasional Good Samaritan but as a lifestyle, deserved the same kind of help if you ever got into trouble. Then last night, you did."

Michael eyed Charlie with a shade of rebuke. "That sounds more like an obsession."

This observation seemed to fluster Charlie. "No, no," he quickly dismissed. "If I've given that impression, I'm overstating things. I didn't shadow you like some private detective. You must understand, I live alone and my simple needs are taken care of. I don't have to work, so I've got time on my hands. I could easily look in on you now and then without disrupting my routine. It's really no big deal."

Michael thought it was, but decided to press on. "It still doesn't explain how you knew my name."

"Everyone at Wal-Mart knows you," Charlie scoffed. "I was even able to get your home address from there."

Michael's heart gave a hammer pound. "You followed me home?"

"Lots of times. Most nights I'd sit in the car listening to the radio until you turned the lights out. It wasn't as tedious as it sounds. KGO radio does some very entertaining stuff in the evenings."

Michael fumed. *Who the hell was this man? What made him think he had the right to stalk a total stranger? Was he some kind of psycho like the guy who shot John Lennon?*

Then, incredibly, it occurred to him that this invasion might deliver an actual benefit.

"Were you ... were you watching at my house last night?"

Charlie nodded. "I saw you come home, then run out the door a few minutes later and drive off like a maniac. Did you know you left the front door open?"

"Vaguely," Michael said. "I was a bit preoccupied."

"No doubt." Charlie grinned. "But I'll have you know I locked and shut it before chasing after you."

"Thanks." And subtly, Michael's anger began to abate. Charlie could be lying about closing the door, but if he wasn't, it was an indication of thoughtfulness and compassion that supported Charlie's explanation of the surveillance. Michael found his spirits remarkably lifted at the prospect that Charlie might be able to corroborate the horrible event in the townhouse and prove that Michael wasn't crazy. He might even have noticed something helpful. And Michael took unexpected comfort in the notion that Charlie had been there, that Michael had not, though he could not have known it at the time, been alone.

"Then did you see—"

"What happened inside? No. Just that it must have been traumatic. That was obvious." Charlie gave his shoulder a couple of pats. "Would you like to tell me?"

"You'll think I'm crazy."

"Give me a try."

Michael took a deep breath and began his story. He told Charlie everything, starting with his purchase of the concert tickets and ending with the convenience store clerk's tip about the bookstore in Sacramento. Charlie, for the most part, sat serenely attentive, even at the part about the tree on the Hendrick lot, but he became visibly agitated when Michael described the encounter in his bedroom.

"Once more," Charlie entreated. "Tell me everything you remember about how this thing looked."

For the third or fourth time, Michael described what he remembered: a dark, rippling female form clad in white, a shimmering mist trailing from the waist down behind it in place of legs, and the eyes, those dark, terrible, soul-piercing, dread-inducing eyes.

"And it couldn't have been the regular stairs inside your townhouse. You're absolutely sure."

"Positive," Michael said firmly. "The bedroom is directly above the kitchen. And anyway, my memory is perfectly clear about how far down it went. It seemed like miles."

Charlie was silent, seeming in a trance. A minute passed by before he queried, "And she said what? As precisely as you can remember."

"By the ..." Michael strained to recall the words. "By the timeless you ... 'By the timeless are you bound this night to Lauria.' That's it, I think."

"You're sure she said 'Lauria'? A hundred percent sure?"

"Yes." Michael regarded Charlie's furrowed expression. "Why? Who is Lauria? What's got you worked up over this?"

"I don't know of anyone named Lauria." Charlie spoke ponderously. "But that whole encounter strikes me as critical to understanding what happened. Maybe even for determining what you should do. And for the life of me, even assuming for the moment that it was in fact paranormal, I can't think of any rational explanation."

"Rational *and* paranormal?" Michael laughed.

"You know what I mean. Rational in the context."

Michael nodded soberly. "But you do believe me?"

Charlie nodded. "I believe you."

WHEN MICHAEL HAD FINISHED HIS story, basking in an unexpected sense of relief at having unburdened himself, Charlie shifted up a mental gear. "So you're going to Boston."

"Unless you have a better idea."

Charlie shook his head. "How were you going to get there?"

"Um, drive?" Michael declared with amusement.

"What roads were you intending to take?"

"I hadn't gotten that far," Michael reminded him. "That's why I was looking for maps in the bookstore."

"Ah, yes." Charlie reached around and retrieved the atlas from behind his seat, thumbing to the two-page spread of the country at a glance. He found Reno and squinted across the page. "Well, it looks like 80 would have taken us to I-90 around Chicago, and that runs all the way to Boston."

"Where do we go from Vegas to get up there? Not back the way we came, I hope."

"No. But taking the straight course doesn't seem to me like the best plan."

"Why not?"

"They'll be watching it," Charlie calculated. "There'll be a nationwide APB by now. Anywhere they suspect you might go they'll be on top of, including the shortest route to get there from San Mateo."

"Maybe," Michael had to concede, thinking of the short Contacts list in his computer and the cache of emails from Dan Hendrick he had saved.

Charlie paged through the book. "Where else in the country do you have friends or family?"

Michael thought, ticking them off on his fingers. "My Dad was from Boulder, Colorado, and most of his side of the family still lives there. My mom grew up in a little town near St. Louis, Troy, Missouri — my grandma still lives in that house. We have some cousins in Pittsburgh …"

"Friends? Girlfriends?"

"No girlfriends." He pondered a moment. "Except for Dan, I've lost track of all my friends that left the Bay Area. I do know some Wal-Mart people at the corporate office in Arkansas that I guess you could call 'work friends,' but …"

Charlie studied the map. "How about Arizona?"

"No."

"Texas? Louisiana?"

"Nope and nope."

"Anywhere in the Deep South?"

Michael thought for a moment. "I went to Charleston, South Carolina once on business. Don't know anybody, though. I believe that's it."

"All right." Charlie eyed the book, tracing the page with his finger. "I think I see how we need to go."

"I don't want to get *too* far out of the way," Michael cautioned. "I don't really feel safe, even in this car, especially now that it's getting light outside and we'll be easy for the cops to see. I'd like to get to Dan's as soon as possible."

"I think we can stick to the freeways. My route shouldn't add more than a day or so." Charlie looked up. "And we could just travel at night. I'll share as much of the driving as you'll let me."

Michael nodded. He hadn't considered it. He had envisioned driving from early morning till about sunset each day, plopping himself exhausted in some ratty motel room to get up half-rested before dawn and repeat the marathon. But as soon as he heard them, Charlie's suggestions made eminently good sense. A circuitous route would dodge the Klieg lights, and the cloak of night would dramatically decrease the chances of being recognized by an alert cop.

"Okay. Yeah." Michael grinned. And for the first time, he was unequivocally thankful to have Charlie Paris along.

It would not be the last.

AROUND HALF PAST NINE, THE audacious jewel of Las Vegas bloomed incongruously before them out of the desert. It was none too soon for Michael. Driving for nearly six hours on four hours of sleep had made him desperately tired again, too tired even to address the empty but apathetic feeling growing in his stomach.

Nevertheless, driving into town infused Michael with a temporary alertness. He had seen Vegas in movies and on TV plenty of times, but had never actually been there. Even from a distance he could clearly see the line of tall buildings he knew must be "The Strip," the famous four-mile section of Las Vegas Boulevard lined with lavish casinos and spectacular hotels.

Michael couldn't resist. When they reached it, he took the exit and drove them south on the storied thoroughfare, drinking it all in with awe.

He was astonished by the theme park atmosphere. He had envisioned a metropolitan canyon of overdone, borderline sleazy glitz. Maybe it had been that once, but no more. What he saw instead seemed more like a grown-up Disneyland.

"What the hell?" Michael was staring upward, disbelieving what he saw. At the top of a tower worthy of the Jetsons, similar to but almost twice the height of Seattle's Space Needle, a roller coaster was racing madly around the pinnacle more than a thousand feet above the ground.

"God, you couldn't pay me enough to get on that." Michael shuddered.

"Aw, it looks like fun!" Charlie marveled.

All along the tour they never once found themselves without something jaw-dropping to look at. There were more coasters rocketing in and out of buildings, the dancing fountains of the Bellagio, glorious cityscapes of Paris and New York that surpassed anything in Epcot's World Showcase, the enormous pyramid and gleaming Sphinx of the Luxor. He found the scene a spectacular triumph of art over the ordinary, captivating him in the same way as his beloved Disney's *Pirates of the Caribbean* ride: a sense of wonder and immersion, an image he knew was gloriously idealized but which fact diminished his enjoyment not a bit.

Michael turned to Charlie. "Should we pull in and hole up in one of these? God, I wonder how much they cost."

"Not as much as you'd think," Charlie said, gawking at the scene with only a shade less of child-like awe. "They make so much money in the casinos they can price the rooms at teaser rates. They know visitors spend most of their gambling money at the hotel where they're staying. But no, I don't think we should stay on The Strip. These places are glutted with cameras and security staff. Better some hole in the wall that's just grateful to have a paying guest and has no particular interest in scrutiny."

Michael nodded wistfully. They weren't on vacation, he hadn't lost sight of that, but for a moment he had relished the prospect of exploring this world-famous spectacle now so tantalizingly close. Any diversion would be welcome, something to rejuvenate his spirit even for just a few hours, charging his mental and emotional batteries for the next leg of their sober and precarious journey. But Charlie was right, and Michael knew it. He sighed audibly as they merged onto I-215 eastbound to reconnect with US-95. Maybe the day would come when he would be free to return for a more leisurely and carefree sampling of Las Vegas's wonders. He certainly hoped so. He found himself dismayed to the point of despair at the thought of a future in which that sort of thing would never become possible.

"FAR ENOUGH?" MICHAEL ASKED A quarter of an hour later as the trappings of the famed city began to thin at the far edge of town.

"I think so," Charlie affirmed.

Michael pulled just off the throughway into the parking lot of an aging two-story motel identified with twenty feet of vertical pink neon as "The Bony Coyote." Even this scab, Michael noticed wryly, seemed to have its own casino, a modest blanched-wood structure on one corner of the property in the Old West motif so prevalent in Reno, a large skeletal coyote with rapturous blue eyes set in relief above its batwing double doors.

He pulled under the portico in front of the motel office, shut the motor off, and started to get out. But Charlie was ahead of him.

"Give me that woman's Visa and go park someplace," Charlie instructed. "I'll get us the room. If there's any trouble, we don't want them getting a look at you."

Charlie emerged a few minutes later with two card keys, handing one to Michael along with the Visa. They were on the second floor of the row of economy rooms. As Michael exited the car for the first time since Mina, he felt physically assaulted by the overpowering heat. He wondered how the locals who faced this day after day could stand it.

The room was modest, but not as bad as Michael had feared it might be. Crucially, the air conditioner was working and had been set refreshingly cool. He slung his backpack onto one of the chairs around the small wooden table, kicked off his sandals, and lay flat on the bed furthest from the door. After a day and a half without a comfortable place to sleep, it felt like the caress of an angel. When after a minute he started to get up, he felt that his legs had turned to lead, his whole body magnetically pulled to the mattress.

"Get some sleep," Charlie encouraged. "You need it bad. We'll get back on the road at sunset. I'll wake you."

"What are you going to do?"

Charlie shrugged. "I'm not tired. I thought I'd have a look around to wind myself down. I'll gas the car, if you don't mind me taking it."

Michael felt a twinge of apprehension at the thought of giving Charlie the keys to his only practical means of reaching Boston. But his suspicion of Charlie had by now dwindled to a whisper, and even that was evaporating away.

"All right." Michael retrieved the car keys and Shell card and extended them to Charlie, then hauled off his jeans, yanked his socks free, and chucked the clothes under the chair where he had set his pack.

"Sleep well," Charlie called as he closed the window shades and then strode toward the door. Michael climbed into bed and gave a little hand-puppet wave before turning on his side and pulling the soft, sweet covers close around him.

CHARLIE AND THE CAR KEYS were still gone when Michael awoke late that afternoon. The clock said 4:36. He'd slept for six hours. Charlie's absence concerned him, but by now he knew it was most likely benevolent consideration. Charlie had probably checked in on him several times, but left again so as not to disturb Michael before he'd had his full rest.

Now he was achingly hungry. He started for the shortbread cookies in his pack, then thought better of it. He had no way of knowing how difficult it was going to be to obtain real meals over the remainder of the trip, and he decided it would be wise to get one now while things seemed, for the moment, relatively safe.

Feeling his shirt clinging to him, he decided it was worth enduring hunger pangs for a few minutes to take a quick shower. The water was hot instantly, and the robust pressure of it on his back felt like an invigorating massage. He soaped himself thoroughly, washed his hair and rinsed off, then just stood there for two minutes with his eyes closed, enjoying the sensation and allowing his mind to clear.

He wrapped the towel around his waist and pulled his toiletry bag from his backpack, sprayed on deodorant, and brushed his teeth. He plugged in his shaver, then looked at it, pulled the cord out of the socket, and put it away. It might not make a difference, but there was a chance that letting his facial hair grow might help keep him from being recognized.

He had considered doing it anyway from time to time, just to see how it would look and whether the feel of it would annoy him, and now he had the best excuse imaginable for cultivating a test beard.

Recalling the heat, he put on a white T-shirt, a pair of light tan cargo shorts, and leather open-toed sandals, this time without socks. He grabbed his wallet and the room card key, and headed out the door.

The sunlight was blinding and the air even more sweltering than before, but after rest and a shower it didn't seem nearly as uncomfortable as it had that morning. Michael made his way across the searing parking lot, taking care not to step in the beads of viscous tar dotting the asphalt, and flapped through the doors into the casino under the bone coyote's neon leer, an unsettling expression that struck Michael as oddly lascivious even for "Sin City."

It was even cooler inside than in his room, and equally dark. There were rows of slots and video poker machines and a felt-top card table in one corner, but the rustic, windowless establishment was at least as much tavern as casino. It smelled strongly of spirits and half the floor space was taken up by knotty pine restaurant seating. Above the bar a large Keno screen displayed a matrix of the current winning numbers, and next to it an identically-sized widescreen television was playing CNN with the sound off.

In spite of its association with the motel, the saloon appeared patronized mostly by locals. The place was almost half full and heavy on old jeans, cowboy boots, and variants of the traditional western hat. He was particularly struck by one man with tussled hair, exaggerated sideburns, and a worn T-shirt from which the sleeves had been torn off by hand. His thick, tanned muscles were evidence of a life under the hot sun, and the handle of a long bowie knife protruded from a leather sheath strapped to his calf. Walk into a restaurant in San Mateo like that, he mused, and you'd be behind bars before the host could flash you a smile.

Michael anchored himself on a stool at the bar and

asked if he could order food. He took a quick look over the menu the bartender produced, then asked for a clubhouse sandwich with potato salad, a slice of blueberry pie, and a large draft beer. The barman scribbled on a ticket pad, then waved a waitress over to take it to the kitchen while he filled a pre-chilled pint glass from the tap. Michael thanked him, left a dollar tip on the counter, and took his beer over to a booth from which he could see the TV and try to lip-read the news.

Privation made the meal taste like the best he had ever eaten. When he was finished, he ordered a second beer and sipped it contentedly as he followed the news. He couldn't make out what the anchor Don Lemon was saying, but the headline ticker at the bottom of the screen provided context for the images shown. Tensions were high in the Middle East and might produce a spike in the price of gas. Michael rolled his eyes. If this was news, the networks should just clone the segment, because they could save money by trotting it out again every day.

Feeling fed, rested, and buoyed by the effects of the beer, he decided to try his gambling luck. He sat on the stool in front of a video poker machine and began feeding in quarters the waitress had kindly obtained for him while cashing his bill. On the third hand, the machine dealt two kings and an off suit 7, 6, and 2. He marked the three low cards for discard and pressed DRAW. To his amazement, up popped the other two kings, and the device began emitting the sound of coins clattering into a payout tray like hail. He printed the paper winnings voucher from the machine, stood up, and started toward the bartender to cash out while he was giddily ahead.

What he saw drained him pale.

On the television, in split screen with the anchor on the left, the right panel showed Eldridge Raymore glad-handing supporters at a campaign event. The display changed to a local news capture of the crash scene from the previous night. And then, incredibly, it was Michael's driver's license photo over the ticker caption: "Eldridge Raymore Jr. dies from in-juries sustained in hit and run."

His stomach lurched up like a high-rise elevator, so violently he had to bite hard on the back of his hand to keep from losing his composure. Heart pounding, using every last ounce of discipline he could summon to keep from running, Michael walked unsteadily to the men's restroom down a hall to the left of the bar. He barely made it into the center toilet stall before his lunch began spewing into the bowl like a fire hose.

He kneeled in front of the toilet for three full minutes, gripping the seat with both hands for stability, vomiting miserably until not even digestive fluid would come up and twice by pure reflex after that.

When at last the nausea dissipated enough for a run to the motel room, Michael flushed and yanked a wad of toilet paper off the roll to daub his eyes and wipe the residue from around his mouth. He was just standing up when he heard the restroom door crash open and something slammed hard against the walls of the stall, followed by the sound of a hand smacking onto the tile floor.

"No!" cried a frightened, young-sounding man's voice.

"You should have listened, you dumb son of a bitch," came a lower, angry tone. "I told you three times not to talk to her. Now I gotta make your ugly face even uglier."

"Look man, I'm sorry. I'm sorry!" the first voice plead-ed.

"Too fucking late," came the attacker's reply, then from the victim in anguish: "Aaaah! Aaaaaaah!"

Michael threw open the stall door. The local with the hand-torn sleeves he had noticed earlier was straddling the chest of a scrawny young man flat on the ground, blood streaming from a notch in the victim's ear and a three-inch gash across one cheek.

Adrenaline gripped Michael before he could think. He couldn't stand to see cruelty like this, it made him physically ill, and letting it go on was not an option.

"Get off him," Michael commanded threateningly, tearing his wallet from his back pocket and flashing it open and shut too fast to be scrutinized. "Federal agent!"

For an instant the man froze, surprised, but as he sized Michael up his composure quickly returned. He stood up slowly, planting a foot on the stomach of the man bleeding on the floor, fixing Michael with a menacing leer as he poised the knife and drawled, *"Buuull sheeeat."*

The door to the stall next to the one Michael had occupied burst open, slamming against the attacker's elbow. Out stomped Charlie Paris.

"You heard my partner," Charlie barked. As the assailant wheeled, Charlie jammed the edge of his shoe into the man's forward instep with such force that they could all hear the bones crack. He yelled furiously and staggered down, the knife flying; Michael quickly retrieved it as it clattered to the tile.

Now it was the knife man's turn to lie helplessly pinned to the ground. "Listen up, cowboy," Charlie menaced, his foot planted firmly on the man's chest. "Your anger management problems have nothing to do with what we're here for, so at the moment we're not interested in you. You would be very wise not to get us interested. Understood?"

The man glowered at Charlie and tried to get up. Charlie knocked him back with a kick to the jaw that elicited another howl. *"Is that understood?"*

The knife man nodded, wincing limply, pain appearing to win out over his defiant anger.

"You gonna be okay?" Michael helped the younger man to his feet and over to the sink.

"Yeah. Thank you."

Michael gave him a smile as the man turned on the faucet and splashed cold water over his injuries. They looked superficial, not as bad as the bleeding had made them seem, and while it was hard to say whether some permanent scarring could be avoided, there was no doubt it could have been much worse.

"Get the hell out of here," Charlie directed the assailant, who slowly got up, eyed the bowie knife in Michael's hand as though about to demand it back, then appeared to think better of it. He ambled to the door and out into the hallway, his posture crumpling and his face contorting with every other step.

"FEDERAL AGENT? THAT'S WHAT YOU come up with, *federal agent?*" Charlie guffawed once they were safely back in the motel room.

"I don't know where that came from," Michael said.

"Well, it worked. I guess that's all that matters. You saved that kid a serious case of bad cosmetic surgery."

"Not me. You did. The guy was about to stab me, too." Michael's gaze narrowed. "Charlie, how the hell did you happen to be in that stall?"

"Keeping tabs on you." Charlie shrugged.

"I could have sworn that stall was empty when I came in the restroom. I looked under the doors. Besides, how did you even know I was in the casino?"

"You weren't in the room. Where else could you be? You didn't have the car."

He wasn't satisfied, but Michael couldn't see any irrefutable rifts in Charlie's explanation. *The guy's been shadowing me for weeks*, he thought. *Maybe the habit dies hard.*

He cleaned the knife thoroughly – it wouldn't do for a maid to discover it with blood still on the blade – then set it down in the trash bin under the sink, careful not to tear the bag. He had thought briefly of keeping it for protection, but realized immediately how ridiculous that was. For one thing, Michael felt very uncomfortable around knives, especially sharp ones. For another, he knew in his heart that he would never be able to use such a thing against another human being, no matter what the circumstances, not even to save his own life.

Suddenly, he remembered the reason for his presence in the restroom in the first place, and was gripped again by nausea and a dread chill. He told Charlie what he'd seen and started to turn on the TV to get more detail, then stopped as he realized he didn't really want to see it.

Charlie nodded soberly. "Let's get on the road," he said. "It's best not to chance some yahoo in that redneck barn making the connection."

THEY DROVE THROUGH THE GAP between Black Hill and Black Mountain as the last of Las Vegas disappeared from view. Where the highway forked, they abandoned 95 and bore east on US-93 toward Arizona. The sun sank behind them as they headed toward a new time zone, another state, and a second night of driving through the dark.

CHAPTER 7
The Desert Flower

CHARLIE DROVE. NOT ONLY WAS Michael feeling weak both from the loss of his meal and the violence of losing it, but he was still recovering from the shock of what he had seen on the TV.

"Charlie, I killed a man," he lamented, his voice soft and cracking.

"You don't know that."

"He wasn't moving, not even a little. Not even when they lifted him up to the steering wheel. He just flopped like a sack of potatoes."

"Yes," Charlie countered, "but he could have been dead already, have you thought of that?"

"They said he died of injuries from the crash."

"From what you've told me, don't you think it's equally possible that that was just a hasty conclusion encouraged by that corrupt police chief? And anyway, you *had* to do it. They would have hit that little boy."

"I know, but—"

"So, stop beating yourself up. Would you rather have the kid dead?"

Michael pondered. "I don't know." What he said felt wrong to him, but it was the truth. "Maybe I'd feel better if I hadn't done anything that killed either one of them."

"Baloney," Charlie scoffed. "You had no choice. And

most people, even if they were inclined, couldn't have made up their mind fast enough to save him. *You* only could because that's your first instinct. You should feel like a hero."

"I can't," Michael agonized. "Everything you're saying is probably true, but it doesn't— holy shit, what is that?"

Rounding a bend in the road, all at once the Colorado River was before them: to their left the terrible grandeur of the Hoover Dam spilling the waters of Lake Mead into the deep canyon below, straight ahead the majestic arch bypass bridge looming nine hundred feet above the thrashing rapids.

Charlie pulled onto the shoulder and brought the vehicle to a stop. "All yours."

Michael grasped the door latch, pulled, then stopped. He began to hyperventilate. He did want to drive, at least he did if they had to cross this chasm at all, but he wasn't sure he could control himself. The lack of body fuel weakened him, his throat and stomach muscles hurt, he was still mentally traumatized from the events in the casino, and on top of that, he remained unsteadied by the alcohol that had made it into his bloodstream before his purge.

He looked at Charlie, who was still waiting patiently in the driver's seat for Michael to decide. He eyed the dam to their left, an imposing colossus wedged between stark red cliffs, great chunks of water cascading from the spillways like someone pushed off a skyscraper. He looked at the bridge, a lithe, elegant span a quarter mile across with lights like fairy lanterns sparkling in the twilight. There were guard rails, four feet high and solid by the look of them. But they paled in comparison to the reassuring cat's cradles of 2 ½- foot-thick steel suspension cable that guarded cars on the Bay Area bridges, and unlike those gargantuan structures, these rails could not keep Michael's brain from conjuring highly unlikely but not impossible scenarios that might toss a car over the edge.

Yet from the events of this day, he had finally come to accept Charlie without reservation as a sincere and compassionate ally. And a resourceful one at that: a reliable, clear-thinking companion with not only his best interests at heart but also an uncanny ability to engage when most needed and to extricate Michael from situations that he would have been gravely pressed to manage alone.

"It's okay." He squeezed the latch, opened and shut the door firmly to ensure it was secured, and motioned forward. "Go ahead."

"You sure?"

Michael nodded, locking his door and closing his eyes as the car rolled forward, casting up a silent prayer.

THEY CROSSED INTO ARIZONA, THROUGH the painted rock cliffs with their peaks on fire in the dusk light, out across the scrubby tree-dotted plateau as the sun disappeared. Michael gazed out the window like a train passenger, shoes off and his seat tipped comfortably back, allowing the ride to jostle him gently like a mother's hand on a cradle.

"Ever been married?" he asked Charlie, a question that arose in his wandering mind for no particular reason. "I know you said you aren't now."

"Nope," Charlie said cheerfully.

"Never wanted to?"

"I wouldn't say that. It just never worked out. Wasn't meant to be, I guess."

"Do you regret it?"

Charlie thought for a moment. "Sometimes," he admitted. "But it doesn't consume me, if that's what you mean. I'm fine with how things went. I've had a happy life."

"Ever come close?" Michael pressed.

"Not really." Charlie shot him a pleasant diverting glance. "What about you?"

"Marriage?" Michael gave a long, slow sigh. "Yeah, I came close. I like to think so, anyway."

"What happened?"

"There was this girl. Woman, I should say. Her name was Vicki Valentine."

"Valentine? For reals?" Charlie laughed.

"Yeah, yeah. Laugh till you choke." Michael smiled, his eyes straight ahead, his mind miles and years away. "She was an art major I met at school in Santa Cruz. God, was she pretty. But not pretentious about it like some women are. She had this natural kind of beauty, not all makeup and salon hair. She just seemed, I don't know, electric with life. Like a bounding gazelle."

"Sounds like your type."

Michael nodded. "You know, I dated all the time in high school and the first two years at Santa Cruz. Never missed a dance, never stayed home on a Saturday night except by choice. I was pretty taken with some of those girls, too. They were all attractive, sexy, interesting in various ways. But at some point there was always a disconnect."

Charlie nodded, unexpectedly rapt.

"For instance, there was this one girl, the daughter of a Navy doctor. Beth McFadden. She had it all going. Straight-A student, president of the Glee Club, varsity tennis player, confident, and good-looking. I took her to Homecoming and we had a thing for a while. I started thinking maybe she was 'the one,' whatever that means when you're fifteen. Then one day, out of the blue, we were talking on the phone and she just started screaming at me. I couldn't for the life of me figure out what I might've done to ignite a tirade. She started yelling that I didn't understand her, that I was completely wrong about her, I didn't know anything, and I had no right to give her advice. Hell, all teenage kids play psychoanalyst to each other. They have to; they believe anyone over voting age is a different species. I was sure I hadn't said anything unusual, or I might have understood why she was so upset."

"I don't think that's exclusive to teens," Charlie countered. "Sounds like some married couples I know."

"Maybe." Michael shrugged. "Anyway, Vicki was dif-

ferent. We weren't identical, we didn't agree about everything, but on all the important stuff we understood each other completely. People talk about having things in common.
With Vicki, it was more than that. It was like we were in each
other. Like we were looking at the world through the same
colored glass. I never had a sister, so I don't really know, and
I don't mean anything weird by this, but Vicki and I seemed
to be made from the same stuff, like siblings. Pieces meant
to fit together, maybe that's a better way of putting it. Before we met, I thought 'soul mates' was just some saccharine
Hollywood malarkey. It's not. We had it."

Charlie nodded thoughtfully. "That much about love,
I know."

"That would have been enough for me, Charlie. More
than enough. I could have been happy the rest of my days
just bringing home her groceries. But completely separate
from that, she was a really good artist. Big gallery quality. Got offered a Master's scholarship, though I think by
that time she'd had enough of school. She painted different
styles, all sorts of stuff, but what she loved to do best were
these unique abstract pieces, not like anything else I've ever
seen. They weren't Rorschach blots or random paint splatters
like Jackson Pollock, hers had recognizable forms – animals,
flowers, writing symbols, stuff like that – integrated into an
abstract framework. They had this magical quality, like you
were looking into some enchanted parallel world. In fact, all
of her work was like that. Even her landscapes and still-lifes
drew you into a sort of hyper-reality. Better than reality, you
know? Enchanting, and … *whimsical,* that's the word. Like
the feeling you get watching the movie *Fantasia.*"

Charlie smiled. "Sounds like the perfect woman. For
you, anyway."

"Well, nobody's perfect. Let's see … she couldn't bowl
worth crap, there was that. Couldn't hit the head pin to save
her life. Gutter ball left, gutter ball right, 4-7-10 split, repeat.
It didn't keep the two of us from having a blast while I tried
to teach her, though. We scored each frame triple her pin

count, and anything over six was a strike. She was a good sport."

"But bowling a legitimate three hundred was not on her Bucket List."

"Nope. Never going to bowl three hundred." Michael laughed. "So not perfect. But she would have been famous, I guarantee that. There's no doubt in my mind. Her art was that good."

"Would have been?" Charlie queried.

"Yeah." Michael slumped with a haunted sigh. "We went out steady for almost three years. When we were about to graduate, we planned it all out. As soon as school was done, I was supposed to get an apartment back in the Bay Area and she was going to move in with me. It wasn't said in so many words, but I think both of us figured we would give that a little time to see how it went, like a dress rehearsal, and if things worked out, we'd get married the following year. In my mind, it was a done deal. I was going to make damn sure everything went right once she moved in. I was ready to cook dinners, scrub toilets, bring her flowers, keep taking her on romantic dates. Make her feel like the most pampered and adored woman in the world. I wasn't going to let her have any excuse to think we shouldn't be together for the rest of our lives."

Charlie smiled. "She must have thought you were Prince Wonderful, right out of a story book."

"Yeah, well ..." Michael smiled fatalistically. "It didn't go that way."

He started to speak, but a little cough choked Michael and he suddenly found himself overtaken by memory. Up to now he had been able to tell the story with detachment, fully engaged but freed from emotional immediacy by the intervening years. Now, all of a sudden, he was awash in the terrible event he was about to describe as vividly as though it had happened yesterday. Twice he began to form words only to have them drop from his lips stillborn. Only on the third try was he able to muster the composure to go on.

"She was packing up," he resumed. "She was on her way to the U-Haul, in fact. She was heading there with a couple of friends to get a truck she'd rented to move some boxes to her parents' house. We couldn't afford much of an apartment and she was going to store everything she didn't need."

Michael bit down, then continued. "Vicki was riding in the back seat when a semi-truck crashed into them from behind. The driver was texting on his cell phone and didn't see the traffic stop. The gas tank blew up and caught the car on fire. The other two girls got out, but the back doors were jammed shut by the impact. Vicki burned to death."

"Oh my God."

For a moment, Michael held it together, eyes blank, saying nothing. It had been a very long time since he had spoken of this. Doing so now, having to recite the details aloud to someone who had never heard them, brought everything back as fresh as it would have seemed to the listener. Anguish filled the space all around him, and he reached for Charlie, burying his face in the older man's shoulder and sobbing quietly, his rib cage wracked with intermittent shudders, utterly unable to out-swim the brutal horror of this reality with which he had never and could never come to terms, this obscene, senseless event that had demolished the blissful life gleaming so clearly ahead of him, so inexplicable, so unnecessary, so incompatible with a world supposedly under the grip of a benevolent and all-powerful Creator.

At last he could cry no more, and the tide of misery began to withdraw. Michael lay back in his seat again.

"I didn't go to the funeral," he intoned flatly. "I couldn't. I didn't read about it in the papers, either. If it came on the news, I changed the channel." He glanced at Charlie beseechingly without even knowing what he was asking for. "I like to think it was quick, you know? That she didn't suffer. I tell myself she was knocked unconscious by the impact and didn't feel a thing."

As he spoke, he knew that articulating this, a narrative

rehearsed in his mind of its own accord as a way of constructing emotional battlements, risked undermining those very fortifications by exploiting their dire weakness to scrutiny. But Michael was past containing himself.

"Because if I knew otherwise, I couldn't help feeling responsible. Like I was her protector, you know? Like I was her protector, and I let her down. I failed the one truly sacred responsibility I ever had in my life. Like I could have done something and didn't, I could have gotten the truck myself and Vicki wouldn't even have had to be on the road that day …"

Charlie reached over with his free hand and patted Michael gently on the back like a parent comforting a sick child. He knew better than to contradict or cut off Michael's diatribe of self-rebuke. As hoped and intended, the nurturing gesture accomplished what verbal interruption would not. Michael's words trailed off and his furrowed brow began to relax. Before closing his eyes to let the angst drain naturally away, he turned Charlie a grateful glance, and was surprised to find that there were tears on his companion's cheeks, too.

JUST AFTER 8:30 P.M. THEY REACHED Kingman, Arizona, once a prime node on the fabled Route 66 from Chicago to Los Angeles and still rife with diners, hot rods, and a myriad other nostalgic remnants of those romantic glory days.

"You need to eat something," Charlie observed. "Real food, not convenience store crap. You can't have got much nutrition from that dinner you donated to the snakes in the Las Vegas sewer. Want to get something here?"

"Sure." Michael's appetite hadn't completely returned, but he had recovered sufficiently for Charlie's suggestion to sound like a good idea.

Charlie took the next exit, where a blue road sign indicated the presence of restaurants. He pulled in and parked in the Denny's lot. "I'll go in and get some take-out. What would you like? Some soup maybe? You look kind of pale. I don't think you should have anything adventurous just yet."

"Soup sounds fine," Michael replied. "Chicken noodle, if they have it. Maybe some pie." He handed Charlie two twenty-dollar bills. "Get something for yourself, too."

"I'm not hungry, but thanks." Charlie took the cash and got out of the car. "What kind of pie?"

He started to say blueberry, but that thought raised an unexpected revolt in the pit of his stomach. Something mild, he thought. "Banana cream would be good."

"You got it." Charlie closed the car door and headed for the diner.

They were parked on the perimeter of the lot, facing away from the restaurant across Devine Avenue toward a railroad right of way. As Michael surveyed the surroundings, he noticed a small fire, of what origin or purpose he couldn't tell, near the train tracks a few dozen yards away.

Unable to come up with a benign reason for a fire this time of night close to a railroad, he realized with alarm that it might be accidental or even an act of arson, and if so, he might have been the first person to see it, and the only one with a chance to get help in time to prevent disaster. He got out of the car, waited for traffic to clear, and jogged across the street.

As he neared it, Michael began to make out a small group of figures lying or seated around the blaze. He slowed his gait to a walk. They were a rough-edged bunch, clothing tattered, hair overgrown, some of them shielding worn backpacks or belonging-filled dumpster bags, a few nursing bottles of liquid intoxicant. Homeless people, he realized, what used to be derided as "hobos" or "bums." Maybe marking time for covert passage on a freight car, as the stereotype went, but more likely just locals of misfortune bedding down in a spot where they hoped they would not be harassed.

He was about to turn around and head back to the car when one of the figures caught his eye. It was a woman, indeterminate in age but at best guess in her forties, a ragged shawl wrapped around her torso as she huddled in a fetal position, long, stringy hair in the dirt, intermittently shaking as though battling a winter chill even though the air was a comfortable sixty-five or so and her spot near the campfire warmer still.

"Are you okay?" Michael asked, kneeling down beside the woman amid looks from the others, all men, ranging from bitter to apathetic.

"No," she rasped gruffly.

"What's the matter?"

"I'm sick," the woman chattered. "Hurt all over. Can't even get fucking warm. God damn this place."

"Would you like me to take you somewhere? To the hospital? Or is there a shelter?"

"Hospital. Shelter." The woman spat the words. "No hospital or shelter is going to fix this. I'm past all that. I'm dying, for Christ's sake. I'm lying here dying like a fucking dog. And I don't even care. I just want the pain to go away."

"Here, Rosie." The man closest to her held out a bottle of generic white rum with three fingers' worth left at the bottom.

"No, Sam. I'm not going to take yours. Besides, that stuff is crap." The woman forced an appreciative smile. "Thanks all the same, though. You're a good man."

"I'd like to help," Michael said gently. "Is there anything I can do?"

"Yes," the woman answered harshly. "But you won't."

"Sure I will. What is it?"

She issued a scornful chuff, but raised a hand and pointed. "See that store over there? Wan Li's? If you really want to help, go get me a bottle of Wild Turkey. Here, I'll even pay." She fumbled inside her shawl and brought out a jangling coin purse with a few wadded bills sticking out. "I'd get it myself but that bastard won't sell me any more."

The last thing this poor wretch needs, Michael thought, is a fresh bottle of booze. But he had an idea.

"I'll buy." He waved the woman's money away. "How about some food, too? Do they have sandwiches and stuff in there? What kind do you like?"

"No food." Now that she could see he was serious, her tone toward Michael began to thaw. "I don't want anything to eat, it won't make any difference. I just want the pain to stop so I can fall asleep and get this over with."

Michael smiled noncommittally and stood up. "Back in a minute."

Wan Li's did have sandwiches, and not the expected kind with meager filling on flavorless bread that were produced in factories and shipped all over the country in stiff plastic packaging. These were soft, fresh creations on styrofoam trays sealed in cellophane, made in the store or at least somewhere locally, plump with hand-stacked meats, vegetables, and cheeses and lavished with wholesome condiments that had never seen the inside of a miserly tear-open pouch.

Michael bought ten of them, taking care to collect an assortment of ham, turkey, and roast beef on a variety of breads. He grabbed two half-gallons of orange juice, too, with a sleeve of picnic cups to pour them in, and finally – after a short ethical discussion in his head in which his original instinct prevailed – one sleek, full fifth of genuine Wild Turkey whiskey.

The expressions of even the most hostile of the fireside companions melted when Michael started handing out sandwiches and pouring juice. He saved himself a turkey on sourdough, extracted two cups from the sleeve before seating himself next to the woman, then got up again temporarily and found a taker for the sandwich he had withheld. Charlie was feeding him, he thought. These poor guys needed that sandwich a lot worse than he.

He offered the woman a juice, but she shook it off adamantly, as expected. He was more insistent that she take a sandwich, and finally she demurred, accepting a ham and

Swiss on marbled rye, which she nevertheless abandoned to a nearby chunk of cardboard as soon as it was in her grasp, full attention on the whiskey Michael was pouring into the two cups he had set at their feet.

The woman drained a long, smooth draft from the cup and closed her eyes, breathing in deeply. A warm, bright smile spread across her face.

"*Sooo* much better," she cooed in a voice infinitely warmer and richer in tone than before. "May the Lord bless you a thousand times."

"You really should eat, too," Michael admonished gently. "It will make you feel better."

"I already feel better." She gave Michael a clear, vivacious smile that outshone her ragged appearance and seemed utterly incongruous with the dim, enfeebled figure she had been just minutes before. "My name is Rosemary, by the way. Rosemary Hart."

"Michael Chandler." He smiled. Only fleetingly did it occur to him that disclosing his name was an indiscretion to be avoided. At least there didn't seem to be any radios or televisions around.

"Chandler. That means candle maker, doesn't it? So what brings a kind, handsome candle maker to the lonely railroad tracks on a summer night, Mr. Chandler?"

"Oh, I was ..." He glanced over toward the Denny's, suddenly mindful of how distraught Charlie would probably be to find Michael missing. "I was just waiting for my friend to come out of the restaurant there, when I saw your fire. I came over to see if there was a problem."

"And there was." Rosemary poked a finger playfully into his ribs before commandeering the bottle and replenishing the serving of whiskey she had already drained. Michael sipped his own, careful not to let the fumes up into his sinuses, and the nasty stuff bit him like a rattlesnake anyway. God, he thought, how can she just inhale it like that?

"You found a girl on fire, and you put her out. You're a regular hero, Michael Chandler. You're like a fireman for girls. A girl fireman. A … girfman." This inane, inadvertent sputter of humor seemed to amuse Rosemary to distraction, and her frame shuddered merrily as she fought to control the giggles and keep from spitting her drink.

"Have the sandwich. At least half." Michael reached around her to the cardboard mat and retrieved the ham and cheese. "It would make *me* feel better."

Rosemary eyed him coyly, playfully, almost lasciviously. "I'll eat half the sandwich," she proposed dangerously, "if you will be my husband. That's the deal. Take it or leave it."

"How do you know I'm not already married?" Michael tried to say seriously.

"I don't care," Rosemary said petulantly. "She can have you back tomorrow. You can be my husband just for tonight."

For a moment he was taken aback. She was playing, that was obvious, but he wasn't entirely sure playing at *what*. What did she mean by "be her husband"? Surely she didn't mean she wanted him to have sex with her … or did she? He didn't want to offend or alienate her before he had the chance to make her eat and get her to a hospital, which had been his plan all along. But he certainly wasn't going to sleep with her, either. What was he supposed to say?

"What exactly does being your husband entail?" he finally replied, trying to match her tone of playfulness.

"You have to hold me." Rosemary took a swig from her cup and pursed her lips out in a kissy gesture. "You have to hold me, put your arms around me, and tell me I'm beautiful. Tell me I'm the only woman you'll ever want. But just for tonight, except don't say that part."

"And you'll eat the sandwich."

"*Half.*"

"Half the sandwich. And if it doesn't taste yucky like you seem to think it will, you'll eat the other half after."

"Half the sandwich." She turned her gaze to the tray, from which Michael had been deftly removing the cellophane to make it more convenient and appealing. For the first time, she seemed to show it genuine interest. She turned back to Michael and resumed the nuthouse negotiation. "And the other half if you kiss me."

Michael laughed. It wasn't so much that she was funny, though Rosemary seemed to find herself hilarious. It was laughter of simple joy. She had seemed so forlorn and wasted when he had come upon her lying on her side in the dust. Now she was so ebullient, so full of life. Like a whole, real person rescued from the precipice of ruin. I *am* a hero, he thought. I *am* a girfman.

"All right." Michael put his cup down, turned to face Rosemary, put both hands on her shoulders, and proclaimed with flat sincerity: "Rosemary Hart, I, Michael Chandler, do hereby accept your proposal and agree to be your husband for a day. In exchange for which, you agree to eat the sandwich of the first part, which you so ungraciously threw on the ground. Forthwith: you are the most beautiful woman I have ever seen, and I shall never want anyone else, so help me God." After a pause during which he drank in her absolutely beaming and delighted gaze, he added: "For tonight."

"You're not supposed to say that part!" she chided, but her faux displeasure melted instantly into a broad, contented grin. She took a sip from her cup and snuggled right up to him, pulling his arm around so she could nestle her head against his shoulder, and bit into the sandwich with a gusto that firmly belied her earlier protestations. It filled Michael with warm satisfaction, and he gave himself permission to savor the moment, however ridiculous and ephemeral it was. He sipped his drink and let a measure of Rosemary's ecstasy wash over him, too.

"I had a real one once," Rosemary told him after the sandwich – the entire sandwich – was gone, her head resting against his cheek now as they sat watching the fire, lumped together like real lovers. "A husband, I mean. His name was Tom Gump. *Gump.*" She giggled, but softly, not like her earlier animated convulsions. She was slowing down now, way down, completely happy, free from pain, drifting in a sunny sort of melancholy. "I kept my old name, cause I didn't want to be 'Mrs. Gump'." She looked up at Michael briefly. "Is that bad?"

"No." He smiled and kissed the top of her head. "I wouldn't want to be Mrs. Gump, either."

She laughed and jabbed an elbow into his ribs. "I don't know if I was in love with him, even. I can't remember. I was ready to get married, ready to start a family and have a real life, and there he was. He had a job and he thought I was pretty, and that seemed enough at the time. So I married him." Rosemary sighed. "You want to know what's ironic? He left me. *He* left *me*."

"I can't believe anyone would want to do that." Michael gave her a gentle snuggle with the arm draped around her. He was vaguely aware that what he was doing wasn't quite right, both because his affection was half contrived and because it was, in equal measure, a heartfelt indulgence of his own need to be loved. But he pushed such thoughts away. There was no real harm in it, he reasoned. *She's happy, I'm happy, these drunks around us seem to think it's just funny and endearing. Where's the sin in people letting down for a bit and enjoying the ride? Besides, she asked for it. And my motives are pure, because the whole point is to get this woman some medical help. It might not take, I won't know since I'll never see her again, she might be right back here in a week drinking herself to death. But I will have done everything I reasonably could. And it* might *work. This little interlude, someone taking genuine interest in her welfare –* and that part, beyond question, Michael was not guilty of faking in the least – *just that gesture of compassion might be enough to push her back over the line to self-respect and hope. It might be all she needs to support a frame of mind receptive to true recovery. And the chance of that is enough to justify whatever frail foundation this crazy bum party rests on. The chance to save a life makes it right.*

"Well, he did. And you know why? Because I couldn't

have a baby. Because I couldn't ... have ..."

Rosemary's words trailed off into a lonely sigh. For the next few minutes she was silent. Whatever she was thinking, she did not shake, she did not cry. She seemed to be actively using the intoxication to her advantage, channeling her thoughts and emotions with the deftness of someone who, over the course of years, had developed methods of self-management as sophisticated and effective as any professional treatment, albeit at a terrible cost.

"It doesn't matter." Rosemary sounded thoughtful, analytical. "In fact it's for the best. It wouldn't do to have children now. At least I won't be leaving someone without a mother. It's a terrible thing, to have your mother die. Especially young. Especially from something that people who don't know a god damned thing about it think can be easily cured."

"Rosemary?" Suddenly Michael was alert. There was something in her voice, something dreadful. His heart began pounding as his brain began piecing together the meaning in her words, the back story that she had been hinting at all evening but he had not picked up on until now. He strained not to show his alarm, not to upset the cocoon of serenity she had constructed for herself using him as the silk. But it was too strong, it was beyond him, and his muscles tensed.

"It's all right, Michael. Don't be sad for me." Now she was consoling him. The world was turning upside down again. Michael found himself shaking his head, involuntarily, willing helplessly and utterly without effect that things should not continue toward the conclusion he suddenly feared.

"Liver failure," she answered his unasked question. "Psoriasis, they call it. Too much poison over too much time. Eventually the poor thing can't do its job anymore, throws its tools down in disgust, and quits." She smiled into Michael's horrified gaze. "Some people get a transplant. The success rate is pretty high, if you get one in time, though you don't live to a ripe old age even then. It's a temporary fix. Good for some people for sure. Gives some mothers a chance to be there for their children a little while longer."

"Rosemary." Michael broke their embrace, turned to face her squarely, gripped her shoulders, and looked intently into her eyes. "Let me help you. I've got a car right over there. Let me take you to the hospital so they can give you proper treatment. You can have a good life again. I'll help you do it. I ... my situation is complicated, but suffice it to say, I have to start my life over somewhere anyway. It might as well be here. Let me help you out of this. I can. I will."

"No, Michael." Rosemary's voice was calm, measured, and firm. *How can she be so placid?* he thought madly.

"I can't afford a transplant, even if I qualified for one. I haven't had insurance for years. Even if I did, there aren't enough livers to go around. Not by a long shot. Anyway, they give priority to people that actually matter. People with families and relationships and important jobs. As they should. When those people die it's like a line of dominoes. Their lovers, their parents, their children, it's like a tornado running over all those lives. I've set things up carefully so that can't happen. No one cares about me. Well, my dad, but he has no idea where I am. I haven't talked to him in years and the last he knew I was in West Virginia."

"Of course he would care." Michael shook her. "You've got to call him. You can't shut him out of this. If he knew what was happening he would do everything he could to help you. Any good parent would."

"Yes. And he would throw the last penny of his retirement down a rat hole for the privilege of knowing his daughter had turned into a hopeless alcoholic, which I have made sure he is blissfully unaware of. And then what? I don't get a liver, or my body rejects it, or I die anyway when it gives out a couple years later, more likely sooner because I can't hack the lame treatment program? Not on my terms, but choking on my own vomit next to some restaurant dumpster?"

Michael tried to speak, but she grabbed both of his wrists in her hands and yanked down to get his attention. "It doesn't matter, Michael. It doesn't. I made my choice a long time ago. I'm not going to take a spot on an organ donor list from someone who hasn't fucked up their life. I don't want people to know what happened to me, ones who might care most of all. My whole life has been like running upstairs backwards, and I just want to go. *I want to go.* Do you understand? It's my life. My decision." Her voice softened and she eyed him beseechingly. "Don't try to take that from me. Please. You don't have the right. It's the only thing left that I have any control over."

"No," Michael commanded, panicky, his head shaking side to side on autopilot, his hands up trying to fend off something unseen that couldn't be countermanded by force. *"No ..."*

"Listen to me, Michael Chandler. Listen well, because I want you to remember. I want you to have this for when you think about me down the road. I don't want you crying for me. I want you to remember our little time together and smile.

"What you did tonight granted my only wish. You took the pain away so I could do this in peace. That was all I needed, but you gave me more. You stayed with me. You comforted me. You made me laugh. You made me feel like somebody actually gave a shit. Don't you see? You've made me happier than I ever could have hoped for when this day came. You are a miracle."

"Rosie—"

She shook her head and placed her forefinger firmly over her lips. "Just ... hold me. I ate the goddamned sandwich. You promised."

She slipped his arm back around herself and cuddled close to him as before. She took a long last drink to empty the whiskey from her picnic cup. She closed her eyes, let her breath out, and relaxed down into him.

When she turned to look at him again, his cheeks glistened with silent tears.

"You were the best husband I ever had." She smiled

dreamily. "Thank you."

She cuddled back down, wriggling into Michael's embrace as though he were a warm, soft bed with freshly laundered covers.

Then she was gone. Sam, who had offered her the last of his rum, wept openly. The other men contemplated their bottles or looked away, having seen drinking lives end before, having known this was coming and prepared for it, or perhaps never having cared that much to begin with.

Michael rocked her. He held her lovingly in his arms and rocked back and forth, stroking her matted hair, kissing her forehead softly, eyes closed and mind blank but for the scent of her skin, the memory of her voice, the peaceful sensation of her still-warm body moving with him. It was as though time had stopped passing, as though the world had paused in its tracks to allow this humble tenderness to run its course.

FINALLY HIS GRIEF WANED ENOUGH for time to start flowing again, and only then did Michael notice Charlie sitting around the fire with the other men.

"How long have you been there?" he asked.

"Long enough." Charlie's face was grim. "Come on, let's get you back to the car."

It was hard for Michael to put her down, and he couldn't bear to lay her head in the dust as it had been when he found her. He cast about irritably, looking for something dignified to put under her, finding nothing except the old clothing in the bags of the other indigents, which he was not about to ask them to donate. There was her shawl, but he couldn't feel right using that because it would leave the rest of her exposed to the air. He knew she was gone, that in a physical sense it would make no difference whether she had the shawl around her – nor under her head, for that matter. But this rationality was powerless over Michael's fierce compulsion to do right by Rosemary, for his own peace of mind if nothing else. He wanted to leave and remember her not as she had first appeared, but in the warm, satisfied, tucked-in state she had cherished at the end.

As if reading his thoughts, Charlie slipped off his Cardigan sweater and held it out. After a moment's reluctance to deprive Charlie of his habitual wrap, Michael nodded in thanks and accepted the offer, resting Rosemary's head on his leg until he had folded the sweater into an appropriate shape and placed it beneath her like a pillow.

"We need to call somebody," Michael said, adjusting the shawl to cover her properly. "We can't just leave her like this."

"I'm sure these gentlemen will see to what needs to be done," Charlie replied. "Won't you fellows."

"I'll take care of her," Sam volunteered in a subdued but resolute tone.

Michael stood up and brushed the dust off his pant legs. For a few minutes he just stared at her, quiet and motionless. It wrenched his heart to turn his back with the emotional investment in trying to save her still so fresh. Finally, he was able to convince himself that she wasn't there, that everything significant about Rosemary Hart had left this husk and gone on to that mysterious land beyond death.

He looked up and gave a barely perceptible nod. Charlie put a hand on his shoulder and they started back toward the road.

CHAPTER 8
A Tiny Life

IT WASN'T AS HARD TO eat soup in the moving car as Michael had thought it might be. It was as thick as stew and, still hot, it was just right for eating without burning his tongue. The generous chunks of chicken and spirals of fusilli pasta seemed even more life-giving than had his lost meal in Las Vegas. The styrofoam take-out box of cherry tomatoes, carrots, broccoli, and cauliflower that Charlie had thoughtfully ordered unbidden also helped a great deal. By the time he had finished the pie, the weak feeling in Michael's arms and legs had dissipated enough for him to take over the driving.

The busy confluence of Interstate 40 and US-93 east out of Kingman ended, and they followed 93 south through a hundred miles of wide desert canyon not uninterrupted by so much as a one-horse town. Joshua trees like long-necked Dr. Seuss creations peppered the terrain and occasionally concentrated into forest-like clumps. It felt odd to be following a course so oblique to any conventional route between the Bay Area and New England, but Michael couldn't argue with Charlie's logic that they should divert as far as possible from any region with which Michael could be associated, no matter how tenuously. And by that standard, they were taking the most sensible path possible short of leaving the country.

They spoke little, and no matter how hard Michael

tried to dedicate his thoughts to planning and preparing for what the next few days might bring, he could not keep his mind from doubling back again and again to Rosemary Hart. He still believed that he had done the right thing, but it was not the kind of black and white moral situation with which he could feel serenely comfortable. She wouldn't have come to a hospital with him voluntarily, but he could have called an ambulance instead of buying the instrument of her demise and helping to administer it like an amateur Dr. Kevorkian. He could have, but every time he thought it through his conclusion was the same. Life might be sacred, but there were principles of virtue higher than that. Among those principles, he believed, was mercy, and close behind it, personal liberty, perhaps not in all circumstances but certainly in most, the freedom for people to make their own decisions and follow their own paths in matters that were pure of conscience and did not directly harm others, accountable only to themselves and to however God might deign to involve Himself.

He had visions of disheveled Sam hoofing it to a fire station, managing after a good deal of insistence to persuade the real-life girfmen that his story of a dead traveling mate down by the railroad tracks had not come from a bottle, of a white and yellow ambulance warbling to the scene with police not far behind, of Rosemary's husk being hefted into it on a gurney after the EMTs had exhausted every reasonable effort to see if she could be revived. He hoped it was like that, but he could just as easily envision her erstwhile companions relieving her of her coin purse as soon as he and Charlie had gone, along with what remained of the Wild Turkey and any other articles she may have possessed that seemed of value to such men, then abandoning her unceremoniously to the elements like an empty pizza box.

He wondered what her father would think, whether he would agonize for the rest of his days over not trying to find his lost daughter and maneuver her into treatment. He could not decide whether in the grand scheme of things he thought it would be better, as she herself had hoped and intended, if

Rosemary's dad never found out what had become of her at all.

SOMETIME AFTER MIDNIGHT, THEY EMERGED from the long gap between the mountains and into Arizona's vast saguaro cactus kingdom. Now they were well and truly in the heartland of the harsh and rugged Old West. The bright half moon gave more than enough illumination to reveal the hostility of the endless landscape. Michael found himself wondering repeatedly what the mindset of settlers in the 1800s could have been, without the benefit of air conditioners, automobiles, or powered well-drilling machines, making a conscious decision to choose this life-threateningly inhospitable place to unhitch their wagons and set to work raising a homestead.

Route 93 terminated at the small town of Wickenburg, yielding to US Highway 60. Not long afterward, they noticed the telltale glow of a metropolis on the horizon ahead, and around 2:00 a.m. they reached the outskirts of Phoenix. Anxious to keep moving for as long as possible, Michael was relieved when they were able to find an all-night gas and convenience store where they could fill up and take on steaming cups of rejuvenating coffee.

Phoenix seemed to go on forever. With the gas stop, it took them well over an hour to get through. But get through they did, emerging back into the desert southbound on Interstate 10 where the saguaro were even larger, some as tall as a four-story building. Michael was dumbstruck. Road Runner cartoons and apocalypse film backdrops could not compare to this reality, and his regard for the pluck of nineteenth-century emigrants grew.

The ferocity of the landscape only seemed to intensify the further south they went. But an hour out of Phoenix the environment began to moderate. By the time they approached Tucson, the surroundings had pacified into a domain of gentle hills decked in dense, close-cropped shrubs and wild grasses dashed with copses of Ponderosa pine.

It was around 4:30 a.m., and Michael was beginning to tire.

"We'll be in town in a few minutes." He prodded Charlie out of his reverie. "Do you think it's too early to stop for the day?"

Charlie was about to answer when Michael let out a gasp. "What the ...?"

Charlie's gaze followed Michael's as both heads whipped back to get a view of what Michael had noticed in the rearview mirror.

Up the road behind them, five miles at most, the stars and everything else had disappeared. Obscuring them was a vast, impossibly high wall of amorphous darkness, moving so fast that they could literally see it gaining on the sky.

"Sandstorm," Charlie said grimly.

"Is that what it is?"

Charlie nodded. "I saw one once visiting my great aunt and uncle in Palm Springs. Came right over the house. One minute it's a nice sunny day, the next it was dark as night and you couldn't see anything out the windows. It made this shimmery rattling sound on the roof and siding. Little boy four or five years old, scared me to death."

"I guess we better find a motel quick, then."

"No." Charlie was somber, his brow furrowed in a rare expression of dire concern. "I don't know how to explain this, but I don't think that thing ... well, I can't say it's not natural, I guess, but either way I don't think we should let it catch up to us. It feels like something's telling us we need to keep moving."

Michael stared at Charlie as intently as was possible while keeping half an eye on the road. "What are you talking about?" he demanded. "You think a sandstorm is some kind of *message* for us?"

"I'm just saying we can't rule that out, and it's not worth taking the chance."

Michael shook his head. Aside from the patent strangeness of everything that had occurred the past two days, nothing truly inexplicable had happened since he had come upon the cypress tree growing in the Hendricks' yard. Now Charlie was implying that putting two days and a thousand miles between themselves and San Mateo had not been enough to shake whatever was pursuing them. It was a depressing and frightening thought.

THEY SLIPPED BRISKLY THROUGH TUCSON, the sky-blocking menace trailing gradually away behind them. An hour and a half later, they crossed into New Mexico with the sun ascending over the mountains before them. Recalling what the road atlas had said about the time zone change this time of year, Michael studied the console briefly to figure out how, then with a bit of trial and error was able to set the radio clock an hour ahead.

The highway ran across flat scrub desert occasionally interrupted by gray rock mountains and cliffs with barely a sign of civilization. Michael was becoming concerned, both by their exposure in the daylight and by their dwindling gas supply, when they finally reached Las Cruces around 7:00 a.m. He was ready to stop for the day, but Charlie thought it couldn't hurt to put a few more miles between themselves and the night's events in order to reach a larger town, where there was less chance of Michael's face or their California license plates being singled out for attention. They paused to gas up at a quaint station in the shape of a teepee, then got back on the Interstate.

Around eight-thirty, they crossed the Texas border into El Paso, and here they agreed to put the anchor down.

Michael pulled into a parking space near the office of a Motel 6 alongside the highway and handed Charlie the Visa card, having by now accepted the familiar drill. He was grateful that Charlie had taken on this hazardous role that would have strained Michael's nerves to the limit. He wondered how Charlie was pulling it off exactly, using a credit card obviously belonging to the wrong name as well as the wrong gender when most lodging establishments required a peek not only at the card but also a picture ID. But Charlie had proven extraordinarily resourceful, and he was back with the key cards before Michael's ruminations could get very far.

As they trudged up two flights of galvanized fire stairs to their room, it occurred to Michael that El Paso was literally just across the border from Mexico, separated only by the breadth of the Rio Grande from the metropolis of Juarez. It was tempting, achingly so, to figure out some way of crossing the river and escaping the reach of U.S. law enforcement for good. But he knew it would be foolish. Even if he could get past the border patrol – and he had no idea how keenly they might be watching for him – he was sure there was an extradition treaty, and among fugitives who might qualify, it went without saying that an alleged political assassin would rate toward the top of the list.

Michael had been awake for sixteen long hours that had included a knife assault, interminable driving, and a woman dying in his arms. He fell asleep almost before he hit the bed.

MICHAEL DREAMED HE WAS STANDING at the edge of a road, his whole body agitated like with a bad case of the flu but with no idea why. The traffic stopped. Right in front of him, a semi truck came barreling down and crashed violently into the rear of a passenger car, which burst into flames. Heart pounding, Michael raced to the car, smashed the rear window with his bare hands and pulled the rear passenger out. She cleared the window, but to his horror, the superhuman strength of his yank threw her behind him, over the trunk, and onto the hard road surface. He spun around to find her motionless, face down in a dark pool of blood. He knelt beside her to see if there was anything he could do, carefully turning her bleeding head to one side.

It was Rosemary Hart. And in spite of his heroic effort, she was dead.

THEY RETURNED TO THE ROAD at dusk with Charlie behind the wheel and Michael reading as far as he could into Dan Hendrick's *All From Nothing* before the encroaching night made it too dark to see. Around 9:00 p.m. they breezed through the town of Van Horn, the signs approaching it reminding Michael to set the clock ahead for their second time-zone change. Half an hour later, they branched off I-10 onto Interstate 20, heading northeast toward Dallas.

The scrub gradually gave way to grassy plains, vast swatches of it grazed by beef cattle and other livestock or planted in alfalfa or cotton. The smells of stockyards and harvested fields were so pervasive that after a while they became unnoticeable, as though these aromas were as natural, timeless, and ubiquitous as sea salt on the California coast.

They gassed the car and switched drivers in Abilene in front of a hacienda-style store with a pair of life-sized wooden Indians flanking the door. Again the temperature at this hour of the morning surprised Michael, but this was a different kind of heat, a humid, clinging sort in contrast to the dry broil of Nevada and Arizona, where, say what you would about its relentless brutality, the air was at least efficient at cooling skin by evaporating sweat. This air felt like it would be so steamy later in the day that it would be a wonder you could even see through it.

An hour on, they were greeted first by a metropolitan glow, then by the dawn spreading and transcending it as it began to fill up the sky ahead.

The full sun was just up when they hit Fort Worth. They continued into Dallas, chucking exact change from the roll of quarters Michael had obtained in Vegas into the automated basket of an untended toll booth.

After about an hour, the metro area began to thin at its eastern edge. Michael pulled off the freeway and followed signs to a Super 8 in the suburb of Mesquite. He held up the credit card and Charlie wordlessly headed inside to set them up.

He was going to need sleep again soon. But since the Denny's takeout at Kingman, the only food Michael had eaten had been travel rations from his sweep through the convenience store in Sacramento. He felt both in need and up to the task, provided it didn't take too long, of searching out some real breakfast before retiring for his vampire slumber.

"I don't know if that's wise." Charlie frowned, studying the control panel, trying to figure out how to cool the lukewarm motel room down. "We've been pretty lucky so far not attracting attention."

But Michael was firm. He was hungry, but it wasn't just that. After all, Charlie was perfectly capable of getting them food without exposing Michael's fugitive visage. But with every mile of separation from California, Michael was feeling less paranoid about being caught, and in addition to breakfast, he just wanted some air. There had been not one minute of leisurely wandering since all this had begun. The constant driving was beginning to cultivate little aches and sores, and a modest walk before the sun became too hot seemed just what he needed to wind down.

"And I want to go solo," Michael insisted over the older man's protestations. "It's not you, Charlie. You've been perfectly helpful. But, for God's sake, we've been cooped up in that car together for three whole days now. I just need some space to myself, you understand?"

"Of course." Charlie smiled philosophically. "I just worry about you, man. I suppose it's all right. Don't be too long, at least. You've got to sit down to eat anyway, just have your nice stroll and then bring the food back here."

THE NOTION "BEFORE THE SUN became too hot" turned out to be relative. At nine-thirty in the morning, this town was already as hot as it ever got at the peak of summer in San Francisco. But at this angle, the surrounding office buildings provided adequate shade, and the ameliorating effects of soft green grass and ample trees flush with summer foliage made the little neighborhood park Michael had wandered into quite pleasant.

He was still looking for a breakfast outlet, in no particular hurry now that he had found this little oasis, when he happened upon a small man in his fifties seated on a wooden bench, dressed in a dark grey business suit and tie with the jacket draped over his left arm, his right hand propping up his bowed forehead just below a patch of hair thinned to no more than a third of what it must have been in its prime. On the seat next to him sat a canvas tote bag of some kind, about the size and shape of a bowling ball case. As Michael approached to determine whether the fellow was distressed or merely deep in thought, he could have sworn he saw the little bag move.

"Pardon me." Michael smiled, and as the man's head came up from his hand, his state of mind became tragically clear.

"Hi." The man managed a weak smile and feeble wave in return, eyes moist and red and puffed around the edges.

"I don't mean to bother you, I was just wondering, do you know any place around here where I could get scrambled eggs and toast or something like that? To go?"

"Hallahan's." The man pointed between the trees and across the street to a sidewalk level corner establishment in one of the brick office buildings, where Michael could barely make out people seated in booths through the large picture windows. "Anything you want, best breakfast in town." The man was still smiling thinly, but the voice could have come from a grade school tike just socked in the gut by the gym class bully.

"Oh, that's great. Thanks man, I really appreciate it. I'm not from around here." Michael looked into the man's eyes warmly and eased his tone. "Hey, I'm not in a hurry or anything, I'm going to take a breather and then finish my walk before I get something to eat. Mind if I ...?"

The man gestured toward the empty spot on the other side of his tote bag. "Be my guest." As Michael sat down, the man added softly, "I could probably use a friend anyway."

"What's going on?" Michael prompted in the gentle, reassuring tone that came to him so naturally.

For a moment the man said nothing, faint hints of emotion playing across his features as though he were sorting things in his head. Abruptly, his eyes welled up and a pair of twin tears erupted, quickly cleared by a pass of his shirt sleeve.

From a distance, Michael had taken the man for a corporate executive, maybe doing some personal shopping on his coffee break. Close up, the picture was quite different. The suit was frayed, possibly the only one this man possessed, without a doubt worn on a regular basis over the course of many years. The tie was homely and made of polyester, the kind more likely found in Wal-Mart than a men's specialty clothier. The sleeves of his shirt were an inch too long, and inside the button holes the color had begun to wear off the thread. As for his ragged-edged shoes, the compulsory wing-tips had been polished so many times that their original color could only be guessed at.

Not an executive, Michael reassessed. Probably a

salesman. Paid on straight commission, a man who did just fine when the economy was good but might go months without an adequate payday in adverse times, putting in all the more uncompensated hours because of it, deploring his job or at least despairing of its futility, yet too invested in his career and the trappings that had accumulated alongside it to compete with younger men in new industries that had passed him by.

"It's this guy." The man reached over and pulled on a zipper that ran down the side of his tote bag. Michael gasped. Inside the bag was an elegant wire cage painted powder blue. And inside the cage, tiny feet grasping a tree branch affixed to the side, was a little green bird.

"Is that a … parakeet?" Michael inquired, fully aware that he wouldn't know a parakeet from a canary from a baby cockatoo, and hoping the man wouldn't be offended if he had guessed it wrong.

"Parrotlet," the man answered. "He's a Pacific parrotlet, the smallest parrot species in the world."

"A parrot? Really?" Michael was delighted. He squinted down at the little bird, viewing its sharp eyes and hooked beak in a new light and envisioning it perched on the shoulder of some diaper-clad pirate.

"What's his name?"

"Beaker." The man brightened. "We were thinking up names when we first got him and I suggested it as a joke. But my daughters loved it, so Beaker he is."

"Does he talk?"

"He does!" The man beamed. "It's not like a Macaw or an African Grey or anything. Parrotlets have tiny little voices like a scratchy whisper. But they do talk." He peered into the cage and gave a soft chirp, which the bird mimicked. Then he focused both eyes squarely on the parrot, and called in a practiced singsong: "Yo-ho, yo-ho …"

In a small, flat voice, the bird unmistakably replied: "A parrot's life for me!"

"Wow!" Michael laughed.

"They can mimic just about any sound they hear enough times. He does this buzzing noise, and for the longest time I thought it must be some call they do in the wild. I nearly split my pants when I realized he was doing my electric toothbrush."

Michael grinned. "I had no idea."

"Parrotlets are a *real* pet. I had a budgie as a kid, but it died before I was out of grade school. These guys can live twenty-five years or more. Heck, he'll probably ..." Sudden emotion choked the man and he fell silent.

"Is something wrong with him?" Michael prodded gently.

The man nodded. "A couple weeks ago he started falling off his perch. We didn't worry about it at first, they sleep standing up on those things and once in a while it happens. But it happened again the next night, then the next day I came home from work and found him lying sideways at the bottom of his cage." He looked at Michael, his eyes overwrought with a childlike sadness that might have looked sweet if it hadn't been so tragic. "They don't just do that, you know. They spend their whole lives up on their perches. They never lie down."

"Did something happen to his leg? Maybe the first time he fell?"

"That's what I thought." The man's composure began to flag. "I thought maybe he'd broken a bone or something. They're hollow, you know, bird bones, that's what makes them light enough to fly. So they're awfully brittle." He looked at the bird again. "So I took him to the vet to see what it was and what they could do about it. They couldn't find anything wrong with his legs, so they did some tests." His lips began to quiver. "They said he has cancer in his kidney. They said it had to come out or he'd die in a few weeks."

"But can they cure it? It is possible to do surgery on something that small?"

The man's eyes pooled and he wiped them with his sleeve again, shaking his head slowly and helplessly. "Yes, but we can't afford it. It costs six hundred dollars. For a bird, for Christ's sake. We've got enough problems affording the things we *have* to have." He threw up his hands bitterly. "Six hundred to take out the tumor. Or one hundred to ... euthanize him. Those are the options. Hell, it's only two hundred for a *new* bird. I thought about doing that, just getting a new one and pretending it was him. The kids wouldn't have to know. I wasn't even going to tell Cherie. But with the cost of putting him down, we can't even afford that."

"Couldn't you put the surgery on a credit card or something?"

"There's no room on my credit cards."   The man slumped and sighed. "Four years ago when I bought this guy, I was grossing twelve hundred bucks a week. I work for a company called TelMet, you heard of it?"

Michael shook his head.

"Business conferencing. Companies buy a subscription, then their people in different offices can connect through our servers and meet on their computers in real time." The man gave a dry chuckle. "When I started there, this technology was cutting edge. I quit a ten-year position in direct marketing to go with these guys. Worked out great for a while, too. Got the kids to Disney World. Bought a parrotlet." He shrugged. "That was then. Five years later, people don't need us anymore. Lot of them do it in house. Ones who can't afford that can use Skype practically for free.

"I get a little residual out of the subscription fees from customers I brought in. Not enough to live on. My main compensation is supposed to come from signing new clients. I haven't had one in four months. And I don't see it getting better."

"You seem like the kind of guy that could find a new job pretty quick," Michael encouraged.

"Used to be." The man smiled fatalistically. "I've been looking since before last Christmas. Not so much as an interview. Not even a 'sorry, the position is filled' call. Nobody wants a short balding guy that needs a living wage to keep his house out of foreclosure. Speak of the devil, I won't be able to fend that off much longer, either." He swallowed and looked Michael tragically in the eyes. "I can barely keep my wife and kids in their house. How can I justify six hundred bucks for surgery on a bird?"

It was a question with no answer. Michael didn't know what to say.

"Know what the worst part is?" the man continued, slipping into a lost and broken demeanor. "It's not even the kids I'm worried about. When we got this bird, it was supposed to be mainly for them – well, and my wife, she's on military disability from the war in Iraq. She's allergic to pet hair, among other things, and we figured out that a parrot was the closest thing to a dog or cat we could actually have.

"Then we found out what parrots cost. Even when things were good, I couldn't afford a thousand bucks for a big Macaw. So when we discovered parrotlets, it was like a miracle from God. Beaker was two hundred. For the same price as a pet store dog, we get a cute little guy that lives longer, doesn't make Mommy sick, and talks." He gave a flicker of a smile. "So it was for the kids, a pet they could have, and to keep my wife company during the day. But guess what? This little guy had his own ideas. He decided he was going to bond to me."

"Bond?"

"Yep. Oh, parrots are very loving. Colonies in the wild are like monkey troupes. They protect each other, bring food when one of them gets sick, mourn just like people do when someone dies. Pet parrots are the same way with humans." He seemed to brighten again. "Ever had one on you?"

"No ..." Michael trailed off warily.

"Here." The man clicked open a small door and stuck his hand in the cage. "Step up, Beaker."

The bright little bird hopped onto the man's finger, clutching it like a tree branch. With the delicacy of a formal tea server, the man guided his hand to a place just behind Michael's left shoulder, issued a birdish chirp, and pulled his finger away. Like a wine glass left on a table after the magician has yanked out the cloth, there the bird stayed, perched contentedly on Michael's clavicle as naturally as if he had a nest there.

"He sits with me like that for hours." The man smiled, for a moment all traces of his anxiety banished. "Working, watching TV, going to the bathroom. It doesn't matter. Sometimes I forget he's even there."

Michael could believe it. He could see the bird, clinging gently to his shirt and spewing delightful little noises not three inches from his face, yet he had to concentrate to feel its weight.

He turned his head so he could watch more closely, and was surprised to see the bird respond. It stopped, turned its own head to regard him first with one eye, then the other, cocking it at different angles as though to catalog every detail about this friendly new giant his flock leader had introduced as benign, anxious to remember so that appropriate favor could be shown should he encounter this stranger again. Michael had always considered birds on the dim side, if for no other reason than the size of their brains. And childhood contact with budgerigars had done nothing to challenge that picture. But there was much more going on in this tiny head, it was undeniable. He could feel it, and that might just have been anthropomorphism, but he could see it, too. There was an intelligence, a purpose, a thoughtfulness in Beaker's eyes that he had never before paid a bird close enough attention to detect. Their legacy was ancient, he reminded himself; they were of truly regal lineage, these beautiful, delicate descendants of the dinosaurs. It filled him with humility and a sense of wonder.

"And that's the problem," the man said brokenly, spiriting Beaker back onto his own finger and gently kissing him on the back. Michael was amazed any bird would tolerate that.

"He was a playmate for the kids, a compromise for poor Cherie, and he's been great for all of us. But for whatever reason, right from the very first day, he singled out me. He starts hooting and chirping the minute I come home from work, he rides around on my shoulder constantly, he curls up in my shirt pocket when he's tired. He plays with everyone, but when he's not distracted, it's always me he comes to."

He rubbed his forefinger back and forth about the bird's head, barely touching the tiny feathers. Beaker craned his head forward so that the affectionate stroking became a little neck massage.

"I got sick one time," the man related, eyes on the bird. "Real sick with pneumonia. I was three days in the hospital and home in bed for two weeks after. The doctor said if I had put off treatment even a few days longer, I would have died. God, it was awful. I couldn't get comfortable no matter what I did. You romanticize calling in sick to work, you know, sometimes you just think, 'I wish I would catch something, then I could sit home watching TV in my underwear and get out of here for a few days.' Then when you really *are* sick, you remember *why* you can't work, and you realize you can't do any of that stuff that sounded so good, either."

He smiled. "I moved his cage into the bedroom and left his door open so he could come visit me while I rolled all over the bed. You know what this guy did? He started bringing me food. This little bird took chunks of chopped vegetables and sprigs of millet spray out of his own feeding dish and flew them over to me. He wanted me to get well. He cared so much he was bringing me his bird food to help me get better."

The man reached down and carefully let the parrot back into the traveling cage. "There's no way to be sure, but you know what I think? I think he remembers it was me who came to the PetCo. I think he remembers who bought him a cage four sizes bigger than necessary and set it up with all those toys, talked to him all the way home so he wouldn't be scared in that little cardboard box they put him in, took him out of that place full of rodent smells and barking dogs and gave him a calm, loving place to live. I think he really knows."

He peered down at the cage, and his eyes watered again. "I know it's stupid. I know it's just a bird. But I can't help it. Beaker's not an animal to me. He's my friend. He's … I just … I *love* him."

He patted the cage, gave Beaker a little wave, then carefully zipped the canvas bag shut again.

"That's the vet place over there." He pointed toward a wood-frame structure at the edge of the park. "Today was the day. I made the decision, I set up the appointment. I brought him there this morning to have him put down. I walked right up to the door. God, if they had been open yet I might have gone in, paid the hundred dollars, and been done with it. But now that they are, I can't. I just *can't*." The anguish began to flow freely, the man so awash in it that now he was forgetting to wipe with his sleeve. "But I *have* to. I don't want him to die in pain at the bottom of his cage. God, oh God, I don't know what to do!"

Michael swallowed. It was all he could do to hold back tears of his own. His comprehension of the man's suffering went beyond empathy. It evoked acute memories of a tightly bonded pet in his own life, an atypically warm and placid Siamese cat named Alex that had been rescued by his mother when a co-worker moved to an apartment that forbade animals. Like Beaker, Alex had been a family pet not intended specifically for Michael or his brother, both in grade school at the time. And like Beaker, the cat had nonetheless of its own accord, and for reasons that defied discovery, adhered with obvious preference to one family member over all the others: Michael.

It had matured into a joyous, life-affirming symbiosis. Wherever Michael went, the cat could be found, perfectly content as long as it could be near him. Alex had established ingenious habits to manifest his affection in ways unobtrusive yet intimate, nesting himself in Michael's lap while he watched TV, squeezing into the gap between the chair and the small of Michael's back at homework time, draping himself on Michael's pillow each night like a set of warm, hypnotically breathing earmuffs around his master's head.

Then, when the boys were in high school, Alex had developed lesions. A patch of skin on his left hindquarter had erupted in a bloody sore the size of a quarter, which gradually grew into an agonizing malignancy affecting the entire limb. By that time the cat could only drag the leg around. Nothing could be done, and at last Michael's near-hysteria at the thought of life without his companion was overtaken by a resolve to end his misery. As much as it hurt even to think about, Michael felt he had no choice but to be with Alex for the euthanasia; and as it turned out, when the day came, only Michael was able to go. Alone in the parking lot afterward, Michael had collapsed onto the asphalt in a seizure of anguish, his keys hanging from the car door, such a forlorn spectacle that the vet's receptionist had abandoned her desk to come out and hold him reassuringly until he regained enough composure to drive.

"Listen." Michael gripped the man firmly about the shoulders. He felt galvanized. He knew people would think him crazy but he didn't care. They were wrong. Every fiber in him knew it with steel certainty.

"First, my friend, what name can I call you?"

"Will." The man sniffed. "Will Reims."

"Glad to meet you, Will. My name is Michael. Now here is what you're going to do." He reached into his back pocket and took out the wallet full of vacation cash. Without hesitation, he counted out five hundred dollars, leaving behind two twenties and a few small bills. He pulled the astonished man's hand up and pushed the money into it.

"Beaker is going to have his surgery. You're going to march into that clinic and tell them to free up the best doctor they have, because you've got every cent for the treatment in cash. You're going to wish him well and then go walk around the block, have some coffee, read a newspaper, get a muffin, and throw some crumbs to the wild birds while you wait. Get some lunch if it goes that long – have yourself a beer, for God's sake. If you get bored, write silly poems on the back of a coaster. And when it's done, you're going to thank the doctor, leave a respectful little tip, and make a mental note to mail him a Christmas card. Then you're going to take Beaker home, better than he ever was, and he's probably going to end up living longer than you."

Michael was prepared for the response. Fleetingly, he recalled the last time he had forced money into a stranger's hand for a good cause, perhaps the only time. He had not thought about that incident in years, but he did remember. The face of that little boy beaming with the turtle and the cow snuggled against his chest and the angel-sweet sound of his mother's "I love you" would never fade from Michael's memory. But he also remembered what had come before, and he was ready for it, that inevitable, all too human pushback against any charity that seemed too extreme, that strident protest as though there could be such a thing as too much kindness, as though empathy and compassion were comparable to an intoxicant of which modest amounts could warm your mood and extend your life but using it in excess could kill you outright. As clearly as Michael knew that nothing could be further from the truth, he also understood it was a natural, maybe even involuntary, reaction that it was to be expected, braced for, ascetically weathered, and allowed to stand down in its own good time.

But it never came. For a long time Will Reims just looked at the money, not securing it but also making no effort to give it back, regarding it thoughtfully while the expression on his face metamorphosed from uncomprehending to stunned, to disbelieving, to resistant, to unsure, to reasoning, and then, finally, to acceptance and then joy, where it settled in for keeps like Goldilocks having found the Just Right Bed.

"Thank you," came the man's tiny voice, barely audible and yet redolent with earnest gratitude.

From the bench behind him, an even smaller voice affirmed: "A parrot's life for me!"

CHAPTER 9
Charlie

BACK AT THE MOTEL, CHARLIE listened without expression as Michael related the events in the park between mouthfuls of hash browns, scrambled eggs, and toast. Michael fully expected an incredulous and unbridled rebuke for wasting his few precious resources on a bird. What he got was quite different.

Charlie gazed at Michael as though seeing him for the first time, grasping Michael's fundamental nature with newfound reverence and awe.

"Michael Chandler," Charlie said, his eyes welling, "you are a good man. A good, good man. May God bless and ever protect you."

Michael gave an embarrassed half-smile. "Eat your breakfast," he dismissed, and flipped on the television to stifle any further discourse on the subject.

NO BLAZING CARS OR HAUNTING corpses disrupted the deepest and most contented sleep Michael had gotten since the ordeal began.

That was about to change.

It was 5:00 p.m. when Michael rose to prepare for the night's drive. Charlie was absent as usual, but Michael had ceased concerning himself with that. Just as usual, he had no doubt that his companion would show up around sundown and they would get underway on time.

He was standing in front of the motel sink trimming his emergent beard, window shades closed for privacy and to block the overbearing sun, listening to an episode of *I Love Lucy* on the TV. He had never worn facial hair in his life – well, there *had* been that ill-advised experimental mustache when he was sixteen – but he was coming to approve the look of his current growth. Kept trim, he thought it might give him a kind of edginess he was prepared to embrace. He smiled impishly at the rascal in the mirror, thinking it might—

The electricity went dead.

The television spat static and winked out, along with the lights, his shaver, and the air conditioner.

The hair stood up on the back of his neck. His reflection in the darkened mirror was not alone.

The other reflection stood behind him at the foot of his bed, features half hidden in the gloom.

Its otherworldly translucence and malevolent aura were hideously familiar. But it was not the apparition from his bedroom in California. That one's face had been beautiful in a purely aesthetic sense, albeit desecrated by terrible evil. This one made no such pretense. It was a male form, horribly disfigured, its eye sockets empty, skin an unearthly pale blue, hair matted and disheveled, a strip of torn flesh hanging off its face to reveal half a mouth of uneven yellow teeth. Great splotches of blood darkened its clothing like burn scars. And everywhere there was mold or something like it, a sickening green growth appearing to feed on the blood and the half dead skin.

And it was *angry*. It spoke not a word, but its expression, even with the dark void where eyes should be, seemed more irrational and infuriated than a human face could possibly manage.

Michael turned, not to face the apparition but to run from it, to streak past it, fling open the door, and sprint out into the sunlight.

It was right on top of him. In the instant it took Michael to spin, the thing had somehow closed the distance between them and was now practically standing on his toes, its black not-eyes gaping into his face only inches away.

The power snapped on. Every light bulb in the room shattered. The TV roared at full volume, the channel somehow changed to CNN, the anchor's words harsh and gritty to the point of hurting his ears, so distorted they could barely be understood:

"POLICE SAY THE SUSPECT, MICHAEL CHANDLER, WAS SEEN IN A LAS VEGAS BAR WHERE HE IS SAID TO HAVE ATTACKED A PATRON IN THE RESTROOM BEFORE DISAPPEARING WITH AN ACCOMPLICE. A LARGE KNIFE WITH TRACES OF BLOOD WAS FOUND IN THE NEARBY MOTEL ROOM WHERE THE SUSPECT WAS STAYING. SECURITY VIDEO SHOWS ..."

The apparition was gone.

Michael stood frozen in shock for half a minute before regaining enough composure to snap off the blaring TV. He raced to the door and burst outside, lungs heaving as he gripped the metal handrail, shaking uncontrollably.

HE WAS STILL STANDING ON the motel balcony with hands on the rail, numb and completely oblivious to how much time had passed, when Charlie nudged him from the side. It startled him so violently his heart nearly exploded. He had not noticed the older man approaching at all.

"Oh God, Charlie. Oh God. It happened again."

Charlie's expression went dark. "What did?"

"There was another … apparition. Like the thing in my townhouse. Only this one was even worse."

They entered the motel room just long enough to retrieve their belongings, then made straight for the car as Michael recounted what had transpired.

"I just don't know," Charlie apologized. He looked gravely concerned. "I wish I could give you answers. I know this crap is wearing you down, the 'not knowing' most of all. But whatever else this means, it's a clear warning that we need to keep moving. Whatever's going on, we have to get you to Boston as soon as we can."

THE SKY WAS DARKENING, AND not just from the departure of the sun. To the west, great columns of angry clouds were forming up like soldiers preparing for battle. Michael couldn't help wondering if the atmospheric violence was just weather, or if it had something to do with the apparition in the motel.

Charlie drove, but once they were clear of city lights, the brewing thunderstorm made it impossible for Michael to continue reading Dan's book. He wished to God it hadn't. Focusing on the text, fully engaging his left brain, had provided life-giving respite from reverberations of the shock he had just been through.

They drove fast, but not fast enough. Steadily the sky contorted and the wind strengthened, gusts nudging the car sideways as though it was mounted with a sail. Lightning spattered the horizon behind them, and seconds later a long, broad rumble like massed artillery caught up with them and boomed past, shaking the road.

Then the rain came. For a few seconds there was just a trickle, then without warning it crashed onto them, heavy drops falling hard and close together, pelting every inch of the vehicle and roaring like a car wash. The windshield wipers could barely keep up.

"You might want to slow down," Michael proposed, watching the speedometer with alarm. "I don't know what the limit is, but I'd say eighty miles an hour is a hair fast for this much rain."

"It's seventy-five, and we're fine," Charlie said. "This thing has front-wheel drive. Almost as much traction as a four wheeler."

"Well, could you slow down anyway? For me? It makes me nervous."

"There's nothing to— oh, nice. Good. Great." Charlie was looking in the rear-view mirror, speaking sardonically. "We're safe now, looks like we have a police escort."

Michael turned around in his seat to look out the back window at what Charlie was seeing. Red and blue lights strobed behind them through the curtain of rain, a quarter of a mile back but gaining.

Michael's heart pounded. He was seized by sudden, overwhelming despair. *So this is how it ends, he thought. All that planning, all that driving, all the care to avoid being seen. Everything foiled by a stupid traffic stop.* Charlie would pull over, and their goose would be cooked. As his fate again felt bound and controlled by forces beyond his reach and he remembered the options presented by Ridge Raymore, despair turned to panic.

What Charlie did utterly shocked him. Charlie did not pull over and park on the shoulder to wait for the inevitable. Instead, he floored the gas.

"Charlie!" Michael cried, but his driver stared straight ahead and continued to accelerate, switching the lights off and ordering: "Keep your head down."

On came the siren.

Charlie zoomed off the highway down an exit ramp and looped back under, northbound past a sign that read "Tyler State Park." He jerked the wheel sideways, taking the first fork off the park's main road, then a spur off of that.

The wood made it darker than a moonless night and the rain crippled visibility further, and yet somehow, impossibly, Charlie was driving full tilt as though the way was lined with NASCAR lights.

For a few moments, trees blocked their police pursuit from view down the winding road. They came to a parking lot for campers, illuminated by a single street light. Charlie veered into a parking space among the other cars and cut the engine.

"Get down," he hissed. Michael obeyed.

Their margin of error had been razor thin. Michael's head was barely ducked below the window when the screaming police car burst around the curve, lights flashing frantically on the trees. Michael braced for a squeal of brakes, preparing to leap out and dash for the woods on that signal.

It never came. The cruiser flew past them without hesitation, through the parking lot and away around a curve at the far end.

Charlie waited a beat, then restarted the car and backed out, reversing their course up the narrow lane toward the freeway. He kept the headlights off. As to how in the world he could see well enough to stay on the road, Michael was utterly baffled.

Charlie navigated back to the main road and around to the freeway ramp. Only as they merged onto I-20 did he turn the lights back on.

Michael looked out the back window. The way behind was clear. He watched the on ramp they had used until he could no longer see it.

Just as the ramp faded from view, a pair of headlights appeared there. If it was the police car, the siren and flashers were off. They had escaped.

THEY CROSSED INTO LOUISIANA IN the dark of night, out of the dry lands for good. Rain was still falling but it was down to a murmur. They drove in silence for over an hour through forested bog lands. Silent, but far from serene. Slowly, methodically, Michael retraced everything he could remember since he had taken Charlie on in Sacramento: the cryptic comments, the odd behavior, the coincidences that strained credulity to the breaking point. And a picture began to coalesce, a picture both wondrous and terrifying. At last, Michael felt he had organized his thoughts as best be could, and it was time to have The Talk.

"Charlie," he began, "you're ... not ... human, are you?"

Charlie laughed melodiously. "Well, if that's true, my mother is in for a shock."

"Your mom's still alive?"

"Very much so. Doing great, too. She lives in Mendocino now, cute little rental house and a good job at a nursery. She always did love flowers."

"She's still working? How old is she?"

"Getting on, like everyone else. She's in great shape for her age, though. Gets hit on by the fellows constantly."

"Your dad's gone, then?"

Charlie shrugged. "I wouldn't know. I never met him."

Michael took a few minutes to ponder this. Charlie seemed sincere enough. But there was something strange still about his replies. He couldn't put his finger on it, but it wasn't merely the statement that his mother, who had to be in her eighties at least, was supposedly still working, while Charlie himself had retired. Something else beneath the surface was bothering him about the way Charlie spoke, and his words failed to assuage the concerns that had led Michael to broach this. He was answering the questions, and he didn't seem to be lying, but even so, Michael had the nagging sense that somehow, in spite of his agreement to Michael's demand for disclosure, Charlie wasn't telling the truth. And to his own frustration, Michael felt unable to press the point further because he wasn't entirely clear himself as to the root of his suspicion. The intuition was strong, but trying to articulate it felt like grasping at jellyfish in murky water.

"I'll take your word like I said I would. But I've done a lot of thinking, and I can't get over a few things. You wouldn't mind if we just talked them out, would you?"

"Go right ahead." Charlie seemed amicable, unconcerned, and yet there was something else there, a ... flatness? Maybe just a bit too much nonchalance? As though, apologies to Shakespeare, Charlie doth *not* protest *enough*?

"I guess it starts with the bookstore," Michael said. "You said you'd been tailing me. Really? From my house to the car crash, from there to the Marriott to the airport to the parking garage, which even the police weren't able to do, then all the way to Sacramento? I'm sorry, Charlie, it just doesn't add up."

"It's the truth." Charlie shrugged.

"Then there was the gas station in that little town in Nevada. You never did explain how you got the pump on."

Charlie was silent.

"And the episode in Las Vegas. Maybe you found me in the motel casino because it was the most likely place I'd be, but that doesn't explain how you appeared like magic in the bathroom stall. I know the place was empty when I went in."

"I came in after you."

"I didn't hear anything."

"You wouldn't." Charlie smiled. "You were too busy tossing your cookies."

"But how did you even know I was in there? If you had been in the place before then, I would have seen you. Even if you came in just looking for me, you couldn't have seen me through the stall door."

"Even retching, you can tell a familiar voice," Charlie said.

"So why hide in the stall? Why not just tell me you were there?'

"No point horning in until you were done with your business."

Far from being convinced by Charlie's replies, Michael found himself less and less satisfied with these answers.

"Any one of those I could swallow by itself," he pressed. "But taken together, Charlie, I don't think so. Too many coincidences. Too many thin explanations. And it's more than that. The entire time we've been together, I've never seen you eat. I guess you didn't think I'd notice the breakfast I brought you rolled up untouched at the bottom of the trash bag. I've never seen you sleep. I've never seen you use a bathroom. In fact, don't take this the wrong way, man, but you've never even changed your clothes, let alone taken a shower, and you don't smell bad. Not even a little. You don't smell like *anything*."

Again, Charlie said nothing.

"And back there." Michael gestured down the road behind them. "That wasn't just some fancy driving, it was *impossible*. There's nothing wrong with my eyesight and I couldn't see the road at all. You must have been going fifty miles an hour, lights off in the pouring rain, making every turn perfectly in the pitch freaking dark. That was the last straw."

He paused, looking for any sign on Charlie's features, any flicker of anger, nervousness, or embarrassment that might shed light on how Charlie was feeling about all this. There was nothing, and that, Michael understood, was a response in itself. Charlie was unperturbed, if anything, upbeat, and Michael was surprised to find himself suddenly fearful. He had wanted answers, real answers, had needed them, but now, poised ever closer to confirmation that there was something truly out of place with Charlie and not just a baseless paranoia in Michael's head, he was afraid.

"What are you, Charlie?" he said with terrible softness.

"What do you think I am?"

Michael looked inward for a moment. He hadn't spent much time trying to pin it down, but his subconscious had done plenty of pondering. Tentative, he forced out the question that had been circling in the back of his mind for days.

"Are you an angel?"

Charlie didn't seem surprised. "I don't seem to have wings." He grinned with a glance at his shoulder.

"How would I know whether real angels have wings? Supposing they did, how do I know if I could see them?"

"The Bible says angels have wings. There are lots of examples. In those passages, the people can see them just fine."

"Yeah but back then, everybody believed in that stuff. We have science now. In the movies these days, angels usually look like ordinary people."

"You think movies are right, and the Bible has it wrong?" Charlie laughed.

Michael was consternated. "No, I just mean maybe angels can control their appearance. So they can do their business without being recognized."

"Look at me, Michael." Charlie turned his full gaze on his passenger, glancing forward intermittently to keep them in their lane. "Look me over real hard. Do you think I'm an angel?"

Michael looked. Angels weren't perfect, only God was perfect, he was aware of that dogma. In fact, the Bible seemed to indicate that a third of the angels had fallen with Satan at the beginning of the world. Michael had always wondered about that. Had those angels embraced evil willingly, or were they helpless pawns in some Grand Scheme in which they had no choice? If it was deliberate, what could possibly have influenced them to abandon paradise for a side they surely knew, with their assumedly privileged knowledge, was foreordained to lose?

But the details of the fall from grace were irrelevant to the subject at hand. The point was simply that angels were not perfect. Yet there was a certain divinity about them that should be readily apparent, something Michael was sure transcended any state a living person could imitate.

He made a concerted effort to block out all notions of angels instilled by books, movies, or medieval art, focusing on what he could remember of pure Biblical description. And after a moment, the distinction manifested. There was a clarity in angels, Michael thought, a certitude born of knowledge far beyond the reach of God's earthly flock. Angels did not speculate; they proclaimed. There was never any hedging or uncertainty when angels spoke, at least not on their end. They saw everything with a clarity like calm water and with such power that the Angel of Justice, if it existed, its eyes blinded, could nevertheless see perfectly well.

And Michael felt certain, though he could not say why, that wings or not, camouflage or not, angels could not mask the transcendence and purposeful conviction that shone in their eyes. *Maybe it's hard-wired in us like a fear of falling or snakes*, he thought. *Maybe we retain a genetic memory from the time when angels walked openly among us.* And Charlie's eyes were all too human.

"No," Michael replied at last. "I don't think you are."

Charlie smiled the smile of a sensei whose Grasshopper has shown enlightenment. "Good choice, my friend. You are correct."

"But you're not human," Michael persisted. Then a black and horrifying notion came over him. "Are you ... a demon?"

"What do *you* think?"

It took longer this time. Again he tried taking a step back from cultural depictions, hoping to glean whatever kernels of truth might lie at their heart. But most Biblical mentions of demons were short on descriptions of physical appearance, and it didn't help much.

"I ... don't ... think so," he said uncertainly, alarmed that Charlie had left this possibility open. "Are you?"

"Look at me again."

Michael appraised Charlie more thoroughly this time. No horns, no tail, no cloven feet unless he had them stuffed somehow into a pair of clever custom-made shoes. But none of that convinced him. What did was Charlie's earnestness. It was a trait Michael knew well, including how to scrutinize it for cracks, and if angels couldn't lie with their eyes, he was not sure the fallen ones, no matter how glib, could convincingly fake baby powder innocence.

"You're not one," he said tenuously.

"Two for two!" Charlie beamed.

But Michael's mood remained dark. Angels never lied, at least he couldn't recall ever encountering such an act in two full read-throughs of the Bible. For demons, on the other hand, bald-faced deception was coin of the realm. That Charlie might be a demon could not, from his mere denial anyway, be ruled out.

But tabling that for later consideration, it was down to one possibility, at least in terms of what Michael could come up with. He played his final card.

"Are you a ghost?"

This time it was Charlie's turn to ruminate in silence. After a minute he asked, "What do you think a ghost is?"

"The spirit of a dead person." Michael shrugged with a hint of annoyance at being asked to state the obvious.

"More specific. What they look like, what they do, why they do it, et cetera."

"Well, they ..." Michael trailed off as he realized with consternation that, come to think of it, Charlie did not conform to his notion of a ghost. It surprised him to find that he had concrete opinions in this regard, considering that up until four days ago he had dismissed their very existence.

He had little to go on, since among these three types of supernatural entities the Bible mentioned spirits least of all, and those references contained nothing like Jacob Marley or Scrooge's guides in *A Christmas Carol*. When it came to ghosts, Michael didn't feel even the tepid confidence he held in his intuitions pertaining to angels and demons. Nevertheless, as he thought about it, he discovered that he *did* assume certain characteristics of ghosts, if they existed. Charlie didn't exhibit any of them.

And yet …

"I don't see how it matters what I think. I have no way of knowing. But I guess if they did exist, I'd expect them to be transparent, or at least physically insubstantial so you could put your hand through them or they could walk through walls. I'd expect them to be self-absorbed and not talk very much. I guess I'd also buy the notion that they would manifest themselves only around locations that related to something powerful in their mortal life."

Charlie eyed him thoughtfully. "Do you believe in such things?"

"I didn't a week ago. But after that thing in my townhouse, I don't know what to think."

"But you don't see me as that."

"You're not," Michael said simply. "The last thing I'd expect a ghost to do would be to abandon its obsessions and take a wild road trip just to help a living stranger. But for all I know, my entire concept of ghosts is wrong."

"Well, let's say you're not wrong. If there are ghosts, pretty much like you described, you can see I'm not one of them."

"But you're *something*, Charlie." Michael spoke low and warily, suddenly feeling paranoid that strange supernatural entities might be lurking around unseen, creatures from whom he felt impelled to hide this conversation.

"When I said it before, you made it into a joke. But Charlie, I *know* you're not human … at least not like I'm human. You're from over there, I can feel it. You're something from the other side … of … death."

Charlie nodded solemnly. "Yes."

And at that blatant confirmation, Michael went pale. The bile rebelled in his gut and he started having hot flashes. His vision blurred and he started to panic. With one word Charlie had settled the question that had been circulating nervously in the back of Michael's mind since they had first met. And he had well considered the possibility. He had spent long stretches of the drive pondering what was possible, then sorting through those possibilities to decide which were the most likely. And those musings had led invariably, inescapably, to supernatural conclusions.

So Charlie's declaration had in no way snuck up on Michael. But the psychological impact of having his driver's nature confirmed turned out to be far more traumatic than merely nosing toward it in suspicion.

He stared at Charlie in horror. There, sitting three feet away, and in control of the car he was imprisoned in, was a bona fide paranormal being of unknown nature and purpose, an alien entity that was dead, or worse, with supernatural abilities and a demonstrated capacity to lie, manipulate, and overpower for its own inscrutable reasons.

Michael was terrified, even more so than he had been in his townhouse that night, because at least then there had been something he could do. He wanted to get out, to jump from the car and run as fast as he could like he had run from the Raymore crash, to get as far away as possible from this hideous thing that had held itself out as his protector and friend, to run through the dark and rain as far and long as necessary until he found someplace to hide. But he couldn't, because, bailing out onto the highway at this speed, the asphalt surface would shred skin and bone like a power sander. And even that, he realized horribly, might not be enough to free him from whatever kind of creature Charlie was.

He had accepted Charlie's story and claimed benevolence, Michael realized, partly from evidence but in large part simply from wanting it to be true, needing desperately for someone to share his burden and stave off abject loneliness. He had known all the time that it didn't quite feel right and that his companion might be very different from what he appeared. Now, that acquiescence felt like the most colossally blind and foolish decision of his life. If he had read Charlie wrong, he realized grimly, Eldridge Raymore's frame job might seem generous in comparison to what he was in for now.

CHAPTER 10
The Curtain Stirs

MICHAEL EXPECTED SOMETHING TERRIBLE TO happen at any minute.

When it didn't, a new feeling began to develop, a wave of anger building alongside his fear until finally it crested above everything else and surged out of Michael like a tsunami making landfall.

"I want you out, Charlie!" Michael declared harshly, his tone masking the unsteadiness he felt inside. "Not here, but I want you gone at the next town. And I don't want you following me, or trying to find me, ever again."

Now Charlie reacted. He eased on the brakes and pulled the car over toward the shoulder. *Oh God, here it comes*, Michael thought, his heart thundering so fiercely he felt like he was going to pass out. *I shouldn't have said anything. I should have waited until we stopped for gas and just ditched him there.*

Charlie parked, leaving the engine running. "I'll go now," he said quietly. "I really want to help you, God knows I do, but I don't want you hating or being afraid of me. I won't trouble you further if that's what you truly want."

Michael studied him. The look on Charlie's face showed the same innocence he had seen the first time Charlie had sat where Michael was now. In fact, now that he knew Charlie better, that expression seemed not just innocent but positively child-like: apologetic, worried, helpless.

When Michael said nothing, Charlie found the door handle and began stepping out, casting him a last sad and painful glance.

"Wait." Michael called out. "I said I wouldn't force you out here. How about you let me drive and we keep talking. If nothing changes by the time we get to Shreveport, we go our separate ways."

Charlie nodded.

They switched places, and Michael pulled back onto the road. Charlie's contrition had diluted Michael's concern, and being in control of the car eased it further.

"All right, Charlie. If we're going to have any chance of continuing together, I've got to know what you are. Don't keep making me guess. Just tell me the truth."

"I have been."

"Damnit, Charlie!" Michael smacked the steering wheel so hard it made Charlie jump. "You've been lying to me the whole damn time. I told you that first day, on the way to Las Vegas. I said if I was going to trust you, you had to be straight with me. And you said you would."

"I have been," Charlie repeated. "I did lie once to you, Michael. I admitted that at the time and I told you why. But I've kept my promise. Everything since that story about needing a ride to Reno to be with my daughter in the hospital has been the truth."

"That's a technicality!" Michael fumed. "You haven't told me the whole truth and that's the same as lying. I'd say the fact that you're some kind of supernatural thing is rather significant, wouldn't you? You said you'd tell me everything!"

"Everything I *could*," Charlie corrected. "And I have been."

"Bullshit." *If this continues*, Michael thought, *I'm going to grant his wish and dump his ass right here.*

"I can't tell you everything, Michael. There are constraints."

"You mean you *won't*." Michael shot him a glare. "All this time you've been saying you were my friend and that your only purpose was to help me. Now you're saying you can't tell me things I desperately need to know. Which is it, Charlie? Are you here to help me, or does your loyalty belong somewhere else? Who are you working for, that thing on the stairs?"

"It's not a matter of loyalty." Charlie looked pained, his voice pleading. "The constraints are absolute. I can't tell you anything you don't already know. If I tried, something would happen to prevent it. *Physically* prevent it. Remember that sand storm behind us in Tucson? I was about to tell you something then. I had worked my way up to thinking that maybe it would be okay. That storm was telling me otherwise. If I'd tried, that thing would have swallowed us up, or we might have been struck by lightning. I don't know if you noticed, but it was gaining on us. Got closer and closer until I changed my mind, and when I did, it fell back. Immediately."

"But you *have* told me things I didn't know," Michael accused. "You did it just now. I didn't *know* you weren't one of us."

"Didn't you?" Charlie challenged. "In the bottom of your heart, you must have. You don't have to know it for sure. It just has to pass the gun-to-the-head test."

"So you would tell me, but then you'd have to kill me," Michael mocked.

"No, no, no." Charlie shook his head. "What I mean is, I can confirm something as long as it's what you'd say if your life depended on it. Even then I can't volunteer it. You have to ask."

Michael pondered this. Charlie was right. Michael had come to a position of believing that there was something supernatural about his passenger. But that was as far as it went. He couldn't say specifically what Charlie was, only what he *wasn't*.

"But you also told me there are constraints," he pressed.

"I didn't know that. There's no way I could have."

"You're right," Charlie said. "I should have clarified. I can tell you *some* things you don't already know. I just can't say anything that would help you make a choice."

"What the hell good is that?" Michael cried. "Besides, you did that, too. You persuaded me to go along with your route to Boston."

Charlie shook his head in frustration. "I sure am bad at this," he admonished himself. "I should have said, things that would help you make a *moral* choice. I can't help you distinguish between right and wrong, or decide what God wants from you."

Michael started to reply, but suddenly, the full implications of what Charlie had revealed set him awash in joy.

"So there *is* a God?" He gazed at Charlie in wonder, eyes wide, a joyous smile erupting across his face.

"Yes. There is a God."

MICHAEL HAD ONLY EVER WANTED two things of enduring importance. The first was romantic fulfillment, hopefully in the form of a lifelong and happy marriage. The second – even more crucial, as much as he longed for the first – was to know whether God existed, and if so, what it was in specific, unambiguous terms He wanted the earthbound, particularly Michael himself, to do.

In his youth, he had sought this knowledge relentlessly. His mother was Lutheran; his father kept his beliefs to himself, though when asked, he dutifully accompanied his wife to the more prominent church ceremonies and events. Michael was swept into these, too, but by age twelve he was already questioning aspects of the orthodoxy he had been fed in children's "Bible School".

At thirteen, he began attending other churches with

his friends, to which his parents for the most part did not object. By fourteen, he was actively seeking alternatives on his own. He tried the Nazarene and First Congregational, which he found suited to his age but a bit light on answers. He went to several Catholic ceremonies and was awed and delighted, but not converted, by the rich iconography. He attended a few Baptist services with the Hendricks, finding them definitely not for him. Once, he let a pair of Jehovah's Witnesses into the house only to have them exit hours later clearly exhausted by his depth of reasoning and facility for debate.

He was a borderline Mormon for six months, owing to a romance with a sharp and pretty girl two years ahead of him whose family had displayed surprising tolerance for her involvement with an unconfirmed believer. *Ah, Susan Best*, he thought, a love of bittersweet memory even now. He recalled her as the first woman he had actually proposed to, though it would have had to wait at least a couple of years. She might even have said yes, but church doctrine heavily favored marriage within the faith, and strictly required it if the wedding was to be performed at the hallowed Temple in Salt Lake City, which for Susan was a non-negotiable lifelong dream. But by that time, Michael had encountered numerous aspects of Mormonism he could not accept. At year's end, she had graduated and gone off to Brigham Young University, and the attention of older men of proper faith was the last torpedo, sinking their relationship for good.

In each case, Michael had extricated himself when eventually and, it seemed, inevitably, some core element of doctrine struck him as fatally flawed. Obviously, the churches involved would have disagreed on the point, but he was equally sure that each church would have similarly dismissed the charters of every other that contradicted their own, oblivious to the irony. He found it strange, hypocritical even, that churches with contradictory tenets tended to close ranks and disavow mutual criticism on certain moral and political issues, even though (and never mentioned) by their own standards, adherents to other dogmas were at least guilty of misinterpreting scripture, and at worst, eternally damned.

In college, he had even gotten into Baha'i, and a radical, quickly abandoned new age phenomenon called Eckankar, with forays into Buddhism and Hinduism mainly from curiosity. But whether close to the Christian center of gravity or diametrically opposed, in every case he at some point encountered elements of belief that he simply could not adopt.

Michael prayed, but never for himself, at least not for personal gain. It was his belief that earnest Christians should involve their own fortunes in prayer only to thank God for their blessings and to seek enlightenment, and he certainly had spent hours praying with an open heart for illumination of the One True Path that never came. For others, he prayed routinely, even for unfortunates he knew only from seeing their plights on television, asking that a man who had lost his whole family in a tornado be comforted, or that a severe burn victim be granted a merciful death. For himself, he felt that God would properly account for humble faith, and that to let Him do so in any way He saw fit, without solicitation, was blessing enough.

He had no qualms, however, about appealing for guidance. *Dear Lord,* he had mouthed earnestly on many an occasion with head bent and eyes closed, *please light the path to salvation. Just tell me what to do and I will do it.* But the Path, if there was one, remained dark. And eventually, some while after graduation, he had quit looking in the world around him and had transferred his soul search to inner contemplation. That this shift occurred within the time frame of Vicki's death he was aware, and he sometimes wondered whether this was coincidental or significant. That answer too eluded him, though from time to time he suspected that in the recesses of his subconscious, the cruel senselessness of her loss had created a kernel of resentment and hostility which, combined with years of ecumenical futility, had alienated him against organized religion, and to some degree against any form of faith at all.

Yet this disillusionment did not change Michael's basic behavior. He did not believe that morality depended on the existence of God. He was of firm conviction that doing the right thing carried its own validation; in fact, one of his objections to canon was the concept that moral behavior should be motivated by the promise of serene immortality combined with fear of eternal torment. To act justly in exchange for a sublime reward or to avoid punishment, he thought, was of no intrinsic merit at all, and proved not one thing about an individual's worthiness. Good should be practiced for its own sake. As he had once explained to his Wal-Mart buddy Carl Adams, he didn't believe Karma was real, but he did believe people should conduct themselves as though it were.

Nevertheless, if God existed – which Michael hoped and believed, in his heart at least – it remained of paramount importance to determine what He intended of His mortal charges and to follow it explicitly. This did not invalidate nor conflict with the principle of good for its own sake. Pure good still applied, but Michael knew he was fallible, often failing even his own standards. And divine guidance would be not only corrective, but comforting. It would at once promote his salvation and relieve the burden of relying on his own judgment in matters where his resources were often no more profound or reliable than simply consulting how he felt.

And so his fidelity to personal principles and failure to find a compatible formal church did not diminish his yearning for the truth. If anything, they compounded it. If the soul was truly eternal, then the four score years of mortal life were utterly trivial except for the choices you made that impacted your existence after. If not, if your time on Earth from cradle to grave turned out to be all there was, the significance of those choices became absolute. On some level, both possibilities came to the same thing: choices mattered.

And investing in a belief system to inform those choices was the only alternative to pure blind luck. That was at the core of Michael's youthful seeking. Conscience must rule, that was immutable, but a conscience fed thoughtful philosophy and fearless examination stood the best chance of pointing to truth.

AS TEENAGERS, THERE HAD BEEN one particular discussion with Dan Hendrick, really more of a debate, that stayed with Michael ever afterward and recurred to him from time to time almost verbatim.

It was a late spring evening and they were circling the Embarcadero in Michael's '66 Mustang, as they often did, for no particular reason except to have such talks. It had started on the topic of animals. There had been a story in the news that day about whether "actual cash value," meaning the cost of a replacement minus depreciation based on age, was a fair way to compensate people whose pets had died as a result of someone else's negligence or willful deeds. Predictably, Michael felt that it wasn't, that for many, pets were only a half rung lower than human family, and people were entitled to something for the anguish caused by their untimely death. Dan replied that according to the Bible, as he had been taught, animals had been placed on the earth solely to serve the purposes of man, and that their intrinsic value could not, in any context, be considered qualitatively comparable to that of human beings.

This led to a discourse about whether pets had souls, which progressed to the question of what becomes of human souls after death.

"I mean, think about it," Michael was saying. "I don't know what it takes for a human being to get into Heaven, let alone dogs. There are so many differences between denominations that it's impossible to know which is right. But let's work through a couple of examples. Some churches believe the ticket to salvation is baptism. They consider it an absolute, and in some churches, baptism is the *only* requirement. So what happens to babies that die right after birth? Children of any age for that matter? Or abortions, if you buy the notion that life begins at conception? Do they burn in Hell just like serial killers and Adolph Hitler? Does a child rapist that has a jailhouse conversion get saved, while a two-year-old whose parents never had him baptized gets tortured for eternity?"

"I don't think that's how it works," Dan said.

"Then how does it?"

Dan shrugged. "I don't know. It probably has to do with the nature of time. Time isn't what you think it is."

"Really? What is it?"

"Just another dimension," Dan replied. "From God's perspective, the passage of time is an illusion, and the past, present, and future are fully known. The universe is finite, even though infinities exist within it."

"That can't be right. How can anything contain something larger than itself?"

Dan paused to call up an illustration. "Suppose you have a hollow sphere. The volume of the sphere is finite. But if you put an ant in there and trace its movements, it will never run out of paths it hasn't walked before. It might *appear* to have exhausted all paths at some point, after billions of years, but only at a level of resolution down to what science calls the Planck length -- that's the shortest distance possible between quantum particles, about 10-35 meters. And space-time goes absolutely haywire at that level."

"How does that pertain to Hell?"

"It shows that even infinity can be limited. And eternity is nothing more than an infinity in a temporal dimension. So there is a sense in which 'eternal' damnation can nevertheless have an end."

Michael shook his head in frustration. "I'm not following you."

"You really can't if you don't grasp the math. You don't

have Calculus, right?"

"No, I do not," Michael confirmed. "And I'm not going to, either. I can barely stomach algebra."

"Well, there are limitations to the human mind. You know, dogs can't distinguish quantities above the number four. If you put out two groups of identical treats with no more than four of them in each pile, the dog will go for the larger group every time. You do the same experiment with say five and six, the dog will choose at random. Four is four, five and above they just see as 'many.' All intelligent animals are like that. For us it's just a higher order of magnitude. We can't visualize extra dimensions, and we can't truly conceive of infinities, either. But we can manipulate and study them through calculations, and math doesn't lie."

Dan's arcane attempts to clarify weren't making things better. Michael sighed and returned to the original subject.

"Meanwhile, back at the Bible," he resumed. "Every Christian group believes you have to accept Jesus as your savior. Duh, right? But where does that leave people who do good all their lives but genuinely don't know what to believe? Mother Theresa, toward the end of her life, admitted she wasn't sure if God existed because she couldn't understand how He could permit all the suffering she had seen. She spent her whole life providing love and comfort to people with no means to help or even feed themselves. Is the Devil down there roasting her like a marshmallow on a pitchfork?"

"I don't know if she said that exactly," Dan replied. "If she did, I'm sure it was just momentary and her faith was pure when she died. Everybody succumbs to stress once in a while. Even Christ on the cross asked God why He had forsaken him."

"She did say it. But forget Mother Theresa. Set aside whatever particular elements salvation requires. What about a mother that steals food for her family? Or toys she can't afford for Christmas? If that mother doesn't meet the requirements – whatever they are – does she get the exact same punishment as that Nazi doctor who conducted experiments to see if there were limits to how much physical abuse a parent could tolerate to stop someone beating their child?"

"Like I said—"

"For that matter, set aside noble motives. What happens to a teenager who steals DVDs or costume jewelry from a department store? Or a cashier that goes home once in a while with a few bucks from the till? Are those people frying in Hell alongside John Wayne Gacy and Ted Bundy?"

This time, Michael didn't even turn an eye for a response from Dan. He was on a roll.

"In fact, what about *those* guys? Think about the very worst crime you can imagine. Think about someone that spent their whole life killing and tormenting people for no reason but their personal psychosis. Forty or sixty years of committing the most heinous crimes. Now put that person in a lake of fire and let them scream and scream in agony for, let's say, an equal forty or sixty years. The same length as their lifetime, without a break. Now let's stipulate that that's not enough punishment for what they have done. Leave them in there for twice that, or even a separate lifetime for each of their victims. If that's still not good enough, how about a *thousand* years? A full thousand years' constant misery for actions that took place over less than a tenth of that time. They're bawling and bawling in there, swearing they're sorry, begging for mercy. Let's stipulate even that isn't enough. Leave them there for a million years. A billion. Or the entire lifetime of the universe. Is that *still* not enough punishment for sixty years of even the most horrible crime? Couldn't you at least just obliterate them at that point, just make them cease to exist instead of continuing to punish them? What on earth is the point, let alone the justice, of torturing anyone *forever*?"

"For someone afraid of drowning forever in a universe full of water," Dan piped up, "you sure seem to be making a case for why that can't be possible."

"I'm not saying what's possible, Dan. I have no idea

what's possible. I'm just asking questions. I'm just trying to understand it, and it seems to me that God would *want* me to understand it, because how else can I use it to make good decisions?"

Michael drummed his fingers on the steering wheel. "Even here, our punishments have a purpose. We put people in prison mostly to keep them from committing more crimes, and to try to convince them not to commit more once they get out. If they behave well and seem remorseful, we let them out early. We allow them to try again. Even our worst criminals, the ones we execute, we don't *torture* them to death. We don't even torture them for punishment until it's time for the chair. If we did, I guarantee all those twenty-year-long appeals would stop."

"No doubt." Dan chuckled.

"So are you telling me that the American justice system is more compassionate, fair, and merciful than God?"

"No."

"Then how do you think it works, mate? You keep shooting down my questions, but I haven't heard any alternatives."

"The Lord works in mysterious ways." Dan shrugged. "With Him all things are possible."

The universal cop-out. Michael smiled to himself. *When he trots that out, I know I've won.*

THOSE DISCUSSIONS HAD BEEN FUN, often enlightening, but they never changed either boy's fundamental beliefs. Michael's earnest anxiety over such matters persisted.

And now, quite unexpectedly and in a way he could never have predicted, all that soul wrenching had been vindicated. There was a God. *There was a God!* And Michael realized euphorically that, unless he was just delusional, this was in no way dependent on who or what Charlie Paris was. Any extra-mortal existence – be it guiding angel, conniving demon, or a festering zombie pirouetting in pink tights on the head of a pin – fundamentally confirmed the existence of God. It wasn't everything, the path remained obscure, the revelation had not been accompanied by a step-by-step User's Manual for the Ecclesiastically Challenged. But it was something; in fact, it was the very most important thing. *There was a God.* And this meant that, found or not, there was also a Path, that a sincere search for it was no fool's errand but rather a noble pursuit, the most and perhaps even the only worthy endeavor in which a person could ever engage.

"So what's it like, Charlie?" Michael asked sedately, still aglow in the radiance of this singular affirmation. "Is it like Earth, or something else? What does God look like? Do you get to meet Jesus?"

Charlie shook his head, grinning. "You know I can't answer. You have no clue about any of those things."

Michael had to concede this, although the distinction between things Charlie could and could not confirm seemed surprisingly thin.

"So whose constraints are these, Charlie?" he said, shifting gears. "Who imposes these restrictions? God? The Devil?"

"A little of both, I think it's fair to say," Charlie replied. "More so God, but not directly. The constraints are indigenous to the world. Woven right into that cosmic fabric your friend Dan talks about."

"The Devil *and* God?" Michael quizzed. "Like in it together?"

"No, no. Not together." Charlie issued a harsh, cold laugh. "As opponents. Like the rules in a football game, except that this is no sporting match. The fate of the world is at stake."

Michael absorbed this. He wasn't quite sure what Charlie meant. In his mind, while the presence and potency of evil was undeniable, there was never any question that good would win in the end. If God's power was supreme, it could go no other way. He knew apocalypse prophecy, he knew there was a monumental struggle, but the outcome of Armageddon could never be in doubt.

Could it?

And how could the fate of everything turn on some arbitrary rule about what creatures like Charlie could and couldn't do to help people like him?

"Why, Charlie? Why would God allow limits on what you can tell people that would only increase their likelihood of doing good?"

"Because those choices *must be your own*." Charlie was gazing directly into Michael's eyes, his own eyes blazing, and he had never appeared more somber. There may even have been a flicker of grim sadness. "It's the choices, Michael. It's all about the choices. *Everything depends on them*."

CHAPTER 11
The End of a Road

THROUGH SHREVEPORT AND BEYOND, PAST corn-
fields and cotton farms and through bogs of blue beech
draped in Spanish moss, Michael's subconscious assimi-
lated and adjusted to his new reality while Charlie huddled
in the passenger seat on his best behavior. Maybe it was
partly afterglow from the confirmation of God, but it was
also because, Michael realized, he needed to resign himself
once and for all to some position on Charlie and let that take
things where it would. This approach seemed eminently apropos given his new foundation for trusting Providence.

Around 1:00 a.m. they crossed the grandest watershed
in the country near Vicksburg, Mississippi. Since he was
driving and the bridge was high off the water, but not so
high you could expect to kill yourself jumping off it, Michael made it across with minimal discomfort. That victory
behind him, he broke the silence.

"So, Charlie, this surveillance you conducted on me ...
you must have done that from the other side, right? Not following me around here like I assumed."

"Nope, it was just like I said," Charlie replied. "Sat in
a car listening to the radio a lot of the time, or pretended to
be shopping at Wal-Mart. I haven't got some magic floating
eye." Michael stifled a laugh at this image as Charlie continued. "I know you were incensed when I told you about it,

Michael, but the truth is that it was mostly concentrated in the last two weeks, and I don't know all that much about you. For instance, it seems strange to me that you've remained unmarried all this time. You're good looking, compassionate, responsible, have a good job. What woman doesn't want all that?"

"Well … I've thought about that, and as much as I hate to admit it, I'm pretty sure it's my own fault."

Charlie raised his eyebrows. "In what way?"

"Well, for instance, that girl I told you about, Beth McFadden? I didn't tell you the whole story." Michael smiled wistfully. He had made peace with the episode he was about to relate, but deep down a few embers of pain still burned.

"We actually met in junior high and tried to have a relationship several times. In between, we were able to stay friends, which is pretty remarkable considering the guy she dated most was this football jock a year ahead of us who used to tackle me in the halls. He did that just to humiliate me in front of her, then he'd say he was just joking around so Beth wouldn't see him as a bully. Even then, I used to wonder if she was only using me when things were on the outs with him. But I kept after it. I badly wanted something more than friendship, and I pursued her time after time. That phone call I told you about was only the last one.

"God, it was mostly misery, to tell you the truth, even when we were romantically involved. She never cared as much as I did, and I lived in constant fear of losing her. Feeling like that made me possessive and jealous, and in all honesty, I think the stupid things I did as a result were what doomed us."

He paused for a moment, the past rolling in his mind's eye like an old movie.

"So here's the rest of it. We were in one of those periods of going out together. Beth's sister Jackie was at the University of Oregon at the time, and she came down with her boyfriend to watch a basketball game against UC Berkeley. She was trying to persuade Beth to follow her to Oregon, so they took her to the game and Beth invited me to go. I was really pumped, because it was always me and never her that set up things to do together, and her taking the initiative for once really felt good.

"It sounds so stupid now, but once we got there, I started feeling neglected because Beth was spending the whole game talking to her sister and paying no attention to me. Here I had these expectations that she was going to fawn all over me, and instead it was like I wasn't even there.

"Somewhere along the line, I had the brilliant idea to cope with this by secretly rooting for the Bears. The rest of them would clap and cheer every time Oregon did something good, but I just sat there. I didn't make a scene when Cal had the momentum, but I was pumping my fists inside.

"It was working, too. The Bears were crushing them, up by fifteen at one point as I recall, and I was feeling great. I was looking forward to the final buzzer, thinking Beth would be all deflated and throw her arms around me for hugs and comfort.

"Then with about two minutes to go, the Ducks started coming back. I wasn't worried at first, but stuff just kept happening, and I remember tensing up and shaking my head – physically shaking my head, though I don't know if she saw me – and thinking to myself *no, no, this can't be happening.* The Bears must have missed ten or twelve shots in a row. They were still ahead by two points with control of the ball and about eight seconds to go, and every single person in the auditorium jumped to their feet. They got it across the center line and started passing it around the perimeter, just playing keep-away to run out the clock, and all of a sudden some Oregon player punched the ball loose right into another Duck's hands. There was only a second or two left and the guy stumbles over the center line and chucks up the ball, and boom, he hits a half court three-pointer. I bet he could take that shot a hundred more times and never make a one, but there it was. The buzzer went off and the Ducks had won.

"I was devastated. I know how that sounds, but damn

it Charlie, I couldn't help it. I had actually been proud that I had found a way to deal with Beth's inattention without doing anything negative. Now the whole thing had blown up and there was my girlfriend with her sister jumping around, clapping and cheering because their Ducks had beaten my team. I felt slapped in the face.

"So you know what I did, the model of maturity? I tapped Beth on the arm and said, 'I'm going somewhere for a while. Don't try to find me.' And off I stomped to the men's bathroom so I could shut myself in a stall and sulk.

"I don't know how long I was in there … probably a long time. I was really worked up. But I finally felt better enough to call off the strike and let them take me home. Only they weren't there any more. I don't know how I expected them to be after a stunt like that, but I was floored. I looked for them all over the place, in the building, out on the sidewalk, all over the parking lot. At least an hour went by before I admitted to myself that they were really gone. It took me another three hours to find a bus and get back to San Mateo. Three hours sitting alone in the corner of the very back seat absolutely mortified by what I had done."

All Charlie could do was shake his head slowly and whistle. "Man."

Michael nodded. "I didn't call her for two weeks. I was terrified of what she would say, if she didn't just slam the phone down. But it ached inside, wondering if I had really lost her or if maybe there was still a chance. I talked myself into thinking that since I had gotten over it, she probably had, too, and if nothing else I could explain myself and she would forgive me. I couldn't tell her the truth, there was no way to package that without making me look like an ass, so I had a nice lie worked out where I was going to say I must have eaten some stale popcorn and had needed time to sit on the john.

"It seemed to start off well. She answered the phone, she sounded civil, she didn't bring up the game and neither did I. She did sound a bit distant, but I told myself that was because she was feeling like I did, a little awkward and just wanting to be careful not to say anything that would upset me. But it didn't last. I've told you that conversation ended in screaming. I still don't remember exactly what was said that put the match to the powder. But that was the last of me and Beth McFadden.

"Know what's ironic? She never did go to Oregon. About a month later, her dad got transferred somewhere back East. I think I mentioned he was a Navy doctor. Well, he earned a military acclaim far beyond that. He had started out as a fighter pilot flying F-18s off of carriers. He had a real collection of combat medals. I remember staring at them in a display case on the wall of his study. But he was also extremely sharp-minded. So when he retired from active duty, the Navy offered him a civilian consultant position and sent him to some East Coast Intelligence station. And of course the whole family moved. Beth actually stayed with relatives so she could finish the school year in California, but she was applying to colleges back east. I wish she had just gone, it was tough having to watch her mollycoddle that prick Rick DeLeon all spring. If Susan hadn't come along just about then, I would have been a basket case."

"Susan?"

"Susan Best," Michael explained, realizing that his lapse into the memory of Susan had been silent. "A senior I took up with a month or so later. But once school let out, they both went. I never saw either one of them again."

"But you must have had other girlfriends."

"Not really." Michael grimaced. "Not for lack of trying, I didn't stop dating or anything. But I think by that time, I had concluded that every relationship was doomed. And they were. It didn't occur to me then that the main reason was the things I did to ensure failure without realizing it. Sometimes it seemed like it would be better if I just cloistered myself from the pain."

"Why didn't you?"

Michael sighed. "I couldn't. As much as it hurt, I had

no choice really. For one thing, I needed romantic validation to blunt those losses. But none of them panned out. Before Vicki, Beth was the best and longest."

"Well, it only takes one," Charlie said. "A happy marriage is the sole exception in a string of failed relationships."

"Yeah," Michael acknowledged. "But I didn't think like that back then. My senior year, I dated a lot of girls for short periods of time, none of them fulfilling. I don't know what I expected from that exactly, it would have been stupid to marry. Then again, I was the guy who had proposed to Susan the previous year." Michael smiled at that memory, then darkened. "By the time Prom rolled around, I was so disillusioned that I decided not to go. Looking back, it's obvious that I was completely irrational. But at the time, I was afraid that no matter who I took, no matter how well it went, no matter what kind of relationship came out of it, the girl would be gone after graduation. I couldn't face that again."

Charlie looked down, subdued and nodding.

"And that was that ... until Vicki. I think I made the same mistakes with her, at first. But she persevered. After a while, it became apparent that she wanted our relationship every bit as much as I did, and that was something completely new. That's the way to have a marriage, Charlie. Both people equally passionate, and each fearful of losing the other. It was magic having someone feel like that toward me. Someone who would apologize and take the initiative just as often as I did.

"God it was good, Charlie. The Epic Fail bowling nights. Sitting for hours in Barnes & Noble with our coffee drinks reading bestsellers for free. Slipping beef jerky through the bars to the stray dogs in the county animal shelter. All that stuff we did that I can't envision doing with any other woman I met.

"So many things." Bliss lit Michael's face like sun on a beach. "Thinking about Barnes & Noble made me remember this one time. At two in the morning, I get this frantic telephone call from Vicki begging me to come over, saying she'll explain when I get there. She absolutely *refuses* to tell me what's going on. So I throw on some clothes, don't shower or shave or anything, race over to her apartment in my Mustang thinking she's got some medical emergency or one of her parents died or God knows what. And there's Vicki at the door in just a halter top and panties, the place completely dark except for a couple of candles on the nightstand next to her bed, and she's holding this book.

"Vicki had bought some ghost novel, I can't remember the title, maybe something by Peter Straub? Anyway, she'd started reading it that afternoon and got so wrapped up in it she couldn't put it down. And it's scaring the bejesus out of her. She's frightened out of her mind, but she's so desperate to find out what happens that she can't stop reading. And she won't put the candles out and turn on some real lights that might break the mood, oh no. *Her* solution is to get me out of bed at 2 a.m. and have me play combination security blanket and teddy bear. And, of course, I did. She stacked these pillows way up behind us, had me lay back against them, then snuggled up in front of me like I was a bean bag chair and went back to the book. Every so often I could make something out on a page, but mostly I was expected to just sit there. And you know what? I didn't mind one bit. I remember smelling her hair and thinking, *Women – if they only knew how magical they seem to men just in their natural state, they wouldn't feel the need for all that makeup and hair goo.*

"We just sat there for hours, her reading and me playing human bean bag, until finally she finished just at the first glimmer of dawn. Practically the whole night, and we didn't even talk or make love or anything, just sat there together snuggled together like spoons in a drawer." He paused, then reconsidered. "Well, yeah, okay, we did make love later, after we decided to skip class and just hang out watching old movies all day. But not until after the book was done and we'd had a nice long morning nap."

Michael sighed, shaking his head softly. "I felt so relaxed and liberated in those days. Nothing could hurt me when I was with Vicki. Everything was easy. The future was a big, bright sunny sky.

"Then that goddamned truck driver took it away." Michael's face went sour. "You know what, Charlie? For a while I used to fantasize about killing him. It mortifies me to remember it now, but at the time I think my view of the world was distorted by grief. I never got to the point of planning details, not rigorously anyway, but the thought kept entering my brain.

"Eventually, though, I realized it truly was an accident and that he was almost as devastated by it as me. The guy was our same age, for God's sake. Only been driving a truck for a few months. They charged him with vehicular manslaughter, and he couldn't post bail – he sat in jail for almost a year before they reached a plea bargain that canceled his commercial driver's license and put him in a community service program. Vicki's family was incensed that he got off like that. But by that time I was able to see things from his perspective, just a kid without much going for him, not particularly bright, who would never intentionally hurt a fly. The urge to kill him went away. It didn't stop the agony of thinking about her, that has never diminished. But forgiving him set me free. It was the first step toward absorbing this horrible thing and getting on with life."

"It still must have been hard."

"Yes and no. Part of me stayed angry for a long time. But I came to realize that it was what Vicki would have wanted. There's not a doubt in my mind. She was a very caring and forgiving person, that's one of the things I loved about her. She would have forgiven him. And knowing she would have wanted me to do the same made it easier."

"And now?" Charlie probed with concern. "Were you able to heal enough to feel that you could marry some day?"

"God, I hope so," Michael replied. "I think so. But to be honest, Charlie, I'm really not sure. Nothing serious ever popped for me after that. I don't think I'm sabotaging things, consciously or unconsciously, but it just doesn't feel right. I still date, I've had a few amiable relationships, but they've never gone deep and I can't help feeling it's because some part of me is still dead inside. It's like an anchor, except I don't mean in the sense that it's holding me back against my will. I guess what it boils down to, at least what it feels like, is a kind of *loyalty*. There's something in me that just can't let go of Vicki enough to let someone else take her place. Like it wouldn't be right to penalize her for dying. You know how when pro athletes gets injured there's always this debate about whether or not they should lose their job over it? That's how it feels. Like I need to hold her roster spot open."

"No, that's completely different," Charlie observed gently. "Ball players can have surgery, go through rehab, get back out on the field, and show whether or not they can still play. It's not like that with Vicki, Michael. Vicki's not coming back."

"I know."

The rest of that night they drove in silence.

THEY LOST THEIR FINAL TIME zone hour when they crossed from Alabama into Georgia on Interstate 59, about thirty miles southeast of Chattanooga. They stopped in Knoxville, Tennessee at a small owner-operated motel built in the 1940s. Again, Charlie was mostly absent, and Michael no longer wasted any effort speculating on where he'd gone or what he might be doing.

He got as far as he could through Dan's more recent book, *All From Nothing*, before settling in to sleep around 10:00 a.m. It was as fascinating as *The Cosmic Tapestry* had been and five years more current; in the intervening years, several of the questions raised in *Tapestry* had been resolved by new astronomical data and experiments at the Large Hadron Collider near Geneva, Switzerland.

Of particular interest in the segment Michael read that morning was a clear layman's explanation of the phenomenon from which the book derived its title. The focal subject of *All From Nothing* was the origin of the universe, laying out and then evaluating various explanations of the seminal cosmic event known as the Big Bang. The point of the passage was to illustrate how the human mind could understand the sudden manifestation of all the contents of the universe from what appeared to be nothing.

He couldn't follow it completely, but Michael got the gist of it and found it a delightful revelation. In essence, Dan was saying that the appearance of "nothing" could actually hide great opposing forces, strong beyond the limits of human comprehension, *provided they were poised in perfect balance.* Two waves crashing together in the ocean, if they were of equal amplitude and met crest to trough, would flatten the water's surface. Light waves intersecting out of phase would go dark. Opposing sound waves could produce silence. Had their energy vanished? Far from it. These phenomena were time-invariant, meaning they were equally valid whether running backward or forward in time, like the positrons that physicists up to Richard Feynman's stature believed were electrons in reverse. Run the waves backward, and *voila*, you had everything appearing to originate from a singularity. All the energy in the universe could be stored, including matter, which was nothing more than energy congealed – imperceptible so long as it maintained equal and opposite harmony. Such an arrangement of forces, undetectable due to their balance, might have been the seed state of the Bing Bang cosmos. It struck Michael as an elegant and beautiful thought.

AS USUAL, THEY GOT BACK on the road around 7:00 p.m., heading northeast through the Cumberland Gap with daylight fading over the Appalachians in the west.

"I don't want to stop anywhere," he told Charlie as Knoxville trailed away behind them. "We're too close now. I looked at the atlas and I want to try to make it to Boston in one shot."

"It's a couple days' drive by my calculations," Charlie said.

"Yeah, but you don't have to sleep, Charlie. If I'd have known that before, we could have been there by now. I'll drive as long as I can, then you can take over and I'll sleep in the back. I'd be too anxious to sleep in a motel this close to the end anyway."

"I can drive the whole way, if you want."

Michael hadn't considered that. Not only could Charlie go without sleep, he never seemed to get tired at all.

"Naw." Michael smiled and patted the steering wheel. "I need to maintain some illusion of control in my life."

THERE WAS A SPRINKLING OF little towns, but given Michael's mental image of the eastern U.S. as the dense matrix of lights in photographs of the earth's night side taken from space, the drive up I-81 was unexpectedly serene. Glimpses of the forested hills on either side made Michael wish they were traveling in daylight. He marked this corridor, along with Louisiana and Las Vegas, as bits of their route he wanted to return to someday when he could explore and enjoy them at leisure.

A little before midnight, they stopped for gas in Roanoke, Virginia. Again, Charlie offered to drive, but Michael was still comfortable and alert. Adrenaline, probably, he thought, realizing that he had no idea what controlled the actual level of the hormone the body maintained, or for how long a noticeable level could persist.

"Charlie," Michael said as they left town, raising a subject he had been batting about in his mind the past hour or so, "what happens to people who aren't saved? Do they really burn forever?"

Charlie was visibly startled, and not just from interruption of his reverie. "You know I can't—"

"Yeah, yeah. Okay." He had expected this, but felt there was no harm in asking. "I was just thinking about my … I was just thinking about the guy who killed my brother."

"Your brother?" Charlie looked perplexed. "I didn't even know you had one. Geez, I've been thinking all this time you were an only child like me."

The questions that Charlie's last comment begged, Michael let pass. He had been thinking about Max, wondering what it would feel like if it was his brother, instead of the enigmatic Charlie Paris, sharing this crazy drive. And he was feeling a sore longing to unburden himself about Max, to share that tragedy and feel like someone else gave a damn, even so far removed from that awful event in both time and space.

"His name was Max," Michael began. "Two years younger than me, but just as strong and a lot tougher. He was the jock in the family. I used to feel jealous when my dad would go to his football games. He never came to watch me in the Chess Club."

Michael said this with a good-hearted chuckle, and Charlie laughed with him once it was clear that any residual hurt was long gone.

"We were rivals, but it didn't mean I didn't love him. Truth be told, the rivalry was mostly on his end. I never really felt it. But you know how teachers are. I did well in school, and the first thing they'd do when Max showed up in their class was gush about me and make sure he knew how keen they were for him to be just as good. It wasn't just school, either, it was anybody – relatives, my parents' friends, hell, even my parents to some extent. He resented that right from the start, and I don't blame him. He must have felt like no matter where he went or what he did, they'd never see him on his own merits, only as 'Michael's little brother'."

"You would think," Charlie remarked, "that mature adults would know better."

"Yeah. I know it was hard on him, and I think it's what made him scrappy. I don't mean he was a bad kid, not in any sense. He got into fights, but he didn't start them. I never saw him bully anyone. He didn't go looking for trouble. But he wouldn't take abuse or what he perceived as disrespect. He really clobbered people a couple of times, sent one kid to the hospital. They suspended him for that, even though the other kid had started it by pouring milk all over Max's lunch."

"Didn't like that, eh?"

"Nope. Grabbed up his tray and shield-bashed it right into the guy's chest. A pint of milk *and* Max's lunch all over his clothes. Then, while the guy was looking down at himself in complete shock, Max smacked him. Flat out smacked him, right in the face. Loosened four teeth and broke his nose." Michael grinned. "I saw the whole thing from two tables away. You wouldn't believe how fast that tray came up. Probably a good thing, too, that kid was older and outweighed Max by probably thirty pounds. If he'd been ready to fight, he probably would have put Max in the hospital. But Max was like that. He took no crap from anyone, and he was absolutely fearless."

"And did you say someone *killed* him?" Charlie looked both sympathetic and incredulous.

"It was that same kind of thing, Charlie. Except he wasn't fighting for himself. He was sixteen by then. It was springtime and there was a high school dance coming up. Max had asked this really cute girl, Gwen Xavier – one of those chicks so pretty that everyone in the school knows her name, you know what I mean? And he was taking her out to dinner a few weeks before so they could get to know each other. He had it all planned, and then right as he was heading to pick her up, he realized he had forgotten the rose. He wanted to give her a single long-stemmed red rose at the door so she'd know he was something special." Michael smiled. "People thought of him as rough, but Max had a tender streak almost no one saw. He absolutely adored old romantic movies. And he kept a box of milk bones in his Camaro in case he came across a stray dog."

Michael paused a moment to savor the sweet memory of his brother's sentimental side. But that part of Max was not the point of this story.

"There wasn't enough time to get to a florist, and Max was stomping around the house in a huff. Then one of our parents reminded him that the convenience store a few blocks away kept single roses in a refrigerator. My folks, to this day, disagree about which one of them mentioned the store. They each think it was the other, although my dad never presses it because he doesn't want Mom to feel responsible for sending Max to die."

Michael choked back emotion for a moment, then sucked it up. "Anyway, Max parked out by the gas pump and went in the store to get his rose, and walked right in on top of a robbery. A guy with a ski mask was pointing his gun right at the head of this little girl next to the cash register. Everyone else was down on the floor, but this little girl didn't speak any English and she was just standing there crying."

Michael took a deep breath. He was surprised how hard it was to confront this, even now. He shouldn't have been; it always was.

"I don't know what Max was thinking, but the security video shows he didn't pause for a second. He dropped his keys and wallet and made a lunge for the guy. He shot Max right through the chest."

Michael looked down, shaking his head, his eyes welling as he knew they would; no amount of rationalization could overcome it.

"There was a silent alarm," he said after a moment. "The cashier had tripped it. The police came literally as that shot was fired. On the video, you can see the cruiser pulling into the frame even before Max hits the floor." Michael shook miserably. "If he had been one second later. One second, Charlie, that's all he would have needed. Would that have been so hard? Would one second have been so much to ask the world to come up with? God damn it. God *damn* it. *God fucking damn it!*"

The ferocity of the outburst startled Charlie. But Max's death had cut Michael so deep that dwelling upon it, facing its full force in his consciousness, could overpower even his fundamental nature. Partly it was grief, partly it was bitterness at having been robbed of his only sibling both in youth and in the shared adulthood he had hoped for. But on top of that – most powerfully and hardest to face – it made him feel guilty. Guilty for not saving Max, though he was intellectually aware there was absolutely nothing he could have done. Guilty even more so in a feeling of unworthiness, a sense that God had taken Max and spared Michael to some noble purpose that Michael had then failed to perform.

Most of all, he felt guilty at having henceforth gluttonously consumed all of his parents' love and attention, both his own rightful portion and that which belonged properly to Max, and that despite this he had also failed his parents with his inability to replace Max in their broken hearts. None of this was rational, and Michael knew it. But emotionally it was so deeply ingrained that he felt powerless when it came to the fore, and the fury it fueled brought out a side of him utterly antithetical to his ordinarily tender and affirmative air.

And now it set upon him like a tiger. Taking shape in his mind, slowly at first and then coalescing with a fearsome rage was the image of that man, that murderer, that ski-masked son of a bitch standing in a cavern of fire from which there was no way out, his skin burning but not deteriorating, screaming in agony, begging for mercy, but there would be none, no mercy given, no mercy given, BY GOD NO MERCY GIVEN! NO MERCY! NO MERCY! NO MERCY!

And then, at first slowly and then as strongly as it had

coalesced, it began to abate as Michael's stronger force, the mettle of which he was truly made, arose and took charge. No, it proclaimed firmly. *No. I will NOT succumb. You have taken my brother. You have carved an indelible mark in all of us. In my mother you have gouged a wound so profound that her soul is irreparably broken. You have done all this and yet I will not meet you. I will not descend to your level and compound your sin. I will release you. I release you.* I RELEASE YOU.

Like a flower breaking through an April snow, Michael recovered. He was alarmed, though he realized he should not be surprised, to find Charlie staring at him with a look *of call 911* concern. Belatedly, he also noticed Charlie's gentle hand patting his shoulder. He had not even known it was there.

"I'm all right." Michael smiled apologetically. Charlie looked relieved. "I'm sorry, man. We didn't always get along. In fact, I'm not sure Max ever liked me. But I loved him. I couldn't wait for him to grow out of all that baggage I felt partly responsible for and show the world what he could really do. I wanted to play golf with him, go on vacations with his family, have him over to my house for Thanksgiving. After we both grew up, I mean. I actually used to plan for that stuff. It's hard knowing that none of that will ever happen now. Sometimes, when I think about it, it's just too much."

With dawn blooming almost imperceptibly on the eastern horizon, they pulled in for gas and a couple of yesterday's donuts at the edge of Harrisburg, Pennsylvania. At last, Michael gave up the wheel and crawled into the back seat. Emotions spent, physical energy exhausted, the weight of the entire journey seemed to collapse on him at once. He fell into a deep and dreamless sleep.

MICHAEL AWOKE TO FULL, BRIGHT sun and, aside from the daylight, no inkling whatsoever of how long he had slept. He was shocked and became instantly alert when he saw the road sign out the window before he could ask Charlie or take a look at the clock.

Boston – 10 miles.

Ten miles!

"You slept right through New York, tiger," Charlie chided. "I thought about waking you. It was something to see."

The comment barely registered with Michael. Yes, yes, he authorized the spinster librarian in his brain. *Las Vegas, Louisiana, Shenandoah Highway, New York City. Bucket list duly appended. Now go away.*

He had, throughout the trip, pictured himself as piloting them into Boston, rolling triumphantly into the city like one of Patton's tanks entering Messina, half expecting parade music and a shower of rose petals thrown by cheering crowds.

When the moment came, though, Michael was so intent on studying the atlas so he could navigate them to Boston University that the anticipated ritual completely slipped his mind.

"There it is!" he barked excitedly as they dropped off of Interstate 90 at Commonwealth Avenue, the gothic spectacle of Marsh Chapel sparkling against the Charles River backdrop. "Oh God, Charlie, we're here! We're here!"

He looked over at his companion and was surprised by the expression he saw. Charlie was not sharing his giddy spirit. He wasn't tearful, he didn't look upset, but there was a subtle drain in Charlie's countenance that seemed completely incongruous with the joyous circumstance.

"What's wrong, Charlie?" he asked.

Charlie pulled the car over and parked at the curb alongside the college grounds. "Nothing's *wrong*," he assured Michael in a soft but even tone. "I'm just going to miss you, brother."

"*Miss* me? What are you talking about?" Michael demanded. "We don't have to split up. You'll be welcome at Dan's with me, I'm sure. I don't know what sleeping arrangements they have, but that shouldn't make any difference to you."

Charlie smiled. "No, partner, you don't understand. This is it for me. My job was to get you here. You're here. Praise the Lord for that, there were times when I didn't think it was going to happen." Charlie closed his eyes and breathed in, looking sublime. "I did it," he said, seemingly to himself. "I really did it. It's over."

"Over …? Charlie?"

Charlie turned to Michael with a loving gaze. "I guess over's not the right word for it. You've got a bit to do yet, I'd guess. Probably a fair bit. But this is it for me."

"You're … leaving?" Michael was floored.

"Yes." Charlie's eyes were apologetic. "I've already explained that my capacity to help you is limited. There are reasons for that, but I can't explain them to you and I know how ridiculous and unfair that seems, but Michael, that's just the way it is. I've got one last chore to do, and that's disposing of this thing." Charlie gestured around vehicle.

"You're taking the car?"

Charlie nodded. "Now that it's done its job, this baby is going to be reported stolen. Your DNA is all over it now, and I'm going to deposit it as far as possible from where they could actually find you."

"But …"

"Keep the cards for a while," Charlie continued. "Try to be discreet with them, though. Make other arrangements as soon as you can. I wouldn't hold them longer than a few weeks – at some point around then they're going to have to be canceled."

"But Charlie, I—"

"Oh, shoot, shoot! I almost forgot!" Charlie cried. He dug into a pocket of the chinos he had been wearing throughout the entire trip and held out a wad of cash.

"Huh?" Michael gawked.

"Your winnings." Charlie smiled cheerily. "From that jackpot you won on the video poker machine in Vegas. You dropped the voucher on your way to the restroom. I picked it up and cashed it."

A smile matching Charlie's spread across Michael's face. He smoothed the bills flat and tucked them into his wallet, about two hundred dollars on top of the forty-something he had left. "Thank you, Charlie." He did not finish with the obvious *for everything*. He didn't need to.

"Be strong." Charlie clapped him on the shoulder. "Everything's going to be all right."

Michael wrenched himself over and gave Charlie a clumsy hug. When they released, Charlie gave a little wave, and Michael reciprocated as he retrieved his pack from the rear seat and climbed out onto the sidewalk.

Suddenly, an urgent thought occurred to him and he stuck his head down inside the door for one last hopeful question.

"Charlie," he asked, in a voice choked with earnestness and longing, knowing full well that no real answer could possibly come, "did I make it? Will I get to see Jesus?"

Of all the hours they had spent together, among all the laughs and cries and debates and tirades, amidst all the love and hurt and revelations and half-truths, Michael had never seen anything like the expression that now consumed Charlie's face. It was like an anvil thunder cloud taking over the entire sky, pregnant with a destructive power impossible to withstand.

"Michael Chandler," Charlie said, in the darkest, saddest tone Michael had ever heard him utter, "there can be no salvation for you in this world."

For a long moment they just stared at each other. Michael hoped to hear something more, that Charlie might explain or at least offer some words of encouragement that would dampen the impact of the stark and horrible statement he had just made. How could he say this? Had not Charlie only seconds before assured him that everything was going to be all right?

But nothing came. Nor did Charlie look away. He held his gaze on Michael, a look of abject anguish and despair so terrible that finally Michael could take it no more. Numb, unable to begin the process of parsing what Charlie had said, trying to figure out what it could possibly mean if not the certainty of his eternal damnation, Michael shut the passenger door. He watched as Charlie drove the green car that had served them so well back into traffic and out of view down the busy boulevard.

On top of Charlie's words still reverberating in his head like the peeling of the Devil's own bells, the sudden, unexpected ache that now overtook him was so powerful he nearly collapsed. It felt like he had swallowed a bowling pin. Tears began to flow freely as he realized the true value of Charlie's presence during the trip. It wasn't sharing the driving or getting the motels or bringing him chicken soup. It wasn't even saving his life or confirming the existence of God. Those things had been vital – Michael knew well he most likely would never have made it to Boston, probably not even out of Nevada, without Charlie's help. But his true value – what Michael surely would have failed without – had been his companionship. Even with the episodes of mistrust and confrontation, Charlie's presence alone had held his sanity together and kept his hope and determination alive.

It dawned on him that he had been wrong about what Barbara Jordan had said. Barbara didn't know Dan Hendrick – she probably didn't even know *about* him. When she had told Michael to drive east out of California, to find "the friend who is going to help you understand" – she hadn't meant Dan Hendrick. She had been pointing him to Charlie.

Now Charlie was gone. And for the first time since the fateful evening that had begun all of this, Michael Chandler was alone. Alone without the only friend in all of Creation who might truly be able to help him. Alone with Charlie's haunting pronouncement that he had no hope of interpreting on his own. Alone on a hot sidewalk in a city of strangers, with a backpack full of bad food and dirty clothes and little else, clinging to the tattered thread of a once-bright plan whose wisdom and potential for success now seemed frail beyond madness. He had reached his destination, but now that he was here, the prospect that a mere reunion with Dan Hendrick could set right all that had gone out of control struck him as very remote indeed.

CHAPTER 12
A Home Away

IN THAT MOMENT OF CRUSHING loneliness on the Boston sidewalk, what Michael most desperately needed was a fortuitous break, some sign that, despite Charlie's words and the explosion that they had just detonated in his life, the universe had not utterly forsaken him.

He got two.

"Excuse me." He waved down a friendly-looking student traversing the square in front of Marsh Chapel. "I've got a meeting with a professor, Daniel Hendrick. Do you know where I can find him?"

"What does he teach?" The young woman smiled.

"Physics. Or maybe math? Physics, I think."

The woman turned back in the direction from which she had come and pointed toward the nearest building, a large, elegant brick structure. "That's Arts and Sciences. I don't recognize his name, but Physics would be in there."

"Great, thanks." Michael smiled and waved, then took off for the building entrance at a trot.

He was not out of the woods, though, and he knew it. There was no guarantee that Dan would be in his office, or even on campus. It was entirely possible that the fall semester had not yet begun. True, he had just encountered a young woman who appeared to be a student, but the granite-tile courtyard surrounding Marsh Chapel, with its enormous inlay in the shape of a Celtic cross, seemed too empty for a class day. If the school was between semesters, Dan might not even be in Boston, instead enjoying a last week or two of vacation travel. Or he might just be puttering around his house.

And unfortunately, Michael had no idea where that house was. He had been so focused on just getting to Boston that these considerations had never occurred to him. As a result, he realized grimly, he was totally without a contingency plan.

Then, though perhaps not as indispensable as the girl's directions but nevertheless a great relief to Michael in his vulnerable state, the stars tossed him a second kibble of good luck. In an era of campus shootings and post-9/11 vigilance, Michael had wondered whether he would have to find his way around security measures that might expose him to the forces he was fleeing from California – locks or surveillance cameras at least, police or overzealous guards at worst. He uttered a prayer of thanks when it turned out there were none.

He hopped up the short flight of steps and though double-glass doors into the Arts and Sciences hall, found the room number of Dr. Hendrick's office on a large wall-mounted placard, and hiked up the stairs to the second floor. He strode briskly up the corridor, noting the room numbers. Empty classrooms lined the way on the right, with offices, storage, and maintenance rooms on the left. He had gone almost the length of the building when the door to a suite of offices, including Dan's, finally appeared.

His quarry possibly so close, it suddenly dawned on Michael that he might not get the friendly reception he had been counting on. Since Vegas, he had known that the collision with Eldridge Raymore was national news. Surely Dan must have seen it. He felt sure that Dan would believe him no matter what the media said, but that wasn't going to help initially. It was possible that Dan would reject him outright before there was time to explain, having formed an opinion based on the newscasts, a fear that might well have intensified and entrenched itself over the past six days out of concern for his family. For that matter, if Dan had worked himself up sufficiently over the news that his friend had tried to assassinate a candidate for governor, he might even call the police.

Michael started thinking about how he might evade campus security long enough to get clear of this place, and then what would he do? Two hundred-odd dollars wasn't going to buy food and shelter for long. Of course, as he had just realized, there was every chance Dan was not even here, and if that was the case he was going to need temporary living arrangements regardless. How was he going to manage that without revealing himself, in an unfamiliar city, without a car, without ID, and without whatever legerdemain Charlie had pulled to make Barbara's Visa card serve his purpose?

And then, almost shocking in its abruptness, there was Dan Hendrick in front of him, the very object and culmination of his arduous road trip, the Holy Grail that had been driving him ever since that fateful night. He was seated behind a desk working on some papers in a large and well-appointed office, its paneled mahogany door open to reveal a postcard view of the Charles River and the hilly north Boston skyline through the picture window behind him.

Jubilation swept through Michael like a hot flash, and for a moment he thought his legs were going to buckle. But it quickly passed, and a broad smile took over his face.

The reception desk near the door to the outer suite area was unoccupied. Michael strode past it and knocked on Dan's door frame.

"Dr. Hendrick?"

Dan looked up with a faint note of irritation. He was wearing a light gray suit and a yellow tie loosened at the neck, his top shirt button undone, rimless eyeglasses perched on the bridge of his nose. Under the get-up – Michael could not recall ever having seen him in a suit, other than a Prom tuxedo – it was the same old Dan, albeit with the faintest touch of gray hair at his temples and a bit thinner at an age when most people were taking on some weight.

And life had been good to him. The office was so nicely furnished it bordered on lavish. Michael didn't know what research professors made in salary, but there wasn't a single office this nice at UC Santa Cruz, that much he knew for sure.

Dan stared at Michael without a word for three seconds, and it was beginning to look like that half-baked escape plan might be necessary. Then all at once his eyes popped wide, a grin burst across his face, and he stood up from his chair.

"Michael? Michael Chandler? Is that you?"

"Hey, Dan." Michael returned the smile and shook his friend's hand warmly.

"Come on in, come over here, sit down!" Dan pointed Michael toward a small leather sofa and sat himself down in the matching chair. "Sorry, it took me a minute to recognize you." Dan pawed his own cheek in explanation, and when Michael did the same he instantly understood. Six days' worth of unshaved stubble was beginning to qualify as a close-cropped beard, and his hair – in dire need of a cut already before he had left California – no doubt completed the impression of a scruffy over-age undergrad shouldering a worn pack presumably full of books.

"Michael Chandler. Wow!" Dan exclaimed when they were both seated. "Man, it's good to see you. What on earth are you doing in Boston?"

For a moment, Michael just smiled. It was hard not to cry. He had made it. In spite of the scene with Charlie fifteen minutes earlier, here he was, having finally reached the objective he had set out for from his violated townhouse a full week and three thousand miles ago. And far from fulfilling his fears, Dan's reaction was delivering every bit the relief and sanctuary he had been seeking. He felt like letting the tears flow and throwing both arms around Dan like a child nesting into its mother after racing home to escape a schoolyard thug. But he didn't; he wouldn't cry, not here or now. He had to solidify Dan's reception, he needed to appear gracious and stable and as delighted by the reunion as his host, so Dan would be relaxed and in the right frame of mind when Michael related his story in full.

And he would have to be careful. It seemed clear from his greeting that Dan knew nothing of the San Mateo events.

"It's a bit complicated." Michael smiled, forcing a friendly and confident air. "I'll give you the whole run down when you have time. I didn't mean to interrupt, I just came by to see if I could catch you and maybe set a time to meet up later. I can hang out somewhere while you finish your day, or whatever works for you."

"No, it's fine. The quarter doesn't start until next week, most of the kids are just getting here. I'm tweaking my lesson plans with trivial changes to burn the time." He dug his cell phone out of an inner pocket. "Where are you staying? You've got to come over to the house. I want you to meet Melissa. Do you have plans for dinner?"

"Just got into town," Michael disclosed. "I haven't arranged a hotel yet. No dinner plans."

"Excellent." Dan punched a speed-dial number and put the phone to his ear. "Hey, it's me. Guess what, that old school friend from California I keep telling you about, Michael Chandler? He just walked into my office ... Yeah, he's here! Right now! He looks hungry, too. What do you think about having him over tonight, would that screw up anything? ... Perfect. Is there any reason we couldn't put him in the guest room for a couple of days? ... Good, I'll tell him ... Okay, see you in a little while, hon. I think I'm going to close up for the day and take him on a tour ... Love you, too." He clapped the phone shut.

"I didn't mean—"

"Don't start that." Dan waved off Michael's objections. "We live ten minutes from here. Whatever you've got going, our place is as convenient to town as the hotels. And the parking's better." Dan crossed back over to his desk, grabbed a paper, and popped open his phone again. "Let me make a call or two and free up the afternoon. You've never been here before, right? I'd love to show you around the Cradle of Liberty in this nice weather. Assuming you don't need to be somewhere, that is."

"Dan," Michael pressed. "That all sounds wonderful and I appreciate it immensely. But there's something I need to tell you before we do anything else."

Dan's expression turned to concern. "What is it, man?" he asked, sure the answer was some terminal disease or tragedy of equal proportion.

Michael twisted to face behind himself briefly. "Could we shut the door?"

MICHAEL STUCK MAINLY TO THE car crash and cross-continent drive parts of his story. It was a great relief to be able to unburden himself to someone he thoroughly trusted, but he wanted to gauge Dan's reaction before sticking his neck out too far. It also seemed prudent to defer the elements that might land him in a padded cell, if he was going to disclose them at all, until they were in a setting without a brigade of campus police a buzzer away.

Dan listened with grim concern, and Michael was relieved to see that it was clearly concern *for* Michael rather than *about* him. Dan had known Michael as well as anyone else in the world, and he reassured Michael that he believed with one hundred percent certainty that he was telling the truth about the collision with Ridge Raymore.

"That son of a bitch." Dan scowled. "I knew there was something wrong with that guy. Cripes, we have the greatest nation in the history of the world and we can't seem to get a single politician that isn't a crook."

Michael made one exception to the redaction of paranormal detail. Though he hadn't specified what had prompted him to seek Dan's phone number in the first place, he did

tell Dan about finding the tree growing where the Hendricks'
house should be. He fervently hoped, and frankly expected,
that Dan would come back with a perfectly mundane explanation. When Dan instead shook his head and insisted with
puzzlement that Michael was mistaken about where he had
lived, the talk lapsed into an awkward silence. After a few
moments Dan changed the subject, proposing they head out
to his car and get a start on that tour of the sights before rush
hour, and Michael gratefully acquiesced.

"You can stay with us as long as you need to," Dan
assured as he locked his office and led the way toward the
parking garage. "Don't think twice about it."

"Thanks, man." As much as Michael hated to impose,
it was a supreme relief to be in the presence of a friend – a
true, deep friend who understood him implicitly – for the
first time since the whole thing began.

The parking garage was practically empty. As Dan
clicked the locks open remotely from his key ring and
reached for the handle of the driver's side door, he stopped
for a moment.

"That bit about the tree, and where you thought our
house was ... you're *sure* about that." It wasn't a challenge,
just a request for confirmation.

"Positive." Michael hesitated for a barely perceptible
instant, thinking to himself that he couldn't be completely
sure of anything. But all those occasions over all those years,
goofing around and attending Scout meetings and doing
homework in that house, details as specific as the olive color
of the window sill in Dan's upstairs bedroom – those memories were as rich and indelible as he had about anything. Unless he was completely out of his mind, they were true.

Dan nodded and opened the car door. The two of them
got inside and fastened their seat belts.

"It ... wasn't the only thing, either," Michael blurted in
a low, vulnerable voice. "I didn't want to tell you everything
back in your office, man, I didn't know who might be able to
hear. There were other weird things that night ... and since."

Dan turned his friend an intense and sympathetic gaze. He looked like he was going to say something, then thought better of it. "I'll need to hear the whole thing," he concluded, starting the engine with a surprisingly muted purr. "Tonight, after you're rested. For now, how about you let me show you around and take your mind off things?"

Michael nodded back appreciatively. "Yeah. That sounds good, man. Thanks."

MORE SOMBER THAN IT MIGHT have been under normal circumstances, Michael nevertheless enjoyed and appreciated the drive through Boston's history in Dan's comfortable Mercedes. They toured the city's highlights, Dan's guidebook patter interspersed with mutual catch-up on their personal lives, including a reminder that Dan's wife was a psychology professor who also worked at the University of Boston. Michael offered profuse apologies for having missed the wedding because it had conflicted with a Wal-Mart corporate event.

Michael found himself stunned by the size and rough-stone grandeur of North Church, where Paul Revere had lit two candles in a window to warn the colonial militia of an impending British attack. He marveled at century-old Fenway Park, the most venerated stadium in all of baseball, to Red Sox fans nothing less than a holy shrine. They drove past Bunker Hill without stopping while Dan recounted details of its namesake battle, and Michael made yet another mental note to come back here someday if his life ever returned to something like normal. *Damn, there's real history here*, he thought to himself. *Everything on the west coast seems like it was built yesterday.*

His most visceral reaction came as they drove past Boston Harbor, the site of the original Tea Party protest and still sporting period ships for visitors to tour or even sail in. But it wasn't the stately schooners or storied history that got to him; it was the air. The scents of salt and sea life the harbor gave off were the first he had smelled since leaving the Bay Area, and with the hilly surroundings unexpectedly reminiscent of his native environs, he was seized by homesickness.

He needn't have been, if the warmth and welcome of Dan Hendrick's home could stand in as a substitute. The extravagant Victorian in the Brookline district confirmed that Dan had done very well for himself: exotic wood cabinets, a state of the art kitchen, walls mounted with artwork speaking of world travel, and bay windows taking up one entire living room wall with a view of the magnificent Boston skyline.

"It's the books," Dan explained, guessing the cause of Michael's wide-eyed gaze. "BU pays all right, but it's the book sales that bought this place." He picked up a hardbound copy of *All From Nothing* off the elegant coffee table and smiled. "*New York Times* bestseller ten weeks in a row."

"I've been reading it," Michael told him. "I don't get everything, but you did a great job using terms most people can understand. In both books, actually."

"Why, thank you, sir." Dan beamed. "To tell you the truth, without the math you really can't express those concepts properly. But my publisher tells me you lose a thousand sales for every equation that appears in your text." Dan grinned. "I couldn't help putting a few in, but I did my best."

"No worries man, they're very readable," Michael assured him. "That's what I like best about them. It's not the writing's fault if I don't understand something."

A short time later came the sound of the electric garage door opening, and Dan's wife bustled into the kitchen with three bags of groceries and some extravagant-smelling fare she must have picked up at one of the harbor restaurants. She dropped them on a counter and stopped long enough for Dan to introduce their guest.

"I hope you're hungry," Melissa declared, "because I'm starving. I need to throw a few things together, is forty-five minutes going to be too soon?

"Whatever's convenient for you," Michael said.

"Here Mel, let me help put stuff away," Dan said, following his wife into the kitchen with a glance over his shoulder. "Sit down and relax, Michael. I'll be back in a jiff."

Michael didn't need to pick up on Dan's furtive tone to know what that was all about. He plopped himself down into a soft and stylish chair, hoping for the best as the couple's low, animated voices emanated unintelligibly from the other room.

APPARENTLY, "THROW A FEW THINGS together" meant preparing an entire amazing meal practically from scratch with the exception of the entree, which she had called ahead for with special instructions and picked up last on her way home.

Whatever had been said, Melissa remained gracious upon joining them in the living room while the side dishes cooked, the air filling with the scintillating aromas of savory shellfish, spiced vegetables, and fresh bread. Yet something in her demeanor had changed. Her lips were smiling, her tone was warm, but the look in her eyes did not match. What was Michael seeing in that look ... shock? Anger? Fear? He could understand any of those, if the interlude had been used to inform her of what Michael had told Dan about the past week's odyssey. It was impossible to tell, but there was probably nothing he could do about it, anyway. Dan's expression remained warm and sincere, so it was probably a safe bet that they hadn't called the police from the kitchen. *Probably*.

Less than an hour later, they were all seated at the candlelit dining room table with half-filled goblets, a carafe of white wine, and a regional banquet of succulent crab with drawn butter, garlic mashed potatoes, festive sautéed squash, a zesty salad of summer greens, and a basket of bakery-warm French rolls.

"Wow, this is just awesome!" Michael thanked Melissa. He would never have asked for it, but the special treatment and the relaxed, family atmosphere were just the salve his soul had needed. "But I wouldn't have wanted you to go to all this trouble just for me."

"Nonsense, it was my pleasure," Melissa replied with a genuine smile.

"Hey, I forgot to mention, Mel, Michael had tickets to that Beatles Reunion show down at the Hollywood Bowl." He looked at Michael. "Melissa is a *huge* Beatles fan, as I think I said in the car."

"I only wish I had been born early enough to see all four of them live," Melissa lamented. "How was the show? I thought about going when they were here, but I think it would just make me depressed with the two of them gone."

"I didn't get to see it." Michael smiled sadly. "That really bummed me after looking forward to it for six months. But I think it would have been spectacular. What a stroke of genius, getting Julian Lennon and Ralph Castelli to back them up."

"Lennon I get, but who's Ralph Castelli?" Dan inquired, flaking a bit of crab onto the edge of his roll.

"I think he means Jimmy Pou," Melissa corrected. "The guy who plays George Harrison in the Beatles tribute band 'Rain'."

"No, it's Castelli," Michael reaffirmed, puzzled by Melissa's suggestion. "The drummer. Filling in for Ringo Starr."

"I wonder what the *real* Ringo has to say about that!" Melissa laughed. She seemed oblivious to Michael's befuddlement. "I didn't know he wasn't drumming. Is he too old or something? I know it takes a lot of stamina to drum through a two-hour set. So what do they have him do? I can't see him playing George."

"Uh, no," Michael started, speaking very slowly as though it would help get his point across, wondering how much of a fan Melissa could really be if she wasn't follow-ing this. "George Harrison plays himself. Castelli is the drummer ... Ringo Starr is dead."

Suddenly, he realized that it was possible Melissa didn't know this. He didn't know how she could have avoid-ed the news, but then again Starr had died in that freak movie set accident only a few years before, and he guessed that if she had been distracted at the time somehow, she may not have picked it up. He felt a twinge of regret at the anguish he might have caused by telling her.

But Melissa wasn't buying it. For that matter, neither was Dan. They were both staring at him as though he had just brought out a hand grenade, a visible chill in their trou-bled expressions.

"Ringo is not dead," Melissa volleyed, matching Mi-chael's clear and ponderous tone. "It's George Harrison that's dead. And John Lennon, of course. Harrison died in 2001 from lung cancer. Did you not know?"

Now it was Michael's turn to stare incredulously. "George Harrison is alive," he declared, but his tone was no longer steady. "I saw ... I saw ..." He looked to Dan for backup. None came.

"Hold on a sec." Melissa got up from the table, making a stop-sign gesture with the palm of her hand, and disap-peared down the hall and around a corner. A minute later she returned with a small laptop computer. When it had powered up, she swiveled it in Michael's direction.

"Look it up," she invited sympathetically.

Swallowing hard, a sense of dread mounting in him alongside a horrifying conviction as to what he was about to find, he popped open the web browser and keyed "George Harrison" into the search field.

And there it was, in the second entry down from Wiki-pedia. He didn't even have to open the link.

"George Harrison, MBE (25 February 1943 - 29 November 2001) was an English musician, guitarist, singer-songwriter, actor and film producer who achieved ..."

Was.

"Oh God. Oh God. Oh God." Michael felt sick.

"Good lord, you really believed that, didn't you? That Harrison wasn't dead?" Dan eyed his friend with an expression of earnest concern. "Sweet Baby Jesus. No wonder you're frazzled."

"Do you think I'm crazy?" Michael uttered weakly.

"No." And he could see from the look Dan focused on him, squarely into his own eyes and unwavering, that this was true. "In fact, I've got something to show you that may actually shed light on this. Something I've been working on."

Melissa shot Dan a concerned glance, but it appeared to Michael more indecisive than alarmed. What could this "something" of Dan's be that his wife seemed not quite sure about?

"It's a theory," Dan explained, answering the unasked question. "A physics principle I've only recently discovered. I don't want to get into it tonight; it's very involved and you're too tired and stressed to take it in. But tomorrow, for sure. Right after breakfast, if you're up to it."

"A physics theory?" Michael was perplexed. "You've got some physics theory that explains why Ringo Starr is dead to me?"

"That would be more of a music theory," Melissa quipped, drawing chuckles and easing the mood just a little.

"So what, am I in some parallel universe like we used to talk about in high school?" Michael pitched in. He had meant it as a joke, but the way Dan looked at him drained his smile away. *Holy shit*, he thought. *It is something like that.*

"Tomorrow," Dan assured. "For now, if you're up to it I think it would be a good idea to get Mel in on everything you told me this afternoon. I'll vouch for her, and she may be able to help, too."

Michael nodded. A spike of anxiety welled up inside him, but he had known this moment was coming, and he had come all this way for the express purpose of unpacking the whole insane mess for Dan Hendrick to scrutinize and advise upon.

"I've got to warn you," he prefaced, speaking mostly to Melissa, "now that this Beatles thing is on the table and Dan thinks he may have some idea of what's going on ... that's just the tip of the iceberg. It wasn't just the tree that night. We didn't go into it earlier, but like I told Dan, there's been more weird stuff like that. Worse stuff. God, I hope you guys don't just think I'm loony-toons."

After confirming that Dan had indeed prepped Melissa with a cursory outline of his story, the part he had shared with Dan anyway, Michael took a deep breath and recounted the rest of the tale, this time beginning with the diversion to help Steve Shelby and sparing nothing he could remember no matter how bizarre or questionable in significance. Melissa sat spellbound, from time to time agape and more than once looking outright disbelieving. But Dan's patience, faith, and attention fully vindicated Michael's decision to seek him out from the start. In addition – in contrast to his bride – Dan raised his eyebrows a few times but never appeared to doubt the literal veracity of Michael's incredible words.

"We did live on Ventura," Dan confirmed when Michael had finished, going back to the part about the aged cypress growing on the vacant lot and picking up where their conversation in the car had ended. "But not on that corner. Down three houses on the other side, with a narrow driveway between boxwood hedgerows."

"The Haftowskis?" Michael gaped. "With that neat little waterwheel on the creek out back? That's where Dave

Haftowski lived!"

"Not on my watch," Dan said matter-of-factly. "My sisters and I grew up in that house. In fact, Carol still lives there. She bought it from my mom and dad when they moved to Arcata. I think Dave Haftowski lived over on Sycamore. That tree, that cypress you're talking about across from Thackeray's? That's been there forever. For God's sake, Michael, we climbed it together lots of times. You don't remember?"

Michael stared blankly. Until this moment, he hadn't consciously articulated it, but he now realized that all this time, in the back of his mind, he had held out hope that Dan might have some pedestrian explanation for the tree. *Yes, it's extremely tricky*, he had hoped Dan might say, *but my Dad's friends with this horticulturalist at Cal-Poly, and they found a way to transplant that thing when my parents left the property. You know how shrewd Dad is about money. He found this obscure government program that paid double what he could have sold the house for to tear it down instead and convert the lot to a green zone*. That, or something like it, was what Michael had dimly hoped Dan would say. Because as contrived and improbable as that sounded, no matter how ludicrous any other explanation might have been, it was preferable to the alternative, that what seemed to Michael as clear, unassailable memory was in truth complete fantasy and that his thoughts could not be trusted by anyone, least of all by himself.

Melissa spoke up. "In addition to what Dan wants to show you, there's something I'd like to do, too," she told Michael. "Have you ever heard of the MMPI?"

Michael shook his head.

"It stands for Minnesota Multiphasic Personality Inventory. It's the most thoroughly validated psychiatric assessment tool there is. The sheer number of questions can be intimidating, but it's all true or false and only takes most people an hour or two to complete. I've got licensed access to it online. How would you feel about taking it? I don't mean this evening. Tomorrow, maybe. You should be in as normal a state of mind as possible and fully rested."

"Um, sure," Michael returned, taken by surprise. "Will that say if I've lost my marbles?"

He had meant it as a joke, but Melissa looked serious. "It can, yes," she told him. "I don't think you're crazy as in needs-to-be-locked-up crazy, Michael. I think we can safely say that. But the MMPI could be really helpful in figuring out what … what you're feeling, maybe even what might be able to help."

"But at least partly," Michael pressed, the writing between the lines now eminently clear, "it would be to rule out whether I'm hallucinating … or making it all up."

Melissa gave an apologetic but confirming nod.

"Whatever." Michael shrugged, not smiling but not defensive either. "If it might help, I'm all for it."

MICHAEL AWOKE TO THE SMELLS of fresh coffee and sizzling bacon. The Hendricks's guest room – suite, really – was as lavish as any four-star hotel he had seen on travel shows, with a wall-mounted TV, luxurious bedclothes, a breathtaking view of the city, and even, incredibly, its own private bathroom.

He took a quick shower and dressed, grateful to Melissa Hendrick for laundering his clothes while they had sipped wine and played three-handed pinochle the previous evening. The conversation had covered a range of topics, from Dan and Melissa's courtship to catching up on things in the Bay Area to Melissa's groundbreaking research into why certain musical chords produced the same emotions in people the world over regardless of culture or personal background.

"Mel thinks it's biologically based," Dan had offered. "I think it's in the soul."

"Of course it's biological," his wife had scoffed, laying a run of spades on the table and turning to their guest. "As much as he hates people challenging his theories where he's an expert in the field, he can't seem to extend that same deference to others. Was he always like that?"

Michael answered with a grin and a shrug.

The evening had proceeded like that, amiable banter spiked with dashes of light marital barb. Nothing more, however, had been said about Michael's predicament.

He made his way downstairs to the kitchen and was surprised to find Dan minding bacon and pancakes while he sprinkled diced spinach and grated mozzarella into a pan of scrambled eggs.

"She makes you work for your keep, eh?" Michael jostled, taking one of the stools under the breakfast bar. "Good for her."

"Only breakfast, and only on Sundays and special occasions," Melissa qualified, emerging from the hall that led to her den. "Unless there's barbecue involved. Danny loves to burn meat." Her hair was neatly tucked with a barrette and she was dressed in a burgundy no-nonsense business ensemble.

"May I borrow him for a minute?" she asked her husband.

"Of course," Dan replied without looking up from the cakes he was flipping.

"This way," Melissa directed Michael. He followed her down the hall.

"Awful perky for someone who can't have gotten more than a half hour of sleep," she quipped quietly, looking back toward Dan. "He was up all night with his toys."

"Toys?" For a moment, Michael worried she was about to tell him something about Dan that he would rather not know.

"Models. Subroutines. Arcane calculations. It's not that unusual when he's on a trail. And your ... situation, for him, is like a trail to Nessie."

She escorted Michael into a smart office with large teak bookshelves, a matching, stately but not oversized desk, and a lighted tank full of neon tropical fish.

Melissa motioned him to the other side of the desk and had him look at the computer monitor. "Here's the MMPI, all teed up," she said. "When you're ready, just click here." She indicated a button marked [Begin] with her mouse pointer. "It's all true or false questions. There's no time limit, but it probably won't take more than an hour and a half. And Michael ..." She paused to make sure she had his full attention. "It's very important that you answer as truthfully as you can. Don't think about how a certain answer might affect the way someone sees you. Don't try to 'fool' the test. It's sometimes helpful to evaluate certain answers manually, but I won't do that unless you want me to. No one need ever see your specific marks. The computer will score the test and I'll just go by the conclusions it spits out."

"Yes, ma'am." Michael smiled, and they returned to partake of the delightful meal Dan had prepared before his wife left to put her work in order so she could take a three-day weekend.

Not only was the breakfast satisfying, it rejuvenated Michael emotionally. After what he'd been through, it was powerful tonic to feel cared for by the Hendricks, in a way that seemed more wholesome, familiar, and sincere than Charlie Paris's cryptic support.

With breakfast behind them and Dan having dismissed Michael's offer to help clean up, he made his way back to Melissa's office, closed the door to aid his promise not to answer self-consciously, and settled into the posh leather executive chair with a fresh cup of coffee to grind through the MMPI.

He had been mildly apprehensive, but once he started it, Michael found the test fun. And he felt validated by Melissa's taking the time, effort, and interest to explore him so thoroughly, a tangible indication that someone gave a damn about Michael Chandler and wanted to help him. Even the individual questions – and now that he saw them, Michael decided he had no objection to Melissa seeing his answers – gave a sense that someone cared about what he thought and believed, that his opinions and life philosophy mattered.

```
Question 4: I think I would like
the work of a librarian.
```

True. Michael caught himself trying to figure out what the question was intended to get at. *No*, he scolded himself, *stop doing that. This is all for my benefit, and Melissa made it very clear that trying to deconstruct the questions would invalidate the results.*

```
Question 15: Once in a while I
think of things too bad to talk
about.
```

True. His vision of a watery hell was only the most cosmic example. The same applied to hopeless claustrophobic scenarios, like miners trapped by a cave-in or sailors in a submarine stranded too deep for rescue, to terminal medical conditions, to severe pain, or to torture, slavery, or any other form of cruelty. He couldn't stand to see any of it, he was compelled to snap the channel off if he encountered such things on TV whether news or fiction, to walk out if it popped up in a movie, and he had to clear his mind forcibly of them or he became enveloped in panic. Of this question, at least, Michael was pretty sure he understood the purpose.

But he *had* to stop analyzing. *Just take the test, go as fast as you can, don't orbit around any one question or you will start second-guessing and defeat the entire point of doing this.* He forced himself to let it go, and moved on.

```
Question 20: My sex life is sat-
isfactory
```

After a moment's reflection, Michael smiled and marked *True*. He didn't get as much sex as he would have liked, that was for sure. But he blamed only himself, and he felt it would be wrong to characterize as unsatisfactory a condition for which he felt solely responsible.

```
Question 28: When someone does me
a wrong I feel I should pay him
back if I can, just for the prin-
ciple of the thing.
```

False. No hesitation there.

```
Question 33: I have had very pe-
culiar and strange experiences.
```

Michael was rocked by a burst of inadvertent laughter,

snatching a look over his shoulder, hoping Dan hadn't heard him above the clatter of dishes. True.

```
Question 35: If people had not
had it in for me I would have been
much more successful.
```

False. There were certainly times when Michael felt discontent with life, self-critical of his modest career, his meager finances, his failure to find new love in all the years since Vicki. But he never blamed others. Some of his disappointments flowed from caprice, but the vast majority, he knew, were of his own doing. *I could have let go and dated more,* he thought. *I could have saved for a down payment on a house. I could have gone to night school for a job more respectable than flittering like the Good Fairy up and down the aisles of a discount store.* Somehow, whether due to justifiable reluctance or lazy complacence he wasn't sure, all of that had seemed too hard. Hard, but not out of reach. Not the result of being held back by other people. *Nothing but my own damn fault. That is the truth and there's no way around it.* He clicked [F] and went on to the next question.

There were 567 in all. But once Michael got rolling and resolved to stick with his first answer whenever in doubt, the exercise sailed along. He was done in just under an hour, and though not a trace of warmth remained in what was left of his coffee when he finally clicked [Submit], to Michael it felt like no more than twenty minutes had gone by. He was almost sorry for it to end, and even more anxious to hear Melissa's analysis.

He returned to the living room to find Dan sprawled over a sofa watching a program on the NatGeo channel about the most recently published developments in M theory. As

Michael entered, Dan punched the mute button.

"All done?" he asked cheerfully.

"Yep." Michael sat himself down in an adjacent chair, the same one he had used the afternoon before. "Don't let me interrupt your show."

"Bah. It's two years behind and mostly ignorant tripe. You're the show today."

For a few minutes they discussed Michael's MMPI, particularly certain questions that had stuck in his mind. Dan laughed with him when he related the one about strange experiences, which brought Michael back to his host's comments the previous evening.

"So now that I'm done with the test," he posed hopefully, "what exactly is this theory you were thinking might be able to help?"

"I don't want to get too far into that until we've heard Mel interpret your test," Dan replied. "But I can tell you that it has to do with the nature of reality, and it's not like anything you've ever heard before. In fact, if I'm able to prove it – don't take this as self-aggrandizing, I came across it by luck as much as anything – it's practically guaranteed to bring a Nobel prize."

That snippet was as tantalizing to Michael as a New York steak to a dog. "Just tell me," he persisted. "I can't see how a psych test could have anything to do with physics."

"Test results first," Dan stonewalled. "You're just going to have to trust me. It's critical to how my theory might be involved."

THEY DIDN'T HAVE LONG TO wait. Upon reaching her office at the college, Melissa had decided to do only what was absolutely necessary, and was back home before lunch time. She was anxious for the test results, too.

She ate a sandwich at her desk while the men lunched in front of the television. By the time they had finished, she was back in the living room with a printout in hand.

"Well, Michael, first off, I'm pleased to say that we can definitively state that you are not clinically insane." Melissa settled next to her husband on the couch, consulting the papers. "The profile is valid, meaning the test doesn't think you made any effort to 'game' it. And your responses overall were well within bounds for a normally functional person. There are a few noteworthy spikes, though. Let's see ... you have a positive outlook, a good sense of humor, although a few seminal events, maybe in childhood or as a young adult, have made you socially cautious, especially in close relationships. You feel lonely quite a bit, even around others, but that's typical for unmarried people in your age range and it doesn't seem to be overwhelming you. You are inquisitive, logical, skeptical without being closed-minded. You're undergoing some acute, short-term stress ... I don't think we need an explanation there.

"Most importantly – and here's what we were really after, Michael – it's very clear that you are telling the truth about these recent events. I'm not saying they happened, there is still a small possibility you could be hallucinating – the results indicate to the contrary, but they don't rule it out. But what is beyond dispute is that *you believe* they happened. And the most straightforward interpretation of these results, taken as a whole, is that they actually did."

Michael nodded appreciatively, positively aglow with the sweet warmth of this vindication.

"There is one truly remarkable finding, and it certainly doesn't mean you're nuts. It's something to be proud of, in fact. Your empathy for others, Michael, it's off the charts. I've never seen the indicators so extreme. You experience other people's pain with practically the same intensity as you feel your own. And you are extraordinarily sensitive, which makes it worse." Melissa favored him with a tender gaze. "That must be hard."

Michael shrugged. "I'm just me," he said simply.

"Well, there's no doubt it contributes to your stress level. In some ways, this says ..." She waved the test results in the air. "... that you are as 'normal' as they come. But there is definitely a persistent, low-level apprehension in the background, made worse by what you're going through."

"So what does it mean?" Michael inquired. "Do I need medication or something?"

"A mild antidepressant probably wouldn't hurt," Melissa said. "But I tend to recommend against them unless absolutely necessary, and for you I don't think they are. I could set up a trial though, if you want. As for what it means ..." She looked soberly at her husband. "It's nothing definitive, but I have to admit that these results are at least consistent with what Dan thinks may be going on. You'll have to get the rest from him."

Dan took his cue. "Let's go in my office," he beckoned to Michael, planting a kiss on his wife's head as he got up from the couch. "It's going to take some doing to explain my work, and parts of it you really have to see on the computer."

Dan's study was upstairs past the bedrooms to the end of the hall. Michael was surprised to find it bigger than Melissa's. In broad strokes, it was similarly furnished, but unlike hers there were touches of whimsy, including a Magic 8 Ball resting on a bookshelf and several contemporary model airplanes suspended from the ceiling by thread.

Dan was looking at the models, having noticed Michael's interest in them, when he seemed suddenly to make a decision.

"Before we start with the physics, I've got something to tell you," Dan began. "It was supposed to be a surprise, but what the hell. I took the liberty of getting in touch with someone else you know who lives here. Don't worry, I was very cautious. I started out with the pretext of just asking if she had seen your story on the news. She said she had. So I asked what she thought of it. She was absolutely adamant that there must have been a mistake. She said no way could the Michael Chandler she knew ever intentionally hurt or kill someone. Especially over politics. She said that was the most absurd thing of all. I really sounded her out, man, I tested every angle, and she was relentlessly on your side."

"Who?" Michael asked with a powerful combination of excitement and foreboding.

"Beth DeLeon."

For a moment, the name didn't register. Then suddenly, Michaels eyes grew wide with understanding. "Oh my God, Beth McFadden? Are you telling me she *married* that asshole?"

Dan nodded, grinning. "Beth McFadden. Yes. And she wants to see you. She's coming over for dinner tonight."

CHAPTER 13
Many-Worlds

MICHAEL WAS CONFLICTED. ON THE one hand, the chance to see someone else who knew him was a welcome surprise, a salve against his sense of isolation. But on the other hand, he was apprehensive about Beth in particular, considering how their relationship had ended with that screaming phone call, and a little angry at Dan for assuming the right to bring her in without consulting him. But the anger quickly dissipated. He knew Dan was trying to do something good, and the precautions he had taken seemed proper. The anxiety about Beth, though, persisted.

Suddenly, he realized something that sent his anxiety spiking.

"What about Rick?" he asked in alarm. "I guarantee *he* won't cut me that kind of slack."

"I checked that, too, before I said anything about where you were," Dan assured. "She said he was gone on a business trip. 'Like always,' she said. That was the only time she sounded edgy. She was nothing but warm when we talked about you."

Michael nodded, trying to convey an acceptance he didn't feel. There was no point in discussing it further. Whatever harm had been done was irreversible, and he had only two options: to flee right now, sealing himself off from Dan's assistance and trying to find some way out of Boston, or to take his chances that Dan's intuition was well founded. What emerged was the realization that he cared more about finding answers than he did about his own safety. And that reduced his options to one.

"IF A TREE FALLS IN the forest with no one around to hear it," Dan began, "does it make a sound?" He had taken the chair behind his desk and sat Michael in another, turning his computer monitor to an angle where they could both see it, warning that it was going to take some time to establish the background for his theory and entreating Michael to bear with it.

The question seemed to Michael spurious and irrelevant, but he played along. "Simple," he replied. "There's no such thing as a true paradox. All supposed paradoxes reduce to a hidden ambiguity, and once you've found it, the conflict disappears. This particular case turns on how you define 'sound.' If you mean the sensation in the brain produced by stimulation of the auditory nerve, the answer is no. If you mean the propagation of sonic pressure waves through the air, the answer is yes."

Dan smiled approvingly. "This may not be as difficult as I thought. Did you get that in school?"

"It's self-evident." Michael shrugged. "But I did major in philosophy."

"Oh, that's right," Dan recalled. "Excellent, that will definitely make this easier."

Michael felt mildly irritated that Dan hadn't remembered his major. Then he realized with a flicker of a smile that on campus the previous day he hadn't been able to recall Dan's specific field, either.

"Now that I remember your major, I probably should have started with this one," Dan said. "What is the one fact, the *only* fact, that we can ever state with absolute certainty?"

Michael shook his head. "Maybe I was sick that day," he said. *Or lip-wrestling in Vicki's apartment.* He smiled to himself.

Dan retreated to a precursory approach. "You're familiar with the canard about brains in a vat, right? That since all experience takes place in the mind, there's no way to prove we aren't disembodied brains sustained in a vat of chemicals, with our neurons being directly stimulated by space aliens?"

"Sort of like in the *Matrix* movies."

Dan nodded. "Thus everything we see, everything we believe, everything we think we know, could in fact be pure thought and does not require the physical existence of anything around us in the world."

"Is that what *you* believe?"

"No." Dan's eyes narrowed. "But stay with me on this. I assure you it's going somewhere."

Michael nodded.

"So every scientific principle," Dan expanded, "when you trace it back along its chain of logic, ultimately relies on the *unprovable assumption* that our perceptions correspond to real phenomena outside ourselves. An assumption that *fails* if subjected to the very scientific method it's invoked to support."

Michael thought this through, and had to concede the point. "Ironic."

"No doubt. And that's just the start. We can't prove that other people exist; you could be the *only* brain in a vat. We can't prove vats or aliens either, so forget them, too. We can't prove that we aren't all dreams in the mind of God, or some formless intellect suspended in a cosmos *without* a god. Or without a cosmos. Ultimately, we can't prove that anything exists, not even the universe itself — with the exception of this one solitary fact."

"If there's no universe," Michael posed, "what else is left?"

Dan smiled. "Experience."

Michael eyed him with a quizzical expression.

"Experience," Dan repeated. "We know for sure that *experience* exists. We *think* we're having this conversation, we assume each other to be real and separate individuals, that the city out there ..." Dan gestured toward the Boston skyline through the window, "is a real place. But we can't *prove* any of that. All we can say for sure is that the conversation, or the nice view, is being *experienced*. We can't say by whom, by what, under what circumstances, or whether it's a dream or illusion. We can't even say what experience fundamentally is."

Michael smiled. "Doesn't that sort of invalidate your whole career?"

Dan shook his head. "I told you, I don't believe we're brains in a vat. But if you're going to call yourself objective, you have to consider all possibilities."

"So what *do* you believe?"

"We'll get to that." Dan continued. "Do you remember the Heisenberg uncertainty principle?"

That basic tenet of quantum mechanics had stuck with Michael, mainly because it seemed so bizarre and counter-intuitive. He recited: "It is not possible, even in principle, to measure both the position and the momentum of a subatomic particle at the same time." He still found it hard to concep-tualize.

"Almost. You *can* measure both, but not with the same degree of precision. And the encumbrance is reciprocal. The more exactly you measure one, the less exactly you can mea-sure the other. Even in theory."

"Yeah. I remember."

"There's an important corollary," Dan went on. "Even if you only measure one value – say position – you can't pre-dict where a given electron will be, even if you know where it was the second before. All you can predict is its *probabil-ity* of being at various locations. But *that* you can do with exquisite certainty. If you measure its location a statistically-valid number of times, you'll get a very specific breakdown of how frequently the electron appears at each spot. If you repeat that experiment the next day, and the next day and the next, you get the same probabilities every time.

"That probability profile is called the 'wave function.' The electron acts like a 'wave' of particles occupying all possible positions at once. Like a swarm of bees that are actually all the same bee, until you do something to detect it. When you make a measurement, it appears as though the wave 'collapses' to a single point. Like taking a snapshot of the swarm, but when you look at the picture, there's only one bee! I tell my 101 kids to envision a bunch of ghostly football players racing all over the field after the snap. Once the ball is thrown, they all run to where the receiver is and merge together into a single, *real* player. So before, you had a field full of ghosts, and now you have this solitary flesh-and-blood guy. That 'real' guy is like the observed electron.

"And his location on the field is determined by the play call. Now, you can't know ahead of time what specific play will be called on a down. But you *can* know which plays are more *likely*, and which ones less, by a team's tendencies. That's how defensive coaches draw up their schemes. If you watch enough games, you see a pattern emerge: screen to the tight end 10% of the time, flanker post pattern 20%, and so on."

"You still teach freshman physics?"

"Once a week. Usually Mondays. My grad students take care of the rest. I actually enjoy it, you know, introducing fresh young minds to all this cool stuff. God knows if I didn't want to teach, I'd get a gig in the tech industry and make some *real* money. But I do apologize for the trite metaphors. I don't mean to insult your intelligence, I'm just trying to make sure you're with me."

Again Michael nodded, trying to appear interested while fighting a growing urge to demand that his host get to the point already. He knew most of this stuff, if only by rote, or at least recalled it from their conversations as teens. But something new was coming, and he was sure all this background must be necessary, otherwise his friend wouldn't be going to all the trouble to set the stage.

"You probably recall that there are two main interpretations of these phenomena. The original is called the Copenhagen interpretation because it was developed by Niels Bohr and Werner Heisenberg at the University in Denmark. That's the model where the wave function collapses. The electron itself is described not as a particle but as a *probability wave*, a wave with spikes of various magnitudes reflecting where the electron is likely to be found. Not just *modeled* as a wave — Copenhagen says it is a wave. Literally. That the wave is what's real, and the collapsed particle is an illusion."

Michael found this difficult to comprehend, but he had read and understood enough to know that it was, indeed, a well-established and viable explanation of the quantum weirdness.

"The competing view is the 'Many-Worlds' interpretation. You may recall that better, since we discussed it to death as kids." Michael nodded confirmation, and Dan went on. "To oversimplify, it's sort of the mirror image to Copenhagen. Many-Worlds says it's a particle all right, but that it exists simultaneously, with equal reality, in every possible position. When a position is measured, Many-Worlds says it's the universe that collapses, not the electron wave. *But only for the particular observer.* Many-Worlds says that every quantum event splits into a series of equally-real parallel universes, so that when these are taken together, everything that could happen does happen. It doesn't seem so to the observer, because he can only see what happens in his own world. But unbeknownst to him, his exact duplicate in a universe next door measures a *different* position for the electron, and the same goes for every outcome allowed by the laws of physics. What the probability wave represents is not the chances of each outcome in a single reality, but rather the number of *separate* realities in which each outcome appears. The higher the probability for a given location, the more parallel universes there are in which the electron is found there."

Michael smiled. He did remember, with fondness, their excited conversations about the implications of this theory, though full disclosure would reveal a decidedly unscientific bias toward talk of parallel-world encounters with certain female celebrities or classmates, and whether it might somehow be possible to trade places with their lucky doppelgängers in those universes.

In those days of orbiting the Embarcadero together in Michael's car, in the science community at large, Copenhagen had been the dominant view, particularly among elder physicists who had grown up considering it the only model with a pedigree. But in the ensuing years, as the maturation of string theory into M theory and discoveries in cosmology had lent scientific legitimacy to once-scorned 'multiverse' ideas, Many-Worlds had surged in acceptance and begun to overtake Copenhagen as the "standard" in quantum mechanics. Among its attractions, Many-Worlds could solve a number of paradoxes that had troubled philosophers for centuries. It supplied a cogent answer to the question of what would happen if a man traveled back in time and killed his own grandfather before his father was born. The Copenhagen interpretation had nothing to offer beyond the unsatisfying conjecture that nature would simply not allow such an impossible act. Many-Worlds provided a simple, coherent alternative. The grandfather killed was not the *literal* grandfather of the man doing the killing; he was a copy of that grandfather in a different universe. In the world the killer came from, Grandpa remained alive. The killing took place in a separate, but equally real, universe in which no version of his father ever appeared.

"So we have these two interpretations," Dan was saying. "And each of them has its points, yet neither one seems to have the story right. What has always bothered me is the so-called randomness of it. I mean, wave or particle, take your pick, if it were truly random, how could there be a pattern? Over time, a random effect should be distributed evenly among all possible results. This effect isn't. The electron will be *here* 60% of the time, *there* 15%, the other 25% in *this* spot. *Something* must be creating that very precise probability structure."

"I guess." Michael shrugged, lacking the background to evaluate the conclusion.

"There's a superficially-similar phenomenon, one that's truly random, called 'quantum foam.' Do you remember what that is?"

"What is this, mid-terms?" Michael countered, good-naturedly but with a tinge of sincere irritation.

"Sorry." Dan shifted down one gear. "I thought you'd remember. It's a latent energy that exists all through the universe. Specifically, it manifests itself as the spontaneous appearance and disappearance of 'virtual particles' everywhere in space. Even in the 'empty' vacuum between the galaxies. Like normal particles, electrons and positrons and so forth, except that they pop out of nowhere and disappear again in a fraction of a second."

"Like the froth at the seashore. Full of tiny little popping bubbles."

"Good, you *do* know." Dan was satisfied. "They wink in and out of existence so fast they don't have time to impact the world like 'real' particles. And we don't really understand why it happens, or where they 'come from' or 'go to' — not that those terms really even apply."

Michael nodded confidently, and Dan moved on. "Now, before we get to the next part, I need to ask some very basic questions. I believe you know all of this, but I've got to make sure, because if you don't, I'll need to lay more ground."

"Fire away."

Dan fixed his eyes on his friend. "What do you remember about the four fundamental forces? What they are and what they do?"

Michael ticked them off on his fingers. "Let's see ... gravity, electromagnetism, and the strong and weak nuclear forces."

"Correct." Dan looked pleased. "And what do they do?"

"Gravity is gravity," Michael dispensed. "Electromagnetism causes light, x-rays, radio waves, and microwaves ... those are all just different frequencies of electromagnetic radiation. Oh, and magnets."

"And electromagnetism holds atoms and molecules together," Dan supplied. "Now, you said 'gravity is gravity' and I get why, because it's part of everyday experience and you assume everyone understands it. But I'm asking you what gravity *is*."

Michael thought for a moment. "Well, Isaac Newton thought of it as a force between objects, like planets around the sun or the earth and an apple. Then Einstein figured out it wasn't really a 'force' at all, it was the presence of matter distorting the shape of space and time."

"Excellent!" Dan approved. "And how do we know this bizarre idea is right?"

"I think it was verified by some eclipse thing. But I don't recall how."

Dan nodded. "In 1919, they did an experiment using a solar eclipse. Normally, the sun is way too bright to detect stars around it with the instruments they had back then. But the eclipse made it possible. They took nighttime pictures of stars in the Hyades cluster, then photographed those same stars as the sun passed in front of the cluster during the eclipse. And when the pictures were compared, the stars appeared to have moved. Their light was bent by the sun's gravitation in *exactly* the way General Relativity predicted. That's what made him famous, you know. Before then nobody had ever heard of Albert Einstein."

"It would have been sweet to be there."

"Indeed," Dan agreed. "And since then, it's been confirmed a hundred different ways. Even the software in the GPS satellites has to be modified to account for the Relativistic difference in time flow between their orbits and the surface of the earth." Dan forced himself to focus. He could talk about this stuff all day. "But back to business, or we'll never get to your answers. What do you recall about the two nuclear forces?"

"I know they hold stuff together inside the atom," Michael recited. "But I always forget what, exactly."

"One of them does. One holds quarks together inside nuclear particles, the other causes radioactivity. Do you know which is which?"

"The strong force is the quark one."

"Good." Dan smiled, relieved. "Four out of four. It was going to put rather a hitch in things if it turned out those were different for you."

"Different for me? How could they be? It's basic physics."

"The cypress lot, Ringo dead," Dan said dismissively, as if that were explanation enough. "Anyway, as you are no doubt aware, ever since they were discovered, physicists have been trying to prove that there's really just one force. That these four forces are just different manifestations of the same thing."

Michael made a dramatic gesture. "The 'Grand Unified Theory'."

"Right. So in the 1980s, it was definitively proven that the electromagnetic and weak nuclear forces are one and the same. There have been some convincing theories bringing in the strong force since then, but that's still inconclusive.

"Only two credible theories have ever emerged that join all four forces: quantum loop gravity and string theory, which of course evolved into the M theory we have today. M theory is currently more favored, and personally I tend to be in that camp. M theory is just too beautiful to be wrong. It's elegant, simple, and dead-on in describing the data. It's the most successful theory of all time.

"There's just *one* little problem." Dan squinted coyly and made a "teeny tiny" gesture with his thumb and forefinger. "M theory requires the universe to have eleven dimensions, seven more than the length, width, height, and clock time we can see. I won't go into why we don't see them, just take my word that it can be satisfactorily explained. I know how Tinkerbell-ish it sounds, but when you see the math and how perfectly the model works, no serious physicist can doubt there is something very profound going on.

"But that's not the 'little' problem. It turns out that these dimensions require space-time to take the form of a geometric shape called a Calabi-Yau manifold. That's an enormously complex shape, something like a garden hose all squished up into a contorted pile. The problem is that there are 10^{500} possible Calabi-Yau manifolds. That's a '1' followed by *five hundred zeroes*. We tested it in class once and showed that it would take a whiteboard over a hundred feet wide to write out that number. And no one has a clue which specific manifold our universe is."

"Couldn't you just have a computer model them one by one?"

Dan's eyebrows arched up. "That is a very astute question. Are you sure you didn't sneak in some physics classes at UC?"

Michael smiled ruefully. "I actually wanted to, but they wouldn't let me because I didn't have the math prerequisites."

"You could have taken them."

"I'd rather eat broken glass."

Dan burst into laughter so hearty he nearly fell out of his chair. It was a full minute before he regained enough composure to continue.

"The answer, unfortunately, is no. The best computer conceivable – orders of magnitude more powerful than we can build today – would take longer than the entire lifetime of the universe to test them all."

"Jesus."

"Yeah, I'm sure *He* could do it," Dan quipped. "But if I have my way, He won't have to."

"No?"

Dan beamed. "No. Because I've found a shortcut."

CHAPTER 14
Strings

"I'LL NEVER FORGET HOW IT came to me," Dan began as they sat back down. "Melissa and I and some friends were in the elevator going down to the car after an excellent dinner at Top of the Hub. We were all a little drunk, and I'm embarrassed to say that probably helped. I was thinking about something that had struck me, how in watching the conversations it became clear that no two people at the table viewed the world the same way. I started wondering how five reasonable, intelligent people could come to five different conclusions. Maybe partly genetics, but for the most part, I thought, it had to be life experience. People tend to believe the religion favored by the society in which they're raised, and it's no different with any other influence. The world you see around you is the real world – for you, the only world. But it's not objective, because each life takes a different path, and even in the course of an entire lifetime, each person sees only a tiny fraction of what's out there. We take an infinitesimal data sample, and from that alone, we project sweeping generalities with unflappable confidence that we understand things perfectly."

Michael nodded to show he was following Dan so far. He still wasn't sure where this was leading, though.

"In my head, I started seeing 'world lines' projecting from each person at the table. That's the swirly line your body would trace out, like a jet contrail, if you tracked your every movement from cradle to grave. Like headlights on the freeway in a time-lapse photograph. It seemed both elegant and terrible to me – all those colorful lines dancing about each other, colliding and bouncing apart, surrounded and affected by the others, and yet, individually, each person trapped in his own reality that could never truly be shared, and from which he could never leave.

"Something kept nagging me from the fringe of consciousness. I had the sense that some profound truth was staring me right in the face. It was like a little voice saying, 'See this! See this! See it for what it really is!' But I couldn't. The more I tried to focus, the foggier it got. I remember glaring at my glass and thinking, 'Goddamn cognac!' But looking back, if it hadn't been for the cognac, I don't know if the idea would have ever occurred to me.

"Finally, I stopped fighting out of frustration and just let it go. The place was too loud and I was too intoxicated to coalesce the thought by force. In fact, after a while, I completely forgot about it. The rest of the dinner was lovely.

"But Melissa will tell you, the subconscious mind is a *force majeure*. I must have kept working on it in the background. Because there we were in the elevator, and all of a sudden it struck me like lightning. I think I actually yelped. What I had stumbled upon was the profound significance of *experience*. They weren't just motion tracks, each of those 'world lines' was also a continuum of experience. And experience is the only thing we know for sure exists. What if the experience, not the physical motion, was the fundamental reality? What if experience continua were nature's building blocks? You couldn't prove they *weren't*, we've already gone through why that is. So I decided to look for evidence that they *were*."

Michael squinted, playing Dan's words back in his mind exactly as they had been said. His eyes began to widen as the import of what Dan was saying slowly dawned on him.

"Yeah! Yeah!" Dan nodded enthusiastically at the comprehension on Michael's face. "Incredible, isn't it?"

"You don't seriously mean …"

"Let me show you what I found." Dan turned to the computer and busied himself on the keys. The screen divided in half into two spreadsheets, top and bottom, long lines of numbers interspersed with indecipherable mathematical symbols filling each.

"This," Dan swirled the mouse cursor about the upper section of the screen, "is a calculation of how many data bits, expressed as quanta of energy, would be necessary to encode every possible reality-branching event under the Many-Worlds interpretation, assuming a universe of flat topography and a closed time cycle commencing with the Big Bang and ending with the achievement of maximal entropy, but with—"

"Whoa, whoa, slow down!" Michael laughed, waggling his hand.

Dan smiled apologetically. "I just mean that it assumes the most widely-accepted conjectures in the Standard Model. The latest science."

"Okay."

"So it starts by modeling the known universe using the most current assumptions. Most of that, even where it's a bit arcane and not necessarily 'settled science,' is at least empirically physical. That's not enough, though, if you're postulating a role for consciousness. So I had to work in a variant of Drake's Equation. Do you know what that is?"

Amazingly, Michael was nodding before Dan even finished his sentence. "The formula for estimating the number of intelligent species there are in the galaxy. Based on factors like how many stars there are of the right class, what percentage of them have planets, how many of those planets could sustain liquid water, et cetera. First computed in 1961, modified and recalculated every few years to incorporate new discoveries."

It pleased him to see that Dan was caught by surprise.

"Frank Drake is professor emeritus at Santa Cruz," Michael explained. "Everyone there knows his deal. You can't avoid it. They treat him like a rock star."

"I didn't know that."

Michael was hung up on something. "But what does the Drake number have to do with alternate realities?"

"Consciousness," Dan reminded. "This is a cosmological calculation. We're not just talking about earthbound consciousness, we have to factor in consciousness everywhere."

It was Michael's turn to go speechless as his mental image of Dan's vision grew from a house to a skyscraper.

Dan smiled appreciatively. "So we extrapolate the Drake values beyond our galaxy, out across time and space. So far so good, but that's when we run into the real problem. Because we're accepting M theory, and that means the stars we see, the intelligence we can estimate, the dark matter we can only infer from its invisible pull, the dark energy we only discovered a decade ago that's making the whole universe expand – all of that stuff is just the beginning.

"And we're stuck there. No way to go on. No hope of calculating what's really out there, which we can't observe or infer in *any* testable way.

"That is, until we interject an obscure feature of M theory proposed about four years back, by a promising young post-doc who got drafted into government intelligence and was promptly blown to pieces in that Khost fiasco in Afghanistan. You probably saw it on the news — the incident where that Jordanian mole walked right into the CIA base wearing eighty pounds of C4."

"Don't think I've heard about it."

"Christ, that kid was only twenty-four. His first time ever overseas. I don't think he was in country more than a week. Ah, well. At least he left a legacy. If there *is* a Nobel in this, I plan to see what I can do to get his name on it."

Michael grinned. For all his scholarly brilliance, for all his matter-of-factness about the subservience of animals and the righteous appropriateness of eternal hell fire, there was a heart beating under the titanium skin in Dr. Dan.

"It was just a few pages buried in his dissertation. And he had a good bit of it wrong. But something intrigued me while I was proofing it as his advisor, so I kept a copy. And when I got onto this," Dan nodded toward the screen, "something told me to dust it off. It took about four months to work out his errors. But once I did, *boom!* Out popped the Hope diamond."

Dan clicked on one of the fields in the upper partition and a new window appeared, overlaying the spreadsheets. To Michael, it was a worse train wreck of incomprehensible symbology than the others. He could only guess that Dan had pulled it up for himself; he couldn't possibly have expected Michael to make sense of it.

"It's what I call the 'P' dimension," Dan explained, ogling the hieroglyph as though it were his biological offspring. "A second time dimension that runs perpendicular to the clock time we know. If you've absorbed anything of M theory, you know it talks about membranes – or just 'branes', as everyone calls them now. You can envision them as bed sheets hanging parallel to each other on a clothesline, with a separate universe on each one. And the P dimension runs laterally *through* these branes, like a spear through the sheets. It's like a conduit for travel from one reality to another. But not just any other: only to realities on adjacent branes. That's what maintains the appearance of causal continuity: each step from one universe to another is small."

Michael gave a little nod, striving to look engaged, but Dan was losing him. In their youth, M theory had not yet branched out from string theory, at least not in the publications Dan had read. Michael's facility with M theory was limited to snippets he had been able to digest from the past week's forays into *All From Nothing*, and moreover, he was pretty sure his head wouldn't be able to get around it all even if he had read the entire book.

Dan, though, was on a roll. "The P dimension and gravity are the only entities that can transfer energy from one brane to another. This is the reason gravity is so much weaker than the other forces, and so much harder to unify—"

"Weak?" Michael challenged. "Gravity holds the planets in orbit around the sun!"

"Yes, but compare that to the other three. Run a comb through your hair a couple of times and then hold it over a few shreds of paper. The static electricity will pick them up. The tiny bit of electromagnetic force you combed out of your hair is pulling harder on that paper than the gravitation of the entire earth."

Michael was silent. He had never thought of that.

"It's also what holds a piece of firewood together so you can't tear it apart with your bare hands, even though you can lift it against gravity with ease. But the others are worse. The weak force is what powers sunlight and thermonuclear explosions. As for the strong force, nothing can split up quarks, not even our best atom smashers."

Michael grudgingly nodded. "Okay. So gravity is weak."

"And here is the reason. Gravity works through the bulk, the 'space' between branes, although it's not really space at all. This dilutes the power, so that, for instance, if you have a 10-g gravity source pulling through ten branes, the amount of force felt on *each* brane is only *one* g."

Michael nodded, mainly to keep Dan moving. He was once more having trouble picturing what Dan was trying to illustrate.

"And like gravity, the strength of P events is strained. It decreases exponentially with distance through the bulk. So overwhelmingly, with respect to any packet of energy moving along the P dimension, that the chances are high that it will travel no more than one brane away before it settles there without the strength to go further. At that point, the event becomes a quantum of firm reality on that brane. It 'collapses'."

Michael took a chance. "Like the wave function."

"*Bull's-eye!*" Dan swelled with such radiant satisfaction that Michael envisioned him popping into a shower of confetti made of shredded science papers.

"And that is the key. Without the P factor, it would be beyond modern technology to do these calculations. The number of variables and the range of possible values would be completely unmanageable. With it, we're able to focus the hard lifting on a few critical components and then confidently extrapolate. The results can be safely rounded off and generalized. It's the P function that makes this computable in a few seconds rather than eons."

Dan closed the overlay, and they were back to the two spreadsheets. "I wish you had the math background to follow the equation. The framework alone took two years to construct. It correlates a vast array of sub-calculations I've got on other sheets; the whole thing is exponentially more complex than the meta-elements on this page." Dan smiled wistfully. "Ah, well. Half my colleagues wouldn't get it either. Let's just dive in."

Dan clicked a button in the upper partition labeled [Refresh]. After a few seconds, during which various fields slipped through changes in value too rapid to be perceived as anything but flicker, a bold figure appeared in a previously empty cell at the bottom of the divide:

107,892.638371109...

Dan looked at Michael as though the figure should mean something. Michael scanned the digits in a Quixotic attempt to extract meaning. He could not. Someone might as well have rolled his forehead on the keys of a calculator.

"It's a huge number," Dan picked up, oblivious to his friend's consternation, "but it's not infinite. The basic laws of physics, whatever they turn out to be, impose at least *some* limits on what is possible. You'll see with the next equation that it's a lucky thing."

Oh, goody, more fun with numbers, Michael thought. *I can hardly wait.*

AFTER A FEW MOMENTS OF silently admiring his own work, doing nothing at all to lift the tent flap so his guest might get his nose in for at least an orphan's share of the enlightenment, Dan moved his attention to the calculation in the bottom partition.

"Now this one," He moused over the lower display, "is a *different* energy total, but it uses the same units and basic assumptions as the first. So when we get a solution here, we can compare the two numbers, apples to apples."

Michael nodded impatiently, afraid he was going to lose touch with the concepts long before Dan finally ambled his way to the Big Reveal.

"This one is a *bit* simpler, but still no walk in the park. What we're finding here is the total amount of energy represented in the quantum foam. You might think that'd be easy, but it's devilishly tricky. You can't just measure the latent energy in a cubic meter of vacuum space and multiply by an arbitrary size. For one thing, the lifespan of virtual particles is so short it's nearly impossible to get useful readings. Nevertheless, through the magic of mathematics aided by computer power and with a few carefully inserted assumptions, it is possible to refine the measurements you do get into a fair approximation. Nothing you'd want to stake your legacy on if you could help it, but something to work with.

"But that's not the worst of it. It gets infinitely trickier when you want to extend the calculation to 'realities' we can't see. I was gratified and rather relieved to determine that once again, when you plug in the P function, it becomes doable. A whole slew of disjointed variables trending toward infinity can be tamed and coordinated along the P axis. Once those numbers are manageable, we pull the 'real' matter and energy out, and voila – the pristine cosmos."

"I don't get it."

"The empty universe. Maybe I should say 'multiverse,' because it does account for the myriad realities. But I don't like that word much because 'universe' implies everything all by itself. How can you have more than one? But whatever. If every brane has its own reality, maybe what we really need is new terminology for *that*."

Michael frowned. "What does 'universe' even mean if there's nothing in it?"

"A universe of *potential*." Dan stroked the mouse absently with his finger. "An invisible framework set up to bear whatever reality materializes. A cosmic trellis, prepped and waiting for its climbing rose."

Michael nodded. He knew he wasn't grasping it all, he felt a bit like a polar bear stranded on a small berg in an immense sea of ice, but of this part, at least, he thought he caught the gist. It was the universe as a blank slate.

Dan turned to the screen and clicked [Refresh] in the lower display. As before, the fields whirred briefly and a bold figure appeared in a box near the bottom:

$$107,892.633421816\ldots$$

"And there it is." Dan gestured to it. "The total amount of energy implicit in the quantum foam, courtesy of the P function. Now look at the whole thing and tell me what you see."

Michael leaned toward the screen. Again, the formulae meant nothing to him. The Greek symbols might as well have been Martian, and the values in the number fields could have kept flickering like slot machine tumblers with no effect on his comprehension. He strained to discern what was so obvious to Dan, badly wanting to appear at least as rational and attentive as a reasonably intelligent layman could be. But it wasn't—

Then he *did* see. He looked at the two bold figures that had popped up in the result box at the end of each calculation, first one and then the other. The numbers were long, more than a dozen digits each, and at first glance they looked far from identical. But on second look, *far from* was not the right phrase. Because the leftmost portions of each number, the digits left of the decimal point representing the large values, *were* identical. So were the first two digits to the decimal's right. And so was the exponent at the end of each line.

Even without full understanding, Michael felt a prickly sensation at the back of his neck as he compared the two numbers that had been generated by such different and seemingly unrelated calculations. Aside from a smattering of numerals at the far right signifying less than a thousandth's part difference, *the two numbers were the same.*

"So have you figured it out now? Can you see what form of energy the 'P' channel is carrying?"

Michael shook his head.

"Consciousness."

He turned to Dan with a gaze that was both awestruck and lost.

Dan was glowing. He turned back to the PC monitor and gestured with the mouse. "The fractional deviance is meaningless, well within the margin of error. They're way too close for coincidence. The energy supplied by the quantum foam is, for practical purposes, the *exact amount* required for Many-Worlds branching of all sentient consciousness in the universe. It can't be an accident. It means that consciousness – not particles or wave functions – is reality's most basic constituent. *The universe is made of thought.*"

It took Michael a long time to parse what Dan had just

said. Dan waited patiently. As the implication sank in, Michael grew absolutely astonished. Compared to this, the apparition in his townhouse seemed as mundane as a Harry Potter muggle.

"So, are you saying ... that perception creates reality, instead of the other way around?"

"Yes." Dan's smile was broader than ever. "The saying 'perception is reality' turns out to be *literally true*. Except that strictly speaking, it's not perception. It's intelligent consciousness."

"What's the difference?"

"Perception," Dan replied, "implies an external 'something' to perceive. Consciousness does not. Consciousness is like the 'force carrier' of raw experience."

"Are you saying the whole world is just an illusion? That everything we think is real is all in our heads?"

"No." Dan grew somber. "The reality we perceive does in fact correspond to external, physical things – at least *I* think it does. I'm not saying it isn't really there. What the theory is saying is that reality is *personal*. That there isn't one over-arching reality like a pool we all swim in. We each have our own pool. And if we could look objectively – which at present we can't, not experimentally anyway – we'd find that no one else really sees our pool but us." Dan fixed his gaze squarely into Michael's eyes to be sure he was hearing. "That literally – *literally*, Michael – *the world you live in is not the same world as mine*."

There was a long silence. Finally Michael asked: "Then how do we interact with each other?"

Dan frowned. "The pool analogy won't work for that question. I could say the pools are in different dimensions, in a 'Twilight Zone' sort of way, and right on top of each other, but that's not right. For one thing, they're *not* dimensions. Damn, I'm trying to make this simple, but I guess if you haven't been immersed in it neck-deep for months like I have, it's really not." He pursed his lips and stroked his chin, thinking.

Michael was still dwelling on the broader ramifications. "How sure are you of this?" he prodded.

"Ninety-nine percent. I'm still working on that final point."

"But how do you *know*?"

After a few moments of eyeing his friend fretfully, Dan issued a sigh. "I thought I had the perfect way to lay this all out, but it's not going as smoothly as I envisioned. I'm just so close to it that I can't tell the plain from the obtuse anymore." He smiled wanly and chucked his friend on the shoulder. "Let's do this, Michael. Let me finish the rest of the show as I had planned it. An imperfect plan is better than none. The last thing I want is for you to get even *more* lost, and if I go off script that's a real possibility. Just ride along, and we'll go back over whatever you want to, for as long as you want, when I'm done."

Michael smiled. "Okay."

Dan returned the smile and stood, peering critically at the juice glass in his own hand and then pointing at Michael's drink. "Give me that," he gestured. "I know it's early, but if ever there was an excuse to start drinking before lunchtime, this is it. We're going to go visual now, and when you've seen what I have to show you and come to understand how it pertains to your problem – heck, what it means about the lives of every human being that ever lived – somehow I don't think that innocent ice water is going to cut it."

FIFTEEN MINUTES LATER, THEY WERE back in their seats with decidedly more festive refreshments. Dan had even come up with the mixer and lime for Michael to fashion a proper gin and tonic.

"Even in the field," Dan began, "a lot of people have sort of taken for granted that the quantum foam was a curiosity without important consequences. Just a bunch of random, fleeting events with no impact on space-time except in those few instances where they interact with 'real' particles. And for those, you could safely focus on the 'real' transaction, and trust that the overall theory would capture any significant contribution of the virtual background. But that always bothered me. Nature tends not to waste, and this frenzy of subatomic activity that permeates all of existence for no reason seemed like the most colossal waste you could imagine.

"But I have come to believe in an answer more elegant and satisfying than anyone ever dreamed. Because, if my theory stands up, it means that what we perceive as the quantum foam is nothing less than the exchange of energy between one reality and another. That each virtual event – *every single one* – is used by nature as a branch to a parallel world. Just a tiny branch, mind you: a single photon might alter its trajectory by just one Planck length. That is an unfathomably small change. But taken together – on the order of trillions upon trillions of virtual events – all of a sudden you have macroscopic effects, things you don't need instruments to see. Multiply it to permeate all of time and space, and it becomes no stretch to call each branching the birth of a new universe."

"That's sort of what the Many-Worlds concept says anyway, though, right?" Michael posed cautiously, afraid the question was impertinent or stupid but even more anxious for understanding, and feeling somewhat emboldened by the drink.

"Yes, so far as it goes," Dan conceded. "The branching universe bit isn't new. But the standard Many-Worlds hypothesis still assumes physical particles as the building blocks. What's different in my theory is replacing those particles with pure consciousness. Not that particles aren't real, they are – don't lose sight of that. Your chair is real, the floor is real, the earth is real. But quantum branching takes place in the consciousness *first*. *Then* the world responds. It seems simultaneous for all practical purposes, we have neither the senses nor even the instruments to catch the difference. But it's real, and the implications are huge."

"Maybe you should just say what those are," Michael prompted. "I think I'm following you mostly, but I'm a little lost about what it all means in the real world."

Dan opened his mouth, started what was probably going to be a sardonic retort, then yanked it back. "You're right. You've been patient as a saint. Forgive me Michael, I can't help it, sometimes when I get talking about this stuff it just takes over." Dan took a pull of tequila from his shot glass and settled back in his chair, making a few rapid mouse clicks. The spreadsheet dissolved and a new program began booting in its place.

He focused his full attention on Michael while the application loaded. "When people think of parallel worlds – not just scientists, I'm talking about comic books, New Age whack jobs, two kids in a Mustang ..." Both smiled at the reference to their high school antics. "... they usually mean a full-blown cosmos, similar to ours but completely separate, like how Many-Worlds resolves the 'Grandfather Paradox.' The killing happens in a full-size *copy* of the universe the killer is from. That may be what you've been visualizing while I've been blathering on here. But it's the wrong picture. I'll say it again: nature tends not to waste. And what would be the use of an *entire universe* of extra space-time just so one man can prevent the birth of his copy-father? The parallel realities in my theory don't have that problem." Dan turned to the computer and tapped a few commands for the new program. "I've been saying all along how key consciousness is. Now I'm going to show you why."

The screen resolved into a high-definition image of a transparent cube, completely filled with a matrix of tiny, equally-spaced dots. Michael recognized immediately that it could serve as the grid for a 3-D graph. In fact, the definition was so sharp, and the effect so convincing when Dan dragged the mouse to rotate the cube, that he had to look several times before he was satisfied Dr. Dan had not somehow acquired a true 3-D monitor prototype.

"What color do you want to be?" Dan offered, but before Michael could say anything a smooth blue line appeared inside the cube, curving gracefully as it traced a path from one end toward the other, connecting a series of the dots.

"That's your life," Dan smiled teasingly. "I'll be red." Two clicks later, a new line appeared, similar and close to the blue one, intersecting it at some points, superimposed right on top of it for short segments, dancing several dots away from it at others.

"And there you are. Two people whose lives are intertwined, not identical but in proximity. Represented as world lines, much like the ones I imagined in the restaurant. I call them 'strands,' partly because that's what they are and partly to honor Jason Strand, that poor post-doc who died. The blue one is you, this end is your birth ..." Dan rotated the cube so that one end of the blue line was prominent. "And over here, you die." Dan spun the cube to the blue line's other terminus.

"In between, at about age eight, you meet me, *here*." Dan rotated the cube to show the first of several intersections between the blue and red lines. "We're buddies through high school." He scrolled along the world lines and zoomed in on a section where they ran on top of each other. "Buddies, not Siamese twins." Dan grinned and zoomed in even closer. As he did so, Michael could see that the grid of plotted dots was actually much denser than it had first appeared; for visual clarity, the density displayed was scaling up and down with the zoom level. This close up, Michael could see that the lines were not, as they had appeared, actually on top of each other. They ran close to each other, and there were a few intersections, but it was clear at this magnification that each line traced out its own unique and separate path.

"Now, we could go on like this forever," Dan narrated, "and believe me, when I think of all the sleepless nights I've put in on this thing, it feels like I have. But I won't drag you through every nuance." He scrolled out to where the ends of the lines could be seen again. "You get the idea. Suffice it to say that even Siamese twins don't trace perfectly superimposed lines. They look like one line at this level, but when you zoom down, at high magnification even Siamese twins never actually touch. Because yes, these 'strands' look very similar to what you would get if you plotted conventional world lines, tracing the path of your body through life. But what this models is beyond physical. These are experience lines. The path your *consciousness* takes."

"But reality is physical." Michael was beginning to comprehend, and as he did so, he felt less intimidated by Dan's academic prowess and more inclined to press and debate. "You said it yourself. The chair is real, the world is real."

"I did." Dan seemed pleased and not the least bit challenged. "And the physical is in these lines, too. The world around you is in there, Michael, wrapped around your spiritual core like plastic sheathing around an electric wire. These lines have girth, they're not one-dimensional. I never said it was *just* your soul in there."

"Then I don't understand the model. What exactly of the 'real world' is in the line, and what's outside? Isn't the cube the universe?"

Dan shook his head with a delighted look, savoring Michael's growing cognizance, his eyes betraying the childlike wonder these concepts held for him.

"The universe," he uttered softly, "is *here*."

With a mouse click Michael barely registered, the screen changed dramatically.

Now there were hundreds of lines. Thousands. Millions, it became clear as Dan manipulated the display. Billions now. More. Lines in every shade and color, twisting in every shape, beginning and ending at different points but all oriented to run roughly from the bottom of the cube toward the top. Other than this loose alignment, it was a frenetic jumble, an immense braid of incomprehensible complexity.

And they weren't just lines anymore; Michael could see them branching. Like a climbing rose – the analogy had not been just a poetic convenience – each line forked into two lines, each new line forked again, and again, and again like the branches of a tree, so that at maximum distance the whole structure was conical, what looked like a single point at the base splitting into a writhing sea of tendrils at the top, swirling and spiraling and intersecting each other with fractal grace. *Like a light cone*, he thought, picturing the diagrams in Dan's books that showed how "event horizons" evolved in time.

All at once, Michael was struck with an epiphany, a realization that coalesced everything he had read and thought about regarding why time, alone among the known dimensions, seemed in everyday experience to flow asymmetrically, always in one direction and never back.

"That's what causes it," he breathed in wonder, tracing a line in the air with his finger parallel to the flow of the display. "*The branching is the arrow of time!*"

Dan was smiling, his eyes too on the display. "Never fear, entropy is safe. We won't be violating the Second Law of Thermodynamics. Energy still flows from hot to cold, order still breaks down into chaos. But some people I know are going to be very annoyed when they find out that's only a sliver of the truth. And you haven't seen the best part."

Dan futzed with the controls. Suddenly, there was a new line, different from all the others. It was embedded at the very heart of the throng, an iridescent column many, many times the diameter of the other lines. At maximum zoom-out, Michael could see that this new line was the only one that stretched unbroken from the bottom of the cube to the top. And it was the only line whose path never forked into separate branches, never meandered.

As his eyes became accustomed to its appearance, Michael noticed an amazing thing. The surface of this great line was not distinct. Its opacity diminished as its breadth extended outward, becoming more and more translucent along its girth. But the discerning eye could detect it all the way out to the sides of the cube, enveloping all the other lines within itself.

He dared not articulate, even within the guarded sanctum of his private mind, what it was he thought he might be seeing.

It was beautiful. *Beautiful*. Michael had always viscerally understood what scientists meant when they said a concept had the quality of "beauty." It meant a simple structure resounding with profound implications. $E = mc2$. And what he was looking at now was the most spectacular example imaginable.

"The cube is nothing, just a frame of reference," Dan said, circling back to Michael's question. "Even the dots are more real; they at least represent quantum events. But even the dots, outside the lines, are false. There is reality only where the lines cross them."

Dan clicked on a control icon and the cube and dots disappeared. Only the lines remained. "There is nothing outside the lines. No space, no time, no formless void. Nothing. The lines are the universe. As you can see, nothing else is necessary."

He *could* see. And for the first time, Michael began to grasp fully what it all meant.

"Now look at me a minute, and make sure this sinks in." Dan spoke gently but insistently. He needed Michael's full attention for this. "These assumptions pare down the list of viable Calabi-Yau forms considerably. *Dramatically*. Enough to allow computer analysis within human time scales."

Dan's face was radiating like an angel's. "I've started the process. It has to be done reiteratively, so it's taking some time. Six more weeks if I'm lucky, nine weeks at most. I've got it humming along on one of the most powerful Crays in the world. But I've already got results from the first pass. And they indicate there is only *one* Calabi-Yau manifold compatible with these parameters."

"Sweet Jesus." The more he thought about it, the more astounded Michael became. "Are you saying you can actually *prove* that raw experience is the fundamental building block?"

Dan nodded. "Yes. Even if this first run isn't conclusive, I'll have a formal case suitable for peer review in time. But I already know it's right."

Dan's voice sounded ethereal and far away. "I'm on the verge of making my own book obsolete. Behold the *true* Tapestry."

CHAPTER 15
A New Door

HOURS LATER, MICHAEL AND HIS hosts sat in the living room discussing what could be concluded about Michael's situation, sipping espresso made from earthy dark-roast beans the Hendricks had picked up in Ethiopia during Dan's speaking engagement at Addis Ababa University. Dan alone was popping pistachios from a bowl on the coffee table; Michael and Melissa were too captivated by the conversation to eat.

Michael was shocked to learn that Melissa hadn't seen the slideshow yet. "You can see she's resistant," Dan explained. "I didn't want to present it to her until I'd built the most convincing case possible. It would be pointless to lay out a half-baked theory and have her justifiably challenge the weak points. But it was killing me not to show *somebody*. When you came along, it was like a miracle."

"Miracles" seem to follow me around like Marley's chains, Michael thought, thinking not strictly of divine providence but of all the inexplicable or suspiciously coincidental happenstance he had recently experienced, the fortuitous as well as the frustrating. But he said nothing.

"So you're saying," Melissa said skeptically, "that any experience we don't share with another person can produce a *physical difference* between their world and ours?"

"Yes," Dan replied, "but it isn't a matter of 'can.' The

world experienced by each person is theirs alone. We can never truly intersect someone else's world line. At best, we can get infinitesimally close."

"In that case," Michael prompted, "can you explain one more time how it is that we can interact with each other at all? I didn't quite follow the first time."

"Yes, how *does* that work?" Melissa seconded with a hint of scorn.

"I didn't turn it on when we were looking at the graph," Dan said, eyes on Michael, "but each strand has a layer of 'fuzz' surrounding it, about twice the diameter of the solid part. The fuzz represents quantum uncertainty: experience potential. This fuzz on different strands can overlap, and where it does, the people involved have the same experience, differentiated only by personal boundaries. So if a man takes his wife to a baseball game and she sits down on a spilled snow cone, he doesn't feel the cold dampness seeping into his pants, and if she grew up in the opposing team's city, she doesn't feel her husband's exhilaration when the home team scores. But aside from that, they both experience the same game, the smell of popcorn, the gorgeous weather. That's how most of life is. The three of us are sitting here having that phenomenon right now. You two aren't experiencing the delights of the roasted pistachio, but we're all seeing the same room and hearing the same conversation."

Michael nodded, feeling pacified, maybe even a little disappointed. That description didn't seem so bizarre.

"But it only holds true for things we're jointly exposed to. Let's say earlier in the day, the husband's co-worker spilled a cup of coffee on his desk. As long as he never mentions this to his wife, in her world, it didn't happen. I don't mean that she just didn't know about it: *it didn't happen.* In fact, as far-fetched as it sounds, so long as they never talk about it and never see it together on the news, it's theoretically possible for their two worlds to have different presidents of the United States."

"What would happen if they *did* talk about it?" Melissa

challenged. "If there are seven billion separate realities, why don't these discrepancies show up all the time?"

"They *couldn't* talk about it," Dan answered, "because if they did, it would mean their presidents were the *same*. Only the versions of them that shared a president could talk about it. Ipso facto. And the fact is that, in the absence of shared awareness, so long as they don't create an insoluble paradox, the discrepancies *do* show up all the time. For instance, I don't believe in alien abductions, and if someone told me that they had been experimented on by doe-eyed eggheads aboard a flying saucer, I would point them in the direction of the nearest booby hatch. But, in theory, it is possible for each of us to be right. In my world, there are no stethoscope-wearing space aliens orbiting the Earth; in his, there might be. So long as I don't believe him and I never see proof to the contrary, there's no paradox."

"If that's how it works ..." Michael's face had suddenly darkened into a somber brood. "... *then what the hell happened to me?*"

Dan looked at him for a long time, needing no clarification to understand what Michael was asking: the apparition, the cypress tree, the wrong dead Beatle, and more were not debunked by this explanation. Melissa looked at Dan expectantly. At last, he said, "I don't know."

"That seems like a rather severe breach in the dike," Melissa remarked, trying not to sound too hostile. Though still far from convinced, she knew that this theory was her husband's pet project at the moment and that he had invested in it an enormous amount of heart and soul.

"I said I don't know what happened. I did *not* say it invalidates the theory." Dan's face matched Michael's sober affect. "It should never happen, but ... you remember the graph display Michael, how all the strands and sub-strands kept flowing in the same general direction, forward in time?"

"Yeah. Like tree branches, every fork bending up toward the sun."

Dan nodded. "I started running some models last night

that I didn't show you, because I need to complete them and analyze the results. But what I think happened, Michael – what *had* to have happened, really, if we take you at face value – is that your world line somehow got yanked sideways."

Michael looked at him quizzically, and Melissa had to stifle an eye-rolling smirk.

"A lateral move in time, *probably* along the P dimension, although at this stage that's a pure guess. P branching is supposed to be gentle, almost imperceptible — and it's supposed to be entangled with a clock-time component. A normal world line runs from one snapshot of reality to a slightly different one with a tick of clock time, exactly like the frames of a celluloid movie chugging past a projector lens. That's just the standard passage of time. What happened to you appears to be an extraordinarily violent shift with no clock time at all. It's as though that version of you, the one who bought the Beatles tickets and was all excited to go, got jerked out of that world line and attached to a completely different future. Like two of those movies running in a multiplex, and, halfway through, one of the reels gets torn off and spliced onto the film next door. So one minute Tom Hanks is Forrest Gump, then all of a sudden he's Jim Lovell in *Apollo 13*. Underneath he's still Tom Hanks, but now he's a character in a totally different world."

Hearing it put so graphically, how invasively his life had been disrupted, Michael felt sick. "And you said ... this *shouldn't* happen?"

"No. It shouldn't happen. It's not impossible, but the chances are miniscule. I calculated the probability, and the chances of a pure lateral move with detectable resonance – I just mean one that creates blatant artifacts like you remembering a past that doesn't belong to your present – the chances of that happening *even once* within the lifetime of the universe are so small that from a statistical standpoint, it is impossible."

"Then what happened?" Michael felt panic and nausea creeping in, a level of anxiety comparable to sitting in his shattered car waiting for Ridge Raymore and Norman Tuggs to decide how to kill him, completely helpless and with no idea of what to do.

"There are only two possibilities." Dan sounded confident of this, though Michael found it hard to see how he could be. "The first is quantum tunneling. Do you remember what that is?"

Michael started to speak, but Melissa waved her hand and interrupted. "I don't."

"Well ... as ridiculous as this sounds, it has been positively verified in repeatable experiments, and it's what causes the radiation from black holes that Stephen Hawking discovered. What it comes down to is that, because of quantum uncertainty, every so often a subatomic particle will teleport someplace that it should not be able to go. For instance, you could have a photon bouncing around inside a sealed box made of lead with mirrored insides, and all of a sudden, it appears instantaneously outside the box. Photons cannot pass through solid lead, so this should be impossible. But it happens. On a cosmic scale, black holes create such an obscene gravity field that nothing can escape, 'not even light' as the cliché goes. And yet particles do get out — through quantum tunneling. Once in a while, a random electron hopelessly trapped inside the black hole will simply teleport out beyond its event horizon. This is firmly established science. In fact, if it weren't for quantum tunneling, the sun couldn't shine."

"And you think Michael spontaneously 'tunneled' from one universe to another." Melissa was incredulous.

"I didn't say that. And I don't think it, either. I'm simply being methodical, laying on the table the only two possibilities I can see."

"Fair enough."

"So quantum tunneling happens, there's no question of that. But it's one elementary particle at a time. You never see, for example, anything the size of a molecule doing this, even though molecules and everything else are just collections of subatomic particles. The chances of a whole molecule tunneling are not exponentially greater than for a whole person, or a planet, or a star. They are all infinitesimally unlikely. It is physically possible, but given the other option, which still seems incredible but in my view less so, I believe the tunneling idea can be categorically ruled out."

"And the other one is ...?" Melissa pressed.

Dan sighed. "The other one is that this was done intentionally. That somebody, or some thing, *moved* Michael. That for some reason I can't even begin to guess, it was necessary to fuse two versions of Michael Chandler into one. Something took the Michael that attended Cub Scout meetings in a house on the cypress lot, the Michael who was looking forward to seeing George Harrison live on stage, and pulled him *sideways in time* — to *this* reality, where George Harrison is dead, and where that house never existed." Dan eyed his friend with an expression of awe. "So that this man we see before us is a cosmic hybrid. A man with a past in another dimension ... and a future in this one."

Melissa pursed her lips noncommittally. "So, the hand of God."

"The hand of God," Dan agreed. His features sobered. "Or ... something else with godlike power."

"DAN?"

Michael was standing next to his friend at the kitchen utility island, each of them chopping vegetables on separate cutting boards while Melissa, having prepared the chicken and spinach lasagna that smelled delicious from the oven, was putting herself together in the master suite upstairs.

"What's up?" Dan smiled.

Michael looked over his shoulder to make sure they were still alone. "What do you think it was? That thing on the stairs?"

Dan shook his head. "I have no idea, man. I have to admit, of your whole story that's the only part I have a little trouble with. But I do believe you, and we've ruled out insanity. I know you wouldn't lie about something like this. But as for what it was ... hell if I know."

"Do you think it could have ... been a ... demon or something?"

"I just don't know, man. I guess you can't rule that out. Have you thought of talking to a pastor or something?"

He hadn't. "That's not a bad idea. But I don't really know any, not even back home. And ... I don't know if I want to go that public. Just yet anyway."

"They're not supposed to violate confidence."

"Yeah, well, they're not supposed to violate little boys, either."

At that even Dan snickered, although he quickly controlled and suppressed it. Religion was not, in Dan's mind, something to joke about.

After a minute or so of further thought, another question came. "Dan, in your theory ... are all the copies of us the same? I mean, the versions of us in all those universes, is one of them somehow, I don't know how to say it, I guess the ... whatever it means ... the *real* me?"

Michael felt sure Dan was going to confirm his sad suspicion that the answer was no, that all versions of a person were equivalent, of equal merit, interchangeable. He was therefore surprised at the answer.

"I've wondered the same thing, and I have a hypothesis. And it actually seems to be supported by the math." Michael had no clue how mathematics could prove anything about the nature of the soul, but he knew of no one more qualified to judge such a thing than Dan.

"I didn't show you this part on the computer because I only discovered it a couple of weeks ago and I'm just starting the analysis. But here's how it goes. You recall the Prime Strand, that thicker, translucent line in the middle of the graph?"

"Yes." And now Michael voiced the question that had been haunting him for hours. "Is that line … God?"

"I'm not calling it that." Though it was very subtle, Dan seemed uncharacteristically uncomfortable. "I don't know what it is exactly. It just popped out of the math unbidden. But I do think it's some sort of unifying or focusing influence, some kind of collective or fundamental consciousness. And I found something striking. You know the sub-strands, the lines that branch off from a world line's main stock? I don't know if you noticed, but they're all variations of the color at the base, the 'birth' color. Well, it turns out the sub-strands closest to the center – closest to the heart of the Prime Strand – invariably retain the highest proportion of the base color. And the reverse is also true: the base color gets more and more diluted the further a sub-strand branches away from the Prime. So there's definitely something special about the particular series of branches that preserves that color.

"And there's more. I started examining the whole line matrix far off into the future and at closer and closer magnification. There was something that puzzled me: there's a point at which everything but the Prime Strand seemed to disappear. When I zoomed way in on it, though, I discovered that wasn't the case. What happens is that as the strands approach that point, the vast majority of them begin to fade. It's very gradual, but eventually, every branch on the tree disintegrates into nothing. Every branch, that is, except for one. For every world line, one chain of branches remains intact and continues alongside the Prime as far out as the model projects. It's as though each life does break off into an uncountable number of parallel universes, as we've been discussing, but in the end, only one survives. And, as you have no doubt guessed, the chain of branches that survives is the series that preserves the base color. I'd say it's as rational as anything to call that line 'the real you'."

Michael was heartened. If he was interpreting this right, it seemed to go a long way toward explaining what had happened to him, even if it wasn't the scenario he, this copy of him anyway, would have preferred.

"What do you think that means for me? Was the strand I came from the one closest to the Prime? Do you think something yanked me away from it for some reason?"

Dan was thoughtful. "Obviously you *feel* like the one you came from was the 'real' you. After all, you were there your whole life, and you've only been here a week. I can't answer objectively; as the theory stands now, I don't know how to measure an actual person's 'base color' and determine how diluted it is." Dan grinned at him. "But cheer up, man. Don't forget it's just as possible something yanked you *toward* the Prime Strand. If it was God doing the yanking, I'd say that's a good deal more likely."

Michael smiled. Within a few minutes of pondering this, the anxiety was gone.

FROM THE MOMENT SHE ENTERED the Hendrick home, Beth DeLeon owned it.

Michael had been nervously monitoring the clock for twenty minutes. He had heard what Dan said about Beth's sanguinity toward him, but that couldn't chase off his memory of her bewitching kiss, her sensual embrace, her potent emotional explosions. And most powerfully the sting, now recalled to his mind as freshly as if it had happened yesterday, of her rejection every time Rick DeLeon became available to her again, each breakup delivered silky smooth so he couldn't be mad at her, yet leaving him a residual ache, helplessness, and self-doubt.

Of course he could only picture her as she had been in high school, a vivacious debutante oblivious to the army of smitten young men always trailing in her wake. Or maybe she *hadn't* been oblivious. Beth was smart, which intensified her beauty like sunlight through a magnifier, and it was well within her capacity to feign ignorance while stringing them along just because she could.

She's aged, Michael kept telling himself. *Just like me. She's probably put on some weight, a bit subdued by the loss of youth, a more conservative dresser. A bit less sure of herself. No doubt she's cut off most of that luxurious long hair.*

But when the bell rang, what he saw as Melissa opened the door was a nightmare.

He had been right about some things ... but in the wrong way. Her blue satin evening dress and open-toed strap heels were conservative only in the sense that they must have cost a blue-blood fortune. She was the only one so smartly attired, yet she somehow generated the sense that the rest of them were the outliers, that they were all underdressed.

Her figure had changed, but rather than deteriorate it had blossomed from a bud into a flower, separating the adolescent pixie from the fully-formed woman she had become. Her hair was impeccable, a few inches shorter but still draped halfway down her back, and now, in place of the straight brown shimmer he remembered, it cascaded in rich loose curves highlighted with streaks of sunshine that made her look even more dazzling. Far from subdued, she fairly glowed with purpose and confidence.

To Michael's dismay, Beth McFadden DeLeon was more beautiful than ever.

And she had a young girl with her.

"This is my daughter Elise," she said, and the sound of her voice after all these years gouged Michael's melancholy even deeper.

The girl appeared to be eight or nine years old. Her hair was darker, with just a trace of chestnut, and Michael could readily see her mother's beauty reflected. Especially in the eyes, he thought: Beth had passed to her daughter those dark, piercing eyes that could interchangeably captivate or burn a hole through a man's heart. The green floral dress she was wearing was certainly age-appropriate, but it had obviously come from a boutique rack not far from where Beth had acquired her own outfit. Like mother, like daughter, Michael thought; Elise DeLeon was going to grow up to become another man-killer.

Though it was trite and oafish and Michael knew it, he couldn't think of anything better to say. "You look just like your mother." He smiled as he gently shook the girl's hand.

"*And* my dad," Elise returned. Her tone was bright and clear, echoing her mother's self-confidence, and her cultured diction made Michael wonder if he had underestimated her age. Her words suddenly reminded him of who her other parent was, and yes, unhappily, Michael could detect traces of that lineage too, in particular ears that crested in familiar elven points, which he found endearing on the girl, but which had always imbued her father with the air of a mischievous demon.

"Hello, Michael." Beth focused her smile on him and extended a manicured hand. He was both disappointed and relieved that she hadn't presented a hug.

"Beth. You look great." It sounded stupid, but it was the truth. He took her hand, and she squeezed his with surprising strength. It heartened him that she seemed genuinely pleased by his casual compliment.

Beth sparkled with a presence honed in countless society soirées as they exchanged effusive greetings. Dan was gracious and welcoming, but evidenced no trace of attraction. Married or not, Michael couldn't see how any man could be immune to Beth's wiles. *Maybe he's just become good at suppressing it,* he thought. *Maybe marriage does that to you.*

Melissa's face, on the other hand, betrayed the same kind of surface cordiality masking apprehension that Michael had detected the previous day when Dan had told her about his plight. He couldn't tell if there was an element of jealousy or mistrust, or if Melissa's unease was attributable solely to the obvious: an attractive woman from her husband's past surveying her home with a critic's eye. As they moved to the living room, he caught Melissa running a furtive finger over the mantle above the faux fireplace, inspecting for dust.

Melissa checked the lasagna and suggested they pass the remaining ten minutes of cooking time initiating the wine. Dan retrieved four goblets and a bottle of Chianti from a reserve held for company.

"By the way, Michael, let me just get this out: I know you're not to blame for that car crash with Raymore. I'm sure your lawyer will clear it up."

She assumes everyone has an attorney on retainer, he thought glumly, *because in her world, everyone does.* But he said only, "Thanks, Beth."

"He must have made quite an impression on you in school," Melissa probed.

Beth chuckled, shaking her head and flashing her perfect white teeth. "Michael Chandler could never kill anybody. Not to save his own life. He hasn't got the balls."

The moment she said it, Beth's face went dark with horror. She clapped both hands over her mouth, nearly knocking over her wine glass on the coffee table. "Oh my God, Michael, I didn't … I didn't …"

"It's okay." Michael forced a calm-looking smile, desperate to diffuse things so the subject could be dropped. "Besides, it's true. I should probably have my lawyer call you as a character witness."

Beth was nodding furiously, her face still flush, clutching the wine glass in both hands. "Yes. Yes, of course, Michael. You've got to know I'll do anything I can to help."

FOR ITS ROMANTIC ATMOSPHERE AND sumptuous fare, the candlelit dinner might have been set in a bistro in Florence. Beth held court, but spritely Elise was the moon to her mother's sun, actively participating in the conversations and exhibiting flawless table manners. Whatever Rick and Beth had done, Michael had to admit that they seemed to have parented well. It was hard to picture Rick DeLeon as any kind of father, let alone a good one. But Elise's poise and Beth's accoutrements, not least an elaborate white gold wedding ring with a center diamond of at least three carats, proclaimed that like the Hendricks, the DeLeons had done well in life. He was beginning to wonder if, among all the friends and classmates that had seemed in youth to be on equal footing, he alone had failed to achieve anything of consequence.

The feeling was compounded when the discussion turned to what remarkable coincidence had brought them together so far from California. Dr. Dan Hendrick, it turned out, had a pilot's license. And the instructor he had engaged upon deciding to fulfill this lifelong ambition had been none other than Ted McFadden, the one-time Hornet jockey and Navy doctor whose civilian assignment with Naval Intelligence had moved Beth's family to Boston in the first place. Dan had signed up for lessons at a private airfield, and was doing quite well. But when the ground school instructor heard him say he was from San Mateo, and then learned that Dan knew the McFaddens, he had put Dan in touch with Ted. "We're happy to have you here," the instructor had said. "But if Ted McFadden will take you, there's no one better." And that had suited Dan fine, not so much because of the hometown connection but because it was Dan's practice to go first class, as a general principle but even more so when life and limb were involved. Ted McFadden was fully occupied with his Intel work and taught flight only when it suited him, but he had taken an immediate liking to Dan and the training had been enjoyable for them both. Beth had shown up looking for her dad during Dan's third session of air time, and though she had never visited his home or met Melissa, they had stayed in casual contact ever since.

"So on top of all this, you've got a Learjet parked in the garage?" Michael joked.

"Afraid not." Dan chuckled. "We rent a plane at the airfield now and then just to keep up my hours. Sightseeing, mostly, although I have flown us to a couple of domestic speaking engagements. It's nice if the sponsor is willing to pay for the plane and fuel."

Discovering that Dan could fly, on top of everything else, and had a special relationship with Beth's father to boot, did nothing to relieve Michael's feeling of inadequacy. But something else did help, something wonderful that Michael could not possibly have predicted.

Beth warmed to him.

He didn't know if it was unconscious recompense for her insensitive remark. He was certain the wine played a part. It didn't matter. She made a point of sitting next to him, even though that had already been Melissa's loose seating plan, and at times she doted on Michael to almost embarrassing exclusion. By the time Melissa brought out the coffee and crème brûlée, Beth had taken to squeezing his hand, touching his cheek, even shouldering against him playfully when she thought the conversation called for it, or at least provided a veil of justifying cover. Even Elise, at times, seemed to feel compelled to divert the topic of conversation, or if nothing else simply to direct her gaze away from the antics and busy herself with her food.

Had it come toward the beginning of the evening, it might have inspired shock. By the end, though, as Dan moved to refill the wine glasses that for unspoken reasons remained on the table along with the coffee, it seemed almost inevitable.

"Not for me, thanks." Beth waved the bottle away. "It's time we got going. Elise has school tomorrow. It's been a perfectly lovely evening, Melissa, you are a sorceress in the kitchen."

She turned to Michael, who by combination of the wine and her attention had become accustomed to the unexpected but welcome intimacy, and who therefore took it in stride when she rested her forearm on his shoulder and proposed,

"Want to come with?"

Before he could answer, she seemed to become suddenly aware of the social ledge she was skirting and backed up a step, addressing the Hendricks.

"Not for the night. I just want to show him our place. I'll cart him right back as soon as Elise is in bed."

Melissa shrugged and shook her head as if to say, *it's none of our business.* Dan quickly shed the expression of alarm that had crossed his face, and calmly deferred. "Michael?"

It seemed insane. He had spent the past week traveling by night, eating like a lost pet, guarding his location and identity in fear for his life. Now all of a sudden he was the toast of Boston society, at least that segment of it that had been transplanted from San Mateo, beloved by all, feted and fawned over, his time in enviable demand.

To his surprise, from the chair behind Beth's, Elise was eyeing him intently, nodding encouragement, clapping hopefully with her fingertips.

And that settled it. Michael grinned and nodded. "Okay."

MELISSA HENDRICK STARED AT THE door, sipping her wine, for a long time after it closed. Finally, she muttered, "Maybe it's a good thing."

"Mm?" Dan paused halfway to the kitchen, arms loaded with dishes from the table like a busboy.

"She seems to have taken to him. I was careful not to mention it, but didn't you tell me they were romantic once upon a time? I couldn't tell if she was just pulling his strings or if there was some genuine nostalgia."

"They dated," Dan confirmed. "I don't know how serious she was."

"Do you think she's pretty?"

Dan considered. "Sure, I guess. In a Bloomingdales mannequin sort of way."

"But your friend was positively smitten."

"He's a romantic at heart. He wasn't blind to her, though. He openly admitted that he felt she played with him like a yo-yo."

"So she was right. He *didn't* have balls."

Dan returned from the kitchen empty-handed and shot her a look of reprimand. "That's not nice."

"It's the truth." She drained half of what remained in her glass. "I'm just glad *you* didn't go all lapdog for that precious bitch."

"Ease up." Dan reached a gentle arm around his wife's shoulder and kissed her cheek. "Be thankful for what we have. I feel sorry for Michael."

"No one made him go. But you know, it might be for the best. Maybe he can stay with *her* for a while."

Dan frowned. "Of course he can't. He thinks of her husband as his mortal enemy, I told you that. And the guy couldn't be blamed for living the part if he came home from a business trip and found Mr. Chandler nosing through high school annuals with his wife."

"She said he's gone for weeks at a time."

"Melissa …"

Melissa sighed. "I know. But Dan, he can't stay forever. You haven't told me what his plans are. Sooner or later the police are going to come around, and I'm sorry but I am not going to risk the life we worked so hard to build."

"I'll talk to him." Dan put both arms around her and held her in a reassuring embrace. "You bring up a fair point. He needs a plan, and we need to know where we fit into it."

She took Dan's hands in hers and looked into his eyes. "*Promise* me," she beseeched. "Promise you won't keep him here just so you can test your theory."

Dan nodded solemnly. "I promise."

POOR BASTARD, DAN THOUGHT AS he held his wife close, taking his own turn staring at the door. *I wonder where this is all taking him.* For the moment, among all the quantum possibilities, he couldn't conceive of any branching path for Michael Chandler that didn't end badly.

CHAPTER 16
Tinderbox

IF MICHAEL HARBORED ANY DOUBTS that the DeLeons had made it into the economic elite, they were dashed at the sight of Beth's silver Porsche 911 Turbo gleaming under a crescent moon in the Hendricks' driveway. The doors eased shut with a muffled clap, and when Beth turned the key, the 500 horsepower opposed-six engine growled to life and rumbled like a pacing tiger.

"Thanks for coming, Michael," Beth said as they pulled onto the street and headed toward the center of town. "This'll be fun!"

"Thanks for inviting me," he returned.

"And hey, Michael ... I'm truly, truly sorry for what I said."

"It's fine," Michael assured her. It wasn't, quite, but he wanted to put it behind them once and for all. "We had a great time all evening."

Beth smiled wistfully. "You haven't changed a bit," she said. "Same old Michael. I insult you in front of your friends, and you turn the other cheek. God, I love you."

Even though he knew she hadn't meant romantically, Michael's heart jumped at the words. He was grateful that the darkness masked his face.

"By the way," she said, "I didn't want to steal Dan's thunder, but I have a pilot's license, too. And we do have a plane."

Christ, Michael thought, *she gets further and further out of my league by the second.*

A few minutes later, Beth pulled onto I-90, heading east along the river. "Have you seen the tunnels?"

"There's more than one?" Michael assumed she was referring to the "Big Dig," the eight-mile-long tunnel at the end of the Massachusetts Turnpike that ran beneath the harbor between town and Logan International Airport. That was the only one he had heard of, and who hadn't? It was nationally famous, not for its traffic throughput or technical brilliance, but for its design flaws, construction delays, and cataclysmic cost overruns.

"You mean besides the MassPike? Oh yeah. The Callahan and Sumner have been there forever, they just couldn't keep up with capacity. In fact, there's a subway tunnel, too, the first one in the world to run under the ocean. That thing is over a hundred years old."

It amused Michael to think that, if he had Dan's theory right, those other tunnels may not even have existed in his world before this conversation "collapsed" them into his reality. Unfortunately, now they were.

"I haven't seen them, no. But if it's all the same to you, I'd rather not."

It galled him to have to appear cowardly so soon after doing his best to bury Beth's comment, but fear had got the best of him. Waterside roads and inadequately railed bridges were bad enough; tunnels running below a mass of water were infinitely worse. If an accident occurred there, you had absolutely no chance to avoid drowning unless you happened to be driving in scuba gear. In all his years in the Bay Area, Michael had been terrified of the BART. It made him queasy just looking at the station signs.

"No problem." To his relief, Beth was nodding in sympathy. "Lots of people get freaked out by the thought of driving under all that water. I was even a little leery the first few times. We don't have to go that way."

MICHAEL'S SENSE OF BETH'S OPULENCE increased as they turned onto the natural causeway leading out to Marblehead Neck.

"This is our Monorail," Elise declared proudly. Michael had been to California's Disneyland many times, and any resemblance to its famous elevated train that circled the park and connected it with the Disneyland Hotel was faint. But he had been to Disney World in Florida once during a training visit to Orlando, and there he saw the comparison. That system glided mostly over undeveloped jungle and along the shore of the enormous Seven Seas Lagoon, and other than elevation, the drive along the causeway here did evoke a momentary sense of rocketing through untamed wilderness, isolated from both the light-speckled historic district behind them and the subdued night peninsula ahead. He might have enjoyed it had his full concentration not been required to throttle his panic at being hemmed in between Marblehead and Boston Harbors, almost at road level within a few feet on either side of the road. He gritted his teeth and fixed his gaze on the glove compartment, struggling to appear casual. Maybe he could, after all, choke off the supply of supporting evidence for Beth's unflattering assessment of his courage.

Mercifully, the jaunt across the water was brief. As they followed the road up the gentle incline toward the northern tip of the island-like suburb, further confirmation of the DeLeons' financial class appeared in the form of enormous homes on generous tree-sheltered lots. There seemed no end to them, on both sides of the road, from modernized Cape Cod construction to stone-girded Colonial structures that would cost three times their current worth to build from scratch. Beth had said that Rick was in the shipping business, mostly imports from Latin America, and Michael began to wonder what facet of that trade Rick could have lucked himself into that had landed him in such rarified company.

Near the end of the road, Beth turned left onto a short private drive lined with trees and proceeded through the iron gate that slid open automatically at her approach. "What do you think?" She smiled.

Michael would not have used the word "mansion" to describe the Hendricks' Victorian. It was well north of middle-class, no doubt, and made his townhouse look like a tent trailer, but in the end it was simply a very nice house. For the DeLeon residence, the word felt barely adequate. "Manor house" seemed a better fit, and if not properly an "estate," it was certainly pushing that line.

"Wow," was the brilliant assessment that escaped Michael's lips as they paused to let one of four garage doors roll up and out of the way.

The place was magnificent. A domed portico sheltered the section of circular drive that ran in front of the entrance, replica gas lanterns illuminating its pillars and the door and flickering off the quarried stone exterior. The house stood a generous two stories high, ten-foot ceilings, and a third level was created by three large turrets, watchtowers in lighthouse motif, rising high above the slate tile roof: one dominating the left front of the house and two others spread out toward the back, between which Michael could just make out what he took to be an iron-railed widow's walk.

From the garage, they entered a comfortable utility room lined with cabinets and benches and a couple of leather-seated stools, ideal for staging indoor projects or as a temporary drop-off for things brought in from the car. As he closed the door, Michael stole another admiring glance at the black Cadillac Escalade and matching Pantera ocean speedboat parked in two of the bays. The watercraft's sleek bow was filigreed with a stylized gold dragon reminiscent of the hood art on a classic Firebird Trans Am. *Rick always wanted one of those,* Michael recalled. *Now he could buy a fleet of them.*

In the utility room, he noted an anomaly. One of the walls was mounted with guns where tools would have been more at home. They were set two-thirds the way up, safely beyond a little girl's reach, but there was room for an intimidating variety. He wasn't a gun aficionado, and could barely tell a rifle from a shotgun, but he recognized at least one: an AK-47 with its signature curving magazine, the Soviet-invented assault weapon favored by militants the world over for its sturdiness and low cost.

Nor was it lonely. The AK was surrounded by small arms of every stripe *except* conventional hunting rifles: a fully automatic pistol, a nasty-looking sniper, a snub-nosed shotgun with extra shells mounted right on the barrel.

Not very sporting, Michael thought, *but to each his own.* "So Rick's a hunter?"

"Sometimes," Beth replied. "Once in a while he hunts exotic animals in Africa or South America. He says they're not endangered species, but I wonder. He says the main purpose of the guns is protection, but I can't see how he thinks he needs enough to outfit a Navy SEAL team."

A hallway lined with Caribbean art led to the kitchen, past a spacious pantry where Michael could see wine racks and what looked like the door to a walk-in meat freezer amidst a small grocery store's worth of shelved foodstuffs. In general quality, the kitchen was not so superior to the Hendricks', which after all was very nice, but it was three times the size and sported dual ovens, two dishwashers, an eight-burner flattop range, and a large center island with its own sink and a matching grill and griddle built right into the countertop. Aside from spotlights illuminating the work areas, the tone was warm but muted, evocative more of the dining area in a four-star restaurant than of the food prep space. Michael was sure, however, that the lighting could be readily dialed up as circumstances required.

Unlike the Hendricks, whose kitchen windows faced an elegant but smallish back garden, the back of the DeLeon residence commanded stunning views of Marblehead Harbor and the city sparkling on the historic promontory, the red and green running lights of pleasure craft easing across the late summer water in between.

"Shall we do the grand tour?" Beth lilted, looking even more beautiful now that she was in her own element and completely relaxed.

"Lego room! Lego room!" Elise cried, hopping up and down and clapping her hands at the same time.

Beth opened her mouth as if to say something, then changed her mind. "Oh, why not." She smiled at her daughter. "You won't be able to sit still until we do."

Unsure of what to expect, Michael followed the girls through the kitchen and down a run of carpeted stairs that descended from the adjacent hall. How many levels had he counted now in the place, *four*?

They led him through the largest and most elaborate "family room" Michael had ever seen. On the water side, it was a daylight basement, more window than wall to take advantage of the view but with electronically-controlled blinds that Elise demonstrated could be rolled down or retracted at the touch of a button. A side wall boasted the largest plasma screen television Michael had ever seen, a flush-mounted, surround-sound speaker system barely visible in the ceiling and walls, an assortment of designer chairs and sofas sufficient to seat twenty arrayed around it in an arc. A short way to the left stood a leather-rimmed wet bar complete with sink, a full built-in refrigerator, a commercial grade Italian espresso machine, and enough name-brand liquors crowding the heavy glass shelving to stock a public house. Two more shelves hosted an army of cups, glasses, and stemware reflected in antique mirror tiles behind. And below the shelves — could that really be another dishwasher? How rich did you have to be to need three dishwashers in one house?

The extravagance went on and on. Positioned about the room at angles and with plenty of distance between to prevent players from interfering with each other were three billiard tables and one ping-pong – no, wait, one of the felt-covered rectangles was slightly larger with smaller pockets and a jumble of miniature red and white balls — what was that, snooker? And there at the back, along the wall opposite the harbor view and positioned, again, with more than sufficient elbow room ...

"Are you *serious*?" Michael burst out laughing at the absurdity of it. "Beth, a bowling lane? In your house? *Really*?"

"Two," corrected Elise, and sure enough, upon inspection it proved to be a regulation, matched pair of bowling lanes with a ball return in the middle, a Brunswick electronic scoring display mounted above the pin racks.

"He likes to bowl." Beth shrugged. "He says it drains off the tension. They're not as expensive as you might think."

Sure they are, Michael thought. *You've just lost touch with what "expensive" means.*

Elise became insistent now, taking Michael's hand and dragging him purposefully toward one of the many side doors. He came along, miming a giant rag doll, Beth giggling at him in tow.

Elise dropped his hand to open one of the doors and darted inside to flip on the lights. The adults strode in behind her.

At first, Michael mistook the contents of the room for a model train set-up. The half-dozen irregularly shaped tables took up most of the room, and the wondrous miniature displays seemed grounded in the kind of meticulous landscaping a small-gauge hobbyist might take years to construct.

But it quickly became apparent that these were flights of fancy far beyond smoke-stained tunnel mouths and nineteenth-century coal chutes. Perched amid wild tropical cliffs and tucked into dense, forbidding forests were structures worthy of Tolkien. Tiny thatched hovels, elegant stone bridges, worn cobblestone paths. A whole village of erratic tree-houses. A forked waterfall spiraling down a scaled hundred-foot drop to splash chaotically into a pale lagoon. Animals real and imaginary. Elaborate castles with sweeping parapet towers that mocked gravity and yet, in the context of this exhilarating fantasy, seemed as plausible as a toadstool.

There was not a rail or a locomotive engine in sight. And once he got a good look, it became instantly clear that this exotic tableau had not been assembled from craft store sundries or expensive train set paraphernalia. Every last bit of it – from the loftiest spire to the gentle, multicolored undulations in the hillside grass – was made of Legos.

Elise was glowing like a light bulb. And so was her mother. Michael didn't know if he had ever, in all the years they had known each other, seen a look on Beth's face as simple, unpretentious, and sweet as the one bursting from her now.

And the truth dawned on him.

"You made this?" he queried Elise incredulously.

The little girl nodded.

"By yourself? *All* of it?"

She nodded again.

"She says she wants to be an architect," Beth said softly. "If they start putting up plastic fairy palaces in Manhattan, I'd say she has a promising career."

Michael was stunned. Every branch of each hand-crafted tree looked anatomically sound. The structure of the buildings was utterly convincing.

"How on earth did you ..."

Beth put her hand on Elise's shoulder. "You tell him, sweetie," she encouraged. "Michael, I'm going to go change into something—" She choked off the unintended insinuation. "To put on some jeans before we do the rest of the house. Elise can show you if you want a drink or something."

"Thanks, I'll be fine."

"I won't be long."

As Beth exited the room and turned toward the stairs, Elise took a large plastic storage bin brimming with green and brown Legos from a cupboard full of such containers at the back, then sat herself on a little chair facing an area of bare landscape, setting the bin on a folding TV tray table within arm's reach. She began extracting bricks from the container and fashioning them into a tree.

Abruptly and for no discernible reason, she announced: "My dad is a drug dealer."

Michael was taken aback, but quickly realized what she must have meant. "You mean medicine," he corrected. "His company ships medicine so sick people can be cured."

"No, I mean bad drugs. Heroin and marijuana and cocaine."

Michael gasped. He wasn't sure what to make of this. Surely, though, she was mistaken.

"I don't think that's right," he soothed. "What would make you say that?"

"I heard them talking about it. They don't think I hear, but I know all the hiding places."

Michael was dumbstruck. It didn't seem like the kind of thing a fourth grader would make up, all the more so a child of Elise's intelligence.

"Your dad's a good man. I'm sure you're misinterpreting. But even if you weren't, why would you be telling me?"

"Because I think you can fix him."

"Fix him? What do you mean?"

"I don't know." Elise shrugged. "I just know you fix things."

It took several minutes for Michael to digest the situation. Finally, he refocused, anxious to suspend the drug subject until he'd had a chance to think it through and decide how to question Beth.

"You were going to tell me how you make this stuff."

The diversion took. Elise grinned and went back to the supply cabinets, pulling several labeled folders from a file drawer.

She spread a file open for Michael to see. It was packed with pictures cut out of magazines.

"When I see something I like," Elise explained, "I cut it out. Then I just copy it from the pictures."

Michael shook his head in silent amazement. What a

precious, precious little girl. He could only hope his own children one day would be half as gifted.

Beth rejoined them, now barefoot, otherwise clad in designer jeans and a silky blue lace-trimmed camisole.

She had apparently changed her mind along with her clothes. "How about staying the night?" she proposed. "It's a long drive back, and I really don't want Elise staying up another hour and a half."

Michael's heart kicked his sternum. Was she inviting him into bed? Was that what this had been all along? Would he even be able to do it, right here in his adversary's home and with her still married to him?

Beth seemed to pick up on his quandary. "We have three nice guest rooms," she clarified. "You could take your pick."

Michael was aware of the concern both Hendricks had felt but not verbally expressed. Still, he didn't see what harm it could really do. And he was enjoying himself, *really* enjoying himself, for the first time since the night he had fled California. He was also aware, though it must have been subconscious at the time, that this possibility had probably motivated his decision to grab his backpack before leaving the Hendricks, even though he had forgotten by the time they had arrived here and had left it behind his seat in the Porsche.

"All right." He smiled. "Sure, I'll stay."

"Great!" Beth glowed. "I'll call Dan."

WITH THE HOUSE TOUR DONE and Elise safely in bed, Beth settled them in the main living room with a low fire and the lights down to match. They had expected to share a late round of tea and cheesecake and then retire, but as they talked and gestured and laughed about younger days, Mi-

chael supplying fragments of his past week's story carefully
redacted of any supernatural detail, time had gotten away
from them. The dessert lay half eaten and the last of the tea
lifeless and cool by the time they finally parted at 2:30 a.m.

With scarcely four hours' sleep, Michael felt impossibly invigorated as he rose to the late summer dawn and
pulled himself together well enough to join the DeLeon girls
in the breakfast nook for oatmeal and fresh melon. He lingered at the tabletop spyglass to take his first good look at
Marblehead proper across the harbor. It was positively enchanting. The lovingly preserved Colonial architecture nestled into the wooded hillside, dominated by the iconic spire
of Abbot Hall, looked as though God himself had breathed
into a Jane Wooster Scott painting. It was life imitating art
imitating life, and the colorful fishing skiffs and sailboats
dotting the foreground completed a tableau as picturesque as
any Venetian scene.

They dropped Elise, still aglow from the thrill of showing off her young life's work to her mother's handsome
friend, at an upscale private school on the promontory. Michael and Beth spent the next two hours assembling a small
new wardrobe for Michael along with a proper suitcase to
store it in, though only after Beth convinced him she was
serious about refusing to do anything else until he had en-
dured the task.

With Michael freshly clothed – and it was nice, he had
to admit, to feel fully presentable again – Beth drove them
south toward the city, heading for a surprise location where
she promised they would be free to relax and talk.

All of a sudden he remembered something that had
slipped his mind in the glow of last night's fireside reminis-
cence.

"I've been meaning to ask you – and I don't want to
get Elise in trouble, please don't make a big deal out of it –
but last night, while you were getting changed, she made a
comment that her dad was a drug dealer. I said she must be
mistaken, she must mean he helps ship medicine or some-

thing. But she said no, it was stuff like heroin and cocaine."

"That girl." Beth shook her head and sighed. "She feeds that story to anyone who will listen. She won't admit it, but I'll tell you exactly what it is. She doesn't like him being gone all the time. She feels neglected. I think she started it with the idea that if she could embarrass him, or make him feel bad about being absent, he might get a different job or find a way to give up the travel. It was understandable when she was five or six, but I expected she'd have outgrown it by now. She's been talked to over and over, but ... I shudder to think of the phone call if she ever feeds that crap to someone at the school. At this age I'm afraid they'd take her seriously."

Fix him, Michael thought. Elise had said she wanted him to "fix" her dad. It made some sense now.

A HALF HOUR LATER, THEY pulled into an underground parking garage in downtown Boston and crossed the street to the Public Garden, a large wooded oasis in its picturesque late summer glory. Beth led him down a path and across a narrow spot in the lake by way of a suspension footbridge, looking for all the world like a miniature Golden Gate on stone pilings, and to his delight, Michael saw a sight unmistakably familiar even though he had never been here in his life.

"The Swan Boats!"

Moored along a wooden pier were a dozen or so elegant red and green pontoon barges with enough bench space to seat several families at once. At the rear of each craft stood a brightly painted compartment in the shape of a giant white swan, concealing a single seat and a mechanism the operator could pedal like a bicycle. They looked exactly as he had pictured them – or maybe he had seen actual pictures, he couldn't remember – from one of his favorite childhood books, *The Trumpet of the Swan* by E.B. White, who had also penned the cherished volumes *Stuart Little* and *Charlotte's Web*.

"You've heard of them," Beth said in approval. She approached and engaged in muffled conversation with an attendant, and Michael could have sworn it was a hundred dollar bill he saw her lay across the wide-eyed young man's palm.

"Our private yacht." Beth gestured, ushering Michael onto the nearest empty craft, and it crossed his mind that the entitled perspective that moved Elise to view the Marblehead causeway as "Our Monorail" had probably come from her mom.

Beth took a spot in the middle of the front-most bench. The boat did not rock as much as Michael had expected as he stepped aboard and joined her. As the operator settled in behind the swan carving and headed them out into the little lake, Michael felt not the least distress and was conscious, as he always was on such occasions, that his aversion to bodies of water was not absolute. It was all about the risk of drowning. He felt no great anguish crossing the Bay Area bridges, particularly if he was driving; the concrete railings and thick suspension cables made it impossible to flip a car off the edge, and he was aware that they had defiantly weathered every storm and earthquake that had hit town since they were built. The Swan Boat was low to the waterline and could not possibly trap him if it capsized, and the Public Garden Lagoon was shallow and nowhere near large enough to put swimming to safety in doubt.

"This is nice," Michael remarked, angling his elbows over the backrest and making no effort to relocate the part of his forearm that unintentionally touched Beth's shoulder. Nor did she.

"I was hoping we could get one alone." Beth smiled. "These things fill right up in the summer. Half the time there's a line."

It was amazing how free and private the venue began to feel as the craft slipped farther away from the shore. The sounds of traffic and far-off voices were easily suppressed by the simple lapping of the pontoons through the tiny pond ripples, and at conversational level the faceless, voiceless operator behind the graceful carved swan was out of earshot. It gave Michael the courage to finally broach the subject that he had known they would have to deal with sooner or later.

"Beth ... there's something I need to say and I don't want it to upset anything. I've been pondering and things seem to be going pretty well between us, and I just can't keep it in any longer. It's something I should have said – have wanted to say – since before you left San Mateo."

Beth peered at him serenely, invitingly, not the least bit guarded, which he gladly took as encouragement.

"I'm sorry about ... that thing with the basketball game. It was childish and stupid. I even knew that at the time, I think. But it took me years to realize just how wrong it was. Sometimes I think we, that if I hadn't, we might have—"

"Michael." Beth reached an arm over and patted him delicately. "It's okay. Don't worry about it. Let it go."

"But—"

"If anyone should apologize, it's me. What a selfish bitch I was, inviting you and then ignoring you the whole time and then leaving you in Berkeley without a ride."

"No, Beth. You had every right."

"Maybe," Beth allowed. "But having the right doesn't mean you *have* to. I didn't have to leave you, Michael; I *chose* to. And for the same awful reason I always did."

Michael eyed her questioningly.

"Rick, of course." Beth sighed. "Michael, I brought you along that day with every intention of pissing you off. I hadn't planned to strand you, I wasn't *that* cruel. But when you created the opportunity, I didn't hesitate. I thought if you hadn't been put off enough already, that would ice it."

"For ... Rick."

Beth nodded. "I had to break up with you. Rick had

been calling me all week about getting together. Damn you, Michael, you were always too sweet. You never did anything that could justify a real break-up. So I manufactured one. And it wasn't the first time. I always thought you probably knew."

"Yeah." Michael smiled, but was beset with a sharp pang in his stomach. "I did, I guess."

"And you kept coming back." Beth shook her head forlornly. "Michael Chandler, a girl's best friend. Patient and sympathetic when she was with someone else, ready to play the stand-in boyfriend to make them jealous in between." She looked at him sadly. "I used you to get to Rick, Michael. Over and over. It was a selfish and horrible thing to do. You were so wonderful to me, even – no, especially – when you knew you had no chance. And I lapped you up like a kitty with a dish of cream."

Beth gazed off distantly, seeing another time. "The worst part is that you really were my friend. A *great* friend. The best male friend I ever had. God, you put up with me complaining about Rick on the phone for hours. I don't know how I would have gotten through some of those nights if you hadn't been there to bandage my ego. How it must have pained you to do that."

"It's not your fault. I knew what was going on. At least at some level I did. I knew what the chances were, but I kept coming back just in case. You were so ... so ..."

"*Ravishing*," Beth supplied, with a dramatic flourish over a thin smile. "Breathtaking. Irresistible. Goddess-like."

"Yeah." Michael grinned broadly. He looked away at the water. "You still are."

He felt a warm, confident hand take his. "Let's put it behind us." Beth squeezed. "You forgive me, I'll forgive you. Can we do that?"

"Yes." Michael squeezed her hand back. Beth released his hand, reached around him and gave him the warmest, most caring, sincerest hug they had ever shared.

And suddenly, completely unexpectedly, he felt something profound happen. He really *could* let it go. Only now did Michael realize how deeply tortured he had been by the recollection of that awful incident all these years. He had closeted it away like an outgrown suit, except that out of sight had never truly translated into out of mind and it had lain there rotting through the box with no hope or expectation – none whatsoever – that it could ever be resolved. And yet now, here, in one calm, rational conversation catalyzed by the maturity that had blossomed in the intervening years on both sides, it was resolved. Completely. The pain was gone.

Maybe he had been hasty, Michael thought. Maybe he should just let God work things out on His own mysterious schedule. Maybe being stalked by miracles wasn't so bad.

IT HAD BEEN A GLORIOUS day. So good that, hours later, Michael still felt ready to make his peace with God again, to call his life good, all things considered, present circumstances not excluded (his predicament could hardly be ignored) but nevertheless earnestly expected to resolve well, when all was said and done, as a demonstration of renewed faith.

Michael and Beth were seated together on the living room sofa, cocktails perched on sandstone coasters atop the burled wood coffee table, drinks Beth had insisted on making "to celebrate the rebirth of a friendship too long neglected," a ceremony they planned to extend until it was time to pick Elise up from school so she could accompany them on the drive back to Brookline.

The couch and table were strewn with mementos from a decade of exotic travel. There were three photo albums, two finished and a third half begun, but for the most part the photographs, tour maps, and keepsakes were jumbled about in envelopes and shoe boxes. There had simply never been time to sort them out properly.

Suddenly, Beth started. "Did you …"

Her alarm jolted Michael alert. And now he could hear it, too. It was the muffled but unmistakable creaking of one of the garage doors.

"Oh shit. Shit! Shit!"

The sound of an engine swelled, reverberated briefly, shut off.

Beth jumped to her feet, banging a knee on the coffee table and spilling pictures and her drink all over the carpet. "Oh, God *damn* it!"

Out in the garage, a car door opened. A few seconds later it clapped shut.

They were both standing now, staring at each other wide-eyed. "What should I—"

Keys jingled in the utility room door.

Beth's gaze darted feverishly between Michael and the kitchen hall. "Quick, get up to the—" She faltered, turning Michael a look of panicked uncertainty, as though realizing just as he did that her guest had no idea where it might be safe to hide, and that she had no way to tell him.

There was no time. Michael bolted for the staircase as the door in from the garage swung shut and male footsteps began clattering on the hardwood.

"Hey, honey," Rick DeLeon called warmly as he entered the living room. There was a nervous silence, then: "What the hell?"

Harsh footsteps thundered across the carpet and up the stairs two at a time. Beth's feet jaunted behind amid a frenzy of frantic, unintelligible words.

Michael froze in the upstairs hall. Which way? In his panic, he couldn't even remember which door led to Beth's bedroom and which to the one he had slept in.

The choice became moot.

Rick DeLeon halted at the top of the stairs, his tall, athletic frame heaving, nostrils flared,   a picture of incredulous fury. And there they stood, Michael Chandler and his tormentor rival, facing each other ten paces apart for the first time in fifteen years, the chips stacked firmly on Rick De-Leon's end of the table.

Beth rushed up and tried to grab her husband by the elbow. He thrust her savagely away.

"I *knew* it!" he exploded. "I knew you couldn't keep your panties clean! But *this* guy? Really, Beth, this fucking loser? Do you know what he did back in California?"

"He didn't kill that man. You know he couldn't. And for your information, he's just here visiting a friend."

"Don't patronize me, Beth. It's undignified. Even for a skanky bitch."

"God damn it, Rick—"

"Fuck off!" he bellowed. "The both of you, just go fuck yourselves. Have a real good time. You're going to wish to God you hadn't done this." He glared and pointed sharply at Michael. "You're lucky I don't just pop you right now, you son of a bitch."

"*You* fuck off!" Beth roared, but Rick was already stomping back down the stairs. A picture frame scraped loud-ly along the wall and glass shattered on the floor. The gun racks in the utility room shuddered. The side door slammed, a garage door began to roll up, and Rick's car screeched out onto the driveway like a raging harpy.

Beth stood staring down the hall toward the kitchen for a long time. Gradually the red in her face and the ire in her expression gave way to pallor and fear.

"We'd better go," she said finally. Michael nodded.

SHE DROPPED HIM OFF AT the Hendrick house, where Michael resolved not to tell his hosts what had happened. It was all he could do to contain it, but he didn't want to alarm Melissa and risk being put out before he had decided himself what to do.

The fuse was burning short now. Rick didn't know that Michael was staying with the Hendricks; Michael wasn't sure he even knew Dan. That would buy some time. But not much. Rick *did* know about San Mateo, and it was inevitable that he would go to the police. And once they knew Michael was in Boston, it would only be a matter of time until they traced him here. Beth certainly wouldn't betray him, but he couldn't rule out that Elise might say something that revealed his whereabouts, inadvertently or not.

They were just sitting down to dinner when the phone in Dan's pocket rang. He answered it, looked mildly surprised, and held it out to Michael across the table. "Beth calling for you."

He took the phone. "Hello?"

"Michael, oh thank God, Michael, I need you. I need you." Beth was hysterical. "Can I come get you? Please, please, can I come and get you?"

"Of course." Michael tried to soothe her, but her anxiety was infectious. "What's going on?"

"That *bastard*," Beth spat over the phone. "He's stolen my baby. *He's kidnapped Elise!*"

CHAPTER 17
Fire

"WHAT DO YOU MEAN? HOW can a father—"

"*No!*" Michael winced at the sound of Beth's voice screaming at him over the phone. "Don't say anything. You can't let the Hendricks know. It's complicated. I don't have time to explain it now."

Michael was starkly aware of both Dan's and Melissa's gazes fixed squarely upon him.

"Well, I'm going to have to … *something*."

"Say whatever you like. Tell them, I don't know, just tell them Rick's decided he wants to bury the hatchet and you're going to stay with us for a few days and put all that high school bullshit to rest."

Michael exploded in laughter. He knew exactly where Rick DeLeon wanted to bury a hatchet.

"Figure it out," Beth barked impatiently. "Just don't say anything about Elise. I'll be there in forty minutes. And bring your suitcase, we're going to need your clothes."

"All right," Michael replied in as casual a tone as he could manage under the circumstances. "I'll see you then."

"Thank you." She sounded thin and desperate. The call ended.

"Everything all right?" Dan queried pointedly as he restored the cell phone to his pocket.

"Oh, yeah. Good, actually." Neither Hendrick seemed

to be buying it, but he had no choice but to press on. "I guess Rick wants to let bygones be bygones. I'm going to stay with them for a few days, shoot some pool, have some barbecue. Bowl a few lines. At bowling I might actually be able to beat him."

"Do you think that's wise?" Dan pushed, his eyes never leaving his guest's.

"Seems great to me." Michael shrugged. "If Beth's going to be in my life again, it would be nice to be on her husband's good side."

"So she's 'in your life again,' just like that?" Melissa poked. "A married woman?"

Before Michael could answer, Dan interjected, "How do you know he's not just going to turn you over to the police?"

"He knows where I am," Michael fibbed, thinking fast. "If that's what he wanted to do, he could just send the police here."

"*Dan!*" Melissa gasped.

Dan took his wife's hand in his and squeezed reassuringly, eyes still on Michael. "Maybe he wants to watch them take you down."

"Bah." Michael shook his head and smiled dismissively. It was a struggle, but he focused his full attention on maintaining a calm and convincing air. Something told him that following Beth's instructions, even if he didn't understand why, was important.

"We've all grown a lot since high school. Rick's a successful businessman now. He doesn't need to hate me anymore. After all, he got the girl."

"It doesn't sound right." Dan glanced toward Melissa's pleading face. "But you're a big boy. Far be it from me to tell you how to run your life, Michael. But watch yourself."

Michael nodded hastily. "I won't be stupid."

Dan seemed to think of something. He stood up from his chair, wiped the corners of his mouth with his cloth napkin. "Be right back, just a second."

A tense two minutes passed as Dan hopped up the stairs and out of sight, Michael darting glances at his hostess, who was staring past him through the dining room window into their lovely back garden, appearing unable to eat.

"Here." Dan handed Michael his business card as he returned and sat back down. He flipped it over. "That's my cell number. Keep it where you can't lose it. And if anything happens, anything at all, you call me, all right? Promise. If you get into any kind of trouble, I want you to call me."

"I don't—" Melissa began, but Dan cut her off.

"*Melissa.*" Dan's tone was controlled, but it was the first time Michael had heard him address his wife with anything approaching harshness. He turned back to Michael. "Promise."

"I will." And this time Michael's smile and gratitude were genuine.

IT WAS HARD TO LEAVE the Hendricks, especially heading back into the dark unknown of whatever was so complicated about the situation that Beth couldn't tell him about it over the phone. Even Melissa had given him a warm farewell hug at the door, sensing that this might be the last time she or her husband would ever hear from him.

But Beth's raw emotion, the sweet, palpable gratitude and, yes, love, that she turned on Michael the moment they were alone in the car was so intoxicating that five minutes into the drive, all those tendrils of melancholy and doubt were forgotten, swept safely under the couch, and his full attention was focused blissfully on her.

"I'm sorry I couldn't explain things earlier," she began after thanking him profusely with tears beading up in her eyes. "You'll understand when I'm done."

Michael had never seen Beth look so vulnerable. It was

sad and exhilarating at the same time, finally seeing human weakness in her, so antithetical to her signature confidence.

"I lied to you yesterday. Rick really is a drug dealer. No, that's too pedestrian. He is a high-ranking partner in one of the most prolific drug smuggling operations in the world."

"Holy shit." Michael gasped.

Beth continued. "I didn't know at first. Right after graduation, Rick pawned everything he had to come out and move to Boston. Hardly a penny left, and he sacrificed it all for me. You have no idea how compelling something like that is for a girl. And he didn't even propose right away. He said he was intent on marrying me, that no one else in the world could make him whole, but he didn't want to ask until he had established a life he could be proud to invite me into. He refused even to live with me until then. God, Michael, I just swooned. He was saying all the right things.

"He had a hell of a time finding a job. I honestly don't know how he ate during that time. Then one day his family in California referred him to a cousin of his, Fernando Lopez, a guy he had grown up with in San Mateo but hadn't seen since their last family reunion. Fernando said his shipping company needed somebody based in New England and he thought they could fit Rick in. See, Rick's parents had immigrated from Colombia before he was born, which gave him dual citizenship. And he spoke flawless Spanish. Since most of the shipping came from South America, Rick really could be invaluable. And, of course, he took the job. It was actually me that proposed to *him* at that point.

"There actually is a shipping company, Cartagena-Littleton. And it does ship some legitimate goods. But it's all a smokescreen for the drug operation.

"Rick was gone more than he was home, but he was stacking up an unbelievable pile of cash. When Elise was born, he did what he could to be around us more but he was still gone an awful lot. One time I asked if he was piloting the boats himself, and he laughed. He said he was mostly negotiating deals with suppliers, which he felt he could do best in person. That made sense.

"Then one day I found some dope while I was rummaging through the boat for a purse I'd lost. Bags the size of footballs stuffed with coke and smack and dried pot leaves were stashed in the life vest compartment. Not recreational — there was enough junk there to get the whole senior class off for a year.

"When I confronted him, he said that he'd had no choice but to take his cousin's offer. He said he was doing it for Elise and me. He said he had a target number, enough to pay the house off and live well without working ever again, and he had intended from the start to get out of the business as soon as he had saved it up.

"You think our yelling phone call was bad? That little tantrum was a Christmas card compared to the nuclear bomb I set off on him. But when it was over, after we stomped off to separate beds, the reality sunk in that without the drug running, there wouldn't be any Porsche or private school or palace on Marblehead Neck.

"And you know what?" Beth dipped her head and closed her eyes in shame. "The awful truth is that I just couldn't face giving it all up. By morning I had made the decision not to disrupt things. It's terrible, I know. And I knew it at the time.

"So I started rationalizing. I convinced myself that it would be all right, after all he was just providing for his family and that if he really did stop once we were secure, it was even a *noble* thing to do. That drug use was a victimless crime and anyone who took it too far only got what they deserved. And all the charitable donations – Rick did everything he could to maintain a respectable public profile – all of that philanthropy wouldn't be possible without that money. And ultimately, it was all for Elise, so she could have the prettiest clothes, go to the best schools, a whole room for her Legos. That's what I kept telling myself. Can you believe it?" The tears were flowing now. "I should probably go to jail. Maybe someday I will."

Michael reached over and patted her reassuringly. "It's okay. I don't think most people could resist that kind of temptation."

"I don't care what most people would do. It was wrong for me. But god damned if I won't turn him in to the police once I have Elise back. Maybe this little stunt he's pulling is a blessing in disguise. It's woken me up to what a fucking animal he is."

A little smile crept over Michael's face. He knew it was juvenile and petty but he couldn't repel the feeling of righteous vindication Beth's words were evoking in him.

"So what's the plan?"

Beth's expression hardened into a look of indomitable determination. "We're going to go get her."

Michael frowned. "Shouldn't you just call the police?"

"I did." Beth scowled. "They asked if I thought she was in imminent danger. Without thinking about it I said no, Rick was a loving father who would never do anything to harm Elise. They said in that case, there was nothing they could do. It's not illegal for a father to pick his daughter up from school. They said it was a non-criminal domestic dispute and that these things usually resolve on their own. They told me to just wait a few weeks and he would no doubt bring her back. Useless bastards." She shook her head and sighed. "Just as well. I guess it's not in their jurisdiction anyway."

"How come?"

"Listen to this." Beth flipped open her cell phone and retrieved a voicemail, handing the device to Michael.

"This is just to let you know she's safe." It was Rick's voice, saturated with smugness. *"Safe from you and your whole goddamned family. Even your GI Joe father can't bail you out of this one, baby."* The message clicked off.

"Hey, yeah, what about your dad?" Michael hadn't thought of it, but now that he did, it seemed like a Navy Intel operator might have some connections that could get around the inert police protocol.

"No." Beth shook her head firmly. "In the first place,

Rick's right. It *is* beyond Dad's reach. And second, if I told him, he'd pull strings to make sure I couldn't take things into my own hands. He knows Rick won't hurt Elise. But he wouldn't risk the chance that Rick might hurt *me*."

"How can you be so sure there's nothing he could do?"

"Because that message spells out exactly where they've gone."

"You mean like out of the country? You think he's taking her to Colombia?"

"Worse." Beth's expression darkened in disgust. "If it was Colombia, we'd have a chance. Their government's on good terms with the United States."

"Then where do you think they are?"

"Not think. *Know*. There's only one place Rick would feel one hundred percent untouchable. A little island just off the coast of Cuba, *Isla Tesoro* – at least that's what those drug mugs call it. It was a sugar plantation and rum distillery all the way back to the 1700s. The whole island stayed in private hands until Castro took over. The government usurped it, like they did everything else, and the owner escaped to Jamaica. They kept it up as a kind of retreat for the Party bigwigs. Then when the Soviet Union collapsed and the Russian proxy money dried up, this drug cartel – the one that runs Cartagena-Littleton – was able to strike a deal where Castro leases it to them for several million a year in exchange for turning a blind eye. It's neat: the Communists get a nice chunk of funding, the smugglers get a base an hour from Miami that's totally immune to U.S. law enforcement or diplomacy."

"But Guantanamo's right there," Michael observed. "Can't the Army do something about it?"

Beth smirked. "The military doesn't give a shit about drug cartels. Not unless they're funding some anti-American cause. For that matter, neither does the CIA. If they did, every pot farm in Mexico and poppy field in Peru would be scorched flat by drone strikes."

"But your dad ..."

"No good." Beth shook her head. "They've got that covered, too. It seems that right from the start, Cartagena-Littleton has been sponsoring a CIA plant. They couldn't care less about the drugs, and they don't lose much sleep over Cuba itself. But they're very interested in certain traffic that comes through Havana by way of more relevant players like Russia and Venezuela, even Iran, I'm told. So the cartel plays both sides, paying off Castro and funneling intelligence to Washington, and neither wants them shut down. The FBI sure would like a crack at them, but three administrations in a row have designated it hands-off."

"God." Michael had to admit that it sounded like a pretty tight setup.

Only then did his mind fully assemble the picture Beth had been painting. He reeled in shock.

"We're going *there*?" He gaped. "To that island?"

"*I* am." Beth was resolute, but she couldn't keep trepidation out of her voice completely. "For starters, I'm going to Key West. We have a bungalow down there. I've got a couple ideas about how to get out to Tesoro, but I'll need to talk to some people. It might take a day, or a week, it all depends on what I'm able to set up."

She turned her eyes to Michael. "But *you* don't have to." Her voice was soft, her expression compassionate and sincere. "Lord knows, Michael, I have no right to ask. You've got enough on your plate. And you've already helped me more than I deserve. If you don't want to take on my troubles on top of your own, I won't think any less of you." She squeezed his hand for emphasis. "I mean that."

"But you *want* me to go."

"Of *course* I do!" She laughed. "Why do you think I blew two hours detouring all the way to Brookline? I could have been halfway to Florida by now. But I'm serious, Michael, I'll understand if it's just too much. It's going to be dangerous. Just say the word and I'll drop you back at the Hendricks' or anywhere you say."

Michael returned her smile and issued a long sigh. "I

drove three thousand miles through the dead of night to get to Boston. I guess another thousand won't kill me."

"Good!" Beth grinned, patting one hand rapidly against the steering wheel in an uncanny semblance of Elise's finger-clap. "But if you plan to drive, you'll have to meet me there."

"Huh?"

Beth grinned. "I told you we own a plane. What good is a pilot's license if a girl doesn't use it?"

CHAPTER 18
Wing Man

IT WAS TOO LATE TO fly out of Plum Island Airport by the time they reached the vicinity; unless arrangements had been made ahead of time to use it after hours, it would be closed. It was just as well. Beth was IFR certified, but a night departure would require filing a flight plan and she preferred to leave no trace of where they were going. She had the personal phone number of the managing operator, and she called, asking him to have her plane fueled up and out of the hangar by eight the next morning.

They spent the night in the Danvers, Massachusetts Motel 6, the closest thing they could find to the airfield. "Eww. I didn't remember how creepy these places could be." Beth grimaced as they opened the door to the room. It didn't strike Michael that way at all – he remembered the days of antiquated TVs and the coin-operated Magic Fingers vibrating bed "massage" that made you feel like a pebble being shaken in a sluice box. Motel 6 had come a long way since then and now compared favorably with middle-tier lodgings like Best Western and Holiday Inn. He did find it puzzling that the rooms had no alarm clocks – no clocks of any kind, for that matter. But he had always used wake-up calls anyway, never being quite sure if he had set the unfamiliar alarm right or not. At least they didn't have to turn on the television to see what time it was; Beth's cell phone took care of that.

Beth ordered pizza for delivery, and they passed a couple of hours eating it out of the box watching a string of old *Seinfeld* and *Friends* episodes. Michael felt a thrill sitting on the same bed with Beth, their bodies sidled up against each other to balance the pizza box across both of their laps. He had to pass her drink to her from the nightstand. They retired early, however, Michael shuffling over to his own bed. They had slept little the previous night, and they both knew how important it was to be fully rested and alert for the travel and trials ahead.

The next morning, they grabbed coffee and pastries from the meager complimentary breakfast spread on their way out the door, though upon examination Beth decided it was too revolting and chucked her Danish in the trash bin outside the registration office.

Half an hour later, they parked at the small Plum Island general aviation airport, and Beth spoke briefly with the manager before heading out to the plane, which had been faithfully prepared as instructed.

Beth fetched a small clipboard from the map compartment and checked through her pre-flight routine as Michael stowed their luggage and marveled at the sleek Cirrus SR22T. It was a beautiful piece of work, either very new or scrupulously maintained, and sported a custom paint job similar to that of the jet boat in the DeLeons' garage: black on top with a muted gold undercarriage and a stylized dragon face on the nose. It was clear Rick could buy anything he wanted, a circumstance no small number of human beings given the chance would be unable to resist, and Michael almost felt sorry for him that the price in personal integrity had to be so dear.

After ten minutes, Beth was satisfied and directed Michael into the cockpit. He was amazed that, instead of the labyrinth of gauges he remembered from a handful of previous private flights, he saw a dual screen display and projected HUD of the kind generally associated with advanced fighter jets.

"Plum Island, this is Cirrus Niner-One-One," Beth said into the headset. "Request taxi from main hangar, over." Then, after a moment: "Roger Plum Island, Cirrus Niner-One-One cleared for taxi and take-off. Proceeding to runway." She closed her mic and turned Michael a golden smile. "Here we go!"

THE PRECIOUS STRETCH OF HOURS that followed, with Beth all to himself and the hypnotically peaceful plane ride insulating them from the gravity of their mission, was one of the most memorable experiences of Michael's life. He had always been infatuated with Beth, though sometimes intimidated, occasionally scornful of her self-absorption and insensitivity. Watching her pilot the Cirrus, a new perspective developed: unadulterated admiration. She was so capable. There she sat, effortlessly attractive in her sunglasses and jeans, guiding this complex machine with effortless confidence, inspiring a respect so unconditional that it eliminated any fear he might otherwise have had at placing his mortal welfare in another's hands. And it wasn't just the plane. Beth could so easily have become paralyzed or lost in hysteria over her husband's abominable act. She could have disintegrated into a sobbing, ineffectual wreck. Instead, she had commenced a counter-attack, grateful for Michael's company, to be sure, but fully prepared to embark on this difficult and hazardous course alone.

And she had done it without hesitation. She had been practical, forthright, and determined from the start. Amazingly, as highly as he had regarded Beth before, she had found ways to earn an even loftier perch.

More incredibly still, she seemed to be coming around to the kind of feelings for Michael that he had so desperately desired in their youth but never in his heart believed possible.

Maybe he had been wrong in resigning himself to the view that they could never succeed together. Maybe they both had grown enough in their adult years to bridge the gap. Maybe when this was all over, when Elise was safe and the DeLe-ons were divorced and Michael had settled into whatever his new reality would ultimately be, maybe ... just maybe ... He dared not dream it, yet he found himself utterly incapable of turning away the hope that *some*day, *some*how ...

Uncannily, as though she had been mulling over ex-actly the same thing, Beth chose that moment to unburden herself as they soared serenely above the green ridges and checkerboard farms of Pennsylvania.

"You know, when I was younger," she began in a philo-sophical tone, "I wanted a rebel. All girls want that, actually, whether they admit it or not. A guy that makes you faint, who goes where he wants, does what he wants, takes what he wants. Who steals booze and talks back to teachers and defies anyone to cross him. A guy like that sweeps you off your feet when you're young. It's like horses – you know how every schoolgirl swoons over horses? It's the power. It's intoxicating to feel like you have control over such a huge, formidable beast. And that's what we want in a boy. We love to feel like we're desirable enough to hold the reins over a reckless force of nature."

"And that was Rick."

"Yes, it was." For a moment she was distant, her eyes far away. She turned back to Michael. "But we're wrong about that. What young girls don't see is that those guys are *already peaking*. Life will never get any better for them. Ten years down the road, those James Deans aren't cool any more, they're just outliers. Those guys who cut class to go smoke in the parking lot are smoking on lunch break be-hind Burger King. If they have a job at all. And those little nerds who—" Beth checked herself. "Those polite, studious ones who went off to college while the bad boys were seek-ing their fortunes in petty crime, *those* are the ones running software companies and buying McMansions with their six figure salaries."

"Well, I love the parable," Michael offered, "but it sure doesn't seem to have gone that way for me and Rick De-Leon."

"Oh, but it is," Beth countered firmly. "It's just taking a little time to work out. Where is Rick going to be a year from now, care to hazard a guess? In *federal prison*. Or if he's lucky, on the lam in Argentina under a false name and living on beetle burritos."

He didn't mean to, but the image that formed in his mind, of Rick DeLeon crouched in a soggy rainforest wearing Groucho Marx glasses and subsisting on bugs wrapped in edible wild greens, choked from Michael a hideous giggle.

Beth became somber and sad. "I know what I said before, but I don't believe Rick is fundamentally bad. He's been a great father, when he was around, and he's always treated me like a princess. He just got caught up in something a lot stickier than he could have foreseen.

"And he did it for me. He really did, that's the truth. And later for Elise. That's the irony of it. As misguided as it was, this whole thing started out as an act of chivalry. And I certainly can't say he hasn't been a great provider. Not having to work has allowed me to invest myself in all sorts of charities and cultural affairs."

She looked at Michael as though pleading with him to believe her. "He really did mean to quit once he felt we were set. He was never comfortable with it. It's just taken a lot longer than I expected." She issued a forlorn sigh. "God, I wish he'd never done this. If I could do it all over, I'd tell him in no uncertain terms that if he didn't marry me right then and accept help from my family until he found a job, he could forget about it ever happening. I know he would have done it if I'd held my ground. Things could have been so different."

Michael nodded noncommittally. The last thing he wanted to hear was Beth walking back her disaffection toward Rick. It reminded him all too well of their high school days.

"As for *you*, Michael Chandler." She perked up, favoring him with a triumphant smile, "All *you* need is a little ambition. That set-up you told me about at Wal-Mart? That's remarkable. You should be glowing with pride. But that's not the place for you. Their business model won't allow them to pay a decent salary. You need to place yourself on the market, that's all. There must be dozens of Fortune 500 companies that would take on a proven Customer Touch executive. We can't compete in manufacturing any more in this country. That's never coming back. It's a service economy now, and the kind of thing you do can be the difference that separates winners from losers in this competitive environment."

"Sounds great," Michael said, "but I seriously doubt they'd pay enough to afford a beachfront mansion with bowling lanes."

"You don't know until you try." Beth turned him a glance of tender affection. "Besides, Michael, there's more to life than money. I saw a sign once hanging in a friend's kitchen that said: 'Kissin' don't last, cookin' do.' Obviously that was written by some sad heifer who never had great sex in her life. *Good* kissin' lasts forever, and it's worth a barrel of gold." She smiled wickedly. "But you know what *doesn't* last? The appeal of aggression. In high school, a boyfriend who picks fights and kicks ass is a trophy. In a grown man, it's embarrassing."

Michael nodded. It had always seemed that way to him, but it was gratifying to hear it from a woman of Beth's rarefied appeal.

"You are a *good* man, Michael. You always were. Back in school, I didn't understand the value of that, it seemed like a weakness. It looks different to me now."

She reached her arm around and tipped his head over to where she could plant a delicate kiss on his cheek. "I was wrong, Michael. Good men are rare. And I realize now that there's nothing more important in a marriage than that."

THEY LANDED IN MYRTLE BEACH, South Carolina for fuel and took the opportunity to have lunch in the small airport's diner. Michael felt uneasy sitting exposed in such a public place, but tried to tell himself that his beard – he was trimming it now, so it looked intentional and not so much like a fugitive's overgrowth – along with his lengthening hair, which was becoming roguish, provided some measure of camouflage. Being in Beth's company probably didn't hurt, either. She certainly did not look like the type of woman inclined to risk sullying herself by harboring a murderer on the run.

It was almost three o'clock in the afternoon when they crossed Florida's continental shoreline and began to descend over the Gulf of Mexico toward Key West. Even the supreme confidence Michael had come to feel in Beth's flying skills couldn't avert a few minutes of bald panic as they dropped closer and closer to the whitecap waves. But the descent was mercifully brief, and with Beth's expert care they touched down like a butterfly alighting on grass.

At the airport's private aviation desk, Beth set up storage and refueling for the plane, then led the way to valet parking. A yellow Mazda Miata rental had been left for them as arranged. She put the top down and drove out of the aviation complex bearing west.

There wasn't a hill big enough for a hobbit burrow anywhere on the island, but the palm trees and warm salt air nonetheless stirred Michael's nostalgia for home. It was humid, but not nearly as hot as Michael had imagined, and he thought part of the reason might be the roiling dark thunderheads to the east, which Beth had watched with mild concern throughout their last half hour of flight. They looked much nearer now and seemed to be closing in.

She continued west all the way through town along the

north coast, then south to Sunset Harbor. Michael was surprised at how built up it was. He had envisioned the Florida Keys as a remote, even rustic destination, but this looked more like the metro-tropical glitter he had seen in videos of the Waikiki district in Honolulu. It was charming, to be sure, and the casual dress and manner of the folk he saw ambling along the sidewalks or gazing lazily at the turquoise waters did seem to have a touch of "Aloha" in them.

Beth parked in front of a small shop near the pier identified by a chunk of driftwood that had been co-opted into a hanging sign that read, "Swordfish Tony's Bait & Tackle."

"I won't be long," Beth said, which Michael took to mean he should stay in the car. She went inside, and less than a minute later, someone he could not make out flipped the placard in the window from "Open" to "Closed."

Beth stayed inside the shop for a good fifteen minutes. Michael passed this time trying to think through the possibilities, but nothing he could come up with that she might be doing in there made sense. Finally, he let it go and contented himself watching the sea gulls and pelicans wheel and dive for crumbs of ice cream cone or broken french fries dropped by oblivious *touristas*. He found some comfort in that.

He was about to leave the car and knock on the dark shop's door, partly from boredom but mainly out of a mild concern that something might have gone wrong, when a vision across the thoroughfare froze him cold.

Half a city block away, in shade under the eaves of an unsavory-looking spirits and tobacco shop – hard to make out with eyes attuned to the brilliant sunlight – was the very last thing Michael expected to encounter on a resort town public street in the middle of a busy day.

It was the male apparition, that same vile ghost that had spooked him from the mirror in the Dallas motel. Even at this distance, even obscured by shadow, there was no mistaking it. Nor could there be an ounce of uncertainty as to its focus. Its ruined face with its decaying yellow teeth and black-hole eyes was staring directly at Michael's own.

The car radio blared on. Michael jumped so hard he banged his head painfully on the windshield. It was the TV all over again, the volume turned up so high it hurt his ears and made the words almost impossible to discern.

"PHONE IMAGES TAKEN BY THE KNOXVILLE MOTEL MANAGER APPEAR TO SHOW THE FUGITIVE AND HIS UNKNOWN COMPANION. THE MANAGER SAYS SHE BECAME SUS—"

Michael snapped off the radio, then stared at it. Beth had taken the keys. The blasted thing shouldn't have been able to turn on.

His gaze snapped back to the cigar store. The apparition was gone.

Michael began to shudder, panic seeping into him like an injection. Only now did he fully realize what Charlie's companionship had done for him. Charlie in his worst moments was at least a sounding board. Charlie couldn't explain everything Michael told him had happened, but he never doubted it, and there was certainly no danger that his opinion of Michael would be shattered just by the telling. Throughout the road trip, through up and down, Michael had been able to confide in Charlie and it had given him a sense of validation.

It was almost the opposite with Beth. Not only did she know nothing of the paranormal undercurrent his predicament seemed to be trailing; not only did he dare not risk putting in jeopardy the one good thing that seemed to be developing out of all this; but on top of that, unlike his time with Charlie, Michael Chandler was not under the spotlight in the current show. This was about Beth, about saving Beth's daughter, about keeping Beth sane and encouraged and as safe, both physically and emotionally, as he could possibly manage. That was Michael's job, he had assumed it willingly, and there was no room in the equation for tending his own troubles.

Whatever else might be said, through all their time together Charlie had been there for Michael, from the very beginning right to the bitter end. This time, he was on his own.

He had only barely just got his breathing back under control when Beth emerged and climbed back into the Miata five minutes later. By sheer force of will he managed a thin mask of calm and what he hoped would sell as a casual demeanor.

"Are we going fishing?" It sounded to him forced and stiff in spite of his efforts.

Beth didn't seem to notice. She wasn't looking at him, her own body language resolute and all business.

"You could say that. But not for fish."

Michael started to ask what that meant exactly, but stopped short. He was fairly certain he knew the answer. He kept talking anyway, partly because he wanted to know and partly because in his residual state of shock, any human interaction felt like a rescue dog's brandy.

"But this shop has something to do with your plan?"

"I don't know yet. I've got the man who owns the place joining us for dinner tonight, and that will settle it one way or the other."

THE DELEON BUNGALOW WASN'T IN Key West proper, nor anywhere in the cluster of satellite islands whose mail came addressed "Key West." Beth reversed their course and drove east from downtown, back past the airport and across an open bridge that linked to the next islet in the chain. The minimal guardrail made Michael shudder. But worse was yet to come.

When Beth first told him they were going to Key West, Michael had envisioned landing on a quaint little island where they would stay until transit to Isla Tesoro had been arranged. It never occurred to him that he might be exposed to the Overseas Highway, the hundred-plus miles of bridges and causeways that connected the Keys to the Florida main-land. As they passed the lavish Key West Golf Club, Michael gaped in horror as his worst nightmare materialized ahead. It was a bridge fifty feet above the water on concrete pilings, with less than four feet of protective rail and stretching more than a mile.

At least they were well separated from the compan-ion bridge for westbound traffic: they weren't going to be shoved over the side by some tequila-soaked bunghole cross-ing the center line. And it helped that the convertible top was down; one of Michael's most terrifying scenarios was being trapped in a car with water gushing in like a fire hose. But the relief these mitigations supplied was minimal. He turned his head to prevent Beth from seeing his expression and did the only thing he could: he closed his eyes and concentrated hard on containing the vomit that was scrambling to escape his stomach as though he had swallowed an angry snake.

Those sixty seconds seemed to Michael like an hour, and by the time it was over he could feel sweat beads starting to dribble down his forehead. But he had survived.

There were other bridges and narrow causeways, but none took more than ten seconds to cross and he found these easier to manage. He kept waiting for the big one, a cross-ing even longer and less protected, so that each time they encountered a shorter one, there was an insulating sense of relief. But no monster came. The bridge out of Key West turned out to be the worst the drive would have to offer.

They turned south off the highway on an island Beth identified as Sugarloaf Key, and here at last was the isolated tropical beauty Michael had foreseen. She pulled up in front of a beachside hacienda-style dwelling not unlike ones he had seen in Malibu except for the large dormer jutting from the clay tile roof that opened onto a white-railed, second-story deck with a spectacular ocean view.

"I thought bungalows only had one floor," he remarked as he retrieved their luggage from the Miata's trunk. Michael towed both suitcases as he followed Beth past palm and lemon trees through the breezeway to the front door, where he was reminded of something that had struck him when he stowed their bags in Boston. There seemed something wrong with Beth's travel case: it was inordinately heavy. What could she possibly have in there, he wondered, that would pack the heft of a bowling ball? Was her devastating figure so dependent on a fitness regimen that she would haul along free weights on a trip like this?

"It's just a loft," Beth answered.

Just a loft, Michael thought. *Even a standard floor plan beach house in the Florida Keys wasn't good enough for the DeLeons.*

He had expected the best, and he was not disappointed. The place was nearly two thousand square feet, impeccably furnished and decorated in Caribbean colonial style, with sea-glass floats dangling from hand-woven fishing nets beside double doors that looked out on the oval swimming pool and the deserted beach beyond. There were even flourishes nodding to the pirate era: a pair of crossed cutlasses above the volcanic-stone fireplace, a lacquered rum keg repurposed as a side table, a small ship's cannon menacing the room out of one corner with a pyramid of iron ball shot stacked beside its wheels. And a touch only a DeLeon would think indispensable: an exquisite waterfall, issuing from the top of a sculpted rock cliff built seamlessly into the living room wall, garnishing the atmosphere with a pleasant shimmering sound as it cascaded in delicate rivulets through clumps of lush vegetation into a gently lit sand-floored lagoon at the base.

"You'll be here." Beth guided Michael to a generous bed and bath suite decorated, ironically, with vintage travel posters from the inception of air tourism to Cuba in the 1940s.

"No, no, you take it," Michael protested, puzzled and embarrassed. "I'll be fine on the couch."

"Nobody sleeps on the couch, you goofball." Beth laughed. "This is the guest room. The master's up in the loft."

THE DAY WAS EASING DOWN into a magnificent sunset, readily enjoyed through the generous windows that lined every room on the ocean side, when there was a knock at the door. Michael, who had been using powerful binoculars to survey ships that appeared intermittently in silhouette against the fiery horizon, jumped at the sound. But he realized at once that it had to be Beth's friend, the man from the fishing shop, arriving as directed to discuss whatever secret business she had in mind for him. Even so, he slipped discreetly behind the bedroom door as Beth took her hands off the blender she had been using to frappe a supply of margaritas and made her way to the front of the house.

"Tony! Come in. Thank you so much for doing this on such short notice."

Michael emerged to find Beth welcoming their guest with a sisterly hug.

"Anything for you, my friend." The swarthy middle-aged man let his hostess take the two sacks of savory-smelling restaurant food he had brought in and held his hand out to Michael. "Tony Pizarro."

"'Swordfish Tony'." Michael smiled and shook the offered hand. "Pleased to meet you. I'm Michael Chandler."

"Glad to know you, Mr. Chandler. Any friend of Beth's is a friend of mine."

Michael relaxed, feeling a warmth well up in him that he couldn't quite explain. Was it because this man seemed so affable, so genuine, that it felt like yet another trustworthy ally had now entered the complicated picture? Or was it just the unexpectedly potent thrill of being referred to by an outsider as "Beth's friend"?

"But that would be my father." The man's warm smile

took on a touch of sadness. "Opened the original shop over on Roosevelt back in the day. He was Swordfish, I'm just Tony."

"A family business," Michael said with a smile. "Nice."

"Yep," Tony agreed. "Shouldn't have been, by rights. He passed away while I was still in prison. Broke his heart, the mess I made of my life, my mum gone and me his only son. When they told me he'd died I figured that's the end of it, he's finally shed of me now. But would you believe it, the old bugger left me the business. And a handwritten letter in the safe deposit box saying how much he loved me, too." Tony bowed his head with all the reverence of a penitent. "I'll never be the man he was. Don't claim to be. But I try, every day."

"THERE IT IS." BETH POKED a finger confidently at the navigational chart Tony Pizarro had rolled out on the table. The dishes had been cleared, but the smells of buttered lobster, sautéed vegetables, and fresh-baked bread lingered deliciously in the air. This place, Galleons, where Beth had sent Tony for the food, had it aced when it came to presentation and flavors resonating with tropical mystique. Michael longed for a chance to see the place in person, to sit down at a cloth-draped table and watch the mango sunset through shaded glass, sipping a cocktail of his own selection with a proper little parasol in it, waiting for some culinary masterpiece he had chosen off the menu himself. He found himself longing for all those things, the petty poignancies of life, the things any ordinary person at least in the developed world was free to do at their discretion, things they took utterly for granted, things that had been embargoed from Michael Chandler since that night in California when his fate had twisted like a dagger gouging a fatal wound.

"You're sure?"

"Positive. I'm a pilot, remember? Rick only took me there once, but I tracked down the location the minute we got back to Boston. *That* is the goddamned place. *Isla Tesoro.* Shaped like a miniature Minnesota, see?" She stabbed her finger on it repeatedly.

"Good enough for me." Tony eyed the chart critically. "Damn. Right across from Havana. Well sir, *Annie* can get you close enough to go in by inflatable the rest of the way. But it ain't going to be easy."

"Annie?" Michael queried.

"His charter boat," Beth supplied, then turned to Tony. "If you've got a better idea, I'm listening."

"No, ma'am, I didn't mean it that way."

"If you think it can't be done, just tell me. This isn't a death wish, Tony. I want my daughter, but I want her alive, safe, and with her mother. I'm not doing this just to send some histrionic message."

"I know you're not. Beth DeLeon doesn't roll like that." Tony smiled.

"You're under no obligation to get involved, you know," Beth told him softly. "I love you to death, Tony. I'm thankful for your support, but I don't want you or me killed here. It's not worth that. If I thought that was going to happen, I'd hop right back to New England and see if my attorneys know anyone good who specializes in this sort of crap. I'm only down here because the justice system takes the life of Methuselah to get anything done, and I want my daughter *now.*"

Tony grinned. Michael began to see that Tony's regard for Beth was a seasoned version of the respect Michael himself had developed for her only in the last twenty-four hours.

"I got no better idea. And I never said it won't work. You want it done, we'll make it work." He returned his attention to the chart. "We should be able to run right close to the island without being spotted if we launch at dusk. We'll get as far as we dare and set you two down in the raft, then

I'll pull a sensible ways out and pretend to be fishing while you sneak in and grab your girl." Tony grinned. "Hell, I may as well *do* some fishing."

Beth nodded like a field commander preparing for a skirmish. "And you've got things all set so we can signal you to pick us back up?"

"Will have by tomorrow. Can't say for sure on the Zodiac, I wasn't able to track down Freddie yet. But I expect I will. And o' course weather's fickle this time of year, can't much count on that. Still, what say we plan on tomorrow, and if things don't look right by afternoon, I'll give you a call."

Beth nodded, looking almost excited. She eyed Michael as though seeking confirmation, and he nodded, too.

He smiled, but inside he was a dismal wreck. The idea of covering the last few miles to the island in a tiny rubber craft terrified him, and the idea of sneaking around a criminal compound full of heavily armed thugs, hoping for some freak opportunity to snatch Elise and putter back to safety without getting shot, made him positively sick. But he was here, he had made a commitment, and he was going to follow through. He was determined to be ... well, to *look*, anyway, strong for Beth.

Tony winked.

Beth raised her margarita glass over the center of the table. The men clinked their drinks to hers. The conspiracy – and with it, Michael Chandler's fate – was sealed.

CHAPTER 19
Night Cruise

WITH THE PLAN SETTLED, TONY Pizarro stuck around just long enough to partake of the mango sherbet Beth dished up before taking his leave with the promise that he would be up bright and early the next day seeing to the arrangements they had agreed upon. For their part, Beth and Michael cleaned up the kitchen together and then purposefully stayed up late. If things went according to schedule, it would be a vital advantage to adjust their biological clocks for optimal performance in the dark hours.

It was past 1:00 a.m. when they came to the mutual realization that they could no longer fight the exhaustion of long travel and churning emotion. They had been sitting together on the king-size bed in the master loft watching the romance drama *The Lake House* with Sandra Bullock and Keanu Reeves. Michael, but not Beth, had cried silently at the final scene in which the two separated lovers finally found each other. Beth was married and utterly confident of being able to find a replacement mate should it become necessary. For Michael, the story tugged achingly at his longing to share life with a soulmate, and no less the abject agony of his near miss with Vicki Valentine.

The movie ended and Michael rose to his feet. It seemed

like a kiss goodnight might not be entirely out of place, a playful peck at least, but it didn't happen. Michael was torn, but when it came right down to it he was not unduly disappointed. On one level, he would have been thrilled enough not to wash his face for a week, figuratively if not literally. But on another, he felt uncomfortable with even such mild intimacy with a married woman, no matter how doomed her current union might be.

He trundled down the stairs to the guest room. Beth had left the rum keg table lamp on to light his way. He switched it off, undressed save for underwear and a T-shirt, and snuggled into the caress of the cozy bed.

He was just at the precipice of sleep when he heard the faint click of a lockset turning. He opened his eyes and looked in the direction of the sound.

In the open doorway, visible only in silhouette against the faintly starlit background, stood the figure of a woman. She was leaning against the door frame in a posture that managed to be both relaxed and commanding. Even in the dark, one thing was clear beyond doubt from just the outline of her form: she was completely, magnificently, naked.

"Want some company?"

Michael sat bolt upright. He was paralyzed with confusion, both at being roused from the brink of slumber and from the shock of the situation itself. Back in Boston, when Beth had invited him to stay the night, he had wondered whether she was proposing sex. This time, there was no doubt.

"I ..." He faltered, his heart racing. "I don't th—"

"Michael Chandler," Beth chastised in a tone so wicked he half expected her to sprout horns, "are you telling me that you never wanted this so badly you would have done a deal with the devil to get it?"

Michael gulped. He of course never faced that option, but now that she framed it he had to admit, to his great discomfort, that he couldn't answer.

"You're married," he said stupidly.

"Like *hell* I am." The bitterness in her voice momentarily disrupted the carnal electricity. "Do you see a ring on this finger?"

He couldn't have made it out in the darkness anyway, but he took her meaning.

"It's in a zip-lock bag in the glove compartment of my Porsche. The only reason I haven't chucked it in a dumpster is so I can sell it and get *some* value out of the goddamn thing."

"That doesn't—"

"What do you care anyway?" She was moving toward him now. "*You're* not married."

Her sexual aura was overpowering. Michael's heart was hammering like machine-gun fire. It was hard to breathe. He didn't know what to do.

Part of him was exhilarated beyond any feeling he could remember. Here was Beth McFadden – restored rightfully to that name by her own proclamation – not merely the sassy cheerleader but the heart-crushing siren she had blossomed into, standing two feet away from him *au naturel* like Cybill Shepherd and Charles Grodin in *The Heartbreak Kid*, presenting the one thing he had desired more than anything else in life except marriage to Vicki. She was there for the taking, within reach of his hand.

Yet something bothered him. Fiercely. Some powerful force, feeling almost like a conscious entity, was holding him back from this unbelievable opportunity to silence the ghosts of Beth's rejection for good. He sensed it inside him, something he couldn't articulate, something he felt with overwhelming passion but could not find the words to express. Something that made this, just as in that scene from Heartbreak, not the right time.

And then, all of a sudden, it clarified for him and he knew. It hurt like an arrow through the chest, but he understood his feelings and he knew, wretchedly, what he had to do.

"I'm not married," he conceded with quiet, firm conviction. "But someday I want to be. And when I *am* married, I want it to *matter*."

He waited for Beth to respond, expecting her to soften and reward his words with warm encouragement. But Beth was a statue.

"I just ... *can't*," he finally broke in an excruciated tone. "I can't do something I know would be so painful if it were ever done to me." He shook his head in the darkness. "Not even to Rick."

"Rick has nothing to do with this."

Beth's terse words hung in the air unanswered. Three times, the intention to reach out and embrace her left Michael's brain and coursed outward along his neural network, only to expire at his fingertips unfulfilled. If it happened a fourth time, he knew he would be unable to restrain it.

Beth turned without speaking. She strode purposefully to the door, exited the room, and took what seemed like an inordinate amount of care to close it innocuously behind her. Footsteps padded up the stairs, and when the master bedroom door slammed, it appeared that Beth had lost the inclination to temper her humiliation and outrage.

Softly it began to rain. The clay roof tiles absorbed the sound of any falling there, but Michael could hear it pecking quietly on the guest room window. As he nestled miserably back into the bed, he wondered if some of those drops were angels' tears. He turned his face into the pillow and contributed a few of his own.

Half an hour went by. The rain was steady, but gentle. Then all at once the heavens burst in a downpour, sheets of storm water crashing on the roof like a mortar barrage, so thick the white sand beach, visible in the starlight when Michael had gone to bed, could no longer be seen through the guest room window.

The sky flashed and thunder rolled in the distance. Michael, not yet asleep, was snapped fully alert. So it was that he detected the incandescent glow coming in under the door before the knob began to turn once again.

Beth came in bearing a candle burning in a pewter holder shaped like an alligator with its tail curled into a handle. This time she was wearing a white terry bathrobe.

She closed the door behind her, presumptuous perhaps but not mistaken. She sat on the edge of the bed near Michael's feet.

"I won't bother you." Her voice was thin and strained. Her eyes were red and her cheeks looked as grooved as Michael's felt. "I just don't want to be alone, is that okay?"

Michael couldn't keep a smile from breaking out. He nodded and gestured toward the vacant side of the bed.

"We lose power sometimes," she told him, setting the candle carefully on the nightstand and slipping in next to him under the covers. "Being all the way out here, it can take a while to restore. We keep talking about a generator, but by the time we're ready to do something the season's over and we just bag it."

"The power's off now?"

"No. But I like to be prepared." Beth stared at the ceiling and watched the shadows dancing in the flames. "I love candlelight."

"Me too."

She turned to him, hesitated, then let out in a small voice. "Hold me?"

The smile took Michael over completely. He shifted sideways and rolled her facing away from him so they could cuddle with her back against his chest. He lay his jaw over her shoulder and hugged her reassuringly. She melted into him like an egg under a mother bird.

Strange, he thought, harkening to another night in another small town. He had been afraid that Rosemary Hart was trying to maneuver him into a sexual encounter he did not want, and he had deflected her with tact and grace. He had longed desperately for intimacy with Beth McFadden — then when offered he had spurned it in an embarrassingly clubfooted manner. For what, exactly? Why did it matter so much? He was never going to be married. Not if he stuck with this dogged, irrational devotion to a dead girl. *A dead girl*. For that was the truth of it. He was morally opposed to adultery, he hadn't pretended that, but the most compelling force that had held his distance from Beth was not Rick but Vicki. Vicki Valentine, whose face he had not seen and whose sublime skin he had not touched in more than ten years. And never could. Why did it cling to him so senselessly? Why was he unable to let go of her and get on with his life? What was he thinking, what was he hoping for? What was it supposed to accomplish?

He'd found no satisfying answers in a decade. He didn't expect an epiphany now. He settled into his routine, his familiar role: Michael Chandler, the giver. He held Beth DeLeon tenderly, stroking her arm, nuzzling her hair like a mother cat licking her kitten. Visions of Rosemary crept in, but this was different. He wasn't easing Beth's slide off this mortal coil. He had failed to save Rosie at the railroad tracks in Kingman, and it had scarred him; he would never cease second-guessing the choices he had made and what otherwise might have been. He hadn't been able to save Max, and he sure as hell hadn't saved Vicki. But he was damned well going to save Beth. He was going to find a way. He was going to save Beth, save Elise, fend off the best that Rick

DeLeon could dish out, and finish victorious. He *knew* he would. He had never felt so driven and determined about anything in all his life. It felt like a mission from God. *He was going to do this.*

Or he was going to die trying.

WHEN AT LAST EXHAUSTION REALLY did take hold, they slept peacefully and late. It was after ten o'clock in the morning when Beth rose and ambled into the kitchen to start some coffee. There wasn't much to eat – the bungalow was cleared of perishables when the DeLeons weren't in residence. But there was no hurry, plenty of time to find food; they had most of the day to kill.

It was another typical, pleasant summer day in the Keys; the night's storm had left no visible trace beyond a faint humidity haze. Beth let Michael drive the Miata, directing him east to Big Pine Key. There were bridges and causeways along the way, but being in control of the car reduced his anxiety to a whisper. They were no Golden Gate, the guard rails were still too damned short, and he had to suppress the occasional bizarre feeling that he might suddenly lapse into madness and *deliberately* swerve off the road. But he had lots of practice managing that, and they arrived at the Cracked Egg Café without incident.

Tony Pizarro called while they were in the middle of breakfast. Beth conversed with him for a minute, then clapped the phone shut.

"Tony has the Zodiac," she announced, fire in her eyes. "The weather looks fine. We launch on schedule."

THEY SPENT THE DAY TOURING Beth's favorite beaches and funky little shops around the Lower Keys. When Michael was successful in blocking out the overall situation, it felt like being on vacation. When he wasn't, it was still a magical time with Beth, all the more precious because of the danger they would soon be facing together.

They returned to the bungalow around four o'clock, where they each showered and changed clothes. There was no telling when their next opportunity to freshen up would come.

"I take it we're not bringing suitcases," Michael checked.

"We need to run as light as possible. But that reminds me, come upstairs."

Beth plopped her suitcase onto the bed and opened the snaps; to his astonishment, Michael saw what had made it so heavy.

"I don't suppose you've ever used one of these," she said, holding up a frightening black Mac-10 fully-automatic machine pistol. Michael shook his head.

"They're not too bad. You just need to brace it with the folding stock and baby it a little so the recoil doesn't spray all over the place." She reached back into the case and handed Michael the other weapon, a short-barreled SPAS-12 combat shotgun. "This one is easier. It's got a stock, too, but even folded it's pretty well idiot-proof. In close quarters it's practically impossible to miss. The only downside is ammo. It only holds eight shells. Here, let me show you how it loads."

AN HOUR LATER, THEY PARKED at Sunset Harbor and made their way past a dark and locked up Swordfish Tony's Bait & Tackle, proceeding out onto the pier. Tony was waiting for them aboard his pride and joy, a blue and white custom 46-foot Bertram 510 with the name *Queen Anne's Revenge* stenciled in elegant script on the stern.

"Blackbeard's flagship," Beth explained as they boarded.

Tony winked. "Except that the Queen Anne *this* scribble refers to is standing right here."

"God, that *is* your middle name, isn't it?" Michael laughed.

"It is." Beth's dark eyes narrowed and her voice dropped down a notch. "And revenge I mean to have."

The craft seemed more yacht than fishing trawler. The deck was ample, and the bow rails could accommodate an extended family of fishers, but the luxury cabin was over the top for a small charter rig. There was a well-appointed galley, a clean and comfortable head, several built-in tables and chairs, sleeping pods for eight, and a master bed suitable for two more. There was even a little butcher-block station for cleaning and wrapping charter catches for customers to take home.

Michael felt confident in the spunky ship and even more so in her skipper. Even so, he asked, even before the engines were fired up: "Do you have life vests?"

"If I didn't, the Coast Guard would shut me down." Tony led him to a closet stocked with a dozen personal flotation devices of various sizes and shapes. Michael selected a comfortable-looking foam jacket and strapped it on.

"Good idea." Beth followed suit, pulling out a model that fit her but setting it aside on a chair. She then chose a second, smaller model, turning it over carefully to ensure it was sound, and dropped it next to the one she had picked out for herself.

"Looks like we're all set," Tony said. "Before we tie off, Ms. Queen, did you remember about your phone?"

"Oh, god damn it." Beth pawed through the little clutch purse she had brought, containing some cash and bare essentials. "I looked right at it and set it on the counter when I was going through my purse. I must have stuck it in here on autopilot."

"Can't have it," Tony scolded. "Got one all set for you, untraceable like I promised. You want to dump yours in the sea, or shall I call Freddie down here to pick it up?"

"Get Freddie," Beth grumbled. "Like hell I'm going to program a whole new god damn phone."

"Wait." Michael waved at Beth as Tony punched a number on his own mobile. "Before you give that up, can I use it for a sec?"

"What for?" Beth asked.

"I need to call Dan. Don't worry, I'm not going to tell him where we are. I'm not going to tell him anything. I just want to ask something."

Beth shrugged, handing him the phone. Michael stepped out to a corner of the deck and dialed the number on Dan's business card.

"Beth?" Dan picked up, reading the Caller ID.

"Dan, it's Michael."

"Michael!" Dan brightened. "How's it going, buddy? Everything okay?"

"Perfect." Michael strained to maintain an even tone. "Listen, Dan, I want you to do me a big favor."

"Anything."

"I want you to call my parents. I can't— their phone may be tapped and I don't want any record of where I've been. But they must be worried sick and I've got to give them something."

"Sure, man." Michael half expected Dan to ask why he couldn't just have Beth place the call. But Dan didn't ask, and it wasn't surprising. He had offered to help in any way he could, and meant it.

"Here's the number." Michael rattled off his parents' land line. "Only talk to my dad. That's important. If Mom answers, ask for Dad or hang up. Don't say anything to her. I want my dad to decide how he wants her to hear it. Or if."

"Will do." Dan's voice was solemn. "What should I tell your dad?"

"Tell him … I love them. Tell them I love them more than anything else in the world. And not to worry. Don't say where I am, just tell them I'm safe, I'm being well taken care of, and that I'll have everything settled and be back in San Mateo before they know it."

"Will you?" Dan inquired.

Michael sighed. "I've debated over and over whether to call them at all. I can't know what's going to happen, you know that. But the thought of them agonizing over it, worrying that I might be dead — I don't want them suffering like that. I just want them to know I'm still out here doing … fine."

"Are you?"

Michael halted. Tears started welling in his eyes, and at first he didn't understand why. Then he knew. It was nothing more than Dan's concern, the momentary refuge Michael felt in the clear and immediate knowledge that Dan cared. He was sincerely, completely sympathetic — and worried. And Dan's lighthouse of faithful regard in the sea of dark uncertainty made Michael ache so desperately for the unchallenged optimism of their shared boyhood — before Max, before Vicki, before the shattering of his career plans, before his whole world went careening off a bridge just over a week ago — that it was all he could manage to keep from dissolving completely into a puddle of pathetic emotional goo.

But there was nothing more Dan could do to help him now, and the last thing Michael wanted was to leave his friend anguishing over him for no good purpose. He stiffened his lip and answered as cheerfully as he could muster. "Of course."

"Okay." Dan did not sound convinced, but to Michael's relief, he let things lie. "There's an old pub I know in Cambridge that still has a coin-op pay phone. I'll call your dad from there."

"Perfect. And Dan?"

"Yeah?"

"Thanks for everything. Melissa, too. You guys are the best. You made me feel like a person again instead of a mouse on a cat farm. Give your wife a big hug for me. I love you, man."

"Take care of yourself." Bald worry had crept into Dan's voice alongside the support and resolve. "I want you back here as soon as you can."

"You got it."

"I'll hold you to that."

"Goodbye, man." Michael closed the phone thoughtfully and handed it back to Beth, feeling like he was releasing the last frail connection to his old life.

Freddie Wirt, Tony's part-time, habitually bare-chested assistant, who was interested in working only enough hours to stock his bungalow with Spaghetti-O's and beer — and even less work when the surf was good — was already halfway down the pier. Michael, Beth, and Tony converged at the boat's edge to meet him.

"Drop that by the DeLeon place," Tony instructed as Beth handed over the phone. "Don't get distracted and forget about it, okay?"

"Cut me some slack, man." Freddie feigned offense, but the smiles on both men's faces evinced their mutual affection. Tony had spared him juvenile detention for shoplifting an iPod by sponsoring him for a work-release alternative, and Freddie was forever grateful.

Tony turned to Beth. "Where would you like him to leave it?"

"Don't go all the way out there, just keep it in the shop." Beth scoffed. "That's as good as anyplace. We'll be back in a couple of days."

"Got your key?" Tony asked.

"Yeah, yeah." Freddie turned, his flip-flops smacking against the thick dock planks. "Bring back a big one for me!"

"Catch your own!" Tony called. Freddie made a dismissive gesture over his shoulder and was gone.

MICHAEL'S HYDROPHOBIA HAD NEVER PREVENT-ED him from enjoying boats. As long as there were life preservers and he could see the shoreline, the chances of drowning seemed distant. But he had never been out on the ocean. Even the modest seas and swells they were coursing through made the *Annie* feel smaller, and he didn't like it at all when the occasional bad angle splashed seawater up over the gunwales. He felt a flash of panic, too, once they cleared the horizon and for the first time in his life there was nothing but ocean as far as he could see 360 degrees around. But he wasn't terrified, and after the first hour he even felt a sense of pride at having grown "sea legs." He didn't even become nauseous, the traditional initiation of green seafarers, thanks to the prescription-grade Dramamine Beth had thoughtfully brought along and insisted he take as they got underway.

The ride calmed a bit, enough for Beth to invite Michael to join her out at the bow rail, to get some air and enjoy the sunset before the long, dark work ahead.

"So what's the deal with you and Tony?" Michael inquired once they were seated comfortably on the fiberglass prow, seeming to fly magically over the carpet of waves, the soothing whoosh of them shearing off the keel easily overpowering the dim buzz of the twin screws at the rear of the craft. "I take it he doesn't know Rick?"

"Oh, he knows Rick," Beth corrected. "Rick met him first. He went on one of Tony's marlin charters with some of his 'work buddies.' In fact, if I'm not mistaken, it was Fernando Lopez that recommended Tony as the guy with 'a nose for the big ones'."

Michael frowned. "Doesn't it seem a little weird that he would take sides?"

Beth shook her head. "We were all friends at first. Rick chartered a private trip for just the two of us, and Tony brought Freddie for company so Rick and I could be alone. They let us have the master cabin. They brought fishing gear, but it never came out of the bin. We just cruised up and down the Lesser Antilles for two weeks, drinking, swimming, and playing poker. It was a hoot."

"I'll bet."

"You know how it is when you're in close quarters with someone for a long time, even a stranger. By the end of the week we were all great pals. One night Tony got comfortable enough – or maybe just drunk enough – to tell the story about how he had been a drug runner in the '80s moving goods from Yucatan to the Gulf Coast. The problem was, he was a user, too. He wasn't careful, and he'd only been at it a couple of years before he was nailed by Customs. They decided to make an example out of him for Reagan's 'War on Drugs.' He went to prison for six years. It would have been longer if he hadn't been paroled for exemplary behavior. Tony was one of the few who got clean and really did turn over a new leaf. Unfortunately, his dad died less than a year before they let him go."

"That's awful."

"Yeah it is. His mom had died from diphtheria when he was seven and his dad never remarried. Anyway, I told you we drank night and day on that trip; it's amazing our livers didn't burst. And after Tony told his story, Rick decided he needed to show him up. So out came all the yarns about his drug-running 'glory'."

"Sounds like Rick.."

Beth grimaced. "He thought Tony would be mightily impressed. He wasn't. All Tony saw was a guy still playing the game, who still had the chance to cut clean before something really bad happened, and yet not only didn't see the problem, but was *bragging* about it. Tony was appalled. Freddie just kept saying 'Baaad mojo, dude.' I didn't say anything; I just wanted to crawl in a hole.

"And somehow, out of all that, Rick didn't even seem to remember the conversation the next day. He just went merrily along. Is it possible to be so hammered you would have no recollection of something that raw? I don't know. Anyway, nobody else had any desire to dredge it up, so we dropped it. No one said a thing about it. But Tony could see that I had gotten roped in against my will. He was more charitable than I deserved. And after that, Rick, who apparently never did get a clue, kept chartering with Tony and having those guys over to the bungalow. And Tony went along with it, because he thought I needed looking after."

"You did."

"I can take care of myself. I *don't* always, but I *can*." Beth smiled. "But that doesn't make Tony any less dear. And he adores Elise. He's taken her out on the boat lots of times, or just kept an eye on her around the pier to let Rick and I have a break."

Michael nodded. He understood Tony Pizarro's allegiance now. And he had been right in his initial assessment. A new ally had entered the picture. A damn good one.

THE SUN WAS DIPPING, CASTING a blinding cone of reflection across the water from the west, when they sat down to the last real meal Beth and Michael would be able to rely upon. The sea was placid now, and Michael found it astonishing and beautiful that the earth's most dominating force, whose might crashed endlessly against rocky shores the planet over, could out here in the middle of nowhere be as flat and quiet as a garden pond.

"Almost time." Tony checked his watch, only half interested in his share of the gourmet sandwiches and key lime pie he had procured from the *Blue Heaven* at Beth's request. "Once more with the signals. Last time, I promise."

Beth finished chewing and took a drink of her guava juice. The repetitive checking annoyed her, but she understood how important it was to make sure they were all in sync.

"Two rings means come and get us. One means we're doing fine, but need more time."

"And we don't say a word," Michael added.

"And you signal me once a day no matter what," Tony

continued.

"Every day, as close to sunrise as we can," Beth recited.

"Good. And you'll get no signal from me at all until I'm in rendezvous position. Then I'll send a text with just the letter 's'."

"Swordfish," Michael confirmed.

"Then, once you're good and clear of that foul place, you text me your location. Don't get antsy about it, neither. It won't do to ping the coordinates while those bastards are closer to you than me. This bucket's no match for a rumrunner."

Beth nodded impatiently and anticipated Tony's next question by reciting the number of the sterile black market cell phone he had procured for himself, a mate to the one he had given her. "You should have just programmed it in," she complained, returning to her sandwich.

"Leave the shady details to the professionals," Tony chided. "You're not good at it. Now you, Mr. Chandler, in case you have to make the call. Tell me the number."

Michael did. Tony nodded in satisfaction.

"Good. Now soon as we're done here, I'll double check the course and then kill the GPS. Don't turn on your phone, don't light a cigarette. If you need light to piss by, go do it now. From here on in, we run completely dark."

"Don't light a cigarette." Beth eyed him with mock derision. "You're the only one here who smokes."

"Those are *Cuban cigars*. It's not the same thing." Tony glared right back. "Anyway, I'm warning myself, too."

FOR THE LAST HOUR OF the voyage, none of them spoke. No one wanted to. They were rehearsing the plan, each his own part of it, envisioning their actions, thinking through contingencies. Praying.

It was a moonless night, which Tony said he took as a sign that God was on their side. Michael was not inclined to disagree. He knew, however, that divine indulgence was no guarantee against failure.

He had never seen the stars so bright. The Milky Way wove behind them so distinctly it almost looked three dimensional. All those billions of stars, he thought. All those billions upon billions of worlds. Does it really matter, in the grand scheme of things, what happens to us tonight? Can God really be bothered to care what goes on in the individual lives of three tiny motes on a dark speck of rock lost in this vastness?

From his spot alone along the port-side rail on the main deck, he saw a faint glow on the southern horizon. Twenty minutes later, the first ground lights appeared and a dark shape began to rise out of the water. *Havana, Cuba,* Michael thought. *A place I never thought I'd see.* It was the last true vestige of the Cold War, orphaned by the Soviet collapse, a place still forbidden to American travelers and whose own people were so desperate to escape that they would risk the lives of young children trying to cross the ninety miles to Florida on makeshift rafts. The same crossing he had just made in reverse. He felt like Frodo Baggins getting his first look at Mordor.

"This is it," Tony hissed in his ear. It was crazy to think that anyone could hear them out here, their voices on any account muffled by the sound of the motors even at wakeless speed. But he understood Tony's inclination to err on caution's side.

"This is as close as we better get to the island. Even

here their infrareds might pick up *Annie's* motor heat. Come give me a hand with the tub toy."

Michael crossed to the starboard side where the Zodiac dinghy had hung sideways against the hull, pontoons inflated, all the way from Key West. It was designed for two, could safely hold four, but its utility for purposes beyond those meek specifications was severely limited. What it *was* good for was a very low-profile approach, the next best thing for a covert beach landing if you didn't have SEAL gear. Regardless of suitability, it was what they had. *All* they had.

Tony shut *Annie* off completely and joined Michael at the hitches. Beth came out of the cabin to help. Tension mounted as they hoisted the little boat ever so gently down onto the water's surface. He had not taken his life vest off for five hours, but it was all Michael could do to steel himself against what lay ahead. He was frightened. He was *terrified*. He kept reminding himself that he was doing this for Elise, a helpless eight-year-old girl hijacked by her volatile father to some black island infested with career criminals. He tried to think of Beth, of what she was coming to mean to him, had always represented to him, of how liberating it would be to show her in no uncertain terms that he was worthy of her love. That angle faltered; he'd been better off envisioning himself as Elise's Superman. But deep down he couldn't sustain that image either, because he *wasn't* Superman. He wasn't a soldier. He wasn't even a high school jock like his brother Max or his friend Carl Adams or Rick DeLeon. He was Michael Chandler, wanderer of the Wal-Mart aisles, savior of one small green parrotlet and not much else.

Yet Beth had offered him quarter several times, and he had demurred. He could have stayed in Boston and she would have understood. He could have staked himself in the Key West bungalow and she would have been grateful just to have him there waiting for her. He could have convinced her that his proximity was more hazard to her than help given his own bleak circumstances, and she would not have disagreed. She would have left him to his affairs gracefully.

That door was closed. Only one remained before him. It was splashing in the water ten feet below, already bucking uncertainly in seas that were beginning to writhe again, separated from the nearest solid footing by miles of hell-ride in what looked like a glorified kiddy pool with only a hedge trimmer motor to fight the wind and current.

He heard a *thunk* as Beth's duffle bag with the weapons and three days' emergency food bounced onto the Zodiac's belly. "Thanks, Tony," Beth was saying, then flung her arms around the man and held him very, very tight. The sight of her fear magnified Michael's even more.

"Take care of her," Tony told Michael as Beth made her way down the rope ladder, as though Michael were some pillar of strength.

"I will." He embraced Tony. *I'll try. But who the hell is going to take care of me?*

There was nothing left for it. Beth was already strapped into her life jacket and yanking the launch's starter cord. Michael Chandler stepped over the *Annie's* starboard side, gripped the wet strands of rope, and lowered himself down into a nightmare.

CHAPTER 20
The Island

BETH STUDIED HER ORIENTEERING COMPASS, shielding its faint built-in light with her hand, working to get a visual bearing among the dark shapes and anonymous lights on the horizon as the Zodiac's little outboard warmed up.

Tony waited patiently at the *Annie's* wheel station until the little inflatable had lumbered and slid over the swells to a safe distance, then fired the engines and commenced a wide, slow turn that would bear him back north.

From his precarious position toward the bow of the Zodiac, at least a gallon of water already sloshing about underfoot, Michael watched *Queen Anne's Revenge* a hundred yards away arcing back toward Florida and wondered how he ever could have thought of it as unsafe. From this angle three feet above the turbulent waterline, the lightless motor yacht looked as tall and stable as a battleship. Two minutes later, he lost sight of it altogether as it cruised quietly into the enfolding dark.

Beth remained wedged at the stern with her hand on the tiller and the duffle on her lap to keep it dry, her eyes staring intently ahead. A merciless wind blew from the east in cruel gusts. The ocean spat seawater on Michael's face at taunting intervals, and he found that with the swells rolling them sideways and the water surface shifting as unpredictably as a rodeo bull, he could not intuit which direction they were moving, or if they were making any headway at all. He was gripped with panic at the thought that the current might prove too much for the buzzing little motor, that they might be swept all the way out of the Straits of Florida into the open Atlantic, run out of gas, exhaust their supplies, and die a slow, agonizing death from dehydration. It brought home a line of poetry that had stuck with Michael since high school, something like: "water, water everywhere and not a drop to drink." The awful thought occurred to him that as unbearable as drowning was, at least it was over in minutes, not days or weeks. The thought that he might die in the middle of the ocean not from the manifestation of his greatest fear but from its antithesis, a lingering thirst so poignant he might well be driven to drink saltwater, which would only intensify the torture, was too hideous to contemplate.

He tried closing his eyes, but he couldn't. It took all his focus to ride the bucking rubber without being tossed overboard, and what few visual points of reference there were constituted the only way he could maintain any sense of balance or direction.

Unceremoniously and without warning, his stomach seized and ejected its contents despite the Dramamine he had taken just before they separated from Tony's yacht. Only by sheer luck of the boat's motion at that instant did it pitch cleanly over the side and not across their clothes or into the steadily expanding puddle sloshing at their feet.

"Bail some of that, will you?" Beth instructed, seeming not to have noticed his retching. "If the shells get wet, these guns might as well be scrap metal."

Michael cast about for something to scoop with, but of course there was nothing. He crawled over on his knees and started splashing the water back over the side with his hands. It was maddening how half the time, the boat would shift at just the moment he dug forward with his shoveling palms and instead of out, the water would run through his fingers and channel back under him, soaking his pants.

At least it wasn't cold. And there was more utility in it than just keeping the powder dry: it gave him something to do, a purpose, a small but significant sense that he was not completely helpless against these terrifying hazards. It wasn't much, but it was a branch to hold on to, a ritual to chant mantras through and nurture a glimmer of light against the imposing darkness.

"Maybe we'll get lucky," he proposed shrilly, "and a shark will eat us." He had meant it mostly as a joke, although in the depths of his heart, the thought of a nice clean beheading by the jaws of a Great White seemed like a goodnight kiss compared to drowning or dying of thirst. He wondered insanely but with a twinge of earnestness whether it might be possible, in a shark attack, to intentionally position yourself for a fast, efficient death. He almost vocalized this, but at the last moment discretion mercifully intervened.

Beth didn't say a word.

THE ORDEAL SEEMED ENDLESS. TWICE, the boat pitched so steeply that Michael really did roll halfway over the slippery side, and the second one ended with his clothing thoroughly drenched. He shifted to get a start on the bailing; this little maneuver had undone at least three minutes of his work, and he needed to get it out again before another such toss brought in enough ocean to swamp them.

Besides the job as a human bilge pump, two things kept Michael from degenerating into hysteria. The first was his life preserver. It left only a slim possibility that he would drown, and he found this surprisingly comforting. That is not to say he wasn't panicked, but the fear was manageable.

The other factor was Beth herself. Even though he wasn't steering the boat, this was a rare occasion in which he preferred that. He had as much confidence in her at the tiller as he had in the sky, and he also felt with firm conviction that if he had been driving, he would have botched it badly.

There was a contagious sense of focus and determination emanating from Beth, and he found comfort in this, too. It felt like nothing could go wrong – *really* wrong, at least – while he was with her.

MICHAEL HAD LITTLE SENSE OF how much time had passed when he suddenly noticed that the sky seemed preternaturally dark. He paused and, looking up, his mood shifted for the better. It was not hope he felt, nor more than a trace of relief, but it was a sort of welcome resolve.

The sky hadn't darkened. It had been blocked out by an enormous cliff face, its silhouette inscrutable save for the claws of palm fronds jutting into the sky at its crest a few hundred feet above. Michael, his head down and his focus on his tennis match with the sea spray, had not noticed the island approaching.

The Zodiac lurched violently as it hammered into the rocky shore. As the tide receded, Beth hopped out and motioned for help. Michael followed and they dragged the little craft clear of the surf, over a steep grassy berm, and into thick jungle at the edge of the beach.

The dark, wet meander from the cabin cruiser had taken more than an hour. Now with the raft sheltered, their supplies safely ashore, and their feet in contact with firm ground, exhaustion overtook them. Both tossed their life vests into the Zodiac and collapsed, Beth with her back up against a rubbery pontoon and Michael lying flat on a mattress of vegetation, comforted by the breeze and relieved to be free of the constricting flotation garment. Neither of them spoke. For a few minutes of blissful respite, there was no sound except their labored breathing and the rush of the restless sea.

THEY TIED THE BOAT SECURELY to a palm trunk and set off through the jungle along the cliff base, which for a time paralleled the coastline with only a few yards of foliage in between. They split a candy bar Beth retrieved from the duffle. She had left the bag sheltered under the boat with the cell phone, life jackets, and anything else they could do without for the time being, but they had taken with them the guns, pockets full of ammunition, and the binoculars from the bungalow.

Beth extended to Michael a couple of strips of beef jerky, which he accepted but stuffed into his pocket for later. He knew they needed to be smart about managing their energy, but his stomach was still jumpy from the raft ride and it had been all he could do to force half a Snickers down. The very thought of chewing a dried piece of meat made him nauseous.

Ten minutes later, they found their nostrils unexpectedly insulted and pulled up short.

"That smell," Michael said, looking about in the dark and sniffing the air. "Do you know what it is?"

"I don't— no, wait a minute, maybe I do." Beth wracked her memory. "I've never been to this part of the island, but it's got to be the sewer cave."

"Sewer cave?"

"Well, not exactly a cave, I guess. I'd forgotten all about it, but I seem to recall Rick saying that when the place was built, while they were digging for a well they hit a pocket of empty air. It turned out to be an old lava tube about a dozen feet down. They found that a portion of it ran right under the house and drained naturally down to the cliff base, so they took advantage and routed their waste water that way. Then in the 1940s, the owners did a general modernization and ran proper plumbing through it all the way down to the mouth."

"So their toilets dump right into the ocean." Michael wrinkled his nose. "I guess Cuba doesn't have an EPA."

Beth smiled. "Just one more reason to defect."

From there, the cliff veered inland, and they continued to follow it. Beneath the dense canopy, feeling their way along the rock incline, it was frightfully dark. Beth paused now and then to consult her compass, careful not to use even its meager light any longer than necessary. Michael followed blindly in her wake, more than once scraping his face and arms on stray branches invisible in the murk. The footing was overgrown and treacherous, sometimes firm, sometimes sandy, occasionally gooey or even ankle-deep wet, so he learned never to shift his weight too far forward lest his shoe catch in the mud or brambles and pitch him headlong. He was mortally afraid that if he tripped, the weapon he was uncomfortably toting might go off and betray their presence, or even worse, bore a nasty hole through Beth.

He was in fact uneasily aware of the military shotgun. It felt heavy and alien in his hands. Beth had talked him through how it worked, but there had been no opportunity for Michael to test fire. He wasn't confident in his ability to operate it correctly, let alone effectively, should the occasion arise. Though he wouldn't say it to Beth, he was even less sure that he could actually pull the trigger with another human being at the end of the barrel. He hoped to God that such a test would never come.

Their path along the cliff side angled up, and at the same time the height of the rock face began to recede. They were far enough from the ocean now that the rush of the surf was lost completely amid the chirps of night bugs, the wind in the palm fronds, and an occasional unsettling screech or guttural moan that he could not identify. To Michael it seemed they had walked so long that dawn might at any minute breathe life into the gloomy sky and ease their way. He had no idea how far they had actually come and had lost all sense of where they were in relation to the beached Zodiac.

In fact, only a half hour had passed before they reached their quarry, a broad plateau at the island's summit. Beth raised a hand to halt them at the edge of the clearing and got out the binoculars to reconnoiter the compound.

The "house" reminded Michael of the antebellum estates he had seen in movies and in brief glimpses along the southeastern leg of the drive with Charlie. It was large, maybe even bigger than the DeLeon house: two stories of multiple wings with covered decks on both levels that looked like they went all the way around. Wrought-iron gas lanterns dotted the structure like candles, casting a faint, warm illumination down the walls at either side of the double front doors and intermittently between the windows on both floors. It stood on a cleared field surrounded by several outbuildings, one of which must have been the distillery and another, judging by the low hum they could hear when the wind gusted just right, housed a generator. The cliff drop-off loomed forbiddingly to the north. The grounds themselves stretched some twenty acres. He didn't know how much land was needed for a sugar cane farm in pirate days, but he guessed the cleared plateau had once been planted as such. Now it was nothing but wild grass, kept trim nonetheless for an obvious reason: parked in front of a modern Quonset hut, facing north toward the cliff and the open ocean, was a small private plane.

"They have an airstrip?" Michael whispered. "You put us through all that when we could have just taxied up to the front door?"

"Shut up." Beth flashed a glare that made clear she was in no mood for useless diversion. "They keep two planes handy for certain business purposes or to escape in an emergency. Not particularly good ones, though, I think they were acquired from Cuban surplus so they'd be untraceable. You can see the tail number's been painted over. I wonder where the other one is."

She looped the strap over her head and handed Michael

the binoculars, then pointed.

"See that window on the upper left corner? That's the room Rick and I slept in. I'd guess that's where he has her. The door just to the right opens out of it, too. "

Michael surveyed the scene. He hadn't seen a soul, yet it seemed improbable if not impossible that they could cross the bare field unnoticed. Nevertheless, they really had no choice. He was again thankful that God had deemed it expedient to hide the moon on this night when they desperately needed darkness.

"So what's the plan?" he asked.

Beth eyed him evenly. "The 'plan' was how to get on and off the island. I had no way to predict exactly what it was going to take to get Elise," she admitted. "My recollections of the place weren't good enough to plan every detail in advance. Looking at it, though, I wonder if it would be possible to shimmy up one of those deck posts."

"I don't see how with these guns."

"True," Beth conceded. "But only one of us needs to go. The other can keep both guns and watch for trouble."

"What if there's trouble up there?"

Beth smirked. "There won't be from Rick. Not this time of night. He treats this place like a resort. When he's down here, a 'nightcap' means watching *The Tonight Show* in his underwear doing enough shots of Bacardi 151 to kill an elephant. You can't wake him and he snores like a rutting sea lion."

Michael felt a ray of hope. Was it really possible they could liberate Elise and be back on the raft in an hour? It would be a precision strike worthy of Special Ops.

That said, Michael didn't relish the idea of climbing the post himself, let alone being completely ignorant of the situation in that room and with only a slim hope of finding Elise there without Rick. But if just one was going, it only made sense for Beth, less muscled and more experienced with firearms, to remain on the ground as rear guard.

"I'll go up," Michael said with calm resolve.

"All ri–" Beth cut herself off and hastily raised the binoculars. "*My baby!*" she cried softly.

Sure enough, even without the binoculars, Michael could see the diminutive figure that had just come out onto the veranda.

"She knows I'm here," Beth rasped. "She senses me."

Michael began to reply, but decided to keep to himself: *Or maybe God chose this particular moment to make her feel restless enough to give us this break.*

Elise lingered for only a minute, arms over the railing, gaze drifting from one end of the dark clearing to the other. Then she lowered her head and trundled dejectedly back inside, closing the door behind her without a sound.

"We're coming, honey." Beth wept softly.

As anxious as they both were, Beth spent five agonizing minutes surveying the clearing through the binoculars, studying the grassy expanse, the corners of the buildings, the murky tree line on the opposite side. She spotted no enemies; except for wind in the palms, nothing stirred.

Reconnaissance done, there was nothing left to do but go. Beth sucked in a breath and emerged into the open, jogging hunched over as if a lower profile would make her invisible and gesturing for Michael to follow.

Now he could clearly see Havana to the south, its lights just a ferry ride's distance away, though Michael was quite sure no public ferry ran between here and the main island. It wouldn't be needed. Down slope at the water's edge, connected to the upper grounds by a set of worn dirt tire tracks, stood a modern dock complex with the amenities of a small marina. It was sheltered by a sandy breakwater lined with red warning lights – Michael had no doubt that most of the traffic took place at night – and by the light of the tall pole lamps he could see covered slips berthing an assortment of Cigarette speed boats and other elite watercraft.

Their own private port, Michael mused.

They reached the house and knelt below the porch balustrade, barely breathing. There was still no sign of adversaries.

Michael handed Beth the shotgun and started to stand up, eyeing the thick whitewashed column with disdain. He thought he could climb it, but it was going to be a royal bitch.

There was a tug at his sleeve. Beth was pulling insistently, as though she had one last vital instruction. When he knelt back down to oblige, she laid the guns in the grass, gathered him in both arms, and attacked him with a long, sweet, passionate kiss.

It caught him completely by surprise. He didn't know whether it was a true expression of love – it certainly felt like it – or a calculated tactic to inspire courage for what he was about to do. It didn't matter; it succeeded at both.

Their lips parted. Michael allowed a moment to look deep into her eyes. *"When this is all over ..."* they seemed to say.

Michael smiled. He was thinking it, too.

Shimmying up the square post was grueling. It was too wide to get a comfortable grip, the corners gouged his arms and legs, and the need to be quiet made progress maddeningly slow. A hot ache built steadily in his biceps, threatening to unhook his tenuous hold through sheer exhaustion no matter how hard he tried to will it away. But the adrenaline released by the glorious kiss sustained him, and in just over a minute he was grasping the rail and hauling himself up and over onto the second-floor deck.

He feared and felt almost certain the door would be locked, that he would be forced to knock quietly in a gamble that Elise would not only hear but decide to open it without waking her dad. He was shocked, and almost lost his grip, when the handle turned cleanly.

He eased the creaky door open at a turtle's pace, straining against a mad inclination to just thrust it open, vault from the veranda with Elise in his arms, and race headlong back to the raft. The desire to get it all over with was fierce. But he controlled it. The little girl came first, and the whole mission would go for nothing if a commotion was raised and they were caught. He was not about to let that happen.

The gap was almost wide enough for him to slip through when he was startled by a small form appearing abruptly on the other side. Without making a sound, the little figure bounced up and down on her feet and patted her fingertips together in a display of pure joy.

"I knew you'd come!" Elise whispered excitedly.

Michael put a finger over his lips to signal silence. He heard no snoring, but it was impossible to divine what risks to their escape might lay in the gloom behind her. He stepped back onto the veranda and motioned for her to follow.

He was inches away from re-closing the door – already congratulating himself for pulling this off, and thanking God for the good luck – when all hell broke loose.

A dog's bark pierced the air. At first it was distant, maybe a hundred feet away, but it immediately intensified and bounded closer with alarming speed. Then Beth's cry: "Noooo!"

A porch light flicked on. Men's voices and heavy footsteps sounded below.

Michael whisked Elise up into his arms and rushed to the railing.

A bristling Doberman Pinscher was holding Beth at bay six feet away, looking like it might spring at her at any moment with teeth bared. Beth was fussing frantically with the Mac-10, unable in the darkness and panic to get the safety off, the shotgun lying unhelpfully in the grass a few steps behind her.

A flashlight beam streaked sharply across the yard. A firm but remarkably calm voice commanded: "Put it down and I'll call the dog."

"Hey!" a second voice cried out from behind the first. The flashlight beam swung to the veranda, illuminating and partially blinding Michael and his charge.

Elise gripped him tighter than he thought an eight-year-old could. Michael steeled. Time slowed; fear evaporated. He saw everything with perfect clarity. It was the toddler in the San Mateo street all over again.

It was going to hurt, but that didn't matter. All that did matter was that he avoid an injury that would prevent him from running. It was ten feet down and he was carrying an extra sixty pounds, but he would have to do it. He would have to time things perfectly, leap over the rail with as much lateral momentum as possible to shear the angle of descent, coil his knees and ankles to absorb as much of the landing as possible. It was dicey at best, but it was all he could do. He backed up two steps and made a dash for the far corner.

The night exploded with the thunderclap of a .50 caliber shell rocketing from the barrel of a high velocity sniper rifle. The warning shot seared the air so violently they could smell ozone.

"No, Michael!" Beth shrieked. "Don't make them shoot! They might hit her!"

His senses were sharp, his cognition clear, his purpose and determination absolute. And these things told him, without a shade of doubt, that she was right.

He calmly stopped in his tracks.

CHAPTER 21
Trapped

ANY ILLUSIONS OF THE OLD plantation as some kind of resort, or comparable to the DeLeon home for that matter, were quickly disabused. This was a blue collar business site, aesthetically spare, functionally maintained but kept only as orderly as its operational purposes required.

They sat in a drawing room that may once have been elegant but had mostly given over to neglect. The furniture was a variety of badly deteriorating quality pieces and more recent yard sale fare without a trace of artistic sentiment.

Beth and Michael were seated at opposite ends of a rigid plaid couch with Rick's cousin Fernando Lopez in between to keep them apart. They were not roped up or otherwise bound, but the assault rifles in the laps of the two minders sitting opposite them and a third at the shoulder of the man standing in front of the main door were no less effective than iron shackles.

In the center of the proceedings, between the goons and opposite the prisoners, sat Juan Calderon. He was forty-eight years old, nattily attired, shoulder-length hair on the road from chestnut to white gathered in a tasteful ponytail, healthy and manicured and looking like the only person in the room who might be genuinely offended by the facility's aesthetic void. He was executive management in the smuggling operation, CEO of the Cartagena-Littleton shipping concern, and the highest ranking official in the parent criminal enterprise that anyone in the room personally knew.

"Take her downstairs," Calderon directed, addressing the man brandishing an Uzi machine pistol behind Elise.

"Mommy!" Elise screamed.

Beth leapt to her feet. "Get Rick in here this minute, you son of a bitch," she bellowed at the man in charge. "I want him here *now*."

"Don't worry about the young one. Nothing's going to happen to her, and you'll be joining her soon. I just want to have a few words first." He turned to the man hauling Elise away by the arm. "You get that, Javi? Don't drag her like that. Let her walk."

The man dropped his grip on Elise. Instantly she ran back to her mother.

"Please tell her to go," the boss instructed Beth patiently. "There's no need for this to be any more unpleasant than necessary. Don't force my hand."

Beth was livid, her face flushed, her body shaking as she held Elise's head to her breast. "Get ... Rick ... now."

"Mr. DeLeon is not on the island. Believe me, if he were, he *would* be with us. This is his problem, and his to resolve." Calderon nodded toward Elise. "He did not ask if he could bring her here, and I am not pleased he did so. Unfortunately, we had to send him out on business. No one wishes for the girl to be here, but she could not be allowed to go with him and the job could not be delayed. And now it will be cut short, because I've sent word for his return to deal with the crisis you've created." He focused a firm gaze on Beth. "Now please, Mrs. DeLeon, tell your daughter to go with Javier. You will be taken to her as soon as our talk is through. If you don't, there will be no choice but to drag her."

Calderon allowed Beth time to digest the matter. Finally, the color drained from her face and she gave Elise one last squeeze.

"Go with the man, honey. Everything will be all right.

I'll be with you as soon as I can."

"Please Mommy, no," Elise wailed.

Beth steeled herself. Michael could see she was chewing bullets.

"These men are Daddy's friends. They won't hurt you. Now go. I want you to go. I'll be there in a few minutes."

The man with the Uzi beckoned silently. Beth kissed the top of Elise's head and pushed her gently in his direction. "Go."

Elise collapsed into a pitiful sob. Beth physically walked her to the man and once again pushed her toward him. The little girl waddled miserably from the room with the gangster escort, her wails of anguish still audible for most of a minute until finally they passed out of earshot.

"You heartless bastard." Beth glared from her seat, looking barely able to contain herself.

"On the contrary. Those who know me would tell you I'm quite sentimental. I have no personal taste for the sordid parts of this business." Calderon smiled pleasantly. "Speaking of sentiment, you must be the 'prissy cocksucker' Rick can't stop bitching about."

When it became clear that Michael would not rise to the bait, Calderon went on. "Well, I can see why he's torqued up. You don't look particularly worthy of such a beautiful woman. Then again, it's a man's own responsibility to keep his lady happy. If he doesn't, he has only himself to blame when these things occur."

"Just get on with it," Beth spat. "Tell us what you want and let me go to my daughter."

"By all means. I thought you might enjoy an interlude of social civility, but I understand." He focused on Beth, and for the first time his tone became dark. "All I really want to know is how you got here. Who knows about your trip, and whether anybody else is out there trespassing in our private paradise."

"It's just the two of us. We came to get my daughter and go home. That's all we want. Your precious business is in no danger. If I was stupid enough to make trouble I could have done it long ago."

"You could. Then again, there wasn't much to be concerned about while you and Ricardo were kids in love. All of a sudden I have to wonder if the happy family might be coming apart."

"Don't wonder. Rick and I are through."

Michael's heart thumped in alarm. If Calderon came to view Beth's detachment from Rick as a security risk, he might conclude that drastic measures to silence her were imperative. Rick might intervene; they were his wife and daughter, after all. But Calderon was making it sound like Rick lacked the cachet to pull that off.

Belatedly, Beth seemed to realize those same implications of her indiscretion. She hastily softened her tone. "Look, I'm not stupid about the realities here. I've been living with this 'profession' for almost ten years. I've got a Porsche and a nice house and a very comfortable life. I'm as invested in this as Rick is. I can't say anything about the business that wouldn't land me in prison. And I'm not going to. There's plenty of money to split. I'll be perfectly happy to take my half and let sleeping dogs lie."

"I wish I could believe you. It would make things much easier."

"It's not just prison." Beth looked genuinely grim. "Don't think I don't know what happens to people who cross you, Mr. Calderon. I want to live. I've got a daughter to raise. I'll be a good girl."

Calderon smiled. "Well now, that's more convincing." His gaze rolled in Michael's direction. "The prissy cocksucker, on the other hand ..."

"He's got his own problems." Hearing her say this, Michael reeled, incredulous. Beth refused to look at him. She had made her decision that it was their best chance.

She swallowed and went on. "Michael's on the run from the police. His lot is no better than ours. It's probably worse. He's made some powerful enemies on both sides of the law. He doesn't dare surface at all, let alone go to the cops."

Calderon seemed to turn this over in his head like a Rubik's Cube. It was impossible to tell what he was thinking: whether he was deciding if he could believe her, or whether to ask for details, or merely mulling through what the implications might be for him.

He seemed to have worked things out, and resumed his focus.

"I said I wouldn't keep you, and so I won't. Just tell me how you got here, and who else knows, and you can be with your girl."

"Nobody knows. This was spur-of-the-moment, don't you get it? We had a scene at the house, Rick stomped off and grabbed our daughter from school and brought her here. He left me a taunting voicemail making it plain where she was. Frankly, I was foolish. I should have stayed in Boston and lined up the attorneys. I've always been a bit of a hothead, and it's never served me well. There was no planning. There wasn't time."

"Did you parachute in?"

Beth glared at his cheek. "We came from the Keys on a Zodiac. It got punctured on the rocks and sank. I was hoping to get out on one of your boats."

"A Zodiac." Calderon leered. "Punctured on the rocks. What rotten luck. Well, you *are* both quite wet. I should count myself lucky you don't claim you've swum all the way from Boston."

Beth gave him a dark scowl. "I'm telling the truth."

"No doubt." Calderon seemed suddenly pre-occupied, as though something more compelling had usurped his interest in their tale. He stood abruptly, motioning to the armed men to form up. "We'll talk again in the morning after Rick gets here. You may choose to be more cooperative then. There's no sense leaning on you now; that would spoil the test."

"What test?"

Beth tried to twist around and get a read of the gangster's face, but they were being led down a narrow set of stairs and she had to jerk forward to keep from losing her balance.

"Rick's test, of course. I really should thank you, Mrs. DeLeon, your rescue mission has presented me with an unexpected solution to a dilemma. You see, I've had my eye on your husband for some time. He's not really a 'team player,' I expect you know that. I've always suspected he might try to bail on us if he was too well fed. I've seen it before. As you've said, this business really doesn't work that way. It can't. Nobody can become too good for the rest of us; it poisons the well. This is a job for life. There's only *one* way out of a job for life."

The procession wound around the musty basement, down to a large cellar that had served as the curing area for the rum production centuries ago. Even now, the vaguely nauseating scent of sour spirits and degenerate wood remained.

They wound down a short stair into a part of the house that felt truly ancient, with the neglected look and earthy smell of a sunless world long abandoned to spiders.

The lead gunman opened an ancient side door on an even more claustrophobic passage: an irregular stair chiseled right into the raw stone, winding claustrophobically down a rough-hewn descent that made no pretense at refinement at all. It seemed less like a cellar and more like a mine shaft.

"Where are you taking us?" Beth asked in alarm.

"Did Rick forget to share this gem the first time you were here?" Calderon quizzed. "Pity. I think it's the most fascinating feature in the place. Of course, we weren't using it back then. Still, I'm sure it was open."

The stairs ended at yet another impossibly thick door that might have been three hundred years old. Calderon rapped, and Javier Jones, who had taken Elise, let them through.

The way down may not have passed as a bona fide

mineshaft. The floors were largely concrete, the lights were permanently installed, and the walls, rough-hewn though they were, had been polished smooth. There was only one word for the place they found themselves now, however, and it was no mere metaphor. It was a dungeon.

"Slave quarters," Calderon explained conversationally. "They kept two families, each with their own little dwelling, as you can see. Being so close to the main island, there was a fear that if they were warehoused on the surface, some of the Africans might get adventurous and chance a swim across. Keeping them down here removed the temptation. They never lost a one." Calderon smiled pleasantly. "All to the good. Those waters are crawling with reef sharks and man o' war. Not that a half-starved slave runt could swim four miles in a current to begin with."

Beth gaped, speechless. Angry tears burned in Michael's eyes.

On the left side of the passage, two room-sized cavities had been carved out of the rock, perhaps starting from natural crevices, but the floors had been paved smooth with stone. Each of these chambers was walled from the corridor by a grid of iron bars set hard into the solid rock. The iron cell doors must have weighed hundreds of pounds each and might have seemed chillingly romantic in a pirate movie. Knowing the horror they had sustained, seeing them in this real life setting was gut-wrenching.

And this nausea required no imagination. As terrible as they had been, no images of kidnapped Africans long dead, their lives stolen and played out in utter hopelessness, were necessary. Because the cells weren't empty.

Locked behind the ironwork of the cruel chambers, so dim their faces were hard to make out, were what looked like more than a dozen young girls. The eldest couldn't have been more than thirteen. Some were younger than Elise.

And Elise was among them.

"You *animal!*" Beth screamed, wrenching her arms free and getting in one good pelt before Jones and the front guard caught her arms and bent them forcefully behind her. The other guard jabbed the end of his AK into Michael's chest before the sickening bile could raise a similar outburst in him.

"Mama." Elise sobbed, batting savagely as one of the other girls tried to comfort her.

Calderon seemed to have tired of the drama. He pivoted and pointed to the men. There were two more cells on that side, only these were much newer. The bars looked like modern alloy instead of iron, and the composite doors were secured not by heavy rusting keys but by twenty-first century code panels. These were unoccupied, but the material scraps and construction odds and ends jumbled inside them made clear that they had only recently been installed. Cartagena-Littleton, it appeared, was into a new line of business.

And expanding.

"Put these two in the new ones. *Separately*. We can't have any carnal shenanigans. We want our friend Ricardo to see we've preserved his interests. Besides, what would the other guests think."

Beth's outrage could not be contained. Even as the bastards cinched her arms to the point of injury, she could not restrain herself from lashing out.

"*How can you*," she seethed, her breathing heavy from the pain, "*sell children for sex?*"

"Farming's a bitch," Calderon snapped as the guards shoved her and Michael into the two expansion cells. The doors slammed shut with a nauseatingly solid and final-sounding clang. "Twelve-year-olds in Oregon are cooking crystal meth in their bathtubs. Junkies in Cleveland make their own XTC. They have no shipping costs. We can't compete. Hell, how long's it going to be before the states take over pot production? People grow it in their front yards because no one gets arrested anymore." Calderon sounded no different from the corporate brass in any turbulent industry. "The world changes. Businesses that don't adapt go extinct. As they should. *As they should*." He tossed Beth a genuinely indignant glare. "I don't create the markets, twinkle-toes. I simply deliver what the customers will buy."

"Rick can't possibly know about this."

Calderon spun one last time in the doorway. "He doesn't, if that's any consolation. We weren't ready to involve him yet, that's one reason we flew him out of here. Showing up with your girl was very bad timing. But he will come tomorrow, and it's going to be very interesting what he decides. I like Rick, I truly do, rebel or not. The only pure loyalty in this business comes from idiots. We need people like Rick, smart people with his kind of tenacity and resilience. But he's got a choice to make: we don't carry deadweight. He's got to show once and for all that the organization comes first. I hope he commits, but to tell you the truth I don't really care that much. By this time tomorrow we'll be rid of the problem either way. It will be more entertaining if he sides with us, and we'll finally have a real hook in him, but it won't change the outcome. Not for you." He fired a ghastly smirk. "Sleep tight."

JUAN CALDERON STOPPED BY HIS Isla Tesoro quarters just long enough to snatch his cell phone out of the charger. He made his way out onto the veranda. It was a glorious night, pleasant again now that all the unexpected guests had been put to bed, and the staff, save for the dog and the single patrol guard on duty, had made their way to their bunks for the night. It was the kind of warm, starry summer evening that reminded him of why he stayed in the tropics, why he took the steps necessary to gracefully defer overtures by the Organization that would have stationed him in New York or Chicago or Mexico City.

He preferred his villa on Martinique, a Caribbean castle outfitted with a level of taste and style that pretenders like

Rick DeLeon could not even fathom. But he loved Tesoro in a different way. Calderon was a criminal, however discrete, and he could not live anywhere truly in the open. Anywhere, that was, but here. On Martinique, he was an eccentric rich bastard who kept to himself with every thousand-dollar hooker in the islands on call. On Isla Tesoro ... *he was God*.

If he had his way, by this time next year, Isla Tesoro would be unrecognizable from the half-dead plantation it was now. Martinique style from the ground up. And the Organization would pay for it. He had the seed capital for this little investment in the palm of his hand.

When he was positive of his privacy, he punched the California number into the secure mobile. How convenient it was that the Castro spooks were all too happy to run his calls through their scrambler.

He keyed in the signal and waited for the call back. It came five minutes later.

A gruff voice issued from the handset before Calderon even had it to his ear. "I take it this is important."

"I believe so." Calderon relished the suspense. "In fact, you may be cross that I didn't call you sooner."

"Well, what is it, man? Spit it out. What's the crisis this time?"

"No crisis, friend. Quite the reverse. What would you say if I told you ... I have your number one loose end *locked in ice*, right here on Tesoro?"

There was silence, then a cough. Calderon smiled as he heard the unmistakable sounds of his superior chugging a hard shot.

"Don't fuck with me, Juan."

"Am I that guy?" Calderon laughed. "I sent you the message that my man in Boston might have a lead on this Bay Area clown. I didn't believe it myself, I just felt obliged to pass it along. Customer service, you know. But I don't think that anymore. It's a long story, but I've got him. The clown. Michael Chandler. Down in the slave pen under lock and key. And by this time tomorrow, unless you say otherwise … he's going to disappear from the face of the earth."

Another silence. Calderon could hear anxious breathing.

"You're not shitting me."

"You know I don't work like that."

"No, you don't." Calderon could almost hear the smile spreading across the face on the other end of the phone. "God damn. Well *god damn*! No, Juan, I don't have any intention of interfering with your plan. I don't want to know a thing about it. Not now, I mean. You can bet your life I'm going to want to hear every god damned detail as soon as you can get up here after the election."

"I'll commit it to memory," Calderon promised. "There won't be any pictures."

"You son of a gun." Eldridge Raymore had never sounded happier in all his life. "You *son of a gun!*"

CHAPTER 22
The Depths

IN MICHAEL CHANDLER'S THIRTY-TWO YEARS, there had never been a lower time.

When Max died at sixteen, Michael had not believed it. On an intellectual level, he understood it as fact: his brother Max was dead. He never denied to himself or others the veracity of that statement. But his soul refused to cope. When he wasn't thinking about it – and he almost never brought it to mind deliberately – it *felt* as though Max was just around the corner, in another room, joyriding with his friends. Max was dead, but it didn't *feel* like it. The world didn't know it yet. And as far as Michael was concerned, the world could damn well go on in this ignorance forever.

Because Max couldn't be gone. That was just not possible. It was too awful to contemplate, too hideous for God to allow. A sin against the universe. And so Max was dead, in the purely practical sense, but in the ways that really mattered, he lived on. And these contradictory perceptions coexisted in Michael's mind without a bellicose word because the alternative was inconceivable.

He had come out of this deluded rationalization so gradually he didn't even feel it happening. Only from the distance of a decade and a half was he fully cognizant that he had been in mourning and in a profoundly unsettled mental state.

His manifestations of grief had been more acute with Vicki. Having been scarred by death once before, his faculties were better prepared and thus paradoxically less effective in camouflaging the truth. He had cried for Vicki for days on end. He had not attended the funeral – he couldn't. He never made a conscious decision not to go, but simply fell into a catatonic state when the day came around. He had never apologized for this, to himself or anyone else, because he knew with inviolable certainty that Vicki was not in the urn that was consecrated that day, that Vicki was not at the ceremony at all, that funerals were for the grieving and not the deceased and that his grieving was of a nature far too personal to share in a public ritual.

For two years afterward, he had been not so much depressed as simply *numb*. Not numb in the sense of dull and dysfunctional, but rather incapable of feeling or expressing real joy. It hadn't kept him from helping others, hadn't blunted his empathy. In fact, his empathy was no doubt a factor in it – what emotional energy he had was directed toward others, with none left over to serve his own needs.

But over time, his work at Wal-Mart had functioned as a therapeutic salve, drawing him gently and, over time, fully back to the world of the living.

Both had been dark times, and there had been others, some of them within the past two weeks. But nothing that had come before compared to the way he was feeling now. Locked in a cell, an actual prison cell, not only imprisoned but condemned to die, and not as punishment or correction for deeds done wrong but as an unjust penalty for trying to do things *right*. Cramped in a dark stone chamber buried underground with no hope of rescue by some agent of justice because no agent of justice even knew he was there.

He had never felt so hopeless, so helpless, and utterly deprived of personal control. He felt completely and irreversibly defeated. He found to his horror that he could not even muster the initiative to pray.

WITH NO SUNLIGHT, NO CELL phone, no timepiece of any kind, the only way besides dead reckoning to estimate how much time had passed was following the transition between the TV shows the guard was watching on a personal video unit on the small desk he sat behind.

The shows were in Spanish, which would have made it nearly impossible, but Michael had learned enough of the language to help his Latino customers at Wal-Mart. By his measure, six dubbed half-hour American comedies had aired before there was a rattle at the dungeon door and Juan Calderon returned with a gun-toting henchman.

"Get the DeLeon girl," he ordered.

Javier Jones opened the cell just long enough to let Elise out, then locked it again and handed the keys over to the relief guard.

"Take her upstairs," Calderon told Jones. "Give Rick fifteen minutes with her alone, then bring her back here and go get some sleep. This is just to show him she is alive and well, I don't want any pressure taken off. Fifteen minutes, not a second more. Got it?"

Jones nodded. Elise was surprisingly well-composed given the context of the situation, probably at the prospect of seeing her dad. She turned to give Beth a wave and a smile as Jones led her out of the room.

"As you heard," Calderon addressed Beth, "your husband has arrived. He hasn't decided yet what should be done with you, though I suppose he could hardly be expected to sort things out quickly under the circumstances. He's in a bit of shock. I've given him the rest of the day, which will be plenty of time to assess *his* fate even if he can't make up his mind, which would be its own kind of answer, wouldn't it? But he *could* choose in the next hour or the next minute, and I suspect he won't be long once he's seen his daughter.

I would advise you to make peace with whatever god you fancy."

"Killing us will just make things worse on you." Beth scowled. "You've got to know that the CIA won't stand by for human trafficking right under their nose. Ignoring the drugs is one thing, but this crap—" She cast a glance toward the iron cells. "This won't fly."

For a moment, Calderon struggled to divine her meaning. Then all of a sudden he displayed a mirthful grin.

"Morocco Mole, is that who you mean?" Calderon laughed. "I pay him *ten times* as much as he gets from the CIA. That two-faced bastard is in as deep as anyone. He'd be the last one to piss in his own gravy."

Beth sank. It had been the one strand of hope she had been clutching.

"Oh, I almost forgot my reason for coming down in the first place. We found this." Calderon produced a cell phone from his pocket, and Beth recognized it at once. It was the secure device procured for her by Tony Pizarro.

"We found it under your Zodiac, naturally. I have to admit I was surprised to hear you'd told even that much truth. As for the phone ..." He eyed it narrowly. "It's a sweatshop knock-off, probably Brazilian, no serial number, no apps, no speed dial or anything else programmed ... looks like the protocols we use. No doubt for communication with whomever is supporting you on the outside. They do seem to know their stuff."

Beth glared.

"Curious, the Zodiac showed no sign of having been punctured and sunk. It has been now, though." His smile widened as the revelation came home.

"Even if it hadn't, that little pond-skimmer didn't have nearly enough fuel capacity to get here from Florida, let alone to get back. So we know you have an accomplice. We know it's not your military or spy agencies. They would have penetrated personally or just swarmed in with Apache helicopters. Therefore, it has to be some family member or friend. Probably waiting for a call to close in and extract you. So I've had the Cubans put a tap on this. If anyone calls, we'll be able to find their location by GPS, and as backup, I've got a couple of our speedboats out combing for any vessels in the vicinity that look out of place. We keep a few rocket-propelled grenade launchers on hand for just this sort of thing. Hell, I've got the whole staff out patrolling the island perimeter. I'm afraid there won't be any heroics by the cavalry."

The look in Beth's eyes was as pitiful as her daughter had ever mustered. Tears welled up in the corners.

"You could make it easier on them. If you'll tell us who they are and where to find them, I promise we'll shoot them in the head nice and clean after we've had a talk. If you don't, they're going to burn to death or drown. Burn and *then* drown, more likely."

Beth remained reticent, not so much in defiance as in uncertainty about which of these evils would harm Tony less.

"Still no? Well, that won't last much longer. Enjoy your dignity while you can. Rick will get it out of you, if he's smart. And if he isn't, we have some of the best persuaders in the world on staff."

MICHAEL LAY SLUMPED AGAINST THE wall that separated his cell from Beth's. He knew it was irrational and pointless, but he wanted to feel as close to her as possible.

He was lost in thought when suddenly he became conscious of a low tapping sound coming from the other side of the wall. It had been going on for some time in the background, he realized. Now that he was fully cognizant, he found that it was a repeating pattern. Two taps, then four. Two, then four. Two, four. A plumbing drip or mechanical malfunction wouldn't be so regular. It had to be Beth.

What was she doing? Trying to communicate with him? He cursed the fact that he could recall so little of the Morse Code he had learned as a Boy Scout. But no, it couldn't be Morse. Morse Code letters consisted of one to three charac- ters in dots and dashes, never four. He listened intently to see if he might be misinterpreting the pattern. But no, there could be no mistake. Dot-dot ... dot-dot-dot-dot ... Dot-dot ... dot-dot-dot-dot ...

What else could it be? The most obvious possibility was straight numeric substitution. If that was it, two taps would be the letter "B" and four would be "D."

BD.

Beth DeLeon.

Excited, Michael began tapping back. He sounded off in his head as he went: A-B-C-D ... all the way to "M," the thirteenth letter. After a brief pause, he added three taps for "C."

From the other side came a single tap. He waited a full ten seconds for some follow-up. Nothing came.

One tap? He knew Beth was trying to communicate, the two-four pattern had ceased immediately when he began tapping back. But what could one tap mean? The letter "A"? No, that led nowhere. So what was it? Was she just telling him she was lonely?

No. Beth was more practical than that. She had some- thing substantive in mind, he was sure of it.

He had an image of Old North Church in Boston, and Paul Revere's signal code. One if by land, two if by sea. Did she mean to say that a rescue by land was afoot? How could she know? Had she set something up ahead of time without telling him?

No, that made no sense. It would have been pointless and ill-advised to arrange for part of the plan without in- forming Michael or Tony. It was a dumb interpretation any- way – how could they be rescued by land? Calderon had dashed the hope that their one potential ally, the CIA plant, would lend a hand.

Maybe he was thinking too much. Maybe it had been a simple acknowledgement to confirm her comprehension of his "MC." One for yes maybe, two for no?

He tapped back once. Instantly, Beth tapped once in reply. He tapped once again to signal that yes, they were now on the same page.

Michael looked uneasily toward the guard on the other side of the bars. He seemed rapt in his television show. It appeared that the sound of it, and its command of his attention, were sufficient to keep him from noticing the covert exchange.

Beth began tapping a new message. Four dots: D. Nine for I. Nineteen for S. The next one was long and he suddenly lost count. *Damn!* He rapped urgently two times on the wall. Beth responded with one, then a pause, then she started over again. D...I...S...T... There were four more, and then she stopped. This time Michael picked up on them all. The word she had transmitted was "DISTRACT."

He waited several seconds to see if another word would come. There was silence. He tapped back again once to confirm his understanding. Again, silence. The lack of response did not concern him. He had signaled his comprehension, and now she was waiting for him to act. To tap any more would risk confusion or delay.

It was clear enough that she wanted the guard distracted, which meant specifically, Michael surmised, away from her. As it was, his perch behind the little metal desk gave him an oblique view into both of their cells, as well as those of the children. How could he get the man to turn around? And what was Beth going to do if he did? Had she worked her cell door open somehow?

He was eyeing the guard discreetly, casting about for a plan, when he noticed the silver pendant in the shape of a cross hanging around the man's neck. It gave him an idea.

"Hola, amigo, tengo tu permiso para hablar?" Michael waved respectfully, moving to the bars where he could converse with the man more naturally.

"Stick to English, *amigo*," the guard chastised. "Your accent is horrible. You and every other gringo took a couple years of Spanish in high school and think it makes you Emiliano Zapata."

"Prefiero morir de pie que vivir siempre arrodillado," Michael quoted, smiling. *I would rather die on my feet than live on my knees.*

The guard raised an eyebrow. "You know him?"

Michael nodded. "I didn't take Spanish in school. I taught myself, so I could help customers at my job. I rented movies and read lots of books in Spanish. I know I'm not very good, I just think it's beautiful."

The guard nodded his skeptical approval. "Maybe you're not so bad."

Michael leaned as far as he could in the guard's direction and lowered his voice. "Look, I don't mean to annoy you, and I know you don't have to give a shit. But that little girl over there ..." He pointed to Elise, who was curled right up at the edge of the bars in a fetal position, weeping quietly with her eyes fixed on Beth, a posture she had not relinquished since being dragged back in tears from the short visit with her father. It was all Michael could do to bury his anger about the little girl's misery, but he knew that whatever Beth was up to depended on it. So he forced a pleasant tone and went on. "This is the last time she's ever going to see her mother. Have a heart man, put her in with her mom. Let her have a hug to remember her by."

The man said nothing. Michael took that as a good sign.

"You have kids?" he asked gently.

"That's none of your business. Now shut the hell up and get out of my face."

Michael nodded deferentially. "I know, I'm sorry. I just meant ... I had a brother once. Somebody shot him as a kid. My mom went crazy, you know? She never got over it. And the worst part for her – she's said it over and over – was that she never got to say goodbye. She thought she could have accepted it, with God's help if it was His will, if she'd just had the chance to tell him she loved him. He was dead before she even knew it had happened. That just killed her, you know? It would have been so simple. But she never got the chance to say the things she wanted him to know, and it wrecked her for life."

Michael let the words sink in. There was something in the man's eyes, he couldn't tell exactly what, but something was going on behind them.

"I have two," the man said finally. "Used to be three. My son was shot."

"God, I'm sorry." Michael looked down. He didn't have to pretend sympathy. "I had no idea. I didn't mean to make you think of it."

"He was thirteen years old," the guard went on. His eyes had a faraway look, as though he was barely conscious of Michael's presence. "He was so proud. He had just made it into the gang. *Los Águilas.* *My* old gang. They'd just given him the bandana and he was riding his bike to his friend's house to show how proud he was to be like his dad. And some rival banger shot him from a car just for wearing the colors."

The man's features hardened bitterly. "He was just a kid. A fucking kid, man. A good kid. I know what all you pampered white boys think when you hear the word "gang." Well, you don't know a damn thing. In those neighborhoods, you either gang up or you don't make it to eighteen. That's all it was. He was no criminal; he was just getting on with his normal kid life. And some fucker drives by and pops him. A little boy on a fucking bike."

Michael gave a solemn nod, saying nothing.

"My boy did not deserve to die. He never did a god damn thing."

Michael spoke so quietly he almost couldn't hear himself. "That girl did nothing to deserve being here. Just like your son. None of them did. You can't do anything for the rest of them, but you *can* for her. Her mother's right there, and she's only got a few hours to live. You could make the difference."

The guard was silent. Michael held his tongue and held his breath. *Please God*, he prayed. *I know I'm going to die. I'm not asking for myself. If it's Your will, then take me. But help Elise. Help Beth too if you can, but at least help Elise. She shouldn't even be here. Please help this man do the right thing.*

A full minute went by. Then two. Michael cast about in his mind for something to say. Each time he started, he stifled himself before the words could leave his lips. He was terrified of saying the wrong thing, of making just the wrong move and tipping the guard's wavering sentiments down the wrong side of the balance. *Please, God. Please.*

It hadn't worked. Slowly, his gaze never leaving the floor, Michael turned to pace back to his cramped station where the bars met the wall he shared with Beth, feeling helpless and mortally sad.

A chair leg scraped against the stone floor. A key chain jangled. From the corner of his eye, still not daring to look, Michael saw the guard cross to the cell where Elise was being held and unlock the door.

There was a blur, then a sickening thud. The guard crashed into the iron bars as if blown by an explosion, then collapsed like a rag doll, still breathing but utterly unconscious.

A six foot length of alloy bar, left over from the recent construction, protruded horizontally from Beth's cell, its far end caked with the man's blood and hair.

"Jesus Christ!" Michael choked.

"Elise, honey, bring over the keys," Beth's voice barked, low but insistently. "Hurry, honey. Hurry!"

There was a scramble in Elise's cell as seven girls milled about frantically like goldfish in an overcrowded bowl, searching for the dropped keys in the gloom. There was a jingle, a skitter, then: "Noooo!"

"They went down the hole!" one of the girls cried, while another accused, "Tasha, you kicked it!" and a third, all at the same time: "It fell in the potty hole!"

The shrillness in Beth's voice bordered on insanity. "Quick, honey, go through his pockets. Check his pockets and the desk. Maybe he has another set. Do it now, sweetie, hurry!"

"Your lock isn't opened with a key," spoke a clear, tiny voice from the gloom of the iron cell that was still locked.

"What, hon?" Beth asked.

"It's not a key. It's numbers."

"Michael?"

"Oh, shit, that's right," Michael agonized. "Our doors aren't key locks, Beth, they're code pads. Ours are brand new."

"Oh, God damn it. Shit! Shit! Shit!" Beth sounded ready to burst.

"I know what it is," spoke the little voice.

Everyone stopped. Beth tried to regain herself. "What what is, honey?"

"The code. I saw when the man put you in there. He did the cross. Like this." The little girl, about nine years old by the look of her and speaking with an accent that might have been Australian or more likely South African, made the traditional Sign of the Cross over her chest.

"What do you mean, honey?" Beth was frantic again.

"The buttons," Michael interjected. "He did the buttons in that order. Is that right?"

"Yes," the girl agreed. "Like a little Jesus cross."

"Come over to the door," Beth told Elise. "Punch the buttons like the cross."

"I don't—"

"What does the pad look like?" Michael strained. He could not get an angle on the bars of his cell to see either his own door pad or the one on Beth's chamber.

"It's just like a phone," Elise replied. "Mama, what do I push?"

Beth thought to herself, recalling the little girl's gesture. "Okay. Start with two, then ... eight, then four, then six

...? Try that, Elise. Two, eight, four, six."

Elise punched the buttons as she was told, then pulled the lever. It wouldn't budge.

"It didn't work, ma!"

Michael was thinking. The clarity, determination, and single-mindedness that had always manifested in him at such times was rolling in full gear.

"Try the other way," he told Elise. "Two, eight, six, four. That's the way it would look from the front. The way your mom said was backwards because her left is that girl's right."

"Try it!" Beth barked.

Again Elise followed orders. Again the latch stood tight. "It didn't work," she whined, this time starting to cry.

"Use zero," Michael boomed. "Not eight, zero. We've been doing a plus sign, not a cross."

"Two, zero, six, four," Beth affirmed. "Do it, Elise!"

Two, zero, six, four ... Elise gave the handle a third try. And this time, it gave.

"Oh my God!" Beth DeLeon was crying as she burst from the cell and held her daughter for the first time since the ordeal began. "You did perfect, sweetie. Just perfect!"

"Did you see mine?" Michael asked, addressing the girl in the still-locked cell. "What was mine?"

"I didn't see," the girl lamented. "He was blocking it."

Beth released her daughter and regained her focus. They were still a very long way from freedom.

"Maybe it's the same," she said quickly. "What did you do, honey? Two, zero, six ... four?"

Beth punched the numbers and pulled the handle to Michael's door. It, too, swung free.

"Thank God!" Beth almost screamed, eyes skyward. Michael echoed the words silently.

He knelt down beside the guard and felt his neck for a pulse. From this vantage point, the head wound did not appear too severe. "Not dead," he announced. "He won't be out forever."

Beth picked up the bar she had let clang to the floor and hefted it for one more determined blow.

"No." Michael stepped in front of her, grabbing the bloodied instrument with his left hand. "He was letting her out. That's not our way."

Beth glared for a moment, then nodded in self-reproach and set the improvised weapon back down.

"Get the other ones, Mommy." Elise pulled at Beth's shirt sleeve. "We have to save them, too!"

"Oh God," Beth breathed, her thoughts scattered. "Where's the key?"

"It went down the hole," one of the girls reminded.

"Hole?" Beth was perplexed.

Michael entered the empty cell and got down on his hands and knees. Toward the back, the stone masonry floor was interrupted by a circular hole about a foot wide. The smell made its function pungently clear.

"I can't see," he called. "Is there a flashlight or something?"

Beth rifled through the desk and brought him a small box of wooden matches. Michael lit three together and peered down the toilet shaft.

A traditional outhouse setup it was not. The drop was at least ten feet; the match light was inadequate to judge properly. And there was no tank. It was just a rocky cavity, the sides of which he could barely make out, and sewage appeared to have simply splattered on the ground. No keys were visible, but if they had been, they would have been well out of arm's reach. There was no way to retrieve anything from the hole. It was too deep, far too narrow for even a child to drop inside, and even if they could, once down there, there was no way to get back up.

But he did see *something*, something totally unexpected, something so hope-restoring that it made him cry out in joy.

"Pipes!"

"What?" Beth got down on her hands and knees to see

better.

The matches went out. Michael struck another three and pointed into the gloom.

"Do those look like pipes to you? Like plumbing?"

Beth gasped. "It's the sewer cave!"

Michael spoke so fast he was almost unintelligible. His heart was pumping wildly.

"You said it was a lava tube, right? So it's probably big enough to crawl through. And we know it goes all the way to the beach."

"Yeah, but Michael— we can't get down there. None of us. You could barely fit a baby through that."

"Give me the bar. The one you hit him with."

Michael ran his fingers along the masonry seams as Beth retrieved the pole. He couldn't tell how brittle they were by touch, but it was evident that they were very old. A couple of hundred years, quite possibly, and scored with tiny fissures from natural settling of the rock, in addition to whatever deterioration the mortar had suffered from age.

Michael stuffed the match box into his pocket and stood up. He gripped the bar firmly in both hands and lifted it above his head. "Stand back," he warned, and Beth retreated out of his way.

He brought the pole down as hard as he could. It clanged against the rock and shuddered painfully in his hands. He had missed the seam.

He pulled back once more and eyed the floor more carefully. Again he brought the tool down with all his earthly force.

He struck a seam dead-center about six inches from the lip of the hole. There was a satisfying *crack*, and a good ten by twelve inch section of the floor broke free and shattered in the chamber below.

"It worked!" Michael cackled like a madman. "Look, Beth, we can get down there! We can get down there!"

"Oh dear God. Thank you, *thank you* Lord." Beth was breathing fast and heavy, tears of joy pouring down her cheeks.

Michael turned and stuck again. Another chunk of floor dislodged. Now the gash was easily large enough for the smaller girls to pass through.

He struck again. And again. In less than two minutes, he had cleared enough jagged space for them all to slip through.

Michael stepped out into the corridor and looked at the girls in the remaining locked chamber. He spoke to the one who had provided the key code, a pretty, soft-featured young lady still wearing the summer party dress she must have been kidnapped in, her face dirty, hair scraggly, but human spirit burning in her intelligent blue eyes.

"What's your name, sweetie?" he asked.

"Felicity."

Michael knelt down close to the bars and reached out his hands, taking one of hers. It seemed impossibly small.

"Felicity, my name is Michael. You are one special, wonderful girl. What you did today has saved every person in this place. And God will bless you for it."

"Okay." Her voice was thin, terribly lonely.

"Now, I'm going to go down in the tunnel there and get the keys so we can let the rest of you out. Then I'm going to get us out of here, every single one. God is going to protect us."

"Okay." Felicity allowed herself a small, not quite convinced but hopeful smile.

Because I refuse to believe He would grace us with this divine fortune only to feed us back to the wolves, Michael told himself. *Because the God I believe in wants these children free.*

"We'll have you out in a minute," he promised, addressing all of the children in the locked chamber, his voice fierce with conviction. "We're not leaving you here." A couple nodded their heads. A few began to cry. He could see they feared that his words were hollow.

Felicity hunched right up against the iron barrier, crowding it with her belly and face, pressing both palms up against the cruel iron.

"I believe in you, Michael," she said.

He paused one moment longer to stoop down right where Felicity stood and superimposed his palms over hers across the bars. Pulling them off again was one of the hardest things he had ever done. Because while he meant what he was saying, and believed what he was thinking, the bottom line was that you couldn't predict what God was actually going to do. He hadn't saved 'Baby Grace' from that horrific beating in Houston that still haunted Michael just from seeing it on the news. He hadn't saved six million Jews from Hitler's ovens. He hadn't saved Max Chandler for that matter, or Vicki, or Rosie Hart. And all of them had deserved better. Michael wasn't challenging God – in the bottom of his heart he felt there must be reasons for all of this, that some overlying truth must, when properly understood, make those tragedies right. But Michael did not have that understanding, and the lesson was clear: you could never assume that just because something *looked* right, it would receive positive divine support. And without intervention from Heaven, Michael had no clue how he was going to get back here and free these girls.

But none of that was for Felicity to know. "It's going to be all right," he told her softly. "Just hold on."

He returned quickly to the chamber breach. "Listen, Beth," he instructed, now fully on his game. "I'm going to jump down there. Nobody else come just yet. I'm going to find those keys so we can let the other girls out. Then I'll jump back down and you can lower the kids to me, one by one, as far as you can reach. I'll catch them so they don't hurt themselves. Then you'll come last."

"Michael, we don't have time. They could come down here any minute!"

"It'll go fast. Stop talking, just *do*."

Michael lowered himself into the hole, suspended by his elbows. Then he eased himself as far as he could, hanging by just his hands. It was still a long way down, but there was no alternative. And Beth was right: they had not a second to waste.

He dropped.

Even though he braced for it, the hard jolt shuddered his knees. He slipped hard on the film of raw sewage and lost his footing. He went down on his side, banging his left elbow hard enough to cut it on the rocks. But he was all right. He shook off the daze, got to his feet, and managed to light a couple of matches by touch.

Down here, the stench was overpowering. Even with plumbing shielding the waste water from the house, air currents unavoidably blew fumes from the terminus on the beach back up into the tunnel, where rising heat trapped them indefinitely. And weeks of raw sewage from the cells accumulating openly on the tunnel floor created an odor so thick Michael thought he could feel it on his skin.

He cast about looking for the keys. They were nowhere in sight. He cursed the inadequacy of the matches and wished he had even the feeblest kiddy flashlight at hand. He got on his hands and knees, ignoring the wretched filth that was getting all over his arms and clothes.

Still no keys. He was on his third pair of matches and there was no sign of them. He began to fear that they may have sunk into the mud completely out of sight, or wound up under a rock, or even slipped into a crevice in the uneven surface, some niche he would be unable to fish them out of even if he found it. And it occurred to him for the first time that he may not find them at all. It was horrifying. He couldn't contemplate leaving those other girls to the wrath of Calderon and his minions. But searching on hands and knees through every inch of muck where the keys might have caromed to rest would take hours. There was just too much ground and too little light, and—

"Michael!"

—too little time.

"Michael, there's some kind of commotion happening upstairs," Beth yelled urgently. "We have to go *now*."

Michael lit three fresh matches and took a few steps down the passage. Visibility ended in gloom, but the way was open for the short distance he could see. He couldn't be sure, it was just too faint and small, but he thought he could make out a speck of light in the blackness far, far down and away. Sunlight, it would have to be. The way out, if not the way home.

He glanced overhead to make sure. As expected, the locked cell had its own "potty hole." It appeared pretty much identical to the one they had broken, and he could see from the underside that most of the flooring for both chambers had been constructed of masonry laid over massive oiled timbers. It was a stroke of luck that there had been enough space between them to break a hole the right size.

He started to call for Beth to toss the bar down so he could try breaking the trapped girls free from below. But he cut himself off, shaking his head angrily at the futility of it. It had required all of his strength, leveraging the full mass of his body, to effect blows powerful enough to break the mortar from above. Down here, there was no way to muster that confluence of force. The muscles for jabbing upward were a good deal weaker than those for hammering down, the target was too far overhead to maximize even that weaker motion, and his body weight could not be brought to bear at all. As if to discourage him completely, the wood framing intruded so close to the hole that he wasn't sure the girls could clear the beam even if the hole was widened.

"*Michael!*" Beth's voice was frantic, laced with terror now. And even Michael thought he could hear ominous machinations taking place somewhere in the house above them.

It was an agonizing decision. It felt impossible to make, and facing it made Michael feel utterly alone despite the frantic swirl of humanity around him. But ultimately, he knew, there really *was* no choice. To linger would jeopardize not only the girls that remained locked up, but also the ones now clinging to a genuine chance of escape. Tarrying to save everyone might easily wind up dooming them all.

"Give them the bar," he called up with ashen grimness. "At least let them see what they can do with their hole." He felt so dismal he couldn't bring himself even to explain how or shout encouragement to the girls they were abandoning. It wouldn't do any good, and he knew it. They had no light to aim their blows. They didn't have the strength to breach the mortar. And they would break their legs or arms or necks jumping down unassisted even if they did.

It wasn't much better for the rest of them. They had no plan for getting off the island. They had nothing to eat and no fresh water if Calderon's men had trashed or taken their stores when they discovered the Zodiac. They could not hope to prevail without weapons against a camp of armed and ruthless men.

But at least, for the kids that were out, there was *some* chance. And given slim or none, there was nothing for it but to go with slim and give it the best you could.

"Give the trapped girls the bar," Michael repeated, "and start lowering the other ones down. Let's make this count."

CHAPTER 23
Leap of Faith

ELISE WENT FIRST. BETH LOWERED her daughter into the hole until Michael could touch her feet, made doubly sure he was ready to catch her, then with a gasp dropped her into the murk. Michael knew it must be wrenching for her, unable to see into the shaft at all, but there was no choice. It was easier for Michael, who, looking up, could clearly see the girl's outline. Even so, Michael had lifted Elise incidentally a couple of times during their Boston frolic, and it surprised him how much heavier she felt from the short distance drop. He caught her at the waist, narrowly averting a slip on the wet floor that would have brought both of them crashing down. He learned from that, taking a step backward and bracing his feet a bit wider against the rock to keep him from sliding.

For a moment, he was afraid that Beth would jump down next in her anxiousness to get them out of the area. But she dutifully followed with the next girl, one of the eldest and heaviest. *Conserving her strength*, Michael thought admiringly. *She knows she's going to start running out of steam.* He felt sure that if she had gone on pure emotion, the littlest ones would have been first.

It was grueling and at times painful, and twice the catch was so awkward that Michael slipped off one of the rocks. In casual circumstances, they may not have physically been able to do it, but adrenaline served its purpose. Even with momentary pauses between each drop to recharge their batteries, it took only three minutes to get all seven girls down. Beth lowered herself into the hole and plunged blindly into Michael's arms. He stopped her fall only inches from hitting the ground.

"Ugh, the *smell*!" Beth's face contorted in the match light as Michael struck one for illumination and silently counted heads to make sure all the girls were accounted for.

"It's the smell of freedom," Michael chirped cheerily. "Come on, let's get out of here."

Their eyes met, and Beth seemed to suddenly grasp the situation for the first time, to realize that they had made it out of the makeshift prison, that they actually had a chance now to avoid the awful fate that had appeared inescapable just an hour before, and that she could never have gotten out of the dungeon, metal bar or no, without the ingenuity and strength of the man standing before her.

"Oh, Michael, I'm so sorry. I was so *stupid*," she said quietly as they paused to catch their breath. "I didn't know it was in you. If you hadn't come here with me I would have had no chance. I'll never forget this, Michael. Never." There was an unmistakable promise in the tone of her voice: *When we're safe back home, I'll make it up to you. For the rest of our lives.*

"Michael smiled and gave her a quick hug, then struck another match and held the box out to Beth. "I'll lead us down, you stay behind the girls and keep matches lit so we can see. Use three at a time. It's not much, but it helps."

"Just a sec." Beth fiddled with something in her hand, and to his amazement, Michael saw that she was packing Javier Jones's Uzi.

"I found it in a drawer while we were looking for spare keys," she explained. Michael's optimism spiked. *God must be on our side.* He smiled to himself. And though he knew it was no guarantee of success, the thought improved his mood one hundred percent.

Michael got down on his hands and knees while Beth lit new matches. "Hold hands, girls, and follow me. And watch your heads."

He set off down the shaft, feeling his way along the drainage pipe. After ten minutes of slow descent, he caught his first clear glimpse of greenery outside the tunnel. *Twenty yards*, he calculated. *Just twenty yards to fresh air and daylight.*

Harsh sounds erupted from behind and above. The violent shouts reminded Michael of the chaos surrounding his escape from the car crash and put him in the same frame of mind.

"Yell up the tunnel," he instructed Beth tersely. "As loud as you can. Turn your head so they'll hear and yell that we can't get through."

Beth stared at him incredulously. "Are you insane?"

"Calderon said his guys are all out patrolling the perimeter. If he thinks we're down here and having trouble, he'll go upstairs and call them inside to come down after us. It'll clear the grounds and buy us some time."

"Time for what?" Beth tried to keep her voice down, but there was really no way for them to speak without the children hearing. "What exactly are we going to do when we get outside?"

Michael paused, realizing that he had been assuming, frankly without any firm basis for doing so, that Beth had a plan in mind. She was the one who knew the island, and she had been the planner of this caper all along. The fact that she hadn't already figured this out came as a shock. That she was looking to *him* for answers was even more so.

"In the back of my mind I guess I was thinking of the boats," she followed up. "But he's got those patrols out, and he specifically said they were watching the docks. Even if we managed to grab one, they'd just get in the others and come after us with their rocket launchers."

Michael pondered. They *might* be able to sneak past and take one of the boats, and they might be able to get away if it took their pursuers some time to get the weapons. Barring that, they might be able to sneak back into the house, find a phone, and contact Tony or Beth's father, maybe even steal food and guns. They *might* be able to hold out in the jungle until help arrived.

But there was a better idea, one that circumvented all the risks of the above, one that *guaranteed* escape if they could only get to it.

"Does Calderon know you can fly?"

Beth paused. "I don't know. I don't think so. But if you're thinking of the plane, that's already crossed my mind. Who knows if it's unlocked with the keys inside, or has any fuel, or has even been maintained. It's an old piece of junk, I remember that much. And it won't take all nine of us, that, I guarantee."

"Why not?"

"There are weight limits," she said in an exasperated tone, speaking quickly, mindful that precious time was racing by. "And balance. Those little planes are highly sensitive to distribution of payload. There are whole calculations you need to do before attempting a trip with close to capacity weight. And it doesn't matter, Michael, because we wouldn't all fit. You can't cram nine people into ..." She paused, and lowered her voice even further. "It would take the three of us. That it would do. I'd hate to leave these girls, but wouldn't it be better to save some of us than none?"

"No." Michael's voice was firm. "It's bad enough leaving the others back there. We've got to find a way to take these kids with us. Let's at least see if we can get up there and *look* at the plane. Yell up the tunnel like I said, it might help, and it can't make things worse."

"I don't think ..."

"Beth." Michael stood, felt his way to the rear of the procession, and pulled her to him. He laid her head gently on his shoulder and softly patted her hair. "We're going to get out of this. I *know* we are. I can't explain how but I can *feel* it. There *is* a God ... there's no time to explain how I know that right now, but I will when we're safe. And God does not want us to die. God doesn't want these children forsaken. He would not have brought us here and showed us the way out of those cells without a purpose."

He could feel Beth quietly shuddering against him. Her warm tears began to soak through his shirt.

"Let's go look at the plane. His guys will be everywhere *but* around the house. If you still don't think it will work, we'll try to hide in the woods and steal a boat after dark." He gave her one last affectionate squeeze. "Be strong. Have faith. God will protect us."

Beth sniffed and composed herself. She left his embrace and turned back toward the slave pens.

"GOD DAMN IT!" she bellowed, cupping her hands like a megaphone. "IT'S BLOCKED! WE'RE TRAPPED DOWN HERE! *WHAT THE HELL ARE WE GOING TO DO?"*

"Good girl." Michael laughed giddily and returned to his place in the lead. "Okay, kids, here we go. Stay together and move as fast as you can."

Beth didn't bother with any more matches. There was enough daylight at this end of the passage to light their way.

And then they were out. Though he had been here less than a day before, Michael found the surroundings utterly unfamiliar. The jungle looked completely different than it had appeared in the dark, and what was even more disorienting, it was different than he had imagined in his mind's eye. The cliff face was not stark cold stone but instead gloriously draped in lush green growth, and there were flowers – huge tropical blossoms in a myriad of shapes and a rainbow of colors – tucked into cliff crevices, sprouting from the ground cover, hanging from the trees like waterfalls suspended in time.

And there was no need to recognize their surroundings in order to find the way up. The trail of broken branches and trampled grass Beth and Michael had blazed the night before was as obvious as a paved road.

They made much better time in the morning light and with a clearly demarcated path. It took less than a quarter of an hour to get the girls, who were to the very last one brave and discreet the entire time, to the edge of the clearing at the very spot where the two adults had worked out their plan to spring Elise.

The plane was there, parked in front of the Quonset hut exactly as it had been the night before, its nose pointing toward the cliff and to Florida beyond. And again, as the night before, there was no one in sight.

Eyeing the craft in daylight, Michael began to feel his own twinge of doubt. Judging by the undergrowth entangling the landing hear, the plane might not have been used in years. The Quonset was only large enough for one small aircraft, and it looked like the better bird had been kept sheltered while this one languished in the elements. With the plane's faults up close and personal, Michael began to feel genuinely concerned. He did his best to hide it for the girls' sake. The sober fact was that they had no choice.

"Stay with the kids," Beth hissed in Michael's ear. "I'll see if it's unlocked and ready, but Michael, I'm telling you, we can't all fit."

Michael's only reply was to pat her shoulder in encouragement.

Beth turned Javier Jones's automatic pistol in one hand and very deliberately, with what looked like far more force and certainly more emotion than was necessary, snapped the safety to OFF. She extended the stock, then changed her mind and tucked it in again to make it easier to run. She took one last glance right and left to confirm that the coast was still clear, then bolted from the brush like an Olympic sprinter.

Almost immediately, from around the opposite end of the house, out raced the Doberman.

"*No*, Pancho!" Elise screamed.

How he thought of it, he could not have said. All Michael knew was that he was in the zone, that focused, calmly resolute mindset that possessed him invariably at such times. He broke into the clearing in the direction of the dog, waving one arm and shouting for its attention, reaching into his pocket with the other hand.

Instinctively threatened by the motion on its flank, the attack dog checked its stride and turned to face him, teeth bared, growling with unbridled hostility.

Michael sank to his knees, holding his arms apart in an unthreatening gesture. He spoke with a convincing calm that anyone watching would have thought incongruous in the circumstances, if not outright insane.

"It's okay, boy. Come here, Pancho. Look what I've got for you."

The dog rushed him, barking a staccato alarm. Michael stood his ground. The dog was muscular, large for its breed, naturally ruthless. If it chose to attack him full bore, Michael was utterly without recourse to defend himself.

The dog stopped four feet away, eyes blazing, mouth drooling, poised to spring on its quarry like a viper.

"It's okay. That's a good boy." Michael fought to maintain dispassion, brought his right hand around slowly, holding forth the strip of beef jerky Beth had given him the night before.

The dog padded deliberately closer. It was now only two feet away, its eyes level with Michael's in the kneeling position. Michael hunched down even lower to allow the animal a sense of dominance.

"Here you go," Michael soothed, switching his gaze to an oblique angle he hoped the dog would interpret neither as threatening nor fully submissive.

The growling stopped. The Doberman's head moved tentatively in the direction of the food. Michael remained motionless. He tried to breathe easily, to appear neither confrontational nor frozen in terror like helpless prey. The dog was so close now he could feel the heat of its breath on his fingers.

Slowly, keeping an eye on Michael the whole time, the

attack dog lowered its head. The ears like helmet spikes re-laxed. Its front teeth clamped gingerly on the dried meat and tugged it out of Michael's grasp.

Pancho lowered himself onto the grass, gnawing the treat with satisfaction. Michael backed away slowly, careful-ly, never raising his profile, keeping up a continuous patter in low, reassuring tones. When he had retreated about twenty feet without sparking any renewed alarm, he got slowly to his feet, turned his back with a display of confidence he did not feel, and quietly returned to the children.

Beth was making her way back now, no longer running but trotting casually in a conscious effort to maintain the dog's calm, monitoring it with fleeting, furtive glances. She reached Michael and the children just as Pancho appeared to have finished the jerky and was starting to get back up. Michael deftly chucked the remaining piece of dried meat in the dog's direction. It landed near his feet, and Pancho eased himself down again for a second course.

"I hope you have good news." Michael hugged her. "I'm fresh out of dog food."

"The keys are there," she said flatly. "It looks like there's fuel, it wouldn't take much anyway. But Michael—"

"Then let's go." Michael made a gesture to get the girls that were sitting or squatting in the grass to their feet. "Pan-cho won't be my buddy for long. And if any of Calderon's guys show up …" He mimed turning out his pockets with a grin. "I've got nothing to throw them at all."

Beth took one last, hard look at him, her features dark-ening in resignation. She closed her eyes in what might have been prayer, or just a ritual to gird her resolve. When she opened them, she turned to the children.

"Come on."

The nine of them left the safety of the island foliage, moving across the field in a bright daylight that was no lon-ger their friend. They were halfway across, Michael glanc-ing left to confirm that Pancho had not yet had a reversal of mood, when a sprinkle of automatic gunfire erupted to their right, from the direction of the docks.

Michael snapped back just in time to see one of Calderon's personal guards charging up the dirt track road, an AK-47 clutched in both hands. He jerked to a halt and brought the weapon up to firing position.

Beth swung the Uzi up to eye level and squeezed the trigger. A scatter of bright red pimples erupted on the guard's face, spurting blood as he went down in a clump.

Beth froze like a mannequin, her eyes like saucers, her mouth agape in horror. She stared at the Uzi in disbelief, then flung it away, spinning with all her might as though she'd been holding a rattlesnake.

She wiped a trickle of moisture off her cheek with the back of her hand, cursing when she saw that it was not sweat but blood. Apparently the man she had shot had nicked her with a round of his own.

"Get them in," she huffed tersely as she yanked open the plane's left-side door and then raced around it for a frenzied pre-flight check that her discipline would not excuse even in these conditions.

Michael pulled the other door open and hauled the smallest girl in. To his dark dismay, he finally understood what Beth had been trying to tell him.

The little plane was virtually a two-seater, its rear bench capable of accommodating three children abreast but intended more as luggage space than as a seat. The cockpit's ceiling sloped to the point where any adult sitting in back would feel the top of his head would be right up against it. Nine people, even mostly small girls, could never possibly, not in a million years …

Never mind, he told himself. *God will make this work.*

He tucked the first girl onto the floor behind the pilot's seat and told her not to worry, that it was going to be cramped when he fit all the girls in and it might be uncomfortable, but that she should just pull in her arms, close her eyes, and think about how happy she was going to be when they brought her back to her mommy and daddy. The innocent, trusting look on the little girl's face nearly broke his heart. She hunkered down as small as she could get and closed her eyes obediently.

It would be easiest, he thought, to do it left to right, smallest to biggest. That way, he reasoned, any contortions required of the larger girls could be done on his side, where any sitting on laps and encroachment of limbs into the fore compartment would not impair the pilot. So he loaded them in size order; size order, that was, except for Elise. Though his focus remained on the task, Michael could not quite evade the grim awareness that there was an ulterior motive in his seating plan. Beth, he feared, was liable to panic and get the plane going the minute she and her daughter were aboard. She could be forgiven for favoring her own flesh over these strangers. She could, but Michael could not. He could never forgive himself. Helping the ones in the locked cell had been out of his reach, but saving these girls was not. And he was going to make dead sure they hadn't been brought out in vain.

He loaded the girls quickly, helping tuck in their extremities, entreating each girl to be brave and deal with the stifling congestion as best she could, that it would be a short flight and they would be back with their parents in no time if they could only brace themselves and do this one hard thing. The trust in every teary eye was the same. Every girl they had rescued was relying on, believing in, his every word.

Five of them were in now, crammed like turtles into the aft bench area and two with their legs protruding around the edges of Michael's seat. He motioned for the sixth girl, largest of them all, to sit temporarily in that seat while he sat Elise on the grass beneath the wing and mulled over how to fit the three of them into the remaining space.

"Michael!" Beth shrieked at him from the other door. "This is *not* going to work! Pull some of them out and get Elise in here so we can go!"

Finally the strain broke him. He was overcome by that most foreign and terrifying of all his emotions: anger. It was

Rosie in his arms, Max in the mini-mart, Vicki in the fire. Michael Chandler had taken all he could bear of feeling like he had let people down, like he had failed to save an innocent life because of circumstances beyond his control or even worse, because of choices he had made, or could have made but had not. Like hell was he going to stand here one more instant and tolerate obstruction from this woman who, by her own admission, owed her own life to his sacrifice and yet had the gall to tell him he would have to let others die.

"I am *not*," he bellowed, "going to stand by and let you eject *one single girl from this airplane*. Do you hear me, Beth? You think we can't fit everyone in? Then leave me. Just fucking leave *me*. Because I'll be God damned if I'm going to take a ride out of here and leave any of these frightened little girls behind."

Beth glared at him and he glared right back. Five full seconds went by. "Damn you," Beth spat through her tears, jerking herself up into the pilot's seat. And Michael could see, with utter transparency though she would have rather obscured it, that her anguish was not anger or disagreement or even fright. It was admiration. Finally, Beth could see that he was only doing what was right, and her tears came from a mixture of awe-inspired love and bitter shame. How could she have suggested that this man should compromise his principles, this man whose selflessness toward strangers extended all the way to laying down his life? For she had no doubt that he would actually stay behind so the children could go.

Some things, apparently, were worth dying for. Everyone said it, but who had ever had to back it up? Here was one man, Michael Chandler, who would. She loved and hated him for it.

A burst of assault fire perforated the air and a spray of bullets pinged off the fuselage just as the plane's engine spun to life. Michael dove in front of the girls and flung out his arms in a lame effort to protect them. More bullets glanced off the wing. He whirled and whisked Elise into the seat next to the last girl. He had intended to go first, being the heaviest, with the two girls sitting on his lap, Elise on the left so she and her mother could touch. But there could be no deference to thoughtful arrangement now. Michael's body and the airframe itself were all that stood between the gunman and the girls.

Michael jerked his head in the direction of the sound. The man with the assault rifle had pulled it down and was moving in for a closer shot. It was Fernando Lopez, Beth's cousin-in-law. *You black-hearted son of a bitch*, Michael fumed. *You're shooting at your cousin's daughter.*

Behind Lopez, standing at the base of the porch, was another man shouldering a long, sleek sniper rifle. Even a firearms know-nothing like Michael knew you weren't going to miss from this distance with a scope like that. Not if you knew what you were doing.

And he knew the sniper knew what he was doing. It was Rick DeLeon.

Lopez halted twenty yards from the plane. At this distance he could easily target not only Michael, but Beth in the pilot's seat. One shot could bring them all down: if the pilot died, the rest of them would, too. And if Lopez missed, Rick DeLeon surely would not.

Michael had to move. He was under no illusion that he could do anything to stop the gunfire. Nor could he outrun it himself. But if he could shut the door, Beth and the kids would have at least some protection. If he didn't, they would be exposed the minute his body fell.

There was no time. Michael could see the gun poised against Lopez's shoulder. He could see the man's left eye squint as he lined up his shot in the iron sights.

There was a harsh, echoing explosion. It was the same sound as the warning shot that had stopped Michael in his tracks carrying Elise on the veranda the night before, a single .50 cal round bursting from the barrel of an AS50 at nearly three thousand miles per hour.

Fernando Lopez's head exploded like a watermelon hit

with a sledge hammer, and what was left of him flew forward like a running back leaping a goal line pile.

At the foot of the porch, Rick DeLeon took his hand off the trigger and lowered the sniper gun to his waist. He held it harmlessly by the barrel with his left hand, his eyes meeting Michael's with a resigned and weary gaze.

There was no time to wonder, think, or soak in the emotion. Already, other men were pouring out of the house, trying to make sense of what they saw. It would only be seconds before they pieced it together and brought their own weapons to bear.

Michael jammed himself through the door and into a hunch across the two girls' laps. He heaved the door shut and found himself shoved right on top of the center console. There was nothing he could do about it; he had crammed nine people into a vehicle meant for no more than three, and there simply was not one more inch available without breaking a bone.

Beth had the old plane lumbering along the grass runway even before Michael yanked shut the door. In his peripheral vision, he could see that Beth's anxiety hadn't waned. She had resolved herself to try this – what choice did she have? But she was far from happy about it. In fact, if anything, her reasoned protests seemed to have morphed into a kind of fatalistic hysteria.

She seemed to be babbling to herself as the aircraft picked up speed. "A 150. It *would* be a god-damned 150. Of *course* it would. Why else would Castro dump it for a song? Fucking Pinto. Fucking Air Corvair. Come on, baby, come on. You can do it. Get your wings up, girl. Get 'em up nice and high for me. Come on, baby, come on, *come on* ..."

Michael eased himself around so he had an oblique view out the front windscreen. They were almost to the cliff. Almost to the edge, and he could still feel the tires rumbling over the grass. Shouldn't they be airborne by now?

Gunfire commenced behind them. It seemed as distant as a bygone day. A shot pinged off the aircraft's tail, or maybe it was just some mechanical noise. Michael barely heard or cared. It was no longer bullets he was worried about.

"Okay, Michael, showtime," Beth said in her delusional tone. "Tell that God of yours he's on in ten seconds. Tell him to breathe some lift into this barrel of shit, or we're all going for a submarine ride."

Before Michael could even register the horror of what she was saying, the plane went over the edge.

The rumbling sensation ceased. They were in the air. In Michael's limited field of vision through the windscreen, there was only blue. The island was gone.

But something was wrong. Even without visual cues, Michael could feel the aircraft listing. Then all of a sudden he caught sight of the last thing in the world he wanted to see: the azure waters of the Straits of Florida, sparkling gloriously in the sun, crowding out more and more of the sky with every second.

Ahead to the left, a fiery pop exploded at the water's surface. Michael hoped to God it wasn't the *Queen Anne's Revenge* eating a missile. In his heart he knew it probably was.

THE CRISIS SEEMED TO HAVE snapped Beth out of her daze. She was wide awake now, crisp and coherent, frightened to the core. Maybe she had let herself believe, with Michael, that God would make things right. That the overloaded airplane with its ill-maintained parts and insufficient fluid levels would magically elevate to a comfortable 7,000 feet. That the wings which had hewn stubbornly toward terra firma during the run-up would somehow find the lift to resist gravity once the rug was pulled out from under.

Wishes, beliefs, faith, dreams – whatever they had been, they were relevant no longer. No miracle had come to pass. The plane was losing the fight.

Beth poked and pulled frantically on the controls. In a sudden burst of inspiration, she spiked the fuel mixture, nosed the aircraft down, then eased back up, hoping to use momentum to achieve critical speed. It seemed to work. They began to gain altitude, and Beth nursed the fuel feed to what she hoped was optimal, babied the throttle in concert with the flight controls, pulled every trick and called in every chit of luck she might be entitled to in a heroic effort to stabilize their vector. The thought flicked through her mind of talking Michael through placing a distress call, but she discarded it at once. There wasn't time, there wasn't bandwidth, it was taking every ounce of her guile, experience, and physical strength to keep the craft in the air.

They made fifteen hundred feet. Eighteen hundred. Beth might have felt encouraged if she could have afforded the luxury of such diversions. She could not.

The engine was settling down, but she was still fighting the avionics. They hit an air pocket knocking them to the right, shifting every passenger hard in that direction. And suddenly, horribly, she found herself unable to coax them level, hauling on the yoke and crushing the rudder but it *still would not roll true.*

"Oh my God, Michael," Beth blurted, speaking so fast she was unintelligible, heart pounding and lungs puffing in desperate gulps amid the children's frantic cries. "She has the power, I think she has enough power, but Michael there's something wrong with the … no it's the balance Michael it's the balance, we're off balance that way it's too much your side I can't Michael Michael Michael *do something!*"

THEY SAY THAT WHEN A human being is about to die, his entire life flashes before him like a movie on fast forward. No one says it authoritatively, of course, because no one recounting such an experience has actually gone beyond it to die. All that can be said is that it is a common "near death" experience. And it certainly is noteworthy, perhaps even remarkable, that such a phenomenon should manifest to so many people in so many disparate situations.

Some believe it represents a moral accounting. The purpose, they suggest, is to re-acquaint the individual with events long forgotten whose impact nevertheless persists in the destiny of the soul. To prepare, in other words, the transiting person to understand the basis for the divine judgment that is about to be passed upon them for eternity.

There is a more pedantic explanation, some would say more rational, that this stream of images is simply the brain frantically ransacking its contents looking for something in experience that might extricate the person from the dire condition that has placed them "near death." In many ways, this is no less awe-inspiring, and it is certainly, in an objective sense, no less likely.

Perhaps the life-flash is both, perhaps neither, perhaps sometimes one and sometimes the other. Perhaps it happens only to those whose time has not yet come, and never to those whose time it actually is to die.

Its significance in the story of Michael Chandler derives not from the content, but from the *circumstances* of his flash of life.

It is usual for the experience to commence in a moment when the individual feels a total loss of control. This makes sense under either of the common interpretations. The key is that the event has already taken place, the conditions are *already* intractable. The die has been cast and the subject is merely an observer. The movie of life simply plays. It cannot be stopped, it cannot be altered, it cannot be pondered over. It simply is. Then the person wakes up, or enters a period of darkness to emerge later, or whatever the individual case may be. The experience occurs *between* the time when matters have left one's control completely and the time when some measure of control is regained.

Michael Chandler's life passed in front of him *before* he knew he was going to die. He was not, in that moment, panicked. He was in precarious circumstances, there was panic around him, there was certainly justification for a panicked state. But Michael Chandler was suspended in a bubble of calm. The bubble was temporary, maybe even illusory. But what is important is not what was happening around him but what he felt. What is important is how he chose.

MICHAEL LOOKED OUT THE SIDE window. He could see the problem. He was vaguely aware of Beth's frenetic monologue, and he even comprehended the gist of it. Beth was an extraordinarily skilled pilot, a "natural," even if it was her father who said so; he was one who would know. Through a combination of luck and instinct, she had been managing the thrust deficit; she had kept the sorry little plane aloft longer than pilots with many times her flight hours could have done, and it seemed to be improving. She had gained them more than a thousand feet of altitude, which is to say a thousand feet more time and space to work with in her fight to stay airborne. It wasn't so far to Florida, thank God. Half an hour in good conditions, an hour in the worst case. A hell ride, if the entire trip continued as the first five minutes had, but not insurmountable. Beth might be able to stabilize the lift, or she might be able to coax the stubborn craft to the nearest spot of flat land through sheer gumption and will.

She might. She might not. She might also be able to overcome the present crisis, a hard list to the right caused by a gross payload imbalance attributable to Michael Chandler himself. Caused by his ignorant placement of the passengers, no doubt, though his motives had been pure. But caused, too, by the very presence of his own body. *His* weight was the biggest problem. It was the largest factor in both the thrust and the balance dilemmas. This was not intrinsically his *fault*; he simply happened to be the heaviest person aboard. But loading heavy to starboard *was* his doing, innocently or not. The insistence on taking all the girls was most definitely his. And while these contributions to their predicament might be forgivable, to see now a way to resolve it and not act – that would be a different story. And there *was* something he could do, something made simpler by his choice to shield the girls from the gunfire. He had planned to sit in the front passenger seat with the tall girl and Elise sharing his lap, but he had been forced by circumstance to enter the plane last. He was on top of them, and this gave him unfettered access to the door.

His life played out before him as he pondered their predicament in the split second that the plane's list became severe. He saw the floating animal mobile his mother had hung over his bassinet, which played a little Mozart concerto three or four times to fall to sleep by when she pulled the string. He had forgotten all about that. There was Max on his fifth birthday, when Michael had made fun of the paper crown they gave him for it in Kindergarten and then cried miserably and begged for Max's forgiveness when he realized how cruel that had been. Max, verbally anyway, had told him it was okay. There was his grandfather, harshly disappointed by Michael's failure to clear the weeds out of the back garden as he had promised to do after he had been paid for it in good faith, nevertheless assuring Michael, eleven years old and years away from understanding the true profundity of this exchange, that no matter what he had done he was still his grandfather, Michael was still his grandson, and he would not stop loving him over it.

There was Beth McFadden, thirty pounds lighter and two tons more full of herself, abandoning him at Haas Pavilion. Michael tearing flower petals into little pieces at Coyote Point after Susan Best had rejected his marriage proposal.

That first coy look from Vicki Valentine that would be frozen like a diamond in memory forever. That little boy in the Wal-Mart with the stuffed turtle and cow. He hadn't thought about that in ages, but it seemed so *special* as he recalled it now, why should that be?

Everything played for him, all of it. He could not have explained how he was able to perceive each and every incident, in detail and at his leisure, in the fragment of a second it took the mind movie to complete. Nor was he entirely sure why one image, a very recent one in fact, lingered when the slide show was over, hung on him like a heavy medal, a medal perhaps undeserved given the deep and abiding sadness, almost a sickness that it caused. It was the only memory left with him when the reverie broke, when he was back in the plane with the children bawling and Beth filibustering like a mad auctioneer.

It was the image of Charlie Paris, sitting in the driver's seat of Barbara Jordan's forest-green Eclipse, parked along Commercial Avenue near the college on a sunny day in Boston.

There was little Michael, he could see himself in the third person plain as day, looking thin and ragged and uncertain and somehow managing to ask, in his weak and vulnerable voice, a question that should never have been asked, which if not asked would have left him at least ignorantly hopeful instead of devastated beyond repair.

"Charlie, did I make it? Will I get to see Jesus?"

There was Charlie's face, burned into Michael's memory indelibly, that dark and inhumanly sad countenance issuing words that cut like razor wire.

"Michael Chandler, there can be no salvation for you in this world."

And that was the last thought Michael had before he reached for the airplane door. He understood it, and he understood why. He had not sought hard enough. He had not lived well enough. He had not embraced unreservedly even what modest faith he had.

And it didn't matter. Because for all that, even knowing with the cold certainty of having heard it from the lips of an entity from the other side, anguish over the loss of his soul was not strong enough to overcome the nature born into him, his god damned empathy, his compulsion to sacrifice, particularly for the weak and innocent, but for anyone who crossed his path in need, the Beth DeLeons of the world every bit as purely as for a kidnapped child.

Beth might be able to right the plane. But the odds were against it. And they would improve dramatically with a shift in weight.

The eight-year-old Michael, weeping frightened and alone at the end of the diving board, ultimately had come to no real harm. Mercy had intervened. The instructor had fished him out quickly and carried him back to the locker room, and he had never faced the board again.

But that had been childhood, and had revolved solely around him. He was a man now, and the lives of seven children were at stake. Seven children and a woman he loved, after a fashion, who had undertaken this risk against her better judgment, and only upon his insistence. It all rested on him.

And so he fell. With tears in his eyes and Charlie's words in his head, Michael unlatched the airplane door and pitched himself out, as cleanly as he could so as not to skew the balance any further. It was the last thing in his life he could control.

He thought he heard, for one split second, Beth calling after him. "Michael, NOOO!"

Then there was only the whistling in his ears. Michael was alone, helpless as a hanging man, the boundless sea rushing madly toward him.

Nothing in Heaven or Earth would stop it now. Despite a lifetime of fear and vigilance, of taking extraordinary measures to prevent this very thing, in the end it had all gone for naught. Michael Chandler was going to drown.

CHAPTER 24
Where The Lion Sleeps

THE PLANE'S SPEED CREATED THE equivalent of a hurricane wind, banging the door shut again as soon as Michael was clear. For Beth, it felt like slamming a coffin lid. She was at a complete loss, tears flooding her eyes and making it hard to see. Yet she wouldn't wipe them. She let them flow freely, down her cheeks, into the corners of her mouth, down onto her shirt.

She would not hold back the emotion. She *needed* to feel it. Moreover, Michael deserved it. Only now did she fully realize what a precious, beautiful man he was, what a jewel she had passed over in her school-girlish obsession with Rick. Michael Chandler had been a prince, not since grown into but had been one all his life, and the least she owed him was an open and unapologetic display of her tragically belated regard.

She was free to indulge these thoughts because the plane had dutifully leveled within seconds after Michael bailed out, its erratic propeller settling into a well-behaved whir. Except for Elise, the girls stopped crying, sensing that the plane's newfound docility meant their deliverance to Florida was secure.

It wasn't enough for Beth. She wept silently off and on through the entire flight. When at last they came in sight of Key West International, the blur in her eyes was neither joy nor relief. It was raw bitterness at the loss of the shining knight she had come to love too late.

She tuned the radio to 118.2, the frequency of the Key West air traffic control tower, and keyed the mic, her voice cracking from physical and emotional drain.

"Tower, this is Beth DeLeon in a Cessna 150 with no tail number, ten miles out at seven thousand feet, bearing three-one-five degrees at one-two-zero. Request landing. We will need emergency services on touchdown. Repeat, emergency services needed."

"Cessna, this is Key West tower. Descend to five thousand and hold for priority landing instructions. Please confirm the nature of your emergency, over?"

"This is Cessna no-tail, we have six children aboard in need of medical care."

"Roger that, Cessna. Requesting med response."

It wouldn't be a bad idea to have law enforcement, too, Beth thought grimly. *Except that I can't risk being arrested for my complicity in all that criminal shit until I've talked with my dad about what to do.*

"By the way, Cessna, what happened to your tail number?"

"It's a long story," Beth replied. "For now let's just get these kids on the ground."

FROM PURE INSTINCT AND WITH absolutely no hope that it would change the outcome, Michael attempted to orient himself horizontally so he could slow the descent like a sky-diver in free fall. He couldn't do it. The 200 mph wind created by his fall through the hot salt air was too strong for him to prevail. The sting of his shirt whipping against his cheeks and his pants riding harshly up to his inner thighs underscored his total lack of control.

He did the only thing he could to mitigate the terror, what he had done countless times in less dire circumstances: he closed his eyes.

It helped, if only a little. He could imagine himself being held aloft instead of falling, like a balloon balanced on a cushion of forced air, and the minor relief this brought was enough to let him feel emotions other than fear. And what he felt, most of all, was bitterness.

What have I ever done to you? he thought, not daring to acknowledge even to himself that he was addressing God, but nonetheless railing at the universe's unfairness.

"There can be no salvation for you in this world," Charlie had said. Why was that?

If I made some fatal mistake, why did you never show me where I was wrong? I know I'm not perfect, obviously I didn't do all the things you require, but I've done my best to take pity on people. I wouldn't be here if I hadn't. Is that so bad? Is my life so unacceptable for missing some liturgical technicality that it outweighs any good I've done? That it justifies this kind of punishment? Would you be happier if I had let those children die?

Amazingly, he got an answer. Not from God, not from the universe, but from himself.

The answer was that it didn't matter. It didn't matter one bit. What mattered was that he had saved the children. What mattered was that he had returned Elise to her mother. What mattered was that the little bird had received its surgery, that Rosemary Hart had died happy and on her own terms, that the kid lying on the floor in the Las Vegas restroom had been spared serious disfigurement. That Steve Shelby's kids got to stay in their day care and the little boy in Wal-Mart got what his compassion deserved. He couldn't help it if those things didn't count for much with God, or the universe, or whatever. Given a second chance, he would do them all again.

That realization brought Michael some peace. And that was what he was feeling the moment he hit the water and was swallowed whole.

HE FEELS HIS ANKLES BREAK as the velocity of his free fall turns the ocean's surface into a concrete floor. His elbows are smacked as if hit with a baseball bat. Mercifully, when his head reaches the water a hundredth of a second later, his neck is snapped.

Yet like daylight that persists on a planet for a short time after its sun has gone nova, perception lingers. He feels himself plummeting like an anchor, so deep so fast that even through closed eyes he can see the world darken; he feels the temperature drop. Water floods into his nose and down his lungs as if from a garden hose, the very sensation he has feared above all others, except that it happens instantly, far faster than he had imagined. He always envisioned himself choking, coughing the water up only to inhale it again, but he can't. Not only is it happening too fast, but the water pressure at these depths is crushing him like an anaconda. He couldn't draw breath if there was air. The claustrophobia, which he had not expected, threatens to drive him mad.

Yet it could be worse. He knows this. His neck has been broken, and this will blunt and shorten his suffering. Fate has been merciful. Inexplicably, he feels a message – not hears, not thinks, but wordlessly *feels* it. The message says, simply: *God loves you.*

His brain, deprived of oxygen, starts to shut down. The haze of impending unconsciousness clouds the fringe of vision. Sensation is on the ropes. Yet consciousness, a thin thread of it, abides.

It is truly dark now. If he were to open his eyes, the inky black would be absolute. The cold is starting to make him feel numb. He can no longer feel himself falling, at least not in a particular direction. His perception has gone that far askew.

Something is happening, something strange. He is becoming detached, and as he does so amazingly, miraculously, the fear and agony begin to subside. He can sense this physically, as though watching a tide recede, or the last puddle of bathwater shrinking toward the drain. And speaking of baths, he is starting to feel warmer. *I'm at the very bottom of the ocean,* he thinks; *there must be a thermal vent.* And he thinks this calmly and lucidly, because the mental fog rendered by his fear and discomfort has begun to clear. How could that be? Has the connection between mind and body become so frayed that the physical distress is separating like a spent booster rocket, dropping away to liberate his consciousness for uncompromised cognition?

But he still *feels* it, not only in his mind, not even with the limited detachment one experiences on the brink of slumber, but feels it *all*, feels it in his arms and legs, hands and feet, and weren't they numb and drifting away from him just seconds before? No, it wasn't seconds, it was hours. *Hours?* It doesn't take hours to drown. Is he dreaming? He doesn't seem to be. Yet what else can this experience be compared to? *Nothing.* The answer is Nothing. He has no words to describe what he is feeling now, because it is utterly outside of human experience. No language accounts for it. He can only check his way through guesses and metaphors, and he stops doing even that because it isn't helping, and it is not necessary. He doesn't have to understand. It is enough to feel, more than enough; the feeling is *everything*.

Hours? Seconds? Centuries? It's all the same, he sees that now. He begins to understand, without the slightest idea how to articulate it, what Dan Hendrick had truly meant by "time isn't what you think it is." Except that Dan lacked the capacity to understand it fully himself. He did intellectually, of course, to a limited extent, but only at the level of thought experiment. Not with an understanding that originated in your very marrow, or what passed for marrow in this existence. Not an understanding radiating from the soul, resonating in eleven dimensions, as tactile and obvious as sunshine on a summer day.

The warmth blossoms until it envelopes him like a mother's embrace. And incredibly, not only is he no longer cold, he is no longer wet either. He feels a dry soothing in his hands and arms, around his neck, swirling about his feet and ankles, which are no longer broken. No longer? They never could have been; they feel perfectly fine now. Better than fine, they feel vibrant. *Powerful.* And so does every other part of him. For the first time in his existence, he feels *completely alive.*

He is still in motion, but plunging no longer. He is sailing now, soaring maybe, at what seems an impossible speed, though he is not the least bit frightened. And that wind on him – what is that? Not water, that is certain. But not air either. Something more ... more ... he has no word for it, but the closest that strikes him is *genuine.* He is cruising at supernatural speed through something fundamental and ubiquitous, some medium that either is, or is somehow bound up with, the very fabric of the universe. Like the nebulous "ether" of nineteenth century hypothesis, except that after decades of research ether was proven not to exist. Not in the form conceived, anyway, not as a medium for propagating light waves.

But if there is no ether, that doesn't mean space is empty. It is filled with virtual particles, the "quantum foam," that much he knows from Dan, and even thinks he understands. Is he feeling the quantum foam? Or is it something else, the microwave background radiation left over from the Big Bang, or even the mysterious Dark Energy? Could you *feel* any of those things? He has no way to know. All he knows is that he is racing through it, that it feels electric and alive without being the least bit threatening, and that he is exhilarated – exhilarated, he thinks, to the absolute limit, beyond any excitement he has ever dreamt of, basking in a sense of wonder and triumph that could not possibly be topped.

That hyperbole is discarded the moment he opens his

eyes and the experience is topped – big time.

He is flying through the universe, master of speeds far greater than that of light or at least of some mechanism to overcome it. It is a familiar scene in some respects: he picks out bright Vega, Sol's sister Alpha Centauri, gargantuan red Betelgeuse destroying its own solar system in preparation to explode itself. He knows the stars, yet it is not from the constellations he dutifully memorized as a Scout. It can't be, because, coursing through the galaxy like a dimension-hopping excursion train, the relative positions of these heavenly bodies one to another bear no resemblance at all to how they appear from Earth. They are jumbled hither and yon, some larger, some smaller, some slightly different colors, some in different phases of stellar life than he remembers. He finds himself in between Castor and Pollux, one to his left and the other his right, so that the twins of Gemini are actually on opposite sides of the sky. Yet he recognizes them without hesitation. Strangest of all, this does not strike him as the least bit odd.

Much of what he sees is familiar, even though he has never seen it from this vantage or anything like it. But far more of the marvels chased by his captivated gaze are wondrous beyond dream. For he can see everything, not just the bright objects within the Milky Way nor even those extra-galactic sights obtainable in coarse outline on a moonless night using the four-inch Meade reflector his dad had given him for his thirteenth birthday. His vision is crisp and clear and seemingly limitless, better than the Webb space telescope, better even than the LESA array, spanning frequencies from Gamma to microwave that should be invisible to human eyes. He sees the black hole at the galactic center, rich stellar nurseries nestled in Andromeda, dense clusters of nascent island universes in the very vanguard of time.

And he is not alone. He isn't lifting a finger to propel himself, not exerting one iota of the indescribable and limitless power he feels he has. He is being *carried*. The entity – it's a horribly inadequate word, but again, he can think of no accurate descriptor – is enormous, conceptually human in form but much, much larger. It is completely transparent save for the bluish-white neon glow that outlines its form like the surface of a bubble. Although Michael has an unobstructed view in every direction, he can clearly make out his benefactor's face, arms, and gargantuan yet gentle hands cradling him gracefully against its chest like a parent toting a newborn through a magnificent park, holding the little one up so that it can take in every wondrous sight, magical sound, and delicious smell with awe.

He has no clear perception of what the entity is wearing, or whether it is wearing anything at all. It's not that he can't see, because he can – as clearly as he could see a rose held in his hand in broad daylight – but he cannot *describe*, even mentally to himself, what he sees. Not only are there no words, there is no *concept* for it in human thought. But he sees it all the same, and though it defies description the way a snowflake defies capture, he can *feel* it, he *knows* it, and he can say without reservation that it is good.

The entity is male, that is unambiguous. It is not God, or Jesus, or any other religious icon – this he knows beyond doubt, though how he knows he cannot say. He also thinks, though of this he is not *as* sure, that it is not an angel. What he *can* say is that it is a fine, strong, aesthetically beautiful man of indeterminate age – looking perhaps twenty-six or twenty-seven – though as he thinks these numbers he knows perfectly well that "age" is a concept with no application whatsoever to this pearl of creation. It is warm, it is smiling, it is pitying and apologetic and joyful all at the same time. It even seems strangely familiar, though he can't see how it could be.

And it loves him. This entity *loves* him. It feels like parental love, like the most heartfelt, incorruptible, and permanent parental love it is possible to enjoy, and yet this being is not his mother or father, Heavenly or otherwise. It is some kind of embodiment of warm, protective affection focused solely on him. And the sense of reassurance is so enveloping that he ceases to care about the uncertainty. He comprehends what is happening at the soul level. And he is perfectly content simply to smile back and soak it all in.

He is being carried, but he is no passive tourist. He finds that he can control their path. All he needs to do is think, even absently, and the entity takes them. What are the rings around that planet made of? They go weaving through them like a slalom skier. Is that a supernova just starting to erupt? They zoom toward it for a 4th-of-July view. The entity is his engine, but *he* is in control. The experience no longer resembles an infant's first stroll in the park, it has become a glorious joyride on interstellar horseback.

How much time is passing? Has it been decades? Millennia? Eons? He has no sense of it and doesn't care. The measure of it is meaningless. They soar through the cosmos together as on a spring bike ride with pinwheels, on and on until at last he feels totally fulfilled. He has seen everything he could want to for now and knows there is more and more, other wonders beyond imagining, waiting for other times. For now, he is content to wind down. He has no idea what he will do, what he will think about, where or what he is for that matter, although he is not in the least concerned by this. There will be time; understanding will come. For now, he feels he would be happiest just to go home, and he is not concerned by the fact that he has no idea what "home" means in this context. And the entity instantly knows this, without so much as a look between them. As for words, there have been none the entire time.

They focus in on a beautiful blue-white star, the same color as the entity's glow, he thinks. To him it looks like nothing else so much as Pinocchio's Blue Fairy hovering outside the workshop window. As they near the young sun, planets come into view: a small, dark outlier world speckled with some kind of natural luminescence, a red and gold binary pair circled by an impossible-looking figure-eight ring system, a purplish gas giant whose storm patterns mimic the Mandelbrot set. Beyond these is a lush green and blue planet wreathed in streaky light blue clouds, larger than Earth and a bit further from its sun but unmistakably teeming with life.

It is toward this lovely jewel they go, sky-sailing past its blue and silver moons with their own strange biospheres and exaggerated geographies, down through the wispy clouds, across the indigo sky penetrated only faintly now by stars. Below the colors grow bolder, and he can make out thick forests and mountains, streaked rock escarpments impossibly high, between which they zoom toward a tantalizing far-off sea. He glimpses jungle tree-tops, and still they descend, right down into the canopy toward the twilight. Deep through the branches where night is just setting in, enveloped in dark, verdant thickness, and all of a sudden here he is, his feet on the jungle floor, standing in soft grass on trusty ground for the first time since he climbed into the ... into the ...

He can't remember. He thinks there was an island, and a girl. He sees an ocean, beautiful and menacing. He feels like there was something he needed to do, really *needed* to, but he can't remember if he did it, or what it was.

No matter. He is perfectly happy for the very first time. Even the cosmic thrill ride didn't produce this kind of fulfillment. He is home. *Home!* A huge smile erupts across his face as the truth of what has happened finally sinks in. He has died; his mortal life is behind him, never to be visited again. Never to *trouble* him again. And it has turned out – oh my God, it's really true! – that there *is* life after death. Forever life, this time, without a care, without pain, without suffering. He can feel this innately in every fiber of himself. And he has come to the most idyllic, the most pleasing, the most heart-wrenchingly beautiful place he could possibly imagine. A place so perfect, in his eyes, that it seems almost as though it must have been tailor-made *for him.*

And maybe it was, he marvels. As he looks about, he doubts that most people would find this place appealing. It is a world of black interspersed with shadow, although this shadow is not uniform gray. Instead, it is imbued with an alive and subtle color, like wall paint in moonlight. What he can see of the foliage – visibility is lost completely within just a few feet around him – is muted green in every succulent shade, stippled with tropical flowers that seem somehow to retain even in this dimness most of their dazzling hues: delicate purple passion, sprinkles of hibiscus, shameless birds of paradise.

In fact, the jungle is teeming with unseen life. Cicadas chirp in the trees, brush rustles in the distance, tropical night birds croon and call. He glimpses something like a small monkey vaulting through the canopy. The air breathes rose and orchid, fresh rain and warm earth, a menagerie of sultry fragrances as sweet as summer love.

A little stream trickles melodiously, and following the sound, he discovers a delicate waterfall springing out of the rock and splashing into a small, deep pool from which the brook drains off and meanders out of sight. A flash catches his eye, and he is utterly delighted to find the pool swirling with tiny luminescent fish. They put on a light show worthy of a laserium, darting in circles or jumping through the waterfall as if for fun, and he feels like he could sit at the water's edge deep into the night and watch them for hours. Maybe sometime he will.

He tries to put his finger on how the place *feels*, how it can seem so familiar when it is obviously anything but. He can't succeed completely, but he does dredge up a few references that come very close. It's like the picture he sees whenever he encounters the term "Darkest Africa": dense and foreboding, immense beyond measure, brimming with mystery and undiscovered wonders. It reminds him of an Henri Rousseau painting, the darker ones for sure, and evokes in him the same complex emotions.

And that South African song, "The Lion Sleeps Tonight," made famous by The Tokens – it's playing in his head right now – the feeling that song inspires applies perfectly. For this is it, the very "mighty jungle" where that iconic lion sleeps. And he has an epiphany, understands instinctively the reason that song resonates here. It is a connection to a description of Paradise, an element of prophecy known to school children everywhere.

And the lion shall lie down with the lamb.

More than anything, this place matches the images conjured in his mind when his mother had read him Kipling's *Just So Stories:* a pristine jungle of limitless dimensions at the dawn of time, a dominion of animals ruled strictly by the laws of nature in the forgotten eons before the emergence of man. It is a manifestation of nature unsheathed, the purest possible Grand Order of Things.

Some, he knows, might find this frightening. Or too isolated, or too wild. And almost everyone would consider it much too dark.

But not for him.

The entity has departed – when did it go? He hadn't noticed, but he has no memory of its presence from the moment his feet touched down on the jungle floor. Though he is alone now, he feels not the least bit lonely. He knows there are others. For starters, a large, dark panther with emerald eyes silently biding its time at what it believes is a safe distance; he detects it through the murk like clairvoyance, not a lion perhaps but uncannily close. There are people, too, far enough away not to threaten his privacy but somehow close enough to visit, to talk and do things with, when he feels like it. This he perceives telepathically, too. But for now, just existing here, like floating naked in a hot tub with a Mai Tai to one side, is all he wants to feel.

He wonders briefly why this place should enchant him so, why he prefers it over the sunlit vales and celestial landscapes common to the utopian visions of others. He knows the answer. It's because while publicly he has always revered his freakish empathy as a blessing to be cherished, in truth it has been a burden. To be constantly afflicted with the suffering of every troubled person and distressed animal he encounters, to feel like something must be done for each and every one of them, to feel it is his personal responsibility to do it because he alone can – this is an untenable existence, a life of anguish and frustration that can never be relieved for long.

And here, at last, is perfect insulation. The place is dark, it is inaccessible, it is to others even distasteful and foreboding. It is hidden and remote. It is the ultimate retreat, a place where he can't be found, can't be seen, can't even be known about except at his own discretion. Most important of all perhaps, *he* cannot see *them*. He sees no grieving eye, no agonized grimace, no tremble of fear or droop of defeat. He believes this to be a place where such cannot occur, but even if they can, he is beyond their reach. He is alone. He is hidden. He is free.

This miraculous haven is the soil into which the universe has deigned to plant him. He can scarcely believe it. Yes, he knows Charlie had told him as much, or at least that there was a God, so none of this should be a terrific shock. And yet it is. Because it is one thing to nurture a mortal faith, quite another to find himself in the Afterlife feeling no sorrow or pain, surrounded by a living paradise, knowing in his core that he will never have to fear or hurt or worry again. He finds it delighting and devastating at the same time – or perhaps overwhelming is a better word, though the truth lies somewhere between – a soul-deep fulfillment that is truly indescribable, utterly unimaginable in mortal life.

He flings himself backward and bounces into the cool, soft grass beneath the palm-frond canopy and stars he has never seen overhead. It feels as comfortable and safe as a mother's arms.

He thinks he is doing nothing, nothing at all, and he is perfectly content with that. But if he could see himself from the outside, he would see he is wrong. Not every muscle is at rest; the ones in his face are animated without his even knowing. For no matter where his mind wanders, no matter how rudderless his thoughts, on this day nothing can erase his blissful smile.

MICHAEL WAS STILL LYING THERE, splayed in the jungle grass with limbs akimbo, gazing at the stars, when a tall, unassuming man found his way through the labyrinth of sparse paths in the primeval growth to welcome his newly-arrived friend.

And Michael knew him. It took a moment, because the face was younger, the body stronger, the features more handsome. But he could see through to the soul, and there was no mistaking who was reaching down to help him up with an expression of tenderness and joy.

"Charlie?"

Charlie Paris embraced his charge with the warmest, most emotional hug Michael could remember. It was as if all the trials of their road trip together were pouring out until the vessel that had contained them was dry, absorbing invisibly into the sacred ground where they could be forgiven and forgotten for good.

"Welcome home, Michael." Charlie smiled, patting his companion gently on the back. "Welcome to your Place. Welcome to the *real* world."

CHAPTER 25
Place

THERE WAS SOMETHING VERY STRANGE about Michael's recognition of Charlie. Not the *fact* of recognition; his recollection of the road trip was crystal clear. In fact, he had regained all of his mortal memories, including the details of events on Isla Tesoro and the escape flight that had been temporarily blurred by his transition from life to Afterlife. He knew Charlie from their long drive of course, but there was something new here, something he had never felt about Charlie at any time during their week-long journey. It felt as if, in addition to the road trip, he knew Charlie from something else. He had no idea *what*, or why, or why he hadn't perceived this in life. Yet there it was, compelling and persistent. The picture in his mind was of two identical images out of phase, as a falling-down drunk might see duplicates of the same person swimming around each other in his blurry field of vision.

Unable to make any sense of it, he let it drop. Maybe it was just the fact that this youthful Charlie contrasted distinctly against the grey-haired elder that had accompanied him cross-country. In all likelihood, it was just another artifact of the transition. It would pass in time, he felt sure, and expire for good once he became attuned to this new reality.

"So this is Heaven?" he queried when the reunion rituals were over.

"If you mean paradise, maybe yes. If you mean a place in the clouds where God sits on a literal throne with Christ and a choir of angels, no."

"*Is* there one?"

"There is, yeah. I mean, it's not exactly that picture, a throne in the clouds and all, but there is a Heaven. What it is exactly and how a person might get there, that's complicated. I don't fully understand it myself, but you'll meet some who claim to."

Michael pondered. "Well if this isn't Heaven, then is it …" He couldn't finish the question. The thought that this might be Hell was too horrible. He didn't see how it could be; this environment, so finely tailored to his notion of perfect, seemed like the opposite of eternal punishment. But maybe he wasn't seeing the whole picture.

"It's not Hell either, if that's what you're thinking. That ought to be obvious. Although to some people, I'd guess, it feels a bit like that."

"Seriously? Some people hate the dark so much they equate *this* with *Hell*?"

"That's not what I mean." Charlie paused a moment to think about how to explain. "I was speaking of the Afterworld overall. This little part of it, this jungle here, is *particular to you*. It was literally generated by the way you lived your life. Every thing you did *physically* sculpted something here. A stand of trees, a waterfall, a bed of flowers. A volcanic eruption or an earthquake. And more you haven't seen yet.

"It's the same way for everyone. When people die, that tunnel you climbed up toward the light leads each person to a location customized to them. We call it their *Place*. This one is yours."

Michael looked around in astonishment. "My life *created* this?"

In his conversations with Dan Hendrick in front of the computer, Michael had envisioned *consciousness creates reality* in terms of an individual riding along his world line like a rail, "experiencing" what formed around him as a passive observer with no control, his surroundings physically real but no more substantial than the dinosaur and Grand Canyon sets that park-goers rolled through on the Disneyland Railroad. Now all of a sudden his image of the creative power involved multiplied tenfold. The mortal world was a shadowbox compared to this, and while mortal environs certainly had their beauty and charm, they were but preparatory sketches to this masterpiece.

"Yes indeed." Charlie was smiling broadly. "Everyone's Place is created by their actions in mortal life.
Those of us already here can literally watch it happening. You have a sense of the Places of those most dear to you, even while they're still alive. In fact, love acts as a kind of connector. The more love that flows between you and another person, the closer your Place is to theirs. And connected Places form a seamless nexus between them, like an invisible bridge. So you can easily find a loved one's Place and watch it evolve. It's a great pastime.

"While you're inside your own, you are completely safe, and you're going to find that it's almost impossible to feel negative emotions. I wasn't a drinker, but I've been told it's a little like being pleasantly drunk. Everything around you seems extra beautiful and fascinating."

An odd question suddenly entered Michael's mind as if from the outside, fully-formed down to the last word so that he didn't so much say as recite it.

"What about married couples? Do they share the same Place? Is marriage forever or just 'til death do us part'?"

"That depends." Charlie stroked his chin thoughtfully. "Unhappy marriages tend to split completely apart. In content ones, each spouse has his or her Place, but they overlap. The closer they are, the more Place they share."

Michael, who had never been married and now never could be, found this profoundly comforting in a way he couldn't explain.

Charlie went on. "Now, there is a catch to all this. The

nature of your Place is totally determined by how you lived, and the size of it is proportional to how much 'good' you did. Well, for adults, anyway. Infants and young children are credited heavily for their innocence. But for the most part, you Place reflects your life. So some people's Places are pretty bleak and tiny – the worst of them are barely big enough to fit in, like a broom closet."

Michael absorbed this. "So they have to stay in their 'closet' forever? *That's* Hell?"

"No one has to *stay* in their Place. And it doesn't *have* to stay small. But when you leave you become susceptible to normal emotions, the same ones you had on Earth. For most of those closet people, that's unbearable." Charlie smiled. "But they do have recourse. Your Place can continue to change even after you get here. It can never become less than the state you find it in when you die – that's a big part of why mortal life matters. You are guaranteed *forever* that it can't deteriorate below what your mortal life created. You can always retreat to it, and no one can take it away from you. A lot of people rarely ever leave theirs. But as you generate 'good,' even here, your Place can get bigger and more … wholesome? Worthy? That's not exactly it. Maybe a better term would be 'blessed.' It can fall back again, too, from doing the wrong things. But it can never go below your baseline."

"So this is more of …" Michael clutched the air, scrambling for words. "Is it Purgatory? A place to work off your sins? That's what it sounds like."

"I wouldn't say that, no. It's definitely *not* just a way station where you do your penance and then proceed to Heaven like a paroled inmate. There's nothing temporary about it, and nobody has to work off their sins. You're here, you've got the Place you deserve, and that's that. Nothing more is required."

"But people *can* work off their sins."

"You can expand your Place by doing good. I don't think of that as 'working off your sins,' but I guess some people might see it that way. But most people are perfectly content with their Place the way it is. The notion of 'working things off' really only applies to the Darkened."

"The Darkened?"

Charlie went grim. "Some people," he said carefully, "when they get here, are *angry* with God. Some of them were atheists, not the thoughtful kind but the reactionaries, you know, the ones with real hatred in it. Some were self-righteous religionists who got it wrong – there's no shortage of those. Some were just people traumatized by terrible suffering. What they have in common is that they think their mortal lives were unfair, and they can't let it go. They're bitter. Instead of embracing their Place and the wonders of Afterlife, they want revenge."

"Against *God*?"

Charlie nodded. "It's like an obsession. But they're not fully to blame, Michael. Not even half maybe. That kind of perversity can't persist here entirely on its own. But there are dark spiritual forces out there, powerful ones. And those kinds of people are extremely vulnerable when those forces come around recruiting for The Enemy. When that happens, it can turn from obsession into a kind of madness."

"What Enemy?" Michael looked baffled, heading toward overwhelmed.

Charlie took one of Michael's hands in his. "I know it's a lot to digest. You can't do it all in one sitting, Michael, nobody can. You need to take it in doses. There's a lot to learn here, probably way more than you imagine. You're going to get it all; I'm not banned from telling you things anymore, but trust me on this: you've got to let it in sequentially, or you won't have the foundation to understand it."

Charlie looked apologetic and a bit flustered, and it made Michael smile to see his road companion twisted up in the same kind of frustration he had seen so many times in the car. "Well cripes, this is my first official welcoming, man, and it's harder than I thought. I'm probably not doing it very well. Just let me give you some advice I got from a very wise gentleman back when I was new here. He said: 'You've got a hundred questions, son, but there are a million answers.' I didn't quite get it at the time, but eventually I came to understand just how golden true that was. You can't teach a baby Calculus – well maybe here you could, but you'd still have to get him through basic math first. Do you understand what I'm saying, man? Am I making any sense?"

"Yes, Charlie." Michael gave his friend a warm, reassuring hug. He was aware that had this same conversation taken place during their drive across the country, he might have exploded in frustration himself. In fact, he *had* done so in the course of similar talks at that time. But here, in this wondrous Place burgeoning with enchantment and promise, he felt patient and serene. If it made Charlie more comfortable to lay things out in a methodical order, then by all means let it be so. After all, unless he was sorely mistaken, they had an eternity.

Michael reset the conversation in hopes of bringing Charlie back to a calm and confident state of mind. "So back to basics, if that's how it needs to be done. I'm free to wander wherever I want, but I can always come back to this clearing to feel completely at peace. Nothing can hurt me here. Is that the deal?"

"Well, yeah." Charlie perked up, Michael's encouragement appearing to have worked. "Except it isn't just this clearing. Not by a long shot. Have you not seen your house?"

"I have a house?" Michael was delightedly surprised.

"Do you have a house! Oh, man. Come on, you gotta see. Oh, boy, is this going to be fun."

CHARLIE LED MICHAEL CAREFULLY ALONG barely visible trails through jungle so deep and thick that not a smattering of sky could be seen. Neither of them carried a light, yet Michael was able to see faintly their immediate surroundings, making out the shapes of leaves, the pale colors of preternatural blossoms emanating their sultry fragrance, and enough of the path to keep his footing.

Michael hadn't lost his orientation – strange, given the unfamiliarity and gloom – when they came to a thick, irregular wooden door with a wrought iron pull and hinges, the hefty slab set as smoothly as a puzzle piece into a rock face whose dimensions might have been a hundred feet tall and wide, or a thousand – it was impossible to discern in the murk. He reckoned they may have traveled the equivalent of a hundred yards in a straight line, but the winding walk had covered at least three times that.

Charlie touched his hand to a barely visible tiki torch sconce mounted to the right of the door, which instantly flared to life. He followed with a twin torch on the left. Now Michael could appreciate the door for the marvel it was: a generous slab of exquisitely-grained Mopane wood cut to fit seamlessly into a natural opening in the stone, which itself was draped all around in a dense mat of green, fine-leaved ivy. In the torchlight, Michael could finally see that the true color of the rich foliage populating his "Place" was anything but dull. There wasn't a dried fleck or browning tendril anywhere. It felt as though he was seeing real living plants for the very first time.

Michael waited, but Charlie stood aside and gestured toward the handle. Michael gripped it and pulled. To his delighted surprise, the knob felt supernaturally warm and welcoming. It felt like it *knew* him.

The entry was a short passage carved right into the limestone, a hallway that branched into a "T" at the far end. At the head of the T, a sculpture worthy of the ancient Greeks had been carved into the rock like a bust in a niche, an angelic figure from the waist up with its head bowed over a sword and both hands resting on the pommel so that the hand guard formed a cross.

The entry hall sported a single door to the right, a

hefty wooden plank portal with dark iron bracing in medieval style. To the left, a broad gossamer waterfall running the length of the hallway slipped from a crevice in the rock at eye level, pitching smoothly down into a narrow trench lining the base of the wall. The whole scene was moodily lit by more tiki torches, and Michael had no doubt they would operate to the touch just like the ones outside. He did not know, but would discover later to his delight that the level of the flame, and even the color – yes, the very color of the fire – could be adjusted to taste just as simply.

Something caught his attention, and he stared at the sleek sheet of water, trying to put his finger on what it was. All at once it came to him. It wasn't the water he should be looking at: it was his reflection. The wet veil was so sheer that it worked as a sort of mirror, if you permitted your eyes to focus just so. And the man he saw gaping back at him was not precisely what he expected.

It was better.

It was him, all right, his familiar features hadn't been replaced by those of some movie star or model from *Gentlemen's Quarterly*. It was definitely Michael, but it was the *perfect* Michael. Perfect *according* to Michael. He was clean-shaven – he hadn't minded the beard, but it had never felt like him – and his hair was a bit longer, wilder, thicker, shinier. It even seemed to have golden highlights, which he had never had in life. Not the kind a hairdresser might render with chemicals, but rather the kind that might emerge naturally from a healthy life in the sun. It made Michael chuckle. Sun, here? He had never been much of a sun bunny. But he understood that the look had nothing to do with weather. The highlights would persist even if he spent eternity underground.

And if the underground here was all like this magical tiki cave, *he just might*.

Charlie was calling to him from the doorway of the first room, but Michael lingered just a few beats longer. It was fascinating. His figure was lithe and muscular as it had been at the peak of tennis season in high school. His face was young and sculpted and his eyes, one of which in life had sagged just a bit, were bright and symmetrical. He was even a bit taller ... really? Was that a trick of the light? He couldn't tell, but he didn't think so. Could two inches really make so much difference? Even the mole on the back of his right hand was gone, the pea-sized brown mark he had relied upon to tell right from left as a child. His mother would be horrified, but he didn't miss it. Not that it had bothered him, just that given the choice, he would have lived without. And now he could.

"Michael!" Charlie was laughing, but insistent. "What the hell, are you looking at yourself?"

That broke the daze. "Sorry. I've just never seen myself like ... this."

"Of course you have," Charlie corrected. "It's the you inside. It's the guy you talk to when you're talking to yourself. That's who we all are here. The way you look here is the way you *feel*."

After one last wistful, admiring peek, Michael made it to the doorway where Charlie stood waiting, receptive and ready for some new unexpected wonder.

And get one he did.

The room off the entryway was a bedroom, but not like anything he had seen in any house or hotel. The wall opposite the doorway was curved like the hull of a ship, inlayed with rich wood planking of that same motif, and set into it were two cozy bunks tucked with lavish pillows and bedclothes, the upper accessed by a simple wood ladder. In the corner beyond where the ship's wood met stone, an amber window hashed with dark iron mullions breathed in the twilight. It was Michael's romantic image of an eighteenth-century pirate's cabin straight from Disney – Henry Morgan's, no doubt – rendered live.

"But I thought ..." He looked at Charlie timidly, feeling as though he was asking the stupidest question in the world. "We don't have to ... sleep ...?"

"We don't." Charlie laughed. "But we can. And sometimes you want to. Your body will never run down, but sleep
isn't just about the physical. In fact, here it's sort of the opposite. Sleep is a way to get total separation between your body
and spirit. Even mortals use sleep to work things through in
the mind without the distraction of bodily senses and functions. Here, it's even more so. There's a lot to learn here, a
lot to understand, a lot to think about. Having a nice sleep
periodically makes it easier to assimilate all that bewilder-
ing input. It's especially good in your Place. Everything here
vibrates at the same frequency as your soul. Not literally, but
you know what I mean.

"It's kind of like that with food, too, by the way. We
don't have to eat or drink, but it can be good to once in a
while. You still have a physical body, but your spiritual component is much greater here, and that allows you to absorb
energy directly from the environment, like a leaf in sunlight.
But eating or drinking imbues you with some of the energy
of the Place it came from. Like a lot of things, the effect is
most powerful when it's your own Place."

Michael took in the gist of what Charlie was saying,
but he was only listening with half an ear. The sublime surroundings would not release him from their spell.

At the far end of the room stood a small writing desk.
But for the quill and ink, the exotic wood, and the impeccable finish, it was the spitting image of the oak desk with
the secret compartment that his grandfather had hand-made
for him as a boy.

The last wall, the one shared with the entry hall, was
one massive bookshelf. And it was brimming top to bottom,
left to right, with hardbound, hand-inked books.

Michael knew before he even looked that all his fa-
vorites would be there. And they were. Tolkien of course,
and the Narnia set. *The Land of Laughs* and V*oice of our
Shadow* by Jonathan Carroll. *Ubik* and many others by Philip K. Dick. A few Arthur C. Clarke, most of Asimov, and
everything Robert Heinlein had ever penned. *A Wrinkle in*

Time. Alice, Through the Looking Glass, and a thick volume titled *The Complete Sherlock Holmes.* They were all there, meticulously sorted by author and title, every work of fiction he would have wanted if he were stuck on a desert island.

But there were more. At least half of the books – maybe two thirds – were unfamiliar. Some were works by his favorite authors that he had never read. Others were foreign altogether. New adventures just waiting for a stormy night when he could cozy up in whichever bunk suited him and read with a cup of hot cocoa to his heart's content. He had not a sliver of a doubt that each one had been placed there specifically because it was guaranteed to delight him.

"Talking about sleep," Charlie broke in, "I heard of a guy once who slept forty hours straight. When he woke up, he sat down and pounded out an 800-page novel all in one sitting. Completely done in four days. While he was sleeping he'd mapped the whole thing out, every freaking word from Title to The End. And it was a *good* book, too."

"People write books in the Afterlife?"

"Of course. What do you expect dead writers to do?" Charlie grinned. "You've got several new ones right there. A lot of them, in fact."

Michael looked at the shelves more closely. Something caught his eye next to *Return of the King.* He had only glanced at it initially, taking it to be *The Silmarillion* and wondering what an unwieldy albatross like that was doing among these world classics. But it wasn't *The Silmarillion.* It was Tolkien, all right, but the title was different: *The Silmar Door.*

"I've read that one," Charlie affirmed approvingly. "It's the same history as that horrible long thing he wrote that everyone bought and nobody finished, except it reads more like *The Hobbit* and less like a list of Biblical *begats.* He's doing it as a seven-book series and everybody says it's going to be better than *Harry Potter.*"

New Tolkien? New *good* Tolkien? A broad grin creased Michael's face. He was going to like this place. Yes, yes he was.

And now he noticed that there was a little waterfall in here, too. Near the head of the beds on the wall next to the doorway, a quiet foot-and-a-half cascade flowed within a small niche in the stone, the water sparkling as it splashed over a bed of polished rocks at the base of the cavity before draining invisibly away.

"There's more," Charlie called, already out the doorway and into the hall at the T. "Come see!"

The T-branch to the right was a short hall that ended at a rock-carved stair spiraling upward as though inside a tower. At the top was a small observation deck, just large enough for an upholstered love seat, a small writing desk and chair, and ...

Michael gasped.

... a 28-inch university quality reflector telescope, pointed out at a forty-five degree angle through a protective dome, its shell made of a gleaming black material that looked so impervious you could beat it with a sledge hammer and never make a scratch.

Michael made for the eye piece, but Charlie collared him. "Look now, play later," he chided good-naturedly. "You haven't seen *anything* yet."

Down the spiral and along the other end of the T, they passed two closed doors without opening them and discovered a second staircase, this one spiraling down instead of up. It was a much longer shaft, too, hundreds of feet down it seemed, though Michael didn't feel as though trekking back up it would tire him.

When they reached the bottom, he saw that it had been well worth the climb.

The stair let out into a natural cavern the size of an arena. Actually, it was a sea cave, about half of it consisting of tawny sand illuminated by tall tiki torches and the rest a gently lapping saltwater lagoon. An L-shaped pier led from the beach out onto the water, and at the far end of the pier stood evidence that this was no shallow tide pool. Not by a long shot.

There was no other way to say it: it was a pirate ship. It bore the grandeur of a 17th century Spanish galleon in its oversized galley and forecastle, though its agile rigging and sleek black hull looked more frigate of war. Its polished decks and ornate cabins shone with rich lacquered wood grain, the latter festooned with red and gold inlay and spangled with mullioned amber windows matching the ones in his bedroom. It was glorious to behold even at half historical scale, which was still larger than Tony Pizarro's prized Bertram, and Michael hoped, rightfully as it turned out, that this reduction in size rendered the ship operable solo.

Michael walked out a few steps onto the pier toward the fairy-tale craft. Now he could see the cave mouth around a corner of the cavern and the actual ocean reflecting the ebullient twilight sky. To the right, a huge gouge out of the rock wall formed a sort of window, beyond which he saw a sight even more astonishing than the ship: a colonial village sweeping up distant hillsides from a quiet harbor, wisps of smoke and the ember glow of lanterns evincing a centuries-old beach community. And what was that behind it, huge and dark against the dusky sky? A cinder cone, the peak of an ominous volcano, puffing its own trail of gossamer smoke tinged red by an unseen caldera.

It *wasn't* a window, though … was it? Why should he think that? What else could it be? He traipsed down off the pier for a better view. He got up close and reached his hand up, up to touch the …was it glass?

Not glass. Rock. Not smooth, either. And not transparent.

The village tableau and the great sea beyond it, the slow-billowing clouds, the flickering lamps, the tall sailing ships rocking with the swells off-shore, the palm trees blowing luxuriously in the sultry wind — were *painted*. Painted right onto the natural wall of the cave. Painted in some fantastical medium that captured motion, captured time, captured *life*.

Michael was at a loss for words.

"Something, isn't it?" his tall friend admired.

"My God, Charlie, this is beyond ... I mean, who ...?"

Charlie beamed. Michael had never seen him look happier.

"Well, the cave and tunnel structure was already here; in the main rooms the natural contours were just shaved down to make them smoother. So I guess you could say *you* built the basic layout, by your mortal life just like the rest of your Place. But it still took a ton of grunt work to make this a proper house. I helped a little, so did a lot of people. But we were just Christmas elves. The Santa who put this whole thing together was your granddad." He pointed to the vessel at the end of the pier. "Designed and built *that* thing all by himself. Wouldn't take a moment's help from anyone. Can you believe it? I watched it go up. That man is a true craftsman. You couldn't fit a flea's eyelash between the timbers and that was *before* he sealed them up."

Michael stopped cold. He couldn't believe he hadn't realized it before, that he hadn't even thought of the most obvious joy of all. They were here. The people he had lost were *all here*! And his grandfather – the man he had so idolized, who in some respects he had felt closer to even than his own father, whose rare praise had elevated him to euphoria and whose condemnation could crush him for weeks – that giant among men, his Grandpa, was here. And he had seen fit to put the time, trouble, and love into making sure that Michael, when his time came to die, would have this perfect home.

He followed Charlie's gaze to the little galleon, and it was only then that he noticed the name embossed over the dark wood rail in crisp golden script just below the aft deck:

Archangel. A loving reference to his name.

Michael knelt. The emotion overwhelmed him. He cried and cried, both hands to his face, hot tears of disbelieving, unrelenting joy. It was the thought of his Grandpa's doing all this that triggered it, but the fuel burned by this emotional conflagration ranged far beyond. It was everything: his drowning, the knowledge that he had saved those children, the warm and bittersweet love he thought he could feel from Beth even across the boundary of death. His perfect new body, the smell of the night jungle, the glowing fish-like stars doing Busby Berkeley in their galactic pond. The crazy cosmic tour, the pirate bed, the shelves brimming with untold adventures. The telescope and the galleon. Charlie's dog-like loyalty through it all.

More than anything, it was the realization, only slowly sinking in, that mortal life really was over, that hurt and care were behind him. That life had come to something fantastic and wonderful beyond imagining after all. *Everyone probably goes through this*, he thought absently. But the feelings washing through him were so powerfully *personal* it seemed like nobody else possibly could.

Charlie stood by with his hand on his friend's back, patting tenderly. It went on for a long time, but Charlie never flagged, never moved, never tired of comforting. He had perhaps seen this moment coming and been prepared for it. Michael, who definitely had not, thanked God that Charlie had.

"But why you, Charlie?" Michael sniffed as composure began at last to return. "I can see my Grandpa doing this. I mean, I guess I can. I'm a little shocked, I'm humbled beyond belief, but he is my family.

"But you, Charlie? You never knew me in life. I know that crap you spun about watching me in the Wal-Mart, but you and I both knew that was somewhere between half the truth and none. I'm not mad at you, Charlie, dear God, I never could be. Not now. But I want to know. What was it really, man? Why was it you and not my Grandpa that met me by the waterfall? I guess what I'm really asking is ... why *me*?"

Charlie looked at him for a long time. The emotions churning behind the quiet mask looked every bit as complex and difficult for him as the ones Michael had been going through minutes before.

Finally, he spoke. "There's a lot more to see, man."

He smiled, little hints of tears starting to form at the corners of his own eyes. "You've got a really cool Place here. But you know what, Michael, I'm so sick of keeping things from you. You have no idea how agonizing it was for me to sit in that car and not be able to tell you. It was worse for me than it was for you, as hard as that might be for you to believe. Well, that's all over and I did my part. I'm not doing it any more.

"We'll finish the tour later. I've got something to show you. And once you've seen it, all that stuff you steamed over during the car trip is finally going to make sense."

CHAPTER 26
Emergence

THEY LEFT THE PIRATE HOUSE by that same front door, leaving tantalizing passages behind unexplored. Charlie reached for the torches outside, but Michael waved him off. It would be okay, he felt, to leave them on. It would be a cheery sight to return to.

Charlie led the way through the jungle in the direction opposite the pool clearing, a route that seemed to Michael to follow a gentle downhill grade. They had been walking about twenty minutes when the environment started to change. The ground leveled, and the saturation of flora began to subtly thin. Presently, the way ahead began to lighten as though toward dawn. That was odd, Michael thought, because he was positive – absolutely, cinch-lock sure – that the half-light of *his* jungle was not morning, but dusk. It was, of course, because he *wanted* it to be. So how could the sky be brightening? Could it have something to do with those two moons, did they somehow together reflect a concentration of sunlight bright enough to mimic day?

They did not, and that explanation was discarded as they transitioned, so gradually it was almost imperceptible, into majestic redwood forest. Michael gaped in awe at elder trees towering like skyscrapers over a rich, deep blanket of primeval fern, giant lichen, and great drapes of moss. Muted colors were accented toward the east by misty shafts of pinkish-yellow sunlight. This was clearly morning, and had Michael caught his breath long enough to think about it, he would have recognized that it wasn't just the light, he was picking up all sorts of cues. The insect chatter, warm humidity and distant animal calls that dominated the thickness behind them had belonged unmistakably to a jungle evening. Here, the insects were subdued amid scattered birdsong in the utter stillness. It was, without a doubt, the start of a brand new day.

He thought of asking Charlie about it, but checked himself. He had committed to absorbing things all in good time, for his own sake as well as for Charlie's, and he was still content with that.

So he asked instead: "Where are we headed, Charlie? Am I going to get to see your Place? Is that what this is?"

"Just up there a ways. We're going to go by it, and I'll show you the whole thing after. But we're going to take a little detour first."

Michael let it go at that. He'd asked the question, and if Charlie chose not to answer fully now, he would trust that there was good reason. Even if that reason was nothing more than Charlie's emotional comfort. For Michael, that was reason enough.

He did notice something, though. He was still happy, he still felt patient and serene, but things had subtly changed. It had happened as soon as they were into the redwoods, he realized. He could *feel* that they were no longer in his Place. He didn't feel anxious or anything, he didn't feel bad, but a certain buoyancy was gone. He felt normal, instead of feeling elevated. *Yeah*, he thought, *it's like a happy drunk. You don't feel bad when you're not intoxicated, but the glow is gone.* He was still ecstatic about being here – excited, triumphant, even a little euphoric. But there was a definite difference, and from that moment on he knew that he would always be able to feel whether he was in his Place or away from it. He could well understand why some people rarely left theirs.

Suddenly, he realized there was something he very much needed to know.

"How do I find my way home, Charlie?" he posed. "I don't mean now, I'm sure you'll get me back to my Place when we're done, but after that, how do I do it on my own? For that matter, how do I get back to you? I guess I should have been trying to memorize this walk."

Charlie smiled. "You won't have to. First of all, you'll never have trouble finding your own Place. Well, at least what direction it is from wherever you are. It's like a mental compass that always points there. You can feel it right now. Your mind has just been suppressing it because you didn't know what it was. Now that you know, give it a try. Just picture your Place in your head."

Michael did. He closed his eyes and conjured up an image of his Place, and sure enough, he perceived the direction perfectly. He didn't see it, or hear it, or smell it. The pull was invisible, subtle, but unquestionably real.

"There," he told Charlie. "Just a little to the left of that rock."

"Excellent." Charlie shared his friend's triumph. "You can do that from anywhere, no matter where in the universe."

"The universe? There's space travel here?"

"Not exactly." Charlie paused to work out how to explain it. "We're spread all over, Michael. For instance, where we are now isn't on the same planet as your Place. It's, I think, about two million light years away by mortal standards."

"Good God!" Michael was floored. "Then how—"

"You're living openly in six dimensions now. You were in mortal life, too, you just couldn't perceive them. That's how you can home in on your Place. It's also how you can walk seamlessly from planet to planet. This is the real world, Michael, and it never did suffer from those intractable distances. It's empty space that's an illusion. Well, I don't mean it isn't real, just that it's not a true impediment.

"It's the same with people. If you want to find me, just

picture me in your mind and head where it shows you. Gradually, the landscape will change, but your perception evolves along with it." Charlie smiled at Michael's dumfounded look. "It's a bit fuzzy at first, but you'll get it. And you'll need to. You can't much navigate by the stars here, mate. Every time you cross a planetary boundary, they shuffle."

THE TREES OPENED INTO A spacious clearing beside a rushing creek, far larger and more energetic than the trickle that had drained out of his jungle pool. *This* was the kind of stream where you could go fishing. And perched above it, like some Disney fantasy made real, was a treehouse.

And *what* a treehouse! It spanned four trees all told, each of them gigantic redwoods, with about half the living space built on braced decking suspended a dozen feet above the forest floor and the other half right inside the huge trunks, which were connected to each other by covered plank walkways. Michael looked for a ladder, and was delighted and surprised to find that instead, the dwelling's entrance was a subtle door cut seamlessly into the bark, behind which a wooden staircase spiraled up inside the tree.

He turned to Charlie and asked the question whose answer was obvious on Charlie's face. "This is yours?"

Charlie nodded, grinning with pride. Michael looked back up at the structure appreciatively. It was certainly Disney-esque, but it wasn't Robinson Crusoe. It had a finished, permanent look, with none of the gangliness of a makeshift island shelter. It was generously windowed, a kind of cozy very different from his stone-bound pirate cave, and the thick shutters now all drawn aside could be tightly latched against a storm. He found himself wondering what the weather was like here, and discovered a sudden passion to see it at its very worst. What could be more fun than to watch a real gullywasher scouring the landscape from the safety and comfort of your ideal, custom-made abode? God, the thought of lying in his bunk under a blanket during a thunderstorm, with that steaming cocoa, a good adventure book, and the window cracked to let in the sound and smell, was almost too delicious to dwell on.

He started toward the stairs, but Charlie held up a hand and shut the bark door.

"Not yet," he instructed. "I told you there's somewhere else we need to go first. I brought us here because it will make it easier for me to take you. In time, you may learn to do it yourself, but this time you'll be leaning on me, and like everyone else and their Place, my essence is strongest here."

Michael had no idea what Charlie was talking about, and found it remarkable that this didn't bother him in the least. *All in good time*, he reminded himself, a perspective he could not have maintained for long in life. He wondered absently whether the Afterlife was like a drug somehow. Was his patience a display of maturity, or was it simply an intoxicant-like dulling of his normal cognition? But no, it wasn't like that. The feeling that infused him here, and most powerfully within his Place, was not a mask. It was *clarity*. The first true clarity he had ever experienced, perhaps the only such clarity possible. The uncertainty and suffering, the half-blind hopelessness of mortal life – *that* was the mask. Not a mask, exactly, but sort of a mental fog, as the victim of a brain injury might feel. In that jungle darkness, he knew, he had seen more clearly into true reality than he could even contemplate outside it.

"I'll explain it later, I promise. For now, I just need you to trust me. It needs to be absolute, Michael, like 'you fall and I'll catch you.' I'm serious, okay? You've got to put your faith in me, you've got to do it whole-heartedly, or I won't be able to take you along."

"Sure, Charlie." He was not alarmed, but Michael was beginning to feel a twinge of uneasiness at not knowing the reason for Charlie's solemnity. It was perhaps the first trace of negative emotion he had experienced since his passing, something he would not have felt in his jungle. Still, what could happen really? He wasn't going to *die*.

"Take my hand." Michael did as he was told, clasping Charlie's right hand with his left. "Now close your eyes," Charlie continued. "It's not going to blind you or hurt you, there's nothing terrible to see. But we need your mind clear. We don't want it competing with what I'm trying to do. So just relax, close your eyes, try to clear out your thoughts. I know you can't clear it completely, and you won't have to. Just do the best you can."

Michael complied. He closed his eyes, tipped his head forward as in prayer, and imagined a calm and quiet scene. The image that came was of a seashore on a warm blue day, a wide, flat reach of sand with waves lapping gently in and out, the soft, comforting whoosh of its breathing, not a creature or person in sight.

Charlie led them an indeterminate distance over an indeterminate period of time. It might have been five minutes, or it might have been an hour; Michael had no idea, and in his present state he would not have known the difference.

There was a momentary wind, and Michael was so dedicated to maintaining his mental blank that at first he wasn't sure it if was real or an artifact of his conjured image. Then the light outside his eyelids changed abruptly, and the sound and the smell, too, and inadvertently, purely by reflex, he opened his eyes.

The magic was gone. He felt that first, even before he had an inkling of their surroundings. Not "magic," no; the *life* was gone. That sense of extra vitality, that invigorating electricity that permeated the air and every object, living or inanimate, in the Afterworld. Michael had become sensitive to it already, come to take it for granted even, and its absence was palpable. It was as though the air conditioning for the entire universe had been shut off. Charlie had somehow, for some indecipherable purpose, *returned them to the mortal world.*

Immediately, Charlie was in his face, holding a finger up to his lips in an urgent "be quiet" sign. Michael gave a quick nod to show he understood. Charlie kept hold of him with the other hand, and Michael accepted this, assuming there was good reason.

They were in a small house. It was the plainest sort of home, the kind encountered frequently in the course of a life entwined with those of other Wal-Mart line employees, honest working people on the bottom rung of the American dream. As if to confirm this, the treble chatter of a vintage television set sounded from another room, helping to mask their presence.

They were standing in a dim hallway of aged plaster and hardwood that had absorbed eighty-odd years of cooking and pets, living habits and natural decay. They stood at one end with three doors, the left and center ones cracked unremarkably open, the door on the right closed. There was something about that door that Michael couldn't articulate, but he had the strong sense that it stayed closed almost all the time. Maybe there was a barely perceptible layer of dust, maybe the knob looked less worn? Did he really see that, and if he did, could he draw such conclusions from it? He wasn't sure. He was seeing things differently now, that he knew. But he hadn't been doing it long enough to rely on it or to interpret it with confidence. There was something about that door, though, something that in life he was sure he wouldn't have noticed at all.

Charlie beckoned soundlessly, and Michael followed him to the other end of the hall, still holding hands. They stopped short of the adjoining room and peered in.

It was a modest but warmly-furnished living room with a broad old sofa, a matching side chair, and a cheap recliner arranged around a pocked and ring-stained coffee table, all oriented toward the TV. From atop the couch back, a grey cat eyed them with neither interest nor concern.

Sprawled comfortably in the recliner, alone in the room – and for that matter in the house – was a woman in her mid-thirties. She was dressed in worn Levi culottes and cheap baby blue flip-flops, one brassiere strap showing through the open neck of what had once been a fashionable summer-patterned cotton top. She was casually grazing popcorn from a Tupperware bowl on her lap, sighing intermittently at the episode of *Love Life* that was absorbing her full attention. She seemed to be at the end of a long day, if not a long week, of work – Michael found he had no idea of what time or day it was – and the half-drained bottle of Coors Lite perched on a paper coaster within arm's reach had the look of a simple reward well deserved.

The angle was oblique. Charlie made it clear that they were to stay out of sight, but Michael could see that she had been pretty in her day. Not beautiful, but attractive for sure, and her day, come to that, was not quite past. And Michael found – though he had never been here, never seen this house, had no idea even where they were – that somehow he knew her.

Not a name; he didn't have that. Nor could he place the nature of their acquaintance. She wasn't a Wal-Mart employee, not that he recognized anyway. Not a co-worker, yet there was something about her that seemed associated with the store, or maybe just with that time in his life – some mental light that blinked in his head but refused to reveal a connection. Had he dated her? Maybe. He had gone out on occasion after Vicki, and he had met some of those women in the course of his work. That felt closer, but ...He lost the scent. *What the hell was it?* He felt so close to solving the puzzle that the frustration was excruciating. And all the more so because it must be important, or else why were they here, why would Charlie go to the trouble of pulling some teleportation trick and risk discovery ogling her from these tenuous shadows, with no alibi and nowhere to hide if she shifted even slightly in their direction?

He felt a tug on his arm, and Charlie motioned Michael back down the hall. Even at this, Charlie himself lingered a few seconds more, seeming to drink in the tableau like oasis water.

They returned to the back of the hall, pausing briefly in front of the closed door. Charlie gestured toward their clasped hands, repeated his sign for "quiet," and then, swiping the air with two fingers in the direction of the door, gave an unmistakable signal: *We're going in.*

And with that, Charlie, pulling Michael fluidly behind, went – without opening it – *through* the door.

It felt like nothing. It might as well have been a hologram, and for a crazy moment Michael thought that was what it *must* have been. He turned and looked behind him. There it still was, solid as El Capitan, not moving in the slightest, not a mark on it. And he could see, clearly from this side, that the dead bolt was thrown.

He looked questioningly at Charlie, who vigorously shook his head. *Not now.* Silently, he pointed to the room's contents, the very reason they were here.

It was a child's bedroom, a boy's by the furnishings: school age, but only just. It was spare but clean, the folding closet door straight, the dresser drawers flush, nothing poking from under the bed, nothing on the floor except a miniature bench and table streaked with crayon.

There was a fat folio on top of the nightstand. Charlie gestured for Michael to pick it up.

It was a photo album made into a scrapbook, filled with tourist brochures, theme park maps, school awards, and, of course, pictures. The little boy in the photographs jumped out at him, vaguely familiar like the woman but even more so. Still, he found himself maddeningly unable to piece the whole thing together.

On the very first page, there was a yellowed newspaper clipping from the *San Mateo Daily Journal.* The date on the clipping immediately caught his eye. It meant something to him because it happened to be the same week as his Wal-Mart hire, not merely the anniversary, but the actual year. The event memorialized on this paper had occurred the very next day after Michael began his career in the manager's office next to Customer Service.

As he read it, he discovered that even here, with death and worry behind, the hair on the back of his neck was able to prickle.

```
Sunnybrae Elementary first grader
Charles Robert Paris was struck
by a trash collection vehicle in
the 1000 block of South Delaware
Street Wednesday afternoon while
playing with friends in front of
the school. He was pronounced
dead at San Mateo Medical Center
Thursday morning. He is survived
by his mother, Cynthia Reece Bar-
low, 24.
```

On top of the neatly made bed, tucked up against the pillow, lay a family Bible that looked like it had been passed down for generations. On top of it was a pair of stuffed animals Michael had seen before.

They were an unlikely furry, pink and blue pastel-colored turtle and a small, cheaply-made blue cow that had once upon a time been paid for by Michael Chandler and taken home by a beaming, compassionate little boy.

That boy was Charlie Paris.

CHAPTER 27
Revelations

IF CHARLIE HAD KNOWN JUST how liberating it would be to unburden himself to Michael, he may never have been able to keep his silence during the road trip. The cosmic order would have stifled him, of course – as it always must to keep mortals from seeing deep enough into the unknown to alter their moral decisions – but he would have nonetheless tried.

Safe from discovery and overcome with memory and emotion within this shrine to him that his mother had painfully created, suddenly Charlie was transformed, becoming the little boy again. Michael reached down and held him, tears gushing from both of them, quiet and motionless except for the silent sobs that shuddered Charlie's frail frame. Time itself seemed suspended, its passage impossible to judge.

When at last the emotional flood receded, Charlie dried his eyes on his shirt and looked up. "Thank you," he said, and the sound of that innocent little voice not heard in a decade stirred in Michael the same compassion it had inspired all those years ago.

The comforting embrace went on until both of them felt at peace. Charlie released Michael and returned to his Afterlife form. They clasped hands, and once again Charlie led Michael though the locked door. This time there was a windy feel, and they emerged on the other side not into the hallway but back in the redwoods. Michael looked behind them. The bedroom door, the house, and the rest of the mortal world were gone.

Though Charlie had restored himself to his spry adult form somewhere around twenty-eight years old, Michael could see – wondering how he could ever have *not* seen – the first grade kid behind the seasoned eyes. Yet now he realized that he *had* seen, might even have figured it out if his mental energy hadn't been tapped dry by his own troubles. The gentleness, the innocence, the child-like hurt: the little boy whose life was cut short had been in Charlie all along.

"My mom was only sixteen when she got pregnant," Charlie began as they made their way back toward the tree-house through the ancient growth. "The father wanted her to have an abortion." (*'The' father, not 'my' father*, Michael noted sadly.) "So did her best friend. So did her mom and dad. But she wouldn't do it."

Charlie drew inward, and Michael could see from his face that the feelings of guilt between Charlie and his mother ran both ways.

"She had to drop out of school and take a job waiting tables at a pizza place. I think we lived with my grandparents for about six months, then the stress was too much on everyone. She moved us into this dinky apartment that smelled like cat piss, with a girlfriend of hers to help with the rent. That's the first home I remember.

"She worked her tail off for us and still managed to be the best mom you could ever have. There was never enough money, but that's partly because she was always putting some away so I could feel like a normal kid. We had cake and hats for my birthday, a little tree and lots of presents for Christmas, real dyed eggs for Easter that she would hide in the park, then sneak them out of my basket and hide the same ones again to make it seem like more. She even saved enough to take me to Disneyland when I was six. That was the best thing ever. Every day for a week, we got in line a half hour before it opened and didn't leave until they shut down after the fireworks at night."

Michael smiled. "I'm so glad you got to do that."

"Yeah." The magic of that time still showed on Charlie's face. "She was a great mom, Michael. Everyone said it. Everyone but her. She was the only one who couldn't see it. All she felt was guilt. She felt terrible that I didn't have a father, and that we couldn't live in a real house. She hated leaving me in daycare while she worked. Some nights she cried herself to sleep just because she couldn't get me new clothes or something the other kids had for school.

"That day in the Wal-Mart? She used to struggle horribly with stuff like that. She wanted me to have things, but she was always balancing it with what we'd have to go without. She *wanted* me to have that little cow. She *loved* that I cared so much about stuffed animals. She said it meant I was going to be a kind and generous man when I grew up, that I would make a real prince for some lucky girl.

"But she had this exam coming up that week. She'd been studying in the middle of the night for months to test for this government job. Something in the state social services office, I don't recall exactly what. It was going to be the first good job she'd ever had, something with security and good pay and medical insurance. It was going to be our ticket up. But there was a test fee, and she was barely able to save it up in time to pay the day of the exam. That's what she was thinking about when you met us in the store."

"God," Michael said. "If I had known …"

"No, my friend." Charlie smiled reassuringly. "What happened that day was the grace of God. It had to be. Don't even think about if."

"But all I did was—"

"What you *did*," Charlie interjected forcefully, "was spare my mom from a lifetime of misery. Michael, if you had not done what you did, she would have punished herself for the rest of her life over not doing something that meant so much to me when I had only hours to live. She would have seen it as the ultimate proof that she was an unfit mother. She would have been devastated. I mean, not that she wasn't hysterical when I died, of course she was. But over time she was able to deal with that grief. And a big part of it was knowing that she had spent our last hours together making me happy instead of scolding me over a few dollars.

"And there was something else, too. She was deeply affected by seeing a complete stranger display your kind of compassion. You know why she put those animals on the Bible on top of my bed? Because what you did made her feel like in spite of everything, there was true good in the world. It gave her hope that maybe, just maybe, her life could be okay again."   Charlie sobered. "I'll tell you what I think, Michael. I think if you hadn't come along that day, my mom eventually would have killed herself. In fact, I know she would have. I haven't got the slightest doubt."

"Good God, Charlie. I ... don't know what to say."

Charlie shook his head. "You don't have to."

THEY PROCEEDED IN SILENCE, EACH to his own thoughts, until at last the treehouse compound came back into view.

From the safety of this sanctum, it struck Michael that what they had just done constituted a terrible risk. The consequences of being discovered could have been devastating. Encountering some intruder claiming to be her dead son after all these years in the form of an unfamiliar adult phantom, capable of materializing in her home at will – who knew what far-reaching effects that might have had on Charlie's mother?

"They can't recognize us when we go back," Charlie counseled, opening the tree trunk door and leading them up the stairs, as though he could read what was in Michael's head. And who knew, in this miraculous landscape and especially in his Place, maybe he could. "The extra dimensions we manifest in make it impossible, no matter what we say or how close we look to the way we did in life. It even affects *us* a little: you'd find it hard to recognize me in the mortal world if you didn't already know who I was. The eyes see, but the dimensions interfere with how the mind interprets. It has to be that way, otherwise wives would go back to husbands, children would go back ... to ..."

They reached the top of the spiral and walked out onto a covered open-air deck. Charlie gestured and they sat down in the comfortable chairs with a nice view of the river as he took a minute to compose himself. "Just about everyone would go back, and if they could be recognized it would be incontrovertible proof that there is life after death. It would completely undermine the mortal framework."

"*You* went back," Michael prodded. "And just now we *both* did."

"But not *overtly*," Charlie clarified. "I've been keeping an eye on you and my mom for ten mortal years, and neither one of you ever saw me. Well, 'recognized' is a better way to put it. I'm not sure about you, but Mom has made eye contact with me a couple of times. But there was never even a blip of recognition."

It made Michael think of his own parents. *I could go back,* he thought. *He said I could learn how.* The thought of seeing his mom and dad again, even just to watch them from the shadows, made his soul ache. And he wasn't sure he *could* just watch. He would be driven to talk to them, just to see his mom's smile, hear his dad's reassuring voice again after all he'd been through ... except that from what Charlie was saying, it wouldn't be like that. It would be as if they had Alzheimer's; they wouldn't know him, and even worse, they might be hostile toward him. They might see him as nothing but a lying troublemaker. And he couldn't bear that, no, that would make things worse, not better. Yet the temptation was so compelling it brought a physical pain.

He set the notion aside for later pondering. Now was

a time for questions that had been burning inside him and that Charlie could now answer; there would be plenty of time later for soulful rumination on his own. He moved on. "When you found me in the jungle, you said this was your first welcoming."

"The greeting when someone first gets here. Yeah it was. It varies, but ideally it's supposed to be the person here who was closest to you in mortal life. Mainly family members, usually parents or a spouse. Your grandfather wanted to do it. But I persuaded him."

Michael was certainly interested in this line of discussion, but it wasn't his immediate purpose. "The reason I ask is that you died with your mother alive and never knowing your dad. I've just been wondering who greeted *you*."

Charlie smiled. "What's the name on your credit cards?"

"Pfft. Michael Cha—" Suddenly it dawned on him what Charlie meant. "Barbara Jordan?"

Charlie nodded. "The one who intercepted you at the airport. Man, is she ever a nice human being for such a dazzling beauty. Usually those types are so used to pampering, they can't be bothered to help other people. Not her. She was nurturing and sympathetic toward a confused orphan right from the start. Never had kids of her own, I'm sure that was part of it. Resourceful, too. It was no simple matter to arrange for the car, the cards, and the airline credentials. Oh, speaking of which, I've been meaning to show this to you." Charlie reached into a pocket and fished out a wallet-sized card.

Michael's eyes went wide. It was a California driver's license so convincing it looked like it might even fool police. The face was Charlie's, but the name read: *Charles Robert Jordan.*

"You *cheater*!"

"We were going to make it for you," Charlie explained. "In fact we *did* make one with your name on it. But then we realized that exposing your face to motel desk clerks and security cameras would be a bad idea."

Michael marveled, thinking for the first time, now that he knew what was involved, what a monumental task it must have been. Not to mention doing it for someone she'd never met. Beth was resourceful, too, and contributed to a lot of charities. But this compassion for strangers on a *personal* level, he thought, set Barbara Jordan apart.

"I was only with her briefly," Michael said, "but she seems like my kind of lady. I'd like to meet her and thank her sometime. I mean, meet her again."

Charlie looked as pleased as an orphan with birthday cake. "That can be arranged."

THERE WAS SO MUCH TO absorb that Michael found it difficult to remember everything he wanted to ask. He knew there would be time later, but he felt desperate to get as much information as fast as he could.

"So what about those apparitions, that horrible thing I saw in my townhouse and the other one later … what were they?"

Charlie sobered. "The one you saw in Dallas and Key West was a *Darkened*. A dead person who can't let go of resentment. That's what happens to them, their appearance decays to reflect the corruption in their heart. That TV and radio stuff was probably just to unsettle you."

"It worked." Michael shuddered.

"They're nothing you want to mess with, here or in the mortal realm. It's true that for the most part they can't hurt mortals directly, although I've heard of exceptions. But they *can* drive people out of their minds. They *can* inspire murder, or suicide. They can make people's lives a living Hell."

"Why would they pick on me?"

Charlie shrugged. "This one *may* have been tormenting you just for torment's sake. But there's always a *reason*. They don't single people out for nothing. It's possible it was trying to send you a message, although *what* message I can't even guess."

Michael did his best to take it all in. It was a lot to digest. "So, that thing on the stairs in my townhouse ... that was one of these 'Darkened,' too?"

"No." Charlie's tone was definitive. "They don't have that kind of power. They don't have beautiful faces. They don't speak with that kind of bizarre voice you described. And then there's that stairway."

"What about it?"

Charlie pursed his lips. "Well, you know how we can pass through doors because of their archetypal significance? There's something like that with stairways, too. It doesn't apply to regular staircases, like the one your townhouse was built with. But stairs that make no sense, like the ones that lead to a blank wall in the Winchester House — that mansion the crazy lady built in San Jose — ever been there?"

"Sure," Michael replied. "Hasn't every kid in the Bay Area?"

"Yeah." Charlie grinned. "Well, *those* kinds of stairs, ones that shouldn't be there at all, are echoes of the rift between good and evil. They're like a moral 'bridge.' Down leads toward evil, up toward good. The further it descends, the deeper the evil." He sobered. "But I've never heard of one descending so far you couldn't see the bottom. Or that burned a hole in a floor. Or that was surrounded by darkness, like it was crossing the void. The level of evil that implies is mind-blowing. No Darkened could pull that off."

Michael's eyes widened in mounting horror. "What kind of thing *could?*"

"I'm not sure. I know the basics, but I'm no authority when it comes to high order Dark Ones. I try to avoid them whenever I can." Charlie smiled. "But that's what it had to be. Something more powerful and less constrained than the Darkened. Beyond that, I just can't say."

Michael was disappointed. He knew Charlie was telling the truth, but it wasn't the level of certainty and detail he had hoped for.

A lighter question occurred. "If you were seven when you died, Charlie, you'd be about seventeen now. But you look older. Even here, there's something in your eyes that looks as old as you appeared on the road trip. Does just being here age you extra fast?"

"It can, yeah, but that's not what you're seeing. Everybody starts out here with a more or less adult cognition and form. Even infants. It's tough on them for a while, but they get lots of help and it's pretty amazing how fast they adapt. Their minds are extra pliable, I'm sure that helps. And if they choose to, once they're properly oriented, they can remain kids for a while if they want. Indefinitely in theory, although most of them get their fill of it pretty quick. I was that way for a couple of months. But there's so much going on here, so much to explore and do, once they're used to interacting with adults on a peer level, most kids allow their bodies and minds to let it go."

"But you say that's not what I'm seeing."

"Time isn't what you think it is, as your pal Dan loves to say. There are some subtle links between time here and in the mortal world, but for the most part they're independent of each other. I did peek in on my mom as soon as I learned how to do it. I couldn't help it, and thank God I had a saint of a woman on this side to help me through that."

"Barbara Jordan?"

Charlie nodded. "She was invaluable in helping me understand that I couldn't interact with Mom as her son. She helped me see that there wasn't much I could do for her. And most importantly, she helped me see that it was temporary and okay. Mom's going to be here one day, and we'll have all eternity to laugh and love and spend time with each other. In the meantime, she's got her mortal job to do, creating her Place.

"It takes a while, but everyone sees this in time, and it

frees you completely. I gradually started living my life *here*. I kept checking in on her from time to time, but it stopped dominating me. The more I adapted, the more I felt at peace.

"Experience-wise, Michael, I've had more than sixty years here. How you met me in the bookstore, that's how I'd actually look if those years had all been mortal. Not that I had to; with practice, you can manifest any age you like. In fact, that's how I kept you from noticing you were being watched, varying my appearance from one visit to the next. I did that regularly – checking in on you *and* my mom – but that didn't keep me from a full life *here*. I've met tons of people, learned to do new things, had all kinds of adventures. In case you wondered, that's how I learned to drive a car. It's awesome, man, you'll see. You'll feel natural here before you know it."

"Sixty years?"

"Like the blink of an eye," Charlie dismissed merrily. "I'm still a baby. I've met people who've been here for *thousands*."

The enormity of it began to sink in. *They really are all here*, Michael thought. *Every man, woman, and child that ever lived*. It was positively mind-blowing to think of all those lives, the conversations to be had around a low campfire. How had people lived day-to-day east of the Great Rift Valley when the human race began? How did someone with Stone Age mentality conceive of the wheel? How was music invented? Did Plato really have Santorini in mind when he wrote of Atlantis? What happened to Amelia Earhart, and were the Mafia or the CIA involved in killing Kennedy? All the questions of human experience you could ever ask – *the answers were all here*. Just *talking* to people seemed like it could fill eternity.

But not now. For the first time since arriving, Michael found himself tired. Not physically – in that way, his body felt as charged as a Saturday morning despite having not slept for the equivalent of several days. It had been a cacophonous several days, however, crammed to overflowing with things new and exciting, jaw-dropping and barely fath-omable. Now he understood what Charlie had meant about sleep being not strictly necessary, but nevertheless an indis-pensable sanctuary for emotional maintenance.

"Thanks for everything, Charlie. I don't know what I'd do without you. I think I'm all good for now. Frankly, I don't think I could fit one more metaphysical sock in the suitcase without busting a hinge."

Charlie laughed. "I know what you mean, man. It's a lot, and there's tons more. You're welcome to chill here if you want, we don't have to talk. We can just sit and watch the river."

"If it's all the same to you, I think I'll go back to my house. That pirate bed sounds awfully inviting."

"Even better." Charlie stood up from his chair as Michael did the same. "You're going to have a great time ex-ploring your Place. Come get me if you ever want some company for that."   At the head of the stairs, Michael paused. "Funny," he remarked. "Of all the possibilities, I never envisioned Afterlife like this. I always pictured sort of an alabaster cathedral in the clouds where I'd get to see God."

"You don't see God?" Charlie posed.

Michael looked around him. He breathed in the spar-kling river and the shafts of golden sunlight. He marveled at the impossibly huge redwoods. He thought of his tour of the cosmos, his idyllic jungle, his grandfather's unfathomable love.

He smiled at Charlie. "Yeah." He nodded. "I see God."

FULLY CONTENT WHEN HE HAD first arrived in the Af-terworld to be alone with his bliss and wonderment, now Michael found himself desperately desiring someone with whom to share all this joy and discovery. He paused for a moment in the ancient forest, doing his best to detect the departed he loved.

His grandfather was the easiest to find. Michael could sense him ahead and to the right, what felt like about an hour and a half walk, though he had no idea how he could judge that. *I could go see him right now.* He smiled to himself. But he decided to wait until he was rested.

Encouraged, he tried to find Max. At first he picked up nothing at all, but on his second pass there was a faint trace of Max far, far away. He wondered why that would be. He certainly loved his brother. But he realized that for the most part, the feeling had not been reciprocated. *The more love that flows between you and another person, the closer your Place is to theirs,* Charlie had said. Unhappily, it was obviously why Max's signal was so weak.

He had saved Vicki for last because it made him nervous. Despite all he had seen here, he still could not quite come to grips with the idea of a reunion. It wasn't a fear of that prospect – on the contrary, reuniting with Vicki was the most exhilarating development he could imagine. But he had hesitated to pursue it, even mentally, for one compelling reason: a soul-deep terror that it might be hoping for too much.

In life, he had never expected to see Vicki again, at least in his conscious mind. He worried that the intervening decade might have blunted her affection. *Decade?* Who knew how long it had been for her. Time wasn't what he thought it was, and Charlie had passed more than sixty years. Should it be any different for Vicki? The memory of her had been a constant drum beat in Michael's humdrum life, but for her it would be different. Vicki had had the wonders of the universe to explore, and she was the type to pursue an opportunity like that with zeal. What was it Charlie had said? *I've met tons of people, learned to do new things, had all kinds of adventures.* For Vicki, that probably went tenfold, and the prospects for romance here, a universe of supernaturally attractive men, were practically limitless. How could Michael compete with that? How could she think of him as anything more than a fond toy left behind in a distant childhood?

He prayed that it wouldn't be so, that when he reached out he would detect her close by and still as infused with their love as he was. That he would go to her and she would embrace him as if they had parted only yesterday. That Michael's world, for the first time since her best friend had called and told him of the tragedy, would be truly whole again.

But there was nothing. *Nothing*. Michael could sense no sign of Vicki.

It was the absolute worst devastation he had ever felt. Nothing could compare. Not his brother's sacrifice, not Ridge Raymore's threats, not leaving a cell full of doomed girls to their fate. Not even Vicki's own death. That, at least, had been involuntary – she had been gone, but it had in no way tarnished the depth or quality of their love. This, though: this was *abandonment*.

He doubled his pace. He was desperate for the emotional salve of his Place. In the mortal world, he would have screwed the top off a fifth of Jack Daniel's and siphoned it right from the bottle.

THOUGH EMOTIONALLY SPENT, MICHAEL HAD no trouble picking up the way to his Place. Mercifully, it wasn't long before he crossed into the twilight jungle, and from there it was but a healthy stroll to reach the ivied rock abutment that lodged his Pirate House within its carved recesses. Yet even here, his cruel despair over Vicki was so powerful that it left him grasping for reassurance.

It came to him on four legs.

It was so dark he nearly didn't see it, and when he did he pulled up precariously short, narrowly avoiding stepping on the massive black panther lounging at the foot of his door.

He was surprised, but not alarmed. Michael had always loved animals and he knew that this one, despite its meat-hook claws and dagger teeth, despite being size of a Bengal tiger, would do him no harm. And as he gazed into its gem-green eyes, a new perception bloomed: familiarity. It reminded him of how he had seen Charlie, and then Charlie's mother, that uncanny sense that he knew them from some past encounter looming just beyond his mind's reach. Thinking about the answer that had been revealed to those puzzles helped him solve this one almost instantly, and familiarity turned to recognition.

"Alex!"

At the sound of his name, the magnificent beast that had once been Michael's childhood companion issued a rumbling purr.

Michael dropped to his knees with tears forming, both hands reaching out to stroke the massive silky cheeks, which he had been able to do with the fingers of one hand when the animal was an easy-going Siamese in life. Alex had behaved more like a dog than a cat, ever loyal and openly reciprocating of physical affection, in a way that most felines seemed to feel was beneath them. Still, Alex was the last acquaintance he would have expected to find here. Confirmation that pets had a place in the Afterlife was his most joyous discovery yet.

A few mutual hugs and kisses later, Michael rose and opened the chamber door, motioning an invitation for the cat to go inside. Alex, however, simply padded to one side to unblock the entry and settled back down in the grass. Michael could understand this. A normal domestic cat would have a field day in there, napping in the upper bunk or squirreling itself away in some belowdecks cubby of the ship like a small child playing hide-and-seek. In his present form, however, Alex would be hard-pressed just to turn around in the hallways.

"Suit yourself," Michael told him affectionately. "The

offer stands if you change your mind."

During the walk from Charlie's, Michael had half entertained a notion of searching the house for the means to make hot chocolate that he felt certain would be there. But when he actually arrived, the call of the blankets was so compelling that he abandoned all thoughts of detour. He fingered the bedside wall torch down to a whisper of blue flame, closed the door, and buried himself luxuriously in the covers of the lower bunk. Amazingly, but not shockingly – he had almost come to expect such wonders rather than be surprised by them – the bed seemed to rock, swaying gently as a mother's arms, feeling as though he truly were nestled in the cabin of a sailing ship well underway toward some mysterious adventure.

And why not? he mused as slumber rapidly overtook him. It was as true a vision as any.

IT IS JUST THE TWO of them. She stands alone in the rancid cell, hands gripping the cold black bars, her cherubic face calm and trusting. She has placed her faith in him implicitly. A fate worse than death awaits her if he fails.

He darts frantically about the dungeon corridor, casting out for a course to salvation. The desk drawers are full of plastic squirt guns. The two new cells are cluttered with useless trash. The older cell with the open door is completely empty save for the hole in its floor that is their road to freedom.

From the passages above he hears footsteps and voices. They are coming, an army of them. In a minute they will be here, and if he misses this chance there will never be another.

He has no tools, he has no weapon, he has no key. It will have to be brute strength. He will have to summon the courage, the unmitigated commitment, the raw adrenaline-fueled power to do the impossible. It can be done. He knows people are able to heave cars off of accident victims when there is no other hope. He is going to pull the bars apart with his bare hands.

The girl is Felicity. The girl is Beth. He is going to save them both.

MICHAEL SAT BOLT UPRIGHT, EXPECTING to feel cold sweat induced by the nightmare sticking his underclothes to his skin. There wasn't any. He expected to feel drained, too, but he wasn't. He was firmly alert, fit and energetic, ready to move. And he was packed to the seams with purpose.

Because he finally, *finally*, understood.

That's why I couldn't let Vicki go, he thought. It all made sense now. God kept me focused on Vicki so I wouldn't get serious with anyone else. Anyone, that was, but Beth. He had to keep me single and unattached until he could maneuver us back together. Until Beth had reached the point where she would be receptive to me. Where she would need me. Where she could love me. Where she could leave Rick, commit to me for real and for good, and join me in a fulfilling eternal bond.

Then, at that pivotal point, just as Beth and Michael were fusing together, fate had severed them with its harshest cleaver. Whether kismet or dark intent, their budding union had been yanked up before it could take root.

And that separation might have ended the courtship for another man. But not for Michael Chandler. His destiny revealed, he would never let it languish now. Not even through death. This was the final test, he knew. That was *what* it was, and *all* it was. A final ordeal to see if he was worthy of this precious gift.

And worthy he would be. He would correct his mistake. Vicki had been delivered to him by divine grace and he had failed her. He was not going to fail Beth.

The first trial, as stiff as it seemed, had been easier. All it would have taken was to extend his natural chivalry. If *he* had rented the truck, if he had worked things out to help her move that day, Vicki would be alive. Vicki would be alive and the two of them would be married and their children would be in elementary school. They would have a nice little house near a park in San Mateo with a nice little dog running around a white-fenced yard. Just one decision would have changed the world.

It was too late for Vicki, whom he had let down and who – due at least in part to that very failure, he was beginning to suspect – had moved on in the Afterworld and left their relationship behind. This test would be harder, but it was no more than proper penance for his shortfall. And a fair price it was for the sublime reward. Michael and Beth, bound in eternity. Life and love and joy beyond measure. All his longings fulfilled.

All it would take was fifty-odd years of care and finesse. Most of a lifetime, but trivial against eternity. Fifty years, or whatever remained of Beth's mortal existence, watching over her and doing whatever was necessary to nurse her love. It would be difficult, seeing as how in a sense he wouldn't be there, not to Beth. Not as her Michael Chandler. And it was impossible to predict what circumstances might come up to lead her away from him. Other men, surely, that was a certainty. No woman of Beth's appeal could navigate life unnoticed. Health problems, possibly. A fair ration of little tragedies, guaranteed. But Michael could do it. He *would* do it. He would pull it off if it required every ounce of his energy, every scrap of his wit, every minute of his time. And at the end, he would be repaid a thousandfold. Beth's time would come, she would join him in this Afterlife, and she would be humbled and overwhelmed with delight at the wondrous home he had erected for them in her Place. All he had to do was make sure she still loved him, still wanted to be with him above all others, when her moment came.

It was a monumental job. He didn't know how he would do it. He only knew he *would*.

But first things first. There was the small matter of a cell full of little girls in a tropical hell called Isla Tesoro. He had made a promise he intended to keep.

"I NEED TO GO BACK."

They were seated on a rock overlooking the river near Charlie's treehouse, Alex curled up in the grass at its base with his emerald eyes closed.

Michael's voice was amiable, but there was no mistaking his tone of determination. He was not going to be deterred.

Charlie tried anyway. "It's not a good idea," he cautioned grimly. "For one thing, your ability to help is limited. You can pass through doors, you're strong and durable, but that's it. You don't have superpowers. You can talk to people, but you can't tell them anything they don't know if it might affect their moral decisions. People you know won't recognize you and won't be persuaded if you try. And you can't kill anyone."

"I don't plan on killing anyone."

"It's still a bad idea," Charlie persisted. "There's one thing you need to think long and hard on. Any interaction you have with a mortal can alter their decisions even if you don't tell them anything. And if that happens, there's a chance it will damage their soul. Not physically, but it can have a deleterious effect on their Place. Believe me, you don't want that haunting you."

"You know me as well as anyone, Charlie. Do you honestly think I'd do something like that?"

"Not intentionally, of course not. But even for us, the mortal world is basically beyond our control. It's easy to stumble and knock someone's destiny off-kilter. In fact, that's why most people who do it go back – to change the life of a loved one. Friends, family members, children. And it *can* help, but it's just as likely to hurt. Given the restrictions, even the positive effects tend to be minimal. After a while, everyone who goes back ultimately gives it up. A lot of times it's due to frustration. Usually, though, it's because they finally realize that all true destiny lies in the Afterlife, and their loved ones will get here eventually. Once they embrace that, interfering with mortals seems pointless and irrelevant."

"All that didn't keep *you* from doing it, Charlie."

"Yeah, but it's not the same. For one thing, for most of that time I was totally passive. It's true I was watching you, you and my mom, waiting for an opportunity to help. But I was lurking in shadows. I never made myself known."

"Until the road trip." Michael held him to his account.

"Yes." Charlie smiled wistfully. "And *that* part was an exception. I don't know if I ever would have figured out how to make a difference on my own, but we *weren't* on our own. We didn't just pop in on your life and fumble around. We were directed."

"What do you mean, 'directed'? By whom?"

Charlie smiled. "Well, God, ultimately, I'd say. But in the immediate sense … an angel."

Michael was stunned. "An angel? Seriously? An *angel* told you to help *me*?"

"We would have tried anyway, once we saw what was happening. But that might have been too late. I was checking in on you regularly, but it wasn't constant. I probably wouldn't have been watching your place that night if I hadn't been told."

Michael felt dazed. "What would an angel want with me, Charlie? I don't get it."

"I don't know completely myself. But I'll tell you what

I do know. About two weeks before that night, an angel showed up at my Place. Desedaraya, that was her name. She said she knew I had been watching you. She said something momentous was about to happen in your life and asked if I would be willing to help. I said of course, I had been waiting to do that all along.

"She gave me the date and said you were going to find yourself in serious trouble, running from the law through no fault of your own, and that you'd show up at the Alaska counter at SFO sometime after dark. She said I must make sure you got safely to Boston. That was it; she wouldn't tell me anything more. She wouldn't say *how* to do it, and she wouldn't tell me what it was all about. It was maddening, but you can't negotiate with angels. They're just messengers and they're very literal. What an angel says, simply *is*. So I just asked if I had to do this alone or if I could enlist some help. She said I could let in one person, only one, and that it had to be someone whose commitment and discretion were absolute.

"So Barbara Jordan, who grabbed you at the airport, she and I worked out the best plan we could think of and set about getting things in place. A good deal of it we could only plan as contingencies, because, of course, the one factor we couldn't control was a big one: *you*. We decided that she would give you the cards and get you on the road east, on the theory that a beautiful woman would have an easier time gaining your trust. I was to be the escort because I'd be less conspicuous and less of a distraction for you. I had my own car, and I was parked just a few spaces away at the airport when you came down to the Eclipse. I didn't approach you then because we thought there was a good chance it might spook you. I actually drove behind you, a good ways back, all the way to Sacramento. I was just about to show myself at the Mini-Mart when that cashier mentioned the bookstore. I hid until you drove away and then followed you over there. You know the rest."

Michael nodded slowly in amazement. The whole

thing had been choreographed from the start. No wonder he had felt hounded by coincidence.

And the fact that Charlie and Barbara had pulled it off made him more resolute than ever.

"Well, I haven't had orders from an angel," he told Charlie, "but I'm *going* to go. I *have* to. I heard everything you said, and Charlie, maybe you're totally right and I'll find that nothing I do can make a bean hill of difference. But I've got to try just the same. I need to know I did everything I possibly could to free those little girls we left behind. I won't be able to live with myself if I don't. I'll be stuck in my Place like one of those Darkened things because I won't be able to face the regret."

Charlie eyed him appraisingly, sucking in and letting out a resigned breath. "All right, Michael. I can see you've made up your mind. You've got my warning, but who knows? I can't predict the future. Maybe you will do some good. If nothing else, at least it will get it out of your system. Come on, I'll explain how it all works and how to focus so you can go back if you're hell-bent on it. May God be with you."

Charlie started to get up, but Michael waved him back down. "Just one more thing, Charlie, and I think we'll be done with questions for a while. I keep meaning to ask, but there's been so much going on."

"Sure, what is it?"

"That last day in Boston, at the end of our trip. You told me something just before you drove away, remember? You said there could be no salvation for me in this world. *That* world. And then you took off without a word of explanation. I stewed over that, you could probably guess. And I have to say, if this …" He gestured at the world around them. "If this qualifies as 'no salvation,' brother, I'll take it. I'm not knocking the gift horse, but I still want to know. What was that all about?"

Charlie broke down. It was clear this was the very last subject Charlie wanted to think about, and he practically disintegrated at its very mention.

"Oh, God, Michael, you've got to forgive me. Please, *please* forgive me. I didn't want to do that. I *hated* it. It was the most awful experience of my life. But I had no choice. She *made* me do it."

"Barbara?"

"The angel. Desedaraya. She told me you might ask about the status of your soul. And she told me exactly what I was to say if you did. They were her words, Michael, not mine, I recited them verbatim. I had to promise, and then, when I actually had to do it ..." Charlie sniffed and batted tears off his checks with the back of his hand. "It was even worse than I thought. It made me *sick*. As soon as I had the car out of your sight, I pulled off and threw up all over the curb."

"Oh, Charlie." Michael reached out and gave the man a comforting hug, setting aside for the moment the questions that Charlie's account naturally begged.

"She said," Charlie blubbered, "it was *imperative* that you not be reassured. Something about multiplying the power of your sacrifice. I didn't understand it, and I still don't. You've got to believe me, Michael. I would have given *anything* not to have to do that to you."

"It's okay, Charlie. It's not your fault. You did the right thing. You don't need forgiveness, but if it makes you feel better ... I forgive you."

Charlie squeezed him like a grateful schoolboy, mumbling in a thin voice, "Thank you."

After a long minute they separated, and Michael made an attempt to lighten the mood. "So an *angel* made you lie to me."

"It wasn't a lie. Angels *can't* lie, and telling me to would amount to the same thing."

"But ..."

Charlie shook his head. "I can't say for sure what she meant. She never did tell me. But it had to be true somehow. All I can think of is that maybe it's some kind of technicality, like maybe things were still in flux until you made the decision to jump out of that airplane. Or later, because I guess you might have been rescued. Maybe it wasn't final until the moment you actually died." Charlie wiped the last of his tears dry. "If that's it, then you *weren't* saved in *that* world. It wasn't official until you climbed the tunnel and came out into the light."

"What tunnel?"

Charlie frowned. "The tunnel. The dark tunnel where you see the light up ahead. Everybody has it, even people with near-death experiences. The tunnel is your passage to the Afterworld and the light leads to your Place. That's what I'm talking about."

"Charlie ... there was no tunnel."

"Of course there was. Have you forgotten it? Is that even possible? I guess it might be, but I've never heard of it."

Now Michael became alarmed. He wasn't at all sure what to make of this. "Listen to me, Charlie. I didn't forget. I didn't climb any tunnel. My memory is perfectly clear. On the way down I closed my eyes, and that's how I hit the water. I went way, way under with water shooting up my nose. I had no control over anything. The water got cold, then it started getting warm again. All of a sudden I was dry, there was no more pain, and it felt like I *was* flying. I opened my eyes and I was flying. All over the universe, Charlie, I could see planets and supernovas and galaxies. And I still wasn't in control, something was carrying me. A big, huge transparent ... I don't know what, in the shape of a man. I thought it might be an angel, but it didn't have wings or a halo or anything, and I could see right through it. And it was *massive*, Charlie, it was holding me in its hands like a little newborn. It flew me all over the place, wherever I wanted to go, just by thinking about it. And when I felt like stopping, it carried me right down here. I saw the star, I saw the planet from a distance, and all the way down into the jungle in one continuous motion. Then the thing was gone and I was down here under the trees, and you came."

Charlie was dumbstruck. When Michael was finished, he continued to stare, speechless, frozen.

"I didn't dream it," Michael declared, mostly just hoping to break Charlie's trance.

"I'm sure you didn't." Charlie's voice was low, slow, almost monotone. "Because you couldn't possibly have made that up."

"I didn't."

Charlie's eyes never left Michael's, his voice continuing its deliberate tone. "What you are describing," he droned, "is a Nivulum. That's the only thing it could be. You couldn't possibly have known about them because no mortal does. They've never been seen or revealed or written about in the mortal world. I've never seen one myself, as far as that goes. But that's what you saw, beyond a shadow of doubt. You described it perfectly."

"What's a Nivulum?"

"No one really knows. No one I've talked to, anyway. All you hear is that the Nivulem are some kind of advanced beings higher than angels, though they were created later. After Man, in fact. True free moral agents, not like angels who just have that messenger role. Nivulem are free to roam space and time at their whim. What they are, what their purpose is, nobody knows. People speculate, but they've got nothing to base it on. The fact is that they're a total mystery."

"They're not demons or something?"

"No. They're not evil, though they have the capacity for evil just like we do. But nobody talks about them ever *doing* evil. I've always been told the Nivulem have successfully *overcome* evil. Like they're capable of it, but they never succumb. I have no idea if that's true. I have no idea what it means if it is true."

"How do you know they exist at all if no one knows anything about them?"

"There's no trace of them in the *mortal* world. *Here*, the legends about them go back to the dawn of history, and they *are* occasionally seen. They have their scholars, people devoted to studying them, although I've never met one. There are supposed to be books. I never gave it much thought because you just don't encounter them in the normal course of things. I suppose they're a little like the Loch Ness monster, except that Nivulem are real."

"What do you think it means, Charlie? Why would a Nivulem—"

"Nivul*um*," Charlie corrected. "Nivulem is plural."

"Why would a Nivulum give me a piggyback ride through space?"

"I don't know." Michael could see that Charlie was, emphatically, at a complete loss. "I haven't got the slightest clue."

HOURS LATER, MICHAEL CHANDLER AND his three-hundred-pound kitty made it back to the twilight jungle. His patron safely home, Alex peeled off the path and bounded into the darkness to do whatever big cats in the Afterworld did to amuse themselves. He may as well have disappeared. Michael saw the end of his tail ripple like a bullwhip, then he was gone without a sound.

As he opened the tiki torch door, it occurred to Michael that he didn't need to go inside. Charlie had advised him to make the jump from his Place, but the jungle itself counted for that. So why was he here ... force of habit? Did his subconscious feel like he needed to stop by his house and pick up his spiritual car keys?

No, he thought, it was something else. Something was *pulling* him here. And as he allowed this thought to germinate, he perceived that the something was not quite right. He didn't know *how*, but the impression was palpable.

It didn't take long to find out.

He stood in the doorway and froze, gripped with as

much alarm as his Place, his sanctuary, could possibly allow. But for the mental insulation, he would have felt every bit as panicked as he had that night in his townhouse.

There in his home, in the shadows at the "T" end of the hall, stood a murky figure. It was the same entity he had seen in the Texas motel mirror and again on the sidewalk in Florida. The same ragged clothing, the same blood-stained chest, the same yellowed teeth and dark-pit eyes staring from the same hideously abraded face.

Across light years, across the boundary of death, the Darkened had found him.

CHAPTER 28
Dark and Light

THE DARKENED CHEAT.

Charlie had explained this inconvenient and annoying fact during their session preparing Michael for his journey back to the mortal realm. Now Michael played back this exchange in his mind, frantically rummaging for anything Charlie had said that might help him deal with the entity at the far end of the hall.

"The first step is to go somewhere isolated," he saw Charlie saying, "so your mind is pure. Your Place is ideal. Then you think hard of where you want to go, which can only be somewhere you've been to where there is at least some trace of sincere love, either for you or by you. Once you're there on the mortal side, you can literally walk though closed doors. But nothing else, you can't go through walls or anything."

"Why doors?" Michael saw himself asking. "They're just a part of the structure."

"Because," Charlie explained, "doors have an iconic meaning. In the archetypal sense, a door is a barrier intended to control access on either side, to let some things in and keep other things out. That has spiritual as well as physical connotations. It's the spiritual component that creates their metaphysical significance.

"You must remember at all times that you can't allow

yourself to be seen doing it. As I'm sure you can figure out, that makes it possible to get *stuck*. If that happens, your only hope is to manufacture privacy somehow so you can wink back to the Afterworld and return to the mortal world somewhere else that's safe. It can be a pain, but at least it's something."

Michael smiled. "I can just picture the look on a guard's face when somebody vanishes out of a locked cell."

"That does happen." Charlie laughed. "It's behind a few of those 'escapes' nobody has ever been able to figure out."

"So I think of where I'm going." Michael put the topic back on track. "And then ..."

"Where and *when*," Charlie added. "Then you instinctively head for it just like a Place or a person here. You will come around a corner, a big rock or the edge of a tree or something, to where this world and the mortal intersect. And you just walk through. It's not all that different from traveling between Places."

Michael nodded to show he understood. Then an inspired question occurred to him. "You said time runs differently here than in the mortal world. How does that work? How do you know 'when' you're popping to?"

"This is a little complicated, so bear with me," Charlie said. "In the first place, you can't go back to a time prior to your own death. And you can't go to the future – well, it's really not the future, but you can't go to a time *later than* the death of the last person who loved you. And each time you go, you can never return to a time prior to that visit. So that's your window for returning to the mortal world: from the time of your death to the death of your very last loved one, and any time skipped between returns is forfeited.

"Within those constraints, you can port over to any time you choose, and to any location where you're connected by love. It takes a little more mind power than Place-hopping here, but you can do it."

Michael nodded. "I think I follow you."

"You'll be fine." Charlie sobered. "There is one more thing to be aware of. These rules apply to ordinary souls. They *don't* necessarily apply to the Darkened. They have some of our same restrictions, for instance they can't go back to before the time of their death or their most recent crossing. But instead of a love conduit, the Darkened can cross to the site of *any* strong emotion, even white-hot hate. And they can persist in the mortal world indefinitely. They often gravitate to locations that relate to their deaths, and if their delusion grows too deep, they can come to regard *that* as their Place, and literally forget their real one in the Afterworld. That's how you get classic 'hauntings.' The worst become so fixated that they can even forget they've died.

"The more enslaved they become to their obsession, the more their corporeal presence deteriorates. They become less and less human, they start to fade visually, and if it goes far enough, they become transparent. At that stage, even the door restriction goes away. The deeply Darkened, what some call the Lost, can pass through anything – walls, rocks, even their coffin lids and the earth on top of them. That's what people see rising from graves. And the very deepest of those can lose their physical form almost completely, eaten away by their own hatred and rage until there's nothing left but a vortex of pure violence. That's what's called a poltergeist. Poltergeists aren't invisible, they're just so faint most people never detect them."

Michael mulled it over grimly. "I'm starting to see how it works. But there's one thing I don't get, Charlie. How is it that these Darkened, these corrupted things, have so much power? It seems like a lot more than we have. Isn't that backwards?"

"It's not that the Darkened have more *intrinsic* power. It comes from that higher order of dark forces that back them. Purely evil entities like what some call demons. We call them the *Fallen*, beings that were created immortal and nearly perfect but became corrupted or embraced evil by choice. The Fallen imbue the Darkened with some of *their* power; that's what enables the cheating."

"You'd think," Michael said with the faintest hint of reproach, "that a God truly against evil might even things up some."

"He won't directly, not like the evil ones do. That would be fighting wrong with wrong, and once you have a full comprehension of what's going on here, Michael, you'll understand how crucial a difference that is. But here's the key. He *did* create the universe, so the 'grid' you might say, the basic structure underlying everything else, is in divine harmony. That causes some compensating factors to emerge from the natural order. For example, the Darkened abhor natural light, especially direct sunlight. It dilutes their power. That's why they stick to night and shadow, especially the really bad ones. The deeper their evil, the worse the drain. The worst of them are sharp and deadly in the pitch black, but they're like malaria victims under full sun.

"They're usually not seen by mortals in any case, even when they're there. Their appearance is so impossible and hideous that the subconscious mind blocks them out. It's like that 'invisible gorilla' experiment I saw on TV once. That made a big impression on me even as a kid. You know the one?"

"I think so," Michael said. "If you're talking about where they show a video of people playing basketball and tell watchers to count how many times the ball is passed from one person to another. All through the video, this guy in a gorilla suit is strolling about in the background. But they're so focused on what they were told to do that nobody notices him. When they're told he's there and watch the clip again, the gorilla seems so obvious they can't believe it's the same tape."

"Yeah, that one," Charlie confirmed. "It's like that with the Darkened. The way they look is so shocking and so contrary to what people expect to see that most of the time, they just *don't*."

"That's just crazy," Michael said. "Kind of a blessing,

though."

"Yeah," Charlie agreed. "Now I'll give you a last one, a real clincher. Because divine love is the door between life and death – don't ask me to explain right now, you'll get it in time – the Darkened *cannot speak to mortals*. Not one intelligible word. Well, except that the worst of them, the Lost, are sometimes able to absorb enough Fallen influence to utter short, distorted phrases that can be laced into broadcast static or common audio ambience, and even caught on recording. That little scrap of cheating gets through, but it's so borderline that the mainstream doesn't take it seriously, and it's mostly ignored. That's one way the universe balances against their efforts to corrupt mortal choices. I don't know if it's a fair trade-off, but it's a significant handicap. It's the best proof that the thing in your townhouse, since it spoke to you, was something more.

"So yeah, one on one against us, the Darkened have the advantage. But when you look at the big picture, I wouldn't want to be in their shoes. They're grabbing for power, and they get some, but it's a trap. It can become like an addiction, where letting go of the obsession feels like withdrawal. Really, it's addiction mixed with madness. They can't be reasoned with, they become oblivious to reality, they can barely communicate even on this side. And that's when the Fallen pounce like the Pleasure Island carnies on Pinocchio. Those poor bastards become their slaves."

Michael was shaking his head. "That's horrible!"

"Yeah. And there's really nothing you can do for them." Charlie paused, then added a warning. "But don't let sympathy blind you, Michael. The Darkened are dangerous. They're a bit tethered in their dealings with mortals, but they have no such restrictions against you and me. You're going to find out that even in the Afterworld, it's possible to be severely harmed. And a hell-bent Darkened with a vendetta against you is an enemy to be feared."

THE CONVERSATION WITH CHARLIE FLASHED through Michael's mind in an instant. He had been trying to recall anything that might explain how, or why, a Darkened could track him down and be inside his home in the Afterworld. He exhausted his memory with no such illumination.

He spun for the door, thinking to bolt outside and somehow call for Alex, as if the former Siamese could psychically hear him and then do something about the intruder – both of which, he realized even as he thought it, were unlikely.

His inclination now was to run through the trees like his life depended on it and try to reach Charlie. But something stopped him. He released the door latch and turned slowly back, picking up subtle cues that told him he need not be hasty. The creature was carrying no weapon, making no threatening moves, maintaining its distance. Its appearance was revolting, terrifying, but its demeanor was not bellicose. The thing definitely radiated negative emotion – what was it, angry? Bitter? Both, Michael decided. But the thing's hostility did not seem to be directed at *him*.

"I am sorry to startle you." The voice was gravelly, the words interspersed with an unpleasant sucking sound.

Michael tried to keep his own voice calm. "What do you want?"

"We have a common enemy." The creature spoke slowly, obviously straining to be intelligible. "I come to propose joining arms against him."

"What enemy?"

"The one that put us here. The contemptible bastard who killed us both."

Michael wasn't following. The decision to drop out of the airplane had been his alone. Was the thing speaking figuratively? Was he talking about Charlie? Rick? Juan Calderon?

"Who are you?"

The voice spat unadorned bitterness. "In life, I was called Eldridge Sidney Raymore after my false father of the flesh. But what was once blood has turned to fire. I am son of that name no more."

ELDRIDGE RAYMORE'S SON.
Panic flared in Michael so fiercely that, if not for the insulation of his Place, he might have passed out.

"I didn't mean to kill you!" he shrieked, on the border of hysteria. "You've got to believe me. There was a baby, this little kid in the road—"

"Be at peace." The thing that Sid Raymore had become held up a gangrenous hand and spoke in a voice that now sounded strangely tired and almost benevolent. "You had no part in my death. It was my father that killed me, the reeking coward who dared to call me son. Though not by his own hand, it was his work nonetheless. It is his debt to pay."

Michael stared at the Darkened uncertainly. The thing seemed to sense his confusion. "Let us sit, Michael Chandler. You risk no harm from me. We have much to discuss. Hear my words, and if having heard well you choose to spurn the offer, I will leave your Place and trouble you no more."

TWILIGHT HAD BECOME NIGHT AGAIN. They sat in the dark, dense jungle near the waterfall pool, able to see each other only in starlight. On the opposite bank, Alex lay licking his forepaws, looking for all the world like a pair of disembodied green eyes that vanished when he blinked.

The Sid-creature – Michael refused to think of it by

its new name – related the events of the night on which he had been beaten by his father's lackey John Burko, suffered a heart attack from the trauma, and died needlessly from it in the back of the car because the elder had chosen to burn precious time driving to a mob doctor instead of calling an ambulance that would almost surely have saved him.

"I died a good ten minutes before the crash," the Sid-thing told him. "I know because I have gone back there. I saw the child in the street. I saw what my father did to you. I have tried to even the score on my own, but I have come to realize that I need another who can walk the world openly. That is what I have come for. In return, I offer you your own justice against him."

Michael nodded, not in agreement but to signify understanding. "Before I answer," he said, "I have a question for *you*. What was with the TV and radio those two times I saw you during the road trip? It scared the hell out of me, and I thought that was the purpose. But now that I know who you are and what you're doing, it doesn't make sense."

"They were warnings," the Darkened explained. "I wanted you to know that the authorities were tracing you. I couldn't speak to you directly. Those stunts were the best way I could think of to help keep you from being caught."

Michael eyed the thing Sid had become as he thought through all he had heard. There was nothing frightening about him anymore; what Michael saw now was a sad, tragic, misguided soul in need of gentleness and companionship.

"What would you have me do?" he asked.

"Help me see to it that he continues down his poisonous path. Everything possible to ensure that he commits ever more sinful and despicable acts. There will be arrangements that can only be made by someone who can talk to people and walk in sunlight."

Michael had been prepared to hear a plan for exposing Ridge Raymore's underside, destroying his political prospects, and possibly landing him in prison. That Sid intended to nourish his father's depravity made no sense.

"I don't understand," he said. "Why would you want that?"

The voice became angry. "Because mortal punishment is nothing. I want him suffering for eternity. I want his Place to be so stifling that it clings to him like skin and consigns him to a region of the dark lands so bleak he would have to walk for ages just to see another soul. Where the hopelessness and oppression outside his Place are so poignant he would go mad before getting that far."

Michael pondered. They were cruel words, terrible words. Yet he could detect a faint murmur of good at the creature's core. *The old Sid Raymore is still in there,* he noted. *Buried under an avalanche of understandable resentment through no fault of his own.*

It was then Michael discovered that even after death, even after coming into his wondrous immortal inheritance, he was the same old Michael Chandler. This pitiful half-man thing needed help. And Michael was going to give it to him.

"All right," he said at last. "I will help you, provided we can agree on a specific plan. But I don't care about payback; I have a different price. You have to help me with something first. I have no love for Ridge Raymore, but there's something more important I need to take care of beforehand. Will you do it?"

This took the Darkened by surprise. At length it nodded. "Yes. Provided we can agree on a specific plan."

Michael smiled at what he took as a playful jab, and he couldn't be sure that the thing's hideous half-mouth wasn't doing the same.

"Fair enough. Let's get planning. I'm sure neither of us wants to waste a second more than necessary."

And so, there in the dead of night, Michael entered into a deal with the Darkened. What would Charlie say? Michael's curse or gift, depending on how the light fell, apparently stretched so far that he could find merit even in a creature as tainted as this.

And he was actually going to *help* him. Help him, yes.

This he had promised.

Just not in the way the Darkened had intended.

MICHAEL MADE HIS WAY THROUGH the night jungle in a new direction, gently downslope in the opposite direction from Charlie's Place, following his travel sense as though homing in on a distant sound, the big cat padding along in tow. After a time, the sky began to brighten – gradually, but much faster than any dawn on Earth – until he was walking in full-on day, shafts of sunlight streaming through the palm fronds, greens muted to turquoise where dense clouds overhead cast their shadows. The ground became sandy and faint whiffs of sea air grew into a ubiquitous beach bouquet.

The route led through a thick stand of banyan, and when Michael tossed Alex a "catch you later" wave and pushed through the curtain of vines, he found himself in a Key West hotel courtyard. He glanced behind him and, as he had known it would be, the primeval jungle was gone.

He was startled by an unexpected sense of alienation. This wasn't his first trip back across; that of course had been the guided look-in on Charlie's mom. But it was his first time solo, and more than that, it was a place he had been to in life. Michael had been post-mortal – the word "dead" just didn't seem right – for something less than a week, subjectively speaking, though how much time had actually elapsed in the Afterworld he could not say. Yet, the transition from mortality had had an immediate and permanent effect. Already, the dark jungle, and even Charlie's redwood retreat, felt like true home. This place, the mortal world, seemed utterly foreign. It made him realize how profound the change had been. Not change around him; the world hadn't changed, or worlds, on either side of mortality. *He* had changed. That wasn't quite right; he was still Michael, his core was still there, but he had *woken up*. Yes, that was it exactly. He felt like a sleeper awakening from a long and lucid dream, a dream so convincing that it takes a few moments to orient himself in the waking world. But once he does, once he is fully cognizant that the dramatic experience he still vividly remembers was all in his head, the dream seems trivial. That was how Michael felt. It wasn't a perfect metaphor, he knew; the mortal world *was* real, and it certainly *did* matter, else he wouldn't be here risking serenity and sanity and who knew what spiritual hazards he didn't even comprehend. But it *did* feel like shadow compared to the Afterworld's light. The change in him was already that advanced.

And there was something even stranger. It was bizarre that, for Michael, no time at all had passed in the mortal world while he had been gallivanting about the Afterworld at leisure. In fact if he had timed this right, a hundred miles to the south, the mortal body he had inhabited for thirty-two years was at this moment drifting lifeless beneath the dim, cool waters of the Straits, so freshly vacated that the warmth of life still huddled in his organs while a plane full of frightened girls stabilized on its way toward the very island he was standing upon. It was a startling and grotesque thought. But he had judged it vital to return to the mortal world as close to the instant of his death as the "rules" allowed. Because every second saved increased the chance that the stock of young prisoners had not yet been slaughtered and dumped in the ocean to dispose of them as evidence.

He crossed the fresh-mown courtyard, entered the lobby through a glass slider, and continued out the front door onto the street. He was relieved to find himself near the Sunset Harbor piers as intended. A short walk past little restaurants and tourist shops took him to Swordfish Tony's. *Thank God*, he murmured when the little OPEN sign came into view. He had worked out what to do if it wasn't, but every second counted now, and any detail that didn't proceed according to plan risked an unthinkable failure.

Freddie Wirt sat on a thatched stool wearing floral-patterned Bermuda shorts and a pair of leather sandals as worn as a baseball mitt, applying a layer of Mr. Zogs Blue to the deck of a sleek Firewire Dominator laid unceremoniously across the cash counter. Michael was a hair's breadth from greeting him as an acquaintance when he checked himself, remembering that Freddie would have no idea who he was.

He had, of course, planned for that. Now he could only hope that fortune would continue to smile on this critical part of the risky caper.

"Morning," Freddie called, barely glancing up from the surfboard and jittering rhythmically to music only he could hear from the iPod clipped to one of his belt loops.

"Yeah, hi, good morning." Michael waved. "You're Freddie, right?"

Seeing that the customer had not come simply to browse, Freddie set down the cake of wax and wiped his hands on a terrycloth towel, popping both buds from his ears with a single yank on the cord so that pinched strains of the Beach Boys' "Kokomo" could be heard.

"Yeah, I'm Freddie. Who are you?"

Michael took a deep breath. "Look, this is going to sound crazy, but I swear to you it's the truth. I'm a friend of Beth DeLeon and Tony. You know they took off in his trawler yesterday."

"Yeah ..."

"Well, they got in some serious trouble. I'm here to get your help with a rescue."

"What trouble?"

"Did Tony tell you where they were going?"

"Nah. Why would he? I know where he takes the charters."

"But you did rustle up a Zodiac for them. I doubt that's standard for a fishing jaunt."

Now Freddie was alarmed, on the verge of open hostility. "How did you know that?"

I'm losing him, Michael thought. *And if I do, unless I can find a way to steal a boat full of gas and navigate to*

Tesoro on my own, I'm screwed.

"They told me what they were doing so I could act as a safeguard," he replied. "For just this sort of thing. Do you have Tony's cell number?"

Eyes never leaving Michael, Freddie dug out a colorful phone and pressed a speed dial button. He held it to his ear for almost a minute, then clapped it shut.

"What about Beth's?"

"Hers is—"

"—right here," Michael finished. "In the shop. She gave it to you before they left."

Freddie's eyes narrowed. "Who *are* you?" he asked again.

"Max Chandler," Michael said with thespian earnestness. He had not planned this; the use of his brother's name as cover simply burst from him on the spur of the moment. Once out, however, Michael found it apropos, even inspiring. The perilous undertaking before him was exactly the kind of thing his brother had relished and been good at. Invoking his name infused Michael with confidence.

"I go way back with Beth and I'm a friend of Tony's, too. But the reason they told me everything as a backup is that my brother Michael was with them."

"Tony would have told me." Freddie remained skeptical, but Michael could hear his mental fortifications beginning to crack.

"They couldn't risk it," he explained. "If the wrong people noticed Tony's yacht in Cuban waters, they'd trace it and kill him and then come after *you.*"

With this, finally, there was progress. Freddie seemed to be studying him, probably perceiving a corroborating family resemblance. "You still haven't said what the trouble is."

Michael pursed his lips. "It wasn't a fishing trip. I know you're going to find this hard to believe, but hear me out."

He related the story faithfully, only omitting his jump from the plane. Freddie listened with growing acceptance. It helped that he knew and cared about Elise, and was already aware of Rick's criminal dealings.

By the time he was done, Freddie's attitude had changed. He may not have been positive that Michael was telling the truth, but he had decided that the chances of it were good enough that he couldn't risk just standing by.

"There it is." Michael tapped Tesoro on the chart of Cuba Freddie had retrieved from a cabinet. "I remember Beth saying it looked like the shape of Minnesota, sort of a "K" with the triangles filled in."

"What do you want me to do?"

"I want you to get a boat." Michael looked pleadingly into Freddie's eyes. "Borrow, rent, whatever you can arrange, quick. It needs to be fast, but able to hold about ten people. I hope to God the *Queen Anne* is still out there, but we can't count on it. You need to run full throttle and get as close to the island as you can, safely. I've got my own way there and I'm going to try to nab one of the gangster boats to get the kids to open water, but if that's not possible we may need you to come in tight to the beach. If worse comes to worst, we'll swim them out to you one by one. Bring lots of life jackets. And some drinking water and candy bars, if it doesn't hold you up too much."

"Your own way there?" Freddie queried skeptically. "And what would that be?"

"Can't talk about it," Michael replied cheerily. "Federal agent."

"Whatever." Freddie eyed him with an air of fluster. "The boat should be no problem, as long as the passengers don't mind riding in the bow compartment. I've got a few rich friends that owe me. How will I know what to do when I get there?"

"Program your cell number into Beth's phone and give it to me. I'll call once we're ready to hook up. If you don't hear from me by nightfall, you're free to go."

Freddie couldn't resist one last skeptical volley. "If you're a federal agent," he inquired, "how come you can't just do this with your own guys?"

"Like I said, the place is officially out of bounds." Michael smiled. "I've gone rogue."

Freddie studied Michael in silence for a long moment, then pursed his lips. "You know, man, your whole story reeks of bullshit."

"I know. But it's the truth."

Freddie sighed. "Well, you've got me over a barrel. I don't even half believe you, but everything good in my life I owe to Tony Pizarro and I'm not going to risk letting him down. I'll do what I can, just on the outside chance that you're on the level."

Michael beamed. "Excellent."

"But if you cross me," Freddie warned, "if this turns out to be some kind of con job, I swear to God, dude, I'm going to kick your ass."

Michael nodded. "Understood."

Freddie set the surfboard in a corner and pulled a set of keys from his pocket. "Just let me close up. I should be on the water in about half an hour."

"Sweet. And how long do you think to get there?"

"Just a second." Freddie called up the weather forecast on a computer sitting to his left on the part of the counter than made an "L" back to the wall.

"Well," he announced, "there's a nasty depression tracking this way from the Bahamas. If I can borrow the boat I'm thinking of and conditions don't get too bad, the run will take probably an hour and a half. Maybe two. These storms are erratic, but two hours should be good enough to beat the worst of it on the leg south. Now, coming back…"

Michael nodded impatiently, deflecting Freddie's concern about the return trip. The challenge of getting the girls to the rescue boat in the first place was absorbing all of his attention. "That's pretty fast, but a long time for a bunch of kids to hide in the bushes. We'll hope for the best and try to hold out until you get in range."

Michael smiled with gratitude and held out his hand for

the surfer to shake. He had secured the assistance he'd come here for. He would deal with the weather and with Freddie's inevitable consternation, once it became evident that Beth and Tony were not involved as he had implied, when the time came.

ANYONE WHO SAW MICHAEL CRAWL into a narrow gap in the coco plum hedge could be forgiven for judging him insane. Had they followed up looking for him on the other side, however, they would have been even more confounded to find him missing without so much as a trace that he had ever come through.

Which, of course, he had not. He emerged back in the Afterworld jungle precisely where he had left it, conjuring up a new destination and following his travel sense.

He had worried that any "love" conduit would be tenuous, if not absent, then perhaps too weak to support a direct crossing, forcing him to sail with Freddie after all and sacrifice hours of precious time. Instead, he found the way unexpectedly direct. He had been traipsing through the pathless growth for less than fifteen minutes before the vegetation, the landscape, and even the smell became unmistakably familiar.

The visual transition was utterly seamless, the crossing so subtle he perceived it only as a step into summer shade. His mission had come full circle, and for the first time he felt a clear sense of just how daunting and uncertain a task he had set for himself.

He was back on Tesoro, alone this time, nestled in foliage at the base of the same leeward cliff he and Beth had skirted in darkness just the previous evening, as time was counted here. For a moment, he half-thought he could hear the drone of a neglected Cessna staggering north like a giant crippled bee.

The wind was calm and the sunlight brilliant, just as it had been when his mortal self had stood on this spot only hours before. But there was something new in the air, a whiff of ozone and perhaps a degree or two of temperature drop. Freddie's storm was coming. Michael could only hope its full fury would be deferred long enough.

Sketching it all out beside the enchanted pool in the celestial darkness, swathed in the aura of invincibility that permeated his Place, the plan had seemed infallible. Now he was assaulted by myriad worries and doubts, wondering how he could have been so glib and naïve. His neat ability to pass through the locked cell door would do its prisoners little good, even if he was able to deflect their vision and the guard's so he could use it. His idea for *opening* the lock, he realized, which had seemed so brilliant and perfect when it occurred to him, was more hope than plan. Yet everything hinged on it, because even if he could get inside with a tool to break the mortar, the configuration of joists underlying the cell where half the girls remained made gouging a drop hole impossible.

Worst of all, and this genuinely terrified him, if Michael were caught, given the day's prior events, he was quite certain that Calderon would assign his most reliable lieutenants to continuous surveillance. Being constantly watched, it would be impossible for him to escape, supernatural powers or no. He knew they couldn't kill him – well, he *thought* they couldn't – but given the little scrapes and pricks he had sustained crawling through the Key West shrubbery, he was pretty sure a torso full of machine gun slugs would make him very unhappy indeed. And if he could feel pain here – just one more validation of the wisdom Charlie said every person came to eventually, that the mortal world was best left behind – and if they could prevent him from returning to the Afterworld by constant observation, that meant he could be tortured. What he could divulge that would be of any use to them he had no idea, but he realized that didn't matter.

What mattered was only what they *thought* he knew. It could be as simple as "How did you get here?" or "Who is working with you?" – information he would be unable to disclose insofar as it revealed the realm beyond.

And a horrible epiphany manifested to him that he wished to God he had considered while he still had time to plan more carefully: you really could get *stuck* here, in a very bad situation, and there was no telling how long you might have to endure it before an opportunity to retreat would emerge. The thought was actually more hideous now, he realized, than it would have been in life. Death, he was only now beginning to see, was the ultimate safety valve against misery. No matter how bad things got, every mortal knew that one day, despite the best efforts of their tormentors and the caprices of fate, there would come an end. For Michael – for any hubris-drunk soul foolhardy enough to return and meddle in mortal affairs as though their ham-fisted interference could improve on Providence – there was no such relief.

Then he thought of the girls, of little Felicity whose keenness of observation had made the rescue of Beth, Elise, and the ones in the neighboring cell possible, she and her fragile companions left behind in the stinking cage who hadn't felt a mother's hug or had a change of clothes, a nourishing meal, or bedding softer than limestone for weeks. As he pictured them, his trademark mindset rose like a gunslinger. He saw clearly what must be done, and as the vision sharpened, all hesitation seeped away. He reproached himself for ever entertaining the doubtful thoughts. This moment, with the die cast, the pieces in motion, and his feet on this mortal soil, was not the time for such thoughts, if there ever had been. He was here to do a job.

The children were waiting. *Along with any nastiness Calderon might dish up.* He steeled himself, whispered a brief prayer, and ducked inside the cave.

CHAPTER 29
The Key

FREDDIE HAD BEEN MAKING GOOD time, running the 35-foot Pantera F2-71 full bore for about an hour, when he noticed a bright orange object bobbing in the moderate swells ahead. At the same time – if he wasn't imagining it, it was too faint to say for sure – there seemed to be a thin, dark haze wafting over this stretch of sea, coinciding with a whiff of diesel fuel and some acrid smell he couldn't place that made him uncomfortable. He kept a nervous eye on the dark clouds and sheets of rain approaching from the east. That low from the Bahamas he had seen on the chart shouldn't have made it this far. How the hell fast was it moving?

He debated whether he should ignore his nagging intuition or slow down and have a look. The storm was nearing, and every second counted, the Chandler guy had made that clear. But the pull of instinct grew eerily stronger the closer he got.

He powered down and looped toward the flotsam to investigate. As he pulled carefully alongside it, he got the shock of his life.

The object was a life preserver, the kind designed to keep your head face up and out of the water even if you lost consciousness. And the face looking up at him, grim and haggard but very much alive, darkened as though a preschooler had colored it using a charcoal briquette and mottled with sickly strips of flesh that looked like burns, was one he recognized.

"Tony?" Freddie dared not believe his eyes.

"Stop gawking and haul me out of here, you half-wit," Tony called good-naturedly, a feat of stiff courage given his condition.

The Pantera was already drifting away. Quickly, Freddie chucked a mooring line ten feet past Tony's head, then reeled it in once his benefactor had a weak but adequate grip.

"Thank God," Tony said, exhausted and for the moment incapable of any more humorous gestures. "I really thought my number was up, there. I'd already mailed it in." He gave Freddie an emotional hug that dampened the younger man's clothes and made Freddie wish he had brought extras, not for himself, but for the saltwater prune Tony had become. He pulled an oversized beach towel out of a side compartment, the best he could do, and handed it to his boss.

"What are you doing here?" Tony queried as he toweled off his exposed skin and started soaking as much moisture out of his clothes as he could. Freddie quickly recounted "Max" Chandler's visit to the shop, the tale of Tesoro he had relayed, and his own role in the plan.

"Sweet Baby Jesus," Tony said, taking in Beth and Michael's story. "Well, we better go through with it. Right here is already too close to be safe, that's how they got me. When I didn't hear from Beth, I tried to sneak in close enough for binoculars, then all of a sudden a couple of Cigarettes showed up and we took an RPG round right amidships. So if they're going to spot us, they already have. There's no point going back." He shook his head, like a wet dog to clear nascent tears. "Man I hated to see *Annie* go down. That was a ship with heart."

"Yeah." Freddie nodded sympathetically, well aware that aside from himself and perhaps Beth DeLeon, the *Queen Anne's Revenge* had been as close to a living family member as Tony had.

"You know, you don't look so good, and *that* thing's

going to be here in no time." Freddie directed a nervous glance toward the storm that now filled a third of the eastern sky. "We should just head back and get you to a doctor. There's no point hanging around here. Beth and the kid and her friend already got out, and there's nothing we can do for those other girls if these guys are cruising around with grenade launchers."

"The *hell* we will." Tony was firm and fiery despite his fatigue. "I ain't gonna pretend I wasn't scared, Freddie, I was *terrified*. You got no idea what it's like to be tossed around like eggs in a mixing bowl with just your head out and nothing anywhere except you and the ocean. You can't see ten feet half the time, did you know that? The waves block your view. You can't rest, cause every time you start riding up a swell, the crest wants to go over your head. It feels like you're the last person on Earth and there's no one out there who even *could* save you. It's the loneliest feeling in the world. It's so bad I half thought of drowning myself just to get it over with. And don't even get me started on the pain. Just be glad you got no idea how saltwater feels on a burn." Freddie shuddered at the thought. "I got no desire to go back in the water, you can bank on it. But we ain't gonna tuck it now. If Beth and that Michael found the stones to take on these guys, we ain't gonna let his brother hang."

MICHAEL HAD EXPECTED THAT THIS time he wouldn't need matches to see, and he was right. The same sort of blanket of dim visibility that he had noticed in the jungle accompanied him up the sewer shaft.

It seemed a shorter trek to him now. He reached the floor below the slave pens, taking pains to be quiet, and sucked in a deep breath. It was one thing to plan, another to do. From this point, everything hung in the balance.

He cast a determined gaze about the floor and was almost stunned at how quickly he found the lost guard keys. It was clear enough why he hadn't seen them before. They must have had some momentum when they were inadvertently kicked down the latrine hole: they had lodged in a little crevice in the tunnel wall about two feet up. He had searched only the floor, and the matches hadn't cast enough light to illuminate this tiny nook.

He smiled as he tucked them into his pocket, careful not to jingle. God appeared to be on his side so far. Now he would see how far he could stretch it.

He eyed the bashed-out hole in the floor of the empty cell above him, taking a moment to study its edges. It was a bit more than four feet above his head. In life, he never could have done what he had planned here, certainly not without months of training. He had thought it through though in light of his now perfect conditioning and had felt, if his memory could be trusted, that it was at least worth a shot. If he failed, he would have to go in the hard way, a *much* harder way, but he would make it happen. The whole plan didn't turn on this, but if he managed it, things would be much less complicated and, more importantly, a great deal faster.

He steadied himself, limbering up his fingers, bending slightly at the knees, giving himself a couple of test bounces. Then, with all the thrust his Afterlife frame could muster, he launched himself straight up.

Amazingly – and so gratifyingly that Michael had to stifle laughter – it worked.

He was hanging in the hole now by the tips of his fingers. He felt superhumanly strong, but he knew it wasn't limitless. He could only maintain this for a minute or two before even these muscles would cry for mercy. So he worked quickly, elevating himself without a sound until his eyes just cleared the edge of the cavity so he could see inside the cell and beyond.

The same guard as before sat at the metal desk, but this time the little TV was silent. Apparently, despite the escape, he had been judged competent to keep watch on the girls, but not with his attention strained. More likely, Calderon had assigned him here as the least critical post in the compound with all that was going on, trusting that even this boob could handle six half-starved kids with the aid of a locked iron door and a gun.

Michael assessed the situation coolly. The door to this cell was shut now, but didn't appear to be locked. Still, he thanked God that he had found the keys. It would have been a huge complication if on top of everything else he'd had to figure out a way to spring the lock next door. Still, he was far from out of the woods. He had been hoping to find the guard station abandoned. He would have to deal with that somehow.

He dropped back into the cave like a cat, making a sound no louder than a bathrobe hitting the floor. He took a moment to find a loose rock the size of a golf ball and stuff it into his pocket. His heart was pounding now, the moment of truth almost on top of him.

He sprang up to grasp the hole edges with his fingers again, and now executed an acrobatic move that would have been impossible in life. Peering up out of the hole, hanging only by his left hand with his chin perched just above it, with his right he took the stone out of his pocket and gave it a hearty heave. He mouthed a silent "thank you" when it sailed between the cell bars and cracked noisily against the wall at the far end of the corridor.

Alert to the point of jumpiness, the guard jolted up from his chair as Michael ducked quickly below his line of sight, still clinging to the rim of the hole. He let one beat pass as the guard's footsteps passed by the cell he was in, then in one impossibly graceful and quiet motion he hoisted himself up out of the cavity and *through* the closed cell door like water through a sieve.

Now the guard heard him. He spun violently around as the little prisoners gasped with surprise and hope. To his chagrin, Michael saw that the man had been sufficiently chastised that he had taken his machine pistol even to inspect this little noise.

The gun started to come up, but like a striking viper Michael seized both of the guard's wrists in his hands and bent them forcefully down so that the barrel faced the floor. For a long moment they struggled like arm wrestlers, the guard refusing to believe that his firearm could be so easily neutralized and Michael just as determined to prove that it could.

As it became clear that Michael had enough strength to deny him, the guard's indignation turned to alarm. He opened his mouth to escalate matters even as his forearms began to falter and shake under Michael's grip.

"No," Michael hissed with a guttural harshness that surprised even himself. "Keep quiet, put the gun down, and I won't hurt you. Force me, and I'll *end* you right here."

He knew this was a hollow threat. Michael was incapable of killing, and Charlie had said the rules didn't allow it anyway. But he also knew that even his enhanced strength couldn't hold up indefinitely. He had to take the gun out of play while he was still in control.

The guard kept struggling, now openly afraid. "You don't know what they'll do to me," he countered in desperation. "It would be better to die."

Michael scrutinized him as the standoff held. He carefully weighed the risks, made his decision, and released the man's left hand while maintaining his clamp on the one holding the gun.

He reached up, causing the guard to wince, and took the cross pendant hanging from the guard's neck between his fingers.

"Does this mean *nothing* to you?" he asked in a quiet voice, shaking the little silver symbol. "Is it just so much empty bling?"

The guard's left hand shot toward his right to transfer the gun. Michael, even quicker, released the cross and batted the man's arm away.

"What does being Christian even mean," Michael persisted, "if not mercy on the helpless?"

The guard let his left hand drop. Michael could feel the intensity in the gun hand slipping   along with the resolve visible in the man's eyes.

"Help me," Michael pressed, "and I'll get you out of here. We'll take you with us."

The man said nothing. Ten seconds went by. Michael could almost see the wheels turning inside the guard's head. He knew it was risky to delay, that at any moment others of Calderon's retinue might show up and that if they did, his presence here would do nothing but accelerate the little prisoners' fate. His judgment, nevertheless, was to stand by a little longer.

Twenty seconds went by. Thirty. Michael recalled the lengthy deliberation this same man had gone through before deciding to open the door for Elise. He hoped things were moving in a similar direction, but as the silence neared forty seconds, his own strength beginning to wane, he realized he could risk no more. He turned his gaze on the gun to pinpoint its location and make sure he could grab it in one forceful snatch, tensed the muscles in his right, and—

The guard thumbed the safety on and let loose his grip. The machine pistol clattered harmlessly to the floor.

The guard's head tilted back and his eyes drew toward the sky that watched down through the two stories of great house and the earthen cellar above their heads, and prayed. "Le pido no protección, pero sólo la dirección."

Michael eyed the man with renewed appreciation and awe, for he understood well both the words and their intent.

I ask not protection, only guidance.

The guard looked back down at the weapon on the floor, then at Michael. "Aren't you going to pick it up?"

"Do I need to?"

The guard stared at Michael in wonder. "No."

Michael released the man's remaining wrist. Tension relieved, the guard instinctively reached back to rub at the base of his skull where Beth had beaned him with the cell bar, no doubt still painful.

Michael held out his right hand. "Max Chandler," he smiled. "What's your name, brother?"

"Manuel Ortego Tejada," the man replied, returning a firm shake. "Just call me Mano."

THEY PASSED THE GIRLS ONE to the other as Beth and Michael had before, except that this time Michael remained above. He trusted Mano, but not to the point of being stupid. Leaving him up top with the girls and his gun would have been too much risk.

With the last girl down, Michael took what he hoped would be his last look at the cruel chamber and began lowering himself into the hole.

"Bring the gun," Mano called from below.

Michael stopped and considered this. He had no intention of shooting anybody, and if the plan worked it wouldn't be necessary. Still, he had to think of the girls, and when it came right down to it, he had to admit that a weapon would provide some insurance against contingency.

He scrambled back out of the hole and retrieved the heavy pistol, double-checked the safety before tucking it awkwardly into his waistband, and dropped himself into the darkness.

As his feet hit the floor, the dim light from the dungeon corridor suddenly winked out and they were left in utter black.

Mano complained with equal parts frustration and fear. "Can't see a goddamned thing." One of the girls screamed, and two more followed as though it were contagious.

"Shhh," Michael cautioned. "It's all right. It's just a power—"

The sound of automatic weapons erupted above them like a chorus of snare drums.

"What the hell?" Mano barked.

"Forget it," Michael shot back. "Just concentrate on what's in front of us."

"But ..." Mano's anxiety persisted, but he let it drop. Michael was right: now that they were down here, there was no point in dwelling on anything beyond the daunting task of making their way through the unremitting darkness.

"Everybody hold hands," Michael commanded. "Make a chain, I'll guide us. I have great night vision." Which was, of course, true.

Despite the lack of match light, Michael's familiarity made this descent of the tunnel faster than before. The firefight sounds grew dimmer and dimmer until they could be heard no more.

A few minutes later, the light of the cave mouth came into view, and all eight escapees physically relaxed. A faint rushing sound grew louder and harsher as they approached. Its source was apparent well before they reached the exit: a thunderous rain was mercilessly thrashing the tropical forest.

Michael made his way to the lip of the long cave, standing just under the rocky cover, and pulled Beth DeLeon's cell phone from his pocket. He punched in the number Freddie Wirt had programmed in and turned his back to the rain.

It was answered on the second ring. "Yes?"

The voice was not Freddie's. Michael was alarmed and confused. Had they intercepted the rescue ship already? Were they searching the island even now?

"Hello, is anyone there?" And now, incredulous, Michael let himself believe that he knew the voice. Not Freddie, but an ally equally welcome. *Better*.

"Tony ...?"

"Who is this?" Now the voice on the phone was laced with concern. And Michael remembered – it was so easy, so natural to forget! – that Tony wouldn't know him.

"Max Chandler," he said, invoking the cover he had, for better or worse, taken on. "Michael's brother. Are you with Freddie?"

"Mr. Chandler. Thank God." Michael could hear Tony's relief over the line. "Yes, I'm with Freddie on some for all I know stolen rum-runner. The little bastard saved my life, and now I'll never hear the end of it. I should just jump back in the water right now."

"Where's your boat?"

"*Annie* went down." The words momentarily dampened the mariner's tone. "Died in a good cause, mind you. And still kept me safe she did, held on with just enough of her above the waterline for me to hunker under till the goons and their popguns were gone."

"I'm sorry to hear that. But glad you're alive."

"Well, good! We have that much in common." Tony chuckled hoarsely. "Freddie's driving, that's why I'm talking to you. He's brought me up to speed."

"Good. Tony, I'm near the beach on what I believe is the northwest edge of the island. The girls are with me and for the moment I think we're safe. It won't last, though. How far out are you? Time-wise I mean."

In answer, there was a sharp crackle from the phone as lightning forked in the northern sky. A few seconds later, a barrel of thunder rolled overhead.

"… minutes if we don't … damn seas …" Tony's voice clipped in and out intermittently.

"Tony, I'm losing you," Michael said, hoping Tony would hear enough to get the gist. "We're going to make a run for the docks and see if we can get out on one of the cartel's speedboats. We'll head due north as close as we can determine. Rendezvous if you think it's safe, otherwise stay out of harm's way. I'll call again once we're on the water."

"… might not … wisest … try to …"

"You're breaking up bad, Tony. Hopefully it will be better when we get in the open. I'm signing off now. Take care, don't put yourselves in danger. We need you alive."

"... Beth was ..."

The call failed. A blinking message appeared on the tiny screen: *Searching for signal.* Michael put the phone away.

Even in the downpour, the track through the thick brush that he and Beth had chiseled at night and then reinforced with their march with the first set of girls remained clearly visible. The plantation complex, however, was not their objective this time.

"You'd better lead," he told Mano. "Can you get us to the docks from here?"

"This way." Mano headed out from under the rocky protection and was instantly saturated with rain. There was nothing else for it; they all followed.

CHAPTER 30
The Sword of Justice

GLAD AS HE WAS TO have them clear of the cave and hustling toward freedom, Michael couldn't help feeling sorry for the little girls, let out of their horrendous cage only to face this slog in unsuitable clothing through cloying mud and rain so thick it was almost hard to breathe.

He heard the splash before he saw what had happened. Felicity's foot had caught in the muck and she pitched forward, adding the insult of mud as thick as peanut butter to the gritty rain soaking her dress.

"Come on, sweetie." Michael smiled and reached out his arms. Felicity grasped him around the neck.

As he bent to lift her, Michael saw that her left foot was bare. He quickly found the missing shoe protruding from a glob of mud. It was so filled with muck that it would be impossible to clean here, and impractical, maybe even dangerous, to wear. In one fluid motion he snatched up the girl and her shoe, wedging the former in one of his pockets so she could put it on as soon as circumstances allowed. He set off with the girl in is arms, jogging to catch up to the others.

Felicity pressed her lips so close to his ear that he could feel their flutter and make out the whisper with its charming intonations over the downpour. "I knew you'd come back."

For a moment he said nothing, taking her faith and gratitude in stride. Then suddenly he realized she should not be able to recognize him as the man who had promised to return.

"How did you …?" He trailed off, unsure of what was all right to say, unsure whether he would be able to say it even if he knew.

"The angel told me," she replied simply, and gave him a magical hug.

"*Angel?*" Michael inquired. Felicity just shrugged. For the moment, Michael stifled the questions her proclamation raised. He had more urgent things to worry about.

It took twenty minutes of trudging through the downpour to reach the southern end of the island, where Michael got his first good view of the marina complex. The docks took a squared-off horseshoe shape, with heavy cleats at intervals along the cross segment and twin piers with covered slips extending out into the harbor on either end.

There were mooring provisions for more than a dozen craft, about half of them currently occupied. There was even a small barge with a commercial tanker truck anchored on board with heavy chains. *So that's how they bring in their fuel,* Michael mused. Not only for the boats and planes, but also for the electrical generator that must power the house. A generator that had somehow, inexplicably, gone dead in the storm at just the right time. Michael smiled to himself.

Half a dozen storage structures of various sizes dotted the shoreline. The door to one of these was open, and two men with assault rifles strapped to their shoulders huddled under the eaves to avoid the rain.

Mano surveyed the scene for a few moments and then turned to Michael, extended his hand. "Give me the gun."

Michael looked at him, hesitated. He hadn't expected this, and didn't know what it meant. Mano had said nothing about the pistol during the rainy march, and Michael couldn't see why he needed it just to talk these guys away.

"The gun," Mano repeated impatiently. "If I don't have it, it won't look right. We're supposed to pack them at all times."

Michael knew that once he handed the weapon over, he would be powerless to save the girls if Mano turned on them. He might be able to stop or disarm the man before too much damage was done, but he could never control Mano *and* two compañeros with assault rifles. Yet if Mano was right and Michael made the wrong choice, if the guard's empty hands set off alarm bells, the sentries would not only remain dockside but would redouble their vigilance, making it even harder to commandeer one of the boats.

He looked at Mano, straining to discern intention in the man's eyes. He looked at the silver cross pendant that hung from his neck, dribbling rain. He looked at the angry sky. He looked into the heartbreakingly innocent and trusting eyes of the little girl in his arms. Then it was back to Mano, now glaring with urgency.

Without looking away, without a word, Michael hauled the hefty killing machine from the waistband of his pants and held it out grip first.

Mano took the weapon with an affirming nod, turned to the jungle's edge, and stepped briskly through the storm toward the makeshift marina.

Michael was not relieved. He had half expected the man to open fire at once, compromising Michael physically at the very least and killing several of the children if that was his intent. It made better sense, though, to collect his backup first, to coordinate with the other two gangsters before turning his coat. Why shouldn't he? It might save some unpleasantness, and either way, what were Michael and six exhausted school girls going to do? They had nowhere to go and no way to get there.

It seemed an eternity, but only three minutes went by before the answer came. Both dock sentries unslung their AKs and took off for the great house at a jog, looking highly annoyed. Mano made a show of looking for something in one of the storage sheds until they had disappeared uphill into the curtains of rain, then trotted purposefully toward the boat slips, gesturing insistently at the party hidden in the brush to come join him *quick*.

Michael beckoned to the girls and they surged out from cover, converging on Mano and the 35-foot Baja Outlaw squeaking against the bumpers in the nearest covered berth.

Mano hopped in over the side and started the engine with a guttural thrum. Michael, who had no idea how to handle a boat with this kind of muscle and had not been looking forward to piloting it by the seat of his pants, was grateful to play first mate instead and busied himself settling the girls into the craft one by one. It wasn't easy with the thing bucking in the stormy stir like a bull in a rodeo chute in spite of the breakwater.

And, dredging up shades of the air escape that had cost him his life, Michael could plainly see that there was not enough room to situate everyone safely. The boat had exactly four passenger seats with little space in between, and unlike the Cessna's enclosed cabin, there was no way to safely stack occupants on top of each other.

Mano saw the predicament and apologized. "Believe it or not, I picked this one because it has *more* passenger room than the faster boats. But some are going to have to ride down there, no way around it." He pointed to the hatch that led to the bow compartment. "At least it's dry."

"Life preservers?" Michael asked, voicing an even more worrying concern. The space problem could be dealt with creatively if it came to that, people *could* squish in tight, sit on each others' laps, and hold onto whatever was handy. But, again unlike the airplane, it was entirely possible that someone could be thrown or fall off the deck by accident.

"There should be one or two, maybe a couple more, in one of the bins down there," Mano replied, again indicating the bow hatch. "Enough for all eight of us, no way."

I could stay behind, Michael considered. *I could hide in one of the sheds or sneak up to the house, maybe find a gun or something, keep the thugs from going after the boat for as long as possible. Lose them in the woods and cross back to the Afterworld once I've done what I can. That*

would leave only four kids sharing their seats. But he knew
he couldn't. As trustworthy as Mano had appeared to be so
far, letting him drive off alone with the girls and his machine pistol was a step further than Michael was willing to
go. Moreover, they *needed* him, the girls and Mano both. He
was a second set of adult eyes and limbs to watch for threats
and deal with any that cropped up. More than that, he had
a couple of unique abilities, ones that could mean the difference between life and death in a conflict with Calderon's
men. No, he was not going to risk betraying Felicity's faith
in him. He would shepherd the girls until every one of them
stood securely on dry, free soil.

He helped the last child into the back of the cabin
and Mano began backing the Outlaw from its slip, bubbles
churning at the stern like the growl of a submerged lion. He
turned to find that Mano had helped one of the girls work
the hatch door open and activate the lights. And now that he
saw how civil the bow compartment really was – a bit com-
pact, no doubt about that, but nicely upholstered, perfectly
comfortable and relatively safe – he changed his mind about
where the passengers belonged.

"In here. Quickly." He motioned, channeling the girls
through the opening one by one as Mano eased the throttle
forward and nosed the speedboat around the docks toward
the gap in the jetty.

"I want to stay with you," Felicity pleaded, standing
barefoot after having kicked off her remaining shoe, which
was nowhere to be seen.

Michael began to say no, but something in her eyes
stopped him. The love and trust embodied in them were inexplicable and heart-crushing. If not for her astute observation of the cell lock combination in the dungeon, this whole
thing could have turned out catastrophically. And one child
riding topside under his care was not going to make any difference in the outcome.

"All right." He nodded and gestured toward the empty
front passenger seat, which the girl settled into at once. "Just

hold on as tightly as you can."

He grasped the eldest girl, thirteen or so he guessed, briefly by the arm.

"Get everybody settled in there, then see if you can find towels or blankets to dry them. And life preservers. If there aren't enough, put them on the smallest ones first. Can you do that?"

To his relief, she seemed to understand English. Her face pallid, perhaps more fearful than the others because she could better understand the realities, she nodded.

Michael closed the hatch behind the kids and took the front passenger seat with Felicity on his lap just as the Baja rounded the edge of the sandbar.

"Hold on tight, amigos," Mano called. Michael held Felicity in place with his right hand and grasped the edge of a side pocket with his left. Leaving his criminal history in their wake, Mano Tejada eased the throttle to full open position and the rum-runner blasted out over the ocean like a doomsday missile.

The boat was moving impossibly fast, astoundingly facile in the roiling seas. It suddenly occurred to Michael how terrified he would have been in life, racing through a storm in the open cockpit with no life jacket and a man he wasn't sure he could trust at the wheel. Amazingly, he felt little of it for himself. The sub-Floridian waters at least couldn't take him a second time, of that he was certain; if nothing else, he could dive out of sight and transit back to the Afterworld.

But he was keenly aware that no one else on board had that option, and though he strained to hide it so as not to alarm them, for the girls he was highly concerned. He couldn't bear the thought of the innocent children suffering the kind of agony that had engulfed him and ended his life.

He looked behind them, hoping the triumphant sight of Isla Tesoro fading in the distance would restore his spirits. What he got instead was a lightning bolt of palpable dread.

Just emerging from the stormy gloom, two long, sleek

craft were bearing down on them from the direction of the island. And they were gaining.

Michael's heart leaped as a horrifying possibility struck him. Had he been thoroughly and fatally duped? Had Mano, instead of coaxing the dock guards to join the others in the great house, spent that conversation coordinating their victory? Had he chosen this boat not for the extra seats, which he must have known with the bow compartment would be unnecessary, but instead to ensure that the "faster boats" he had referred to would be able to catch up? Had Michael walked blithely into their trap, doing the cartel's work for it by bringing the girls out to deep water where they could be thrown overboard and then shot to erase them as evidence of the cartel's foray into the slave trade?

The man in the passenger seat of the nearer pursuit craft raised his head just enough to see over the windscreen. A second later, the modern equivalent of a bazooka came up onto his shoulder.

"Oh, *shit*," Michael exclaimed before he could stifle it. Mano turned toward him, then followed his gaze backward and let out a string of Spanish expletives the Rosetta Stone software didn't cover.

The boat lurched to port in a harsh evasive maneuver, slamming Michael and Felicity against the side and eliciting screams from belowdecks. Three seconds later Mano cranked it the other way, and only Michael's C-clamp grip prevented he and the girl from crashing into their pilot.

Michael tore open the hatch and shoved Felicity into the bow compartment with furious speed. He slammed it shut and turned back just in time to hear a bone-rattling concussion and see a fiery glow like a sun the size of a grapefruit emerge from the tube weapon's barrel.

Mano saw it, too. He wrenched the wheel even tighter, turning sharply across their plane of travel *toward* the direction of the pursuit. It wasn't a death wish or to consummate the conspiracy Michael had momentarily feared. Mano was marshaling all his experience and skills to avoid a hit by the rocket-propelled grenade.

It almost worked. The blazing shell grazed their stern, pitched downward and detonated in the water, kicking up a miniature tsunami that rolled them like a bowling pin. Mano pulled back hard left, but their speed was flagging. To his horror, Michael saw a column of black smoke billowing from the Baja's rear and picked up a sickening burning smell.

"Lost a screw," Mano remarked grimly, coolly working the controls but unable to completely mask the fear that told Michael they were in serious trouble. "God save us if that fire hits the fuel line."

Mano got the Baja pointed north again, still making what would have been excellent speed for an ordinary pleasure boat. But ordinary these were not, and with the Baja's power compromised, the Cigarettes were closing in more rapidly. Michael could do nothing but watch with maddening helplessness as the cartel assassin methodically chambered another rocket and raised the weapon for a kill shot.

He was bracing for the sight of the fiery ignition ring that would seal the Baja's fate when a figure appeared out of nowhere behind the man aiming the RPG launcher. The war piece flew forward with a violent jolt and plunked harmlessly into the sea. The shooter's scream was so pitched and penetrating that Michael could hear it above the storm a hundred yards back.

Mano looked over his shoulder in puzzlement. The Cigarettes were still too far back to make out detail on individual faces. But Michael, whose vision was now something better than 20-20, could have identified the sudden presence even with mortal sight. The haunting impression of empty black eye sockets would have been enough.

The craft that had lost a gun and gained an intruder went into a tight turn of its own and began falling rapidly behind. Michael smiled. He had no way of knowing what exactly was happening to those hapless thugs, and maybe it was best he didn't. *A hell-bent Darkened with a vendetta against you is an enemy to be feared,* Charlie had warned.

Indeed.

That was one down. But the second Cigarette boat was still on their tail, and Michael was fresh out of tamable Darkened hewn to his personal service. The remaining pursuers appeared not to have a rocket launcher, but with one of the Baja's twin engines crippled, the Cigarette would be within small arms range in no time.

"Can this thing be set to hold course on its own?" Michael inquired.

"Sure," Mano replied, "but I don't—"

"Set it up, then get below with the girls," Michael commanded crisply. "Wait three minutes, then look out of the hatch. If you still see me on board, shut it up again and wait one minute more. Keep doing that until I'm gone."

"What the hell?"

"Just do it," Michael barked. "I don't have time to explain and in a minute they're going to be right on top of us. I need you and the girls out of harm's way while I take these guys down."

Mano regarded him with elevated esteem. "If you're planning to fight it out with them, you're going to need me with you. You can't take them two on one."

"You don't think so?" Michael smiled devilishly and gripped Mano's wrist as a reminder.

"You're one strong son of a bitch," Mano allowed. "But they've got guns, and you're not going to have the drop on them like you did me. You're not going to talk your way out of it either, if that's what you're thinking. Those boys are hard core."

"That's exactly the point," Michael told him gently. "The girls can't drive themselves and you're no good to them shot. I can handle myself, but I can't protect you at the same time."

"You don't—"

"Listen, Mano." Michael's body language remained calm, but his voice carried the clipped urgency of an evacuation horn. "I trusted you, remember? I gave you the gun back at the docks when you could have turned us in or just killed us all straight up. I didn't like it, but you said you knew what you were doing, and I let you run with it. You've got to do that for me now."

Mano eyed him unhappily. They had no good options, and he knew it.

"At least take this," he said, resigned, holding out the machine pistol. "Give yourself a chance."

Michael waved it away. "I'm no good with boats and even worse with guns. I believe I can do this or I wouldn't try. If something *does* happen to me though, those kids' only hope is going to be you. I need you to have *your* best chance."

Mano studied at him for a moment more. Then he put the gun away, fixed the tiller on a Florida bearing, and smiled at Michael grimly.

"I was wrong about you, my friend," he said. "Thank you for giving me a second chance. May God be at your back."

"And yours." They briefly shook hands, then Mano disappeared into the bow compartment as he had been told to do.

The timing couldn't have been closer. No sooner had the hatch door shut than a spray of automatic weapon fire zinged off the chrome and fiberglass near the pilot's seat.

Michael glanced back and was surprised to see how close the Cigarette had come in the seconds of conversation with Mano. He ducked below the starboard gunwale where he couldn't be hit and went to work with calculating patience.

Calm and quiet, doing his best not to lose composure when another spread of bullets struck the hull next to him, he eased the hefty wooden emergency paddle he had previously spied out of the side compartment.

He had no idea how much gunfire the Baja might be able to take before its structure would fail and start letting the hot slugs through. He was a little surprised it hadn't breached already. Maybe it was a custom shell, he speculated. It would make sense for the gangsters to fortify their craft with some bulletproofing, if that was even possible. Maybe that was why they kept RPGs on hand, understanding that neither their own craft nor those of their few capable adversaries could be impaired by bullets alone. He didn't know, and it didn't matter; what would be would be, and he didn't need his cover to hold up indefinitely. Not even another full minute, just a few more seconds, just long enough for the remaining Cigarette to come within range. Just close enough for a man with post-mortal strength and a steel determination to free six kidnapped children to make one implausible leap, and then trust God's hand to use him as a divine instrument, to wield him like the Sword of Justice.

Another burst of shot smacked the Baja just above his head, and this time the fiberglass splintered, showering the textured floor next to him with dusty chips and shards. Their trajectory told him it was the moment he bad been waiting for, the window was now. In seconds, the Cigarette would pull abreast and it would be too late. The armed man would cross onto the Baja packing lethal force not tempered by surprise, and neutralizing the other boat would no longer be sufficient to guarantee the children's salvation.

Like a Budo master cleansing before a contest, Michael bowed his head and focused inward, concentrating his *ki*, which for him was that altered sense with which he had been born that had served his personal affairs poorly but never failed to deliver when a stranger's welfare was on the line. Time slept; sound receded; vision sharpened to a clarity that could see forward and backward in time as easily as space from side to side.

And for a second time, uncannily and unexpectedly, Michael Chandler's life began to flash before him. Only this time there were no clippings from the cutting room floor. This time, it was all highlights.

It had always been the "big" things that stuck with

him: the hospital vigils, the unearned forgiveness, the hidden mercies and undeserved sacrifices he routinely made. But now, as if seeing them for the first time – and in a real sense he was, as an outside observer – he began to recognize the soaring power of the *little* things, almost all forgotten yet instantly recognized, resplendent as stars running before him like a string of winking Christmas lights. Each tender word, each casual kindness, each free smile and reassuring hug. Every scrap of jerky smuggled to a shelter dog and every handful of pocket change dropped near some unsuspecting kid. Every piece of someone else's litter he had anonymously cleaned up, every closest parking spot passed by, every last-in-the-store container of his favorite whatever left on the shelf so it could be there for someone else. Every five-dollar tip for a ten-dollar meal, every kind note scribbled for a motel housekeeper, every book he really would have liked to keep donated instead to the charity Bookmobile. And every silent, unsolicited prayer for a lost man across the street, a woman peering anxiously through a window, a child gaping longingly at a simple toy, a baby squirrel frozen in fright at the edge of a busy road.

It was a seamless stream of all he had done that had raised his Place in the Afterworld like tiny bricks burgeoning into Machu Picchu. And finally, *finally* he saw the truth, the only truth, the golden truth his heart had sojourned after since he was old enough for lucid thought. *It's all that matters. I see it now.* The floor cuttings from the movie of life are trivial. Less than trivial, less than shadow. In a real and fundamental sense, they do not exist. They have no shape. *All that persists is love.*

He asked not why this should be revealed to him now; it seemed perfectly clear. It was *now, this* moment, *this* place, this thing he was about to commence, that his entire life had been leading up to. He had lived all this time on a dark stage, and now suddenly, brilliantly the lights were on, the curtains were parting, and he was the star of the show. Ironically, he had had to *die* in order to fulfill his life's destiny. Yet it didn't seem odd. He was still here; he had never been *not* here. Death had not been a tragedy, nor a finality; it wasn't something to be mourned. It hadn't robbed him of life; it had handed him new life, revealed parts of life that had been missing. Death had not been a barrier. *Death had been a door.*

And it was a door to *something.* He was freeing the girls, yes. That was imperative, and important. He was freeing Mano, too, or at least helping Mano free himself, and that might be just as important in its own way. He was possibly tugging a few blocks loose at the base of Isla Tesoro's Jengo tower, and if he had a small hand in toppling that monstrosity, so much the better. It was enough – more than enough. For all his angst about love and failed responsibilities, Michael had never truly begrudged his lot in life. He had tried to be a good man, and he thought that overall, he had been. That should be the end of it. He neither asked nor expected more.

And yet, he felt that there was more. That this was only the beginning. That just as Charlie had characterized mortal life as a kind of preschool, functioning mainly to prepare humankind for The Real Show, there was a purpose to Michael's existence of even greater import. He could feel it without seeing it. But he *could* see part of it: the part laid out before him *right here.* Dorothy Gail and Reggie Dwight both knew that the road of yellow bricks had a beginning. And if you ever meant to reach the end, that's where you had to start.

Michael Chandler, welcome to the Universe. Your life begins ... NOW.

All this played out in Michael's mind in an orderly, deliberate fashion, allowing him ample if not leisurely opportunity to understand it, to embrace it, to absorb it completely within the fibers of his soul. In the world outside, the entire reverie consumed only one second of elapsed time.

He sprang.

It was exactly as he had envisioned it, as he had calculated and hoped. The driver's attention was focused fully on maneuvering the Cigarette, which had to be carefully eased alongside, speed and bearing matched perfectly to the smaller craft, to make sure his accomplice ended up on the target's deck and not floundering with the sharks. The gunman himself was hunched at the edge of the foredeck, gripping the spindly bow rail. He was outfitted in a thin combination flak and flotation vest that left his movements unhindered. With his black AR-16 slung securely across his back and a .40 cal Beretta handgun sealed inside a waterproof holster, his hands were free for the jump he was poised to make the instant the Baja came in range.

Which left him, momentarily, defenseless.

Even immune to drowning as Michael believed he was, now that he was actually doing it, the sight of the twelve-foot gap between the speeding boats as he exploded up from the deck induced a wave of panic. Partly it was force of habit, a lifetime of conditioning to avoid such scenarios at all costs and of lapsing into catatonic paralysis when he failed to do so. Partly it was fear not of the water but of the jump itself, one he could never have made in mortal life even on dry land. And partly it was for the brave and trusting souls hunkered in the bow compartment solely at his bidding. He had left Mano with encouragement and the gun, but in his heart Michael knew that the man had little chance of prevailing against these adversaries without him. If he missed his jump – or if once across he failed to neutralize the pursuers – the little girls, and Mano with them, were as good as dead.

The anxiety was strong, but his will was stronger. Daring not to hesitate and lose his margin of surprise, gripping the oar firmly in both hands, Michael jumped.

For a moment, his heightened senses experiencing it in slow motion, it felt like flying. Then he realized with horror that he was dropping too fast to land on the foredeck as he had planned.

He was in the air above nothing but water. There could be no second guessing now. He would have to scramble as best he could.

He ripped his left hand free of the paddle and stretched it forward. It was going to be close. Already he had fallen below line of sight with the driver's head, and the other man was recovering his wits and reaching back for his deadly automatic.

Michael's left palm slammed down on the bow rail hard enough to have broken his hand in life. Before the rest of him could crash into the hull, he pulled as hard as a winch and vaulted himself upward like an Olympian on the pommel horse.

The gunman had his assault rifle in front of him now and was quickly positioning his hands for a shot. Michael swept the oar in a mighty arc and bashed the gun like a tennis ball, connecting with such force that the weapon was knocked spinning over the side.

Anger visibly boiled in the assailant's eyes as he ripped open the holster flap and grabbed his Beretta.

In the same instant, Michael saw what he had to do. He let his body follow through with the torque of the oar blow, his right leg curling, swooping laterally along the same path, then kicking outward like an angry mule. His foot connected hard with the man's ribs, eliciting a cry of outrage and pain as he slipped on the wet fiberglass, then fear as his attempt to regain balance failed and he tumbled over the edge after his gun.

Michael was on fire. He never broke stride, swirling the oar to smash like a baseball bat into the driver's windscreen.

It didn't shatter, but the safety glass fissured so explosively that the driver could see nothing through the spiderweb of cracks. He stood in the cockpit and reached for his own sidearm.

Michael chucked the oar to the Cigarette's cabin floor. He wasn't going to kill anyone, even indirectly, and the gunman in the life jacket was already hundreds of feet behind. He wouldn't need to kill them, but with what he was going to do, the driver would need the oar along with plenty of patience and elbow grease to get the boat back there and rescue his mate.

Michael lunged over the fractured windscreen and cor-ralled the cartel soldier around the arms and head. Twisting, he flung the man aside like a judo throw, hard enough to stun him, and took his place behind the wheel.

He palmed the throttle and jammed it back into neutral position, sending the craft into an abrupt limp as it banged harshly up and down on the waves it had been so elegantly slicing through. He switched off the ignition and yanked out the key, dropped it to the floor, crushed its plastic flota-tion bobber to useless fragments under his shoe, then with a smile chucked it much farther than necessary out over the water, just one more piece of litter he had consigned that day to the silt on the sea floor.

"You dumbass son of a bitch!" The driver recovered himself, fuming and incredulous at what he had just seen Michael do, grappling for his pistol with one hand as he pulled against the seat back to haul himself erect with the other.

Michael glanced over the bow. The smoke trail leaned almost horizontal now, the liberated Baja already so far ahead it was becoming hard to see. The best efforts of Teso-ro's fleetest had gone for naught, and even if its second line appeared on the southern horizon this very moment, they would never catch her now. He smiled, warm and deep and genuine. The game was over; the white hats had won. The satisfaction was sublime.

There was only the small matter of this irate gangster and his nasty Walther to tidy up.

He could have shot me already, Michael mused. The notion seemed oddly unimportant now that the girls were safe. Michael would have tried to prevent it, of course, had he perceived it, but the man had made no such move. He was holding the barrel on Michael, but for the moment he ap-peared content with control. Probably he saw delivering Mi-chael alive, so he could be interrogated and punished, as his only chance to mollify the brass and shield himself from the terrible fallout this fiasco was inevitably going to bring. The keys were gone, but he had a weapon and Michael didn't; he had a life vest, and Michael didn't; he was in friendly waters with allies close at hand, while Michael's compatriots were steaming at sixty knots in the opposite direction.

The cartel man was indeed thinking along these lines. What had happened was embarrassing, but Calderon would have to understand that it could not have been predicted – what this clown had pulled off seemed impossible. In any event it was over, the element of surprise was gone, and now he had the guy nailed. It was going to be highly annoying waiting for the companion Cig, which for the moment was nowhere in sight, or whatever dispatch Calderon sent out when he radioed for backup. But annoyance wasn't catastrophe, and whatever information this prickless acrobat could be made to spill might turn this setback into a windfall. Tweaking it out of him, or working at it even if there was nothing to get, was going to be sweet payback. The bastard would be gagging on his cutesy smile soon enough.

With all that had transpired that day, he would have laid a thousand to one that nothing further could happen that would confound him more or make less sense than what had already occurred. He would have lost that bet.

"I'm truly sorry about the keys, bro," Michael lamented. "Pro organization like yours, though, I'm sure they keep spares on a hook in the kitchen. Now the windshield, that's another story. I hate to say it, but I'm pretty sure my insurance has lapsed."

The man's face darkened with rage. "I'm the one holding the gun, moron. I gotta keep your punk ass warm for the boss, but a few bullets in the leg or the hand ain't gonna kill you."

Michael held up one hand and looked into the man's eyes with such soul-deep penetration that the thug was momentarily paralyzed. There was no need to clamp his wrists.

"I'm not going to let you shoot me." Michael's tone

was warm, even patient. "I know you'll think I'm doing that for me; that's the only way you can conceive of it. But it's not. It's for *you*, my friend. I'm not going to let you shoot me. And there will come a day when you'll shed tears thanking me for it."

The man wavered, whether confused, conflicted, or delirious it was hard to say. Slowly, however, dark pupils returned to his eyes and his native faculties began to resume control. The ruthless grip on his pistol tightened.

Michael saw it coming. He put on that cutesy smile, gave a little wave, and executed a back flip over the side of the boat so deft and unexpected that by the time the gunman regained the presence of mind to peer over the railing, there was nothing in the water to see.

THE STORM WAS ABATING. TO the north, a band of clean blue sky was expanding at a visible pace to confirm that the tropical sun had not truly gone, but only stepped out temporarily for a revitalizing break.

On that calming horizon, a lone watercraft could be seen racing south with all the speed of the defeated Cigarette boats. It was a borrowed Pantera F2-71 out of Key West, Florida, piloted by a shirtless surf bum who could be as focused as a firefighter when it really mattered and bearing his grizzled employer whose resolve was only intensified by shrapnel and explosion burns, homing in determinedly on the beacon of smoke streaming from a hobbled Baja Outlaw's wrecked motor.

It was as glorious and reaffirming as a glinting knight on a snow white horse. Better late than never; the cavalry had come at last.

CHAPTER 31
Redemption

ELDRIDGE RAYMORE WAS BESIDE HIMSELF.

"How could you let this happen?" he barked into the phone. "Last night you call here and tell me you have Chandler and everything's under control. Now the whole operation is coming apart?"

"It's not like that." Juan Calderon's voice was outwardly calm, but he couldn't keep out a flicker of unease. "The boat won't get far. We already burned their extraction craft and we've got Cigarettes running them down."

"But not the airplane." Raymore was seething. "What are you planning to do about that?"

"The CIA will squelch it," Calderon replied. "They've arranged a fake medical transport to pick up the girls at the airport and quietly distribute them back to their families. I hate losing the investment, but shit happens. DeLeon's wife will be thoroughly discredited, and even those who believe her will do nothing."

"How can you be so sure?" Raymore was still fuming.

"She'll have no evidence with the girls gone. It will be interpreted as lies by a scornful wife against her husband in the throes of divorce. CIA will make sure of it. They're not going to shut down their listening post over a few third world street brats. They can't let this get out anyway, they're as dirty as we are down here."

"You'd better be right."

"As for Chandler," Calderon continued, "he's toast. One of my guys saw him fall out of the plane through his sniper scope."

"You're sure?"

"Positive. Dropped a thousand feet into the drink a few miles offshore. Shark food."

Raymore's demeanor ramped down a notch. "All right, okay. Good. But I still want you to take every precaution. Suspend all business and scrub the island clean. *Clean*, do you understand me? And don't start things back up till I give the order."

"Order?" Calderon challenged with a smile that penetrated the distance. "I thought we were partners."

"You know better, you son of a bitch. Don't pretend to forget it."

"I'll make sure it all happens," Calderon soothed. "I'll take care of the details. Go get your beauty rest and focus on your campaign."

Raymore terminated the call.

MICHAEL BURST UP OUT OF the dark pool like a porpoise, scattering tiny neon fish in all directions. His Darkened accomplice was already sitting in the blackness under a tree near the bank, the panther Alex settled in the grass ten feet away watching him like a German Shepherd.

"You're late," Sid Raymore said, deadpan, his grisly voice making it hard for Michael to gauge whether it was an attempt at humor. Yet the tone sounded warmer somehow, more human than before. Was he imagining it, or had Sid softened toward him in the course of their escapade?

"You were brilliant at the plantation house." Michael beamed, toweling himself against the grass as if making a snow angel and delighted at how supernaturally fast the moisture was evaporating. "Your timing with the electricity was perfect."

"I enjoyed it." Sid let the hint of a smile creep into his voice. "It was fun spraying those bastards' ammo all over the place. I just wish I could have shot that rocket launcher through the floor of their boat."

"I wish you didn't think that way."

The Sid-creature scowled. "But I didn't do it, did I? I held up my end. We did that whole thing your way. And now it's time for mine."

"Sid ..."

"Don't call me that."

"Sid," Michael repeated, then stopped. "Oh my God, Sid!"

"What?" The Darkened was exasperated.

"Get up. Come with me."

"What the—"

"Come ... with ... me!"

Petulant, the half-man clambered to his feet and followed Michael through the maze toward the Pirate House. He had fulfilled his end of the bargain, had more than pulled his weight on Michael's behalf, and now he expected to be repaid. His tolerance for petty diversions was going to be thin.

Michael led him past the blazing torches, through the door into the limestone entry. He stopped them in front of the glassy water wall.

"Look."

Sid did.

It took him some time to process what he was seeing, because Sid Raymore had never seen his own death-face. He hadn't needed to. The dark periphery around his field of vision had told him his eyes were empty sockets. He could taste the gritty rot where perfect teeth had been. He could feel torn flesh and the air sucking in and out through the mangled gash in his left cheek. He could see the dark stains and moldy growth on his arms and chest and knew his head could be no different.

He had not seen his face, but he had a clear mental picture. And it was not the picture staring back at him from the waterfall.

As though not believing his eyes, Sid's hand slapped up unconsciously and fingered the surface between his mouth and left ear. Where the gash had been, *the skin was smooth*.

He grimaced like a chimpanzee. His teeth were sharp, but full. Frightening, but healthy. Filled in and almost white.

His eyes were set back in hollows, no mistaking that. But now there were eyes. The dark periphery was gone. His hair was still wild, but it was thick and all there, no longer matted or missing in splotches. It was only the step up from skeleton to Phantom of the Opera, but it was more human by half.

And now that the shock was behind them, both Sid and Michael noticed his clothes. The bloody mess had shrunk to a few thin streaks like the swipe of a claw. There was no sickening mold or grisly infection at all.

"*Look* at you!" Michael took Sid's hands in his. He couldn't have been more proud if his own son had brought home straight A's.

"I'm ... *better*?" Sid's voice was soft and thin, a self-conscious young man's voice, nothing like the ghastly wheeze of their first meeting in this very place.

Sensing a chance to reach Sid that might not remain open for long, Michael looked him in the eyes and pressed.

"How are you feeling about your father?"

Sid's face darkened. "That's a stupid question. Nothing's changed."

It wasn't the response Michael had hoped for. But he wasn't so sure it was true.

"You don't really want to help perpetuate his crimes."

"The hell I don't," Sid snapped. "And I don't like where you seem to be taking this, either."

Michael countered. "Those girls we got off the island,

are you sorry we did that? Do you think we should have just left them there?"

"Of course not."

"That's the kind of pain people like your father create. Do you know everything he's done over the years? Are you *sure* you know what kinds of crimes your dad has committed?"

Sid paused, remembering. "Smuggling, mostly drugs and exotic animal parts. He was even arrested for that years ago, but they couldn't make it stick. Bribery. Extortion. Tampering with the labor unions. Getting his buddies special treatment in prison. That's what I was able to uncover."

"It could be worse." Michael fixed Sid with a penetrating gaze. "Even if it's not, all those things hurt people, Sid. Innocent people. You're sympathetic toward the girls, even toward me, because they're people you know. But they're no different from people you *haven't* met. It's nothing but chance that certain people come in contact with you and others don't.

"The ones you don't know are no less deserving. If you grease the skids so your father can sink even lower and lower, there are going to be *more* victims. *More* overdoses. *More* houses burned to the ground. Who knows what he's into, or will get into with your help. Don't you see? You can't do it without harming innocent people."

"Drug addicts aren't innocent."

"Maybe they are and maybe they aren't, but they certainly don't deserve the fate you're talking about. Is that really what you want to do?"

Sid's voice was weaker than ever now, like a child caught in a misdeed being asked how he should be punished. "No."

"And you don't have to," Michael continued. "Don't sink to his level, Sid. If you focus everything on revenge, you're the same as him. I think you're better than that."

Sid's whole body stiffened. "That's not my fault. It's not me doing it. It's him. It's him!" He was almost screaming.

"It's not your fault," Michael agreed. "Not yet. But it will be if you continue this way."

"He hurt me!"

Michael eyed Sid sympathetically and tried the tack that Charlie had used with him. "I know he did, bro. And you want to hurt him back. I understand that. He hurt me, too. But Sid, it's not good for us to get that involved in mortal affairs. We can have the purest intentions and still make things worse. Besides, it's not healthy. Look around you, man. You're destroying yourself in the mortal world while there's so much to discover *here*. We belong in the Afterworld, not settling mortal scores. Just look at what it's done to you."

"You're a fine one to be talking like that!" Sid was seething. "You just turned that island inside out like some fucking Batman!"

To that, Michael had no good answer. It was easy enough to steer someone else onto the high road, something else entirely when your own ox was being gored.

He softened. "Look, I'm not going to break my promise to you. I can't pretend I don't want to see Ridge Raymore put in his place. But there's got to be another way."

IT TOOK FOUR HOURS FOR them to work out a plan they both found acceptable and agreed had a reasonable chance of success. It was a miracle that their contradictory perspectives could be reconciled at all; it had been contentious right up to the end.

"I still don't see why we have to involve that brainless fuck Burko," Sid spat. "It was my father's doing, but it was Burko's fists that put me here. He needs to be punished, too. He won't do it, anyway, guys like that don't give a shit about anything except their wallets and their dicks. I'd rather just scare his ass to death."

"From what you've told me, it sounds like you've got that well underway," Michael retorted. "And that's exactly why we use him. You've got the guy cowering in his sister's apartment pacing the floor. He's susceptible."

"He won't do it," Sid reiterated. "There's nothing in it for him. You're such a Mary Poppins, Chandler, you don't get human nature."

Michael disagreed, but he could concede the possibility in Burko's case. After all, he had never met the man, and Sid knew him intimately.

"So we give him something. Didn't you say there was some jewelry in the safe deposit box?"

"Not jewelry. Gold. Troy ounce Krugerrands. I did one semester as an exchange student in Johannesburg and picked one up as a souvenir. I thought it was cool and it seemed like a nice investment hedge, so I just kept buying them whenever the price was good."

"Worth enough to get Burko's attention?"

"God, I don't know how much is in there. I can't remember the last time I counted. But there's at least, oh, two or three dozen, I'd say. That would be about ..." He did a calculation in his head. "Fifty grand or so, depending on the sell price. Yeah, that would be enough to interest him for a while. But I really don't want to give them up."

"Why not? You planning to buy something?"

Sid scowled. "That's not the point."

"Well, what *is* the point? You can't take it with you, as they say. Who gets them now that you're deceased? Did you have a will?"

"No. As a lawyer, I'm embarrassed to say it, but no. I wasn't planning on checking out any time soon." Sid mused for a moment. "I suppose when it gets to probate, it would go ... to ..." Sid winced as if he'd just caught a whiff of the world's worst stink. "Probably my dad."

Michael just stared at him, letting the obvious conclusion speak for itself.

"All right. All right." Sid shrugged bitterly. "I guess it's better putting them to some use."

Michael nodded. "Would Burko take them as is, or would he be afraid they might cause him some problems? Do we need to find a way to convert them into cash?"

Sid smirked. "Hell no. A guy with his connections will have no trouble fencing gold coins."

THEY SHOOK HANDS AS THEIR vehicle pulled to a stop in the dark night alley behind an enormous bank in San Francisco's financial district. It felt strange and wonderful to be back in the Bay Area, almost a euphoria, albeit attenuated by melancholy at the circumstances. But there was no time to savor the nostalgia. Sid parked the stolen minibus in front of his bank's emergency exit and they both climbed out. Michael hated that borrowing the tall van was necessary; he had agreed to it only on the condition that they return it with a full tank of gas. For purposes of Afterlife door tricks, the security camera mounted on the opposite wall of the alley was the equivalent of a human witness. Its digital eye had to be blocked so Michael could meld through the locked door unseen. Even then, he couldn't go through until the interior power had been cut to prevent the bank's cameras causing the same problem on the other side. They had considered cutting the juice to the alley cam first, but it was wired to a separate building, and they decided not to interfere with any more circuits than they had to. Limiting the mayhem might buy them precious time before the cops would notice and mobilize.

"Godspeed," Michael incanted as he crouched beneath the camera's sight line. Sid handed him the car keys, then nodded a silent acknowledgement before dashing away toward the building's juncture box.

Crouching as low as he could, Michael hunched himself up against the metal security door and prayed no one would enter the alley. This was the riskiest part of the scheme and it was maddening having to just sit there, one eye darting up and down the empty back street, the other carefully monitoring the subtle night light leaking through the bank's rear windows.

Abruptly, the electricity went off, causing computer and security camera power lights to wink out as Michael sprang through the door. They came on again a second later as the emergency generator kicked in, then this, too, went dark. *Neat trick,* Michael thought in admiration. *I wonder if anyone can learn to do that, or if it's one of those Darkened "cheats."*

Since they couldn't know for sure, they had decided to assume that this might trigger a battery-powered silent alarm and to work accordingly.

In the distance, a siren wailed. Michael knew he would have to move fast.

He made his way to the assistant manager's office, which Sid had designated, thankfully not far from the alley entrance. He dissolved through the door and found the bank's counterpart box key in an unlocked drawer just as Sid had prescribed.

Staying low in case the power came back on, Michael hurried to the safety-deposit vault and passed through its even thicker door into a chamber of utter darkness.

Even with his new night vision, the visibility wasn't great, but Michael was able to pick out the numbers on the secure container drawers. He found Sid's and opened it on a stand-up table using the bank's key together with the one Sid had supplied.

The envelope containing Sid's documentation of his father's misdeeds appeared intact, and the box was indeed lined with gold coins, each about the size of a quarter. He tucked the envelope into his waistband and scooped out the coins, depositing them in his pockets.

Having been emptied of all contents that held practical value, now only sentimental items remained in the drawer. A junior high sports letter. A Pegasus hood ornament. A delicate lace garter. Michael smiled as he imagined what stories these mementos might tell about Sid's tragically abbreviated life.

He slid the box back into its recess with the gentle reverence of a pallbearer. The siren was much closer now. He returned the manager's key and worked his way back out, made sure that the alley was clear, and set off at a brisk pace in the direction Sid had gone.

SIX HOURS LATER IN OAKLAND, a wary Brenda Burko answered her apartment door, wondering what could be so all-fired important that somebody would knock here at daybreak. It was a school morning and she was still in her bathrobe, the sounds of her children bustling about the house and the smell of bacon and pancakes filling the air.

She might have been even more careful had not the stranger standing on her welcome mat been so good looking. Unconsciously, the harried single mother brushed back her hair with her fingers.

"Sorry to disturb you so early. You're Brenda?"

"Who are you?"

"My name is Max Chandler. I'm a friend of John's. I need to speak with him."

"John isn't here. He lives in Alameda."

"I was told he was staying with you temporarily."

"Well, I don't know who told you, but they were wrong. Now if you'll excuse me, I'm right in the middle of getting my kids ready for school."

"I understand, Ms. Burko, but I only want to help John and I know he's here. His Corvette is parked around the corner."

She bristled. "I don't have time to argue. I told you he's not here. Now, get the hell out before I—"

"It's okay, Bren." John Burko appeared in the corridor behind his sister. His face was pale, his eyes bloodshot, whether from lack of sleep or heavy drinking it was hard to tell. Judging from his attire and smell, it was probably both. He looked like he'd been sleeping in his clothes for weeks.

"It's all right, I can't keep on like this. Just let me talk to him. You go and take care of your kids."

The woman eyed both men with suspicion and fear, then trundled off toward the kitchen.

"Friend, huh?" Burko addressed Michael bitterly. "Where am I supposed to know you from?"

"You don't. I'm sorry. I just said that because I needed to see you. But the other part was true. I know you're in trouble and I really am here to help."

Burko smirked. "I been around the block, Nancy. Don't pull that bullshit with me. Just say who you are and what you want so I can decide if there's any reason not to break your nose with this door."

"Yeah, okay. There is something I want." Michael extended the envelope in his hand. "Take a look at this."

Burko kept one eye on Michael as he flipped through the papers. At first, he seemed annoyed and perplexed. Then all of a sudden a light bulb went on.

He looked up and repeated the question. "Who are you?"

"It's all the stuff Sid Raymore got on his dad," Michael pressed. "Payment records, account numbers, business ledger anomalies, the identities of people he compromised. Enough to knock him out of the election for sure, maybe put him in jail if there's a witness around to corroborate it."

Burko broke into a mirthless grin. "You want me to give you Eldridge Raymore?" His amusement became harsh laughter. "You ain't as smart as I thought. You don't just serve up Ridge Raymore. He's got friends. What are you,

FBI? You fucks should know that."

Michael conjured a sober look. He was no actor, but John Burko wasn't hard to fool.

"Look, Burko, the ride is over. This thing is going down, with your help or without it. But most of this stuff is pretty arcane, not enough to hang Raymore immediately. There'll be plenty of proof eventually, but it will take time to develop. Time for Raymore to get wind of it and leave the country. He's got friends here, he's got even better ones in South America. They'll be more than happy to retire him to some estate on the beach. Meanwhile, guys like you will be rounded up and mowed down. That's how it works and you know it."

Burko leered. "I been to jail before. I ain't afraid of it."

"You're afraid of *something*. Why are you living with your sister? Why are you sleeping in your clothes? Why haven't you slept a whole night through or gone a day without a good hard drink for as long as you can remember?"

Burko rasped angrily, "What are you talking about?"

"Did you think they were dreams, Mr. Burko? Nightmares? When you saw it, the thing with no eyes stalking you in the dark? You think it wasn't real?"

Burko said nothing; he didn't need to, and maybe he couldn't. He was starting to shake.

"I also know," Michael said with menace, "that you killed Raymore's son."

Burko went ashen. "The fuck you do."

Michael eyed him evenly. "I'm not here to intimidate you, man. I said I came to help, and I mean it. I can free you from that stalking. I can end it for good. And I can get you out of here, safe from Raymore. That's why I brought these." He dug out a fistful of Krugerrands. Burko gaped, genuinely jarred out of his element and grateful for any departure from the conversation's recent trajectory.

"There's enough here to get you deep into Mexico and to live on quite nicely for a good long while, if you have the sense to keep your head down. You do what I say, I'll stop the haunting and give you half this gold up front. You'll find the other half in a locker at SFO after we confirm you've done everything agreed to."

Burko stretched out a hand, eyes like a dog fixed on a steak, gesturing for permission to touch.

Michael extended the coin pile toward him. "Be my guest."

Burko lifted one of the Krugerrands to his mouth and bit, examined it, then returned it.

"You ain't FBI."

"No, I'm not." Michael affected a dangerous grin. "You'd do well to be on my side, friend. But I won't need you forever. It's got to be *now*. You screw around thinking about it till we have Raymore without you, you go right under the bus."

A satisfied calm, what in John Burko passed for shrewdness, crept over the man's face. "You're the competition," he declared triumphantly. "You want Raymore out of the way. You figure once he's governor, he'll have enough power to put you out of business. So you're making sure that don't happen." Burko was so pleased with this Holmesian deduction that he looked ready to burst.

Michael said nothing to dissuade him. He put on a bloodless glare. "The pitch is over. Are you in or out?"

Burko smiled conspiratorially. It was sickening how quickly his allegiance turned. "Just tell me what you need done. And pull the rest of that shit out of your pockets. I want to count it."

IT TOOK SEVEN STRAIGHT DAYS and late nights of feverish work without a break except to sleep and eat for *Los Angeles Times* reporter Lani Turner to verify enough information from her lengthy interview with John Burko and the supporting documents he had provided to justify going to press. Her editor delayed publication one more day, a day on pins and needles, so that the article could come out on Sunday and reach the largest circulation of the cycle. It went out top of the fold front page under the headline RAYMORE CRIME TIES. The *Times* made a tidy sum syndicating it out to every major newspaper in the country.

It made interesting reading for Ridge Raymore, who was infuriated but not subdued. The *Times* had been chosen to do the story specifically so that as much of the groundwork as possible could be done away from the Bay Area, where it was feared that Raymore's friends in high places might somehow learn of it in time to warn him. But Raymore's influence had tendrils throughout California, and this precaution of centering the effort in L.A. proved insufficient to prevent the investigation from being detected by his allies.

He had scrambled his Learjet pilot in the dead of night, ostensibly for travel to San Diego for a late-scheduled fundraiser. But the plane had broken course and crossed into Mexico before nosing east toward the safest haven he could arrange on short notice. The Lear had never before landed on Tesoro, whose grass runway had never been intended for anything more than small propeller planes, but they were able to touch down safely. A terse call to Havana to arrange a landing there had been Plan B, and Raymore was relieved when that turned out to be unnecessary. Things were chaotic enough without the unseemly wrangling that might have ensued had the Castros perceived an opportunity to profit from the fleeing candidate's misfortune.

Sitting in a wicker chair on the veranda with the paper on his lap, nursing a triple bourbon and a spiced Cuban cigar before a spectacular sunset, Raymore was displeased but not defeated. He had managed to transfer the bulk of his U.S. financial holdings to discreet offshore accounts during the flight. He might have to lay low, maybe for a long time, but that didn't have to be unpleasant. He wouldn't rot on Tesoro; he had always felt frustratingly impotent here from the scarcity of people available to manipulate and abuse. But he had solid connections in Brazil and Venezuela, where he could arrange a reasonably unfettered life so long as he laid low. Maybe he would change his identity – modern medicine and document technology could work miracles if you could pay – or maybe he would just retire. He was contemplating a number of options he considered acceptable, even satisfying, if his aspirations of political achievement had been derailed.

But even so, he was not prepared to give up just yet. Ridge Raymore had not gotten where he was by conceding without a fight in the face of heavy odds. There were tricks to be tried, strings still to be pulled. Marion Barry, the U.S. congressman sent to prison by the FBI and subsequently elected by overwhelming majority as Mayor and City Councilman of Washington, D.C., was a persistent inspiration. That Barry had been convicted merely of smoking crack cocaine and not operating an international crime empire failed to faze Raymore. The point was that in America, anything could happen; you were never down for good. And Eldridge Raymore had never been down at all.

THEY SAT ON DRIFTWOOD LOGS around a campfire in the Pirate House sea cave sipping hot cocoa, celebrating their victory.

"He got away," Sid lamented, his tone fatalistic. Michael noticed the lack of anger with approval. It was immensely gratifying to see the change in Sid and know that he had been instrumental in bringing it about. It was his first good look at the younger Raymore in the form he was meant to take. Gone were the blood, the facial deformities, the general unkemptness. The Afterlife magnified the impression of an intelligent, good-looking lawyer who doubtless would have married well and enjoyed professional success if he had lived.

"No. You said yourself he saw the election as the pinnacle of his life. You took that away from him. Count yourself even and let it go, Sid. You have to. Don't risk falling back into that miserable trance."

"Yeah, I know." The firelight flickered in Sid's hazel eyes, no longer recessed or misshapen.

At length, Sid stood up and Michael followed, taking the offered handshake. It felt thoroughly warm, sincere, *human*.

"I'm going to go find my mom," Sid told him. "I couldn't bear to do it before. Thanks again for freeing me, Michael. I'd been so blind with fury that all I could see was fire. If not for you, I would have kept wandering that horrible place for a long, long time."

"You saved yourself, man. All I did was catalyze what was already in you."

Sid smiled, and this time leaned forward and gave Michael a brotherly hug.

Michael returned the gesture with warm affection. "Farewell, bro. Check in from time to time, will you? It'll make me happy to know how you're doing."

"I will. I want to show you my Place, for one. As soon as I get things settled I'll be in touch." And with that, Sid Raymore strode across the sand to a dark corner far from the fire and disappeared.

For Michael Chandler, the fight was over. He needed it to be. Only now, when there was finally room to breathe, did the full magnitude of his long ordeal begin to tell. With those he cared about now safe and his duty to Sid fulfilled, he wanted nothing more than to relax and let the wonders of Afterlife bathe him like hot springs. He wanted to read his books and play with his telescope, he wanted to hug his grandpa, he wanted to cuddle his enormous cat and watch the neon guppies dance in their pool. He wanted to sail his galleon and lay in the grass of the dark jungle doing nothing at all, just lying there without pain or concern, free of urgencies and obligations, unrestrained by the limitations of time or space or mortality. He wanted rest – he *needed* rest – and he was ready for it.

But there was one more thing he had to do. Because even now, with all that had happened and beyond the boundary of death, as tired of struggle and as desperate for sanctuary as he felt, the call of love was even stronger, an angelic clarion that would not be denied. And now, for the first time in his existence, he had free rein to pursue the romance that in the course of his life he viewed as second only to Vicki.

His path to love, a road he had not sought but that had nevertheless been laid down before him, had been made eminently clear. It was the path that led to Beth.

CHAPTER 32
The Deafening Choice

THOUGH HE HAD SPENT ONLY hours with the DeLeons on Marblehead Neck, his visit had branded Michael with a deep emotional impression, and when he returned there now, the manor seemed as familiar to him as the fading memory of his San Mateo townhouse. That rented home had been lovingly outfitted with furnishings that radiated his personality from every corner, but he had never shared it with anyone else, and as a result, ultimately it was a lonely place. His primary attachment to it came from a sense of security, of reliability – of *function*. By contrast, his brief time in the manor had been all Lego fantasia and pumpkin pie sundaes and Beth's beautiful laughter in the glow of fireplace embers. It had been a taste of the home life Michael had always longed for but never really had, even in childhood. It was a bittersweet compulsion he could not escape no matter how badly he ached. Now here he was, finally at liberty to strip off the bitter and to plant seeds that would bear him sweet fruit when Beth's mortality reached its end.

He had poked his way in the dark through a storage nook in the Pirate House that his grandfather had stocked for him with handmade clothes. He had emerged in the closet of the DeLeon guest room where he had slept, just like the Pevensie children coming through the wardrobe into Narnia. With what he now knew, he was beginning to suspect that C.

S. Lewis's story was actually true.

The fact that he had crossed over from his Afterlife *house*, the most intimate feature of his private paradise, seemed to Michael proof that his bond with Beth – and to a lesser extent Elise – was a fundamental matter of destiny. The love for him here was strong.

But something was wrong. It was the same house, the same people as before even though two of them didn't know the third was present, yet it felt cold and empty. It was not at all the atmosphere Michael had anticipated when he set out to reconnoiter Beth's circumstances as a first step in his campaign to keep her torch for him burning until she could join him in the Afterlife.

He had made his way to the basement to admire Elise's Lego creations when he was startled by footsteps coming down the stairs. Now he lay prone on the cement floor of the nearby wine closet, listening under the door as Beth and Elise cuddled under an afghan watching *The Lion King*. At least they *had* been watching. Now, Beth had muted the sound, and they were engaged in tender conversation.

The four weeks since the Tesoro rescue had taken a grueling toll. First, there had been Rick's arrest as he re-entered the country on a flight into Logan from Bogotá. Next had come two weeks of wrangling over whether Beth should be incarcerated for her complacency. She had been immensely relieved when the decision came down, partly based on her promise to cooperate and thanks partly to her father's influence, that Beth would not be charged. The process and the waiting, though, had been exhausting.

For now, things were stable. But as she sat there in the quiet house listening to her daughter's somber questions, Beth looked as though she had aged ten years.

"What's going to happen to him?"

"I don't know, sweetie. He's probably going to have to spend a long time in jail. We can visit him, though. We'll go as often as we can, I promise."

There was a brief pause, then: "Mama?"

"Yes?"

"Were you going to divorce Dad and marry Michael?"

Beth sighed. "I don't know, baby. I thought about it, but I think maybe I missed that chance even before ... before this all happened." She chuckled humorlessly. "I'm not sure I would have been the kind of woman he deserved anyway."

There was a silent pause.

"I miss him." Elise began to sniffle, rocking herself back and forth in a subconscious grasp at the comfort she had felt when her mother had rocked her as a newborn.

"Me too."

"Not—"

"I know who you meant, honey."

Elise's agony came out in a heart-wrenching, helpless sob. *"I want my daddy!"*

Beth closed her eyes, nodding miserably, embracing her daughter now in a sad, full, tearful hug, patting her on the back as much for her own comfort as Elise's. "I know."

In the wine closet, Michael knew, too. A cacophony swelled in his head, a deafening choir clawing his sanity, so thunderous it seemed to shake the house and so loud he thought Beth and Elise would surely hear it.

He could barely think. He fought desperately to find the rationale for a different course, to justify and revalidate his original intent in spite of what was occurring. It went for naught. He felt sick, lost in a keening loneliness as debilitating as when he had failed to detect Vicki in the Afterlife. His tears welled up so profusely they blurred his vision.

But in his heart, he knew. As devastating as it was, as harsh and unthinkable, Michael knew. And he made his choice. He would enlist Sid to get the wording right and Charlie to supply a fake ID. He would carefully plan, gather the necessary tools, and do what now he knew with painful certainty had to be done.

RICK DELEON SAT ON A hard plastic seat in the visiting room of the Federal Detention Center in Miami, Florida, clad in orange inmate garb and separated by a Plexiglas barrier from the stranger talking to him on the other side.

He had been nabbed at Miami International on a tip from his wife upon debarkation from a commercial flight out of Cozumel, presumably destined for his bungalow in the Keys. It was a route he often took after wrapping up business in the Caribbean, or surreptitiously from Isla Tesoro when direct transit to Key West seemed unwise.

He had hired and met several times with a local attorney, so he was surprised when this man before him, whom he had never heard of before, showed up unannounced presenting Department of Justice credentials. What made them think they could go around his lawyer, he did not know. Why they would initiate the visit at all he could only guess.

Perhaps it should have made him wary, but it didn't. Rick DeLeon had resigned himself to the worst. He had made a huge mistake, he was going to pay for it, and he wasn't going to complicate things and endanger his life by selling out for a plea.

He might have considered it if it would have saved his family. But that ship had sailed. If Beth had been angry about his profession, it was nothing compared to her fury over his running off with Elise. Calderon sticking them in the slave cells – Elise especially, how could that douchebag pull a stunt like that? – had burned the last bridge. Beth would do all she could now to cook him, and deep down he couldn't blame her.

No, that family was history, Beth was now his adversary, and Elise, he was sure, despised him, at least for now. If not, then Beth's aspersions would doubtless poison any remaining affection his daughter might bear. He hoped that would change when she got older, that by the time he got out – what had his lawyer projected, maybe a twelve-year sentence, probably out in eight if he behaved himself? – Elise would be grown by then, an adult or close to it, and maybe the combination of time and maturity would soften her toward him. He surely hoped so. He hadn't been the best of fathers, largely because he was gone all the time, but he truly loved her. He saw in Elise the melding of their strengths, his toughness and tenacity fused with Beth's intelligence and social appeal, a beautiful, living manifestation of their love.

If she came around on her own, he would thank God for the blessing. If not, he would do whatever it took to win back her heart, would work at it the rest of his life if he had to. Beth had been the love of his life – that torch could never relight even if he remarried – but Beth was gone. Elise, on the other hand, was his immortality. She was the "better" he had brought into the world that counter-balanced his own failings. He craved her love and approval with an almost child-like fervor. He could not bear to live with her disdain.

But Elise was a child, one whose respect he had deservedly lost, and until she could separate from Beth and think independently, he held no hope of reconciliation. And with both of his girls out of reach, it would be idiotic to make a deal that would draw the cartel's enforcers. He wanted a normal existence after he served his time, and there was no point in making his life harder to rebuild than it had to be. So what harm was there in talking to this guy, through his attorney or straight up?

"You don't know me," Michael began, "and that's best for both of us. All you need to know is that I am familiar with the events on Isla Tesoro that put you here, I know something of your personal life, and I'm not your enemy. There are things I can't tell you, and you'll need to respect that. Just try to keep an open mind."

Rick said nothing. He was far too jaded to expect anything good to come out of this talk, but there was no need for hostility before he knew for sure. He was prepared to let at least one shoe drop.

"First, I've been in contact with your family. I want

you to know that they miss you."

"I have no family." Rick's voice was soft, introspective, philosophical. "I don't deserve a family."

"That's not for me to judge. But you're wrong if you think it can't be salvaged. Elise is your daughter, for Christ's sake. She's eight years old. She's going to love you regardless. And Beth ..." Michael paused to let the sudden tightness in his chest dissipate, willing his demeanor to calm. "Beth loves you, Rick. Even after all this. She's mad at you, but the fact is she loves you more."

Rick eyed him stone-faced. "Let's get to why you're here."

"Your father-in-law has been busy lately. He's running all over the Navy trying to marshal support to shut Tesoro down. He's very influential, and people are listening. But he can't make the sale. And the reason is that nobody – not even the CIA – has enough 'actionable intelligence' to pull the trigger."

"Yeah, they wouldn't," Rick said. "I don't think they want to. But even if they did, Calderon keeps their mole guy blind. Not from everything, but they never discussed serious business, not in my presence anyway, except while he was in Havana going through Castro's sock drawers."

Michael went on. "In fact, the CIA is resisting. Tesoro's both useful and embarrassing, and they're not sure they want to scrap it in the first place. And *nobody* wants to make an international incident out of it only to come off looking like they were flailing at shadows."

Rick smiled. "Those self-righteous pricks."

"So here's the thing." Now Michael leaned in toward the Plexiglas, speaking quietly, summoning all his persuasive powers and fixing Rick with an earnest, sympathetic gaze. "What Ted needs is someone like you from the inside. He won't approach you directly, partly to avoid publicizing the shortage of evidence and partly because the family connection makes it awkward. But he would very much like to leverage your help covertly. And he's got a deal for you. He's prepared to sponsor you into the Federal Witness Protection Program. A new name, a house, a job, a new life, completely safe from your friends in the cartel. And not just you — Beth and Elise, too. Immediately. They'll drop all charges. You'll be a free man."

"You're shitting me."

"No." Michael shook his head. "I know better than you might think what's at stake if you talk, Rick. I wouldn't be here if there wasn't a way to make that right. And the DOJ is on McFadden's side. They'll make this work."

"Holy Jesus." Rick found himself in such a state of shock that his eyes could barely focus. "You're not shitting me, right? You're not trying to pull something?"

"On my way here, I dropped a sealed envelope by the front desk in your attorney's office. It contains a secure telephone number directly to Ted. If you choose to do this, Ted will set up a private meeting for you and your attorney with a DOJ case officer. Beth, too, if you don't object. *Private*, not like this. They'll spell out all the specifics. After that, you and your lawyer, and your family, can decide yes or no."

"Holy Mother of God!"

"Call them now," Michael urged. "Don't wait on this. We don't get many second chances in life."

"I will." And something happened just then, like a flash of radiance inside Rick DeLeon, a subtle change that would leave his soul permanently brighter. "Thank you, man. Thank you! I sure as hell will."

As Michael stood up and turned to leave, Rick called after him quizzically one last time. "Are you *sure* I don't know you?"

The reply that came would puzzle him for the rest of his life.

"No. And that was the problem," Michael tossed back. "You never really did."

RIDGE RAYMORE AND JUAN CALDERON sat facing each other in the salon of the great house, the former flirting with a whiskey despite the morning hour and somewhat distracted by his impending flight to Maracaibo, the latter alternating between sips of strong coffee and puffs on a cigar. They were engaged in an animated discussion about how to restore the Caribbean branch of Cartagena-Littleton to its former efficacy.

"The future of recreational drugs is legitimacy," Calderon declared. "It's happening all around you. When was the last time anyone did serious time for cannabis in the States? The market is choking. It's *legal* in Washington and Colorado, for Christ's sake. And that's only going to spread. Nobody's going to cover our overhead for something they can buy in a liquor store or grow openly in their back yard."

"I'm not saying you're wrong in principle, Juan. But you can't extrapolate what's happening with marijuana to coke and heroin. You're not going to see *them* on a ballot any time soon. And nobody's refining Afghan-grade opium in their basement. This 'War on Terror' has only strengthened our connections and intensified our importance to them as a distributor. Besides, this sex toy bullshit, that's not the answer. We don't need the complications."

"The profit is incredible, the market is worldwide, and the customers always pay." Calderon exhaled a thick blast of smoke. "And all those Cartegena-Littleton cargo ships give our competitors wet dreams. We have a one-of-a-kind advantage in moving that kind of freight. There are risks, sure, but ..."

There was a knock at the door. One of the two guards inside opened it, and the outside sentry waved Marco Fuentes in. In the past they had never needed such precautions, buried deep in the Cuban sphere of control and enjoying CIA dispassion. But these days, security couldn't be tight enough.

"The Mole." Calderon smiled. "Maybe we should ask

his opinion." He turned to Raymore. "Have you ever met our 'minder' from the Central Intelligence Agency? I can't remember."

Before Raymore could answer, Fuentes cut him off. "I hate to barge in on you gentlemen," he said, "but I have something to say that can't wait."

Calderon frowned. Fuentes might be capable enough, but for obvious reasons he wasn't given critical assignments on behalf of the cartel. His role was to spy on Castro, keep the Agency satisfied that things weren't off the rails on Tesoro, and stay out of the way. He remained a CIA employee, and everyone understood that the relationship was tenuous. Calderon had gone to some lengths to make sure Fuentes got his hands dirty enough to be controllable, and he thought he had struck a proper mix. But it was unlike Fuentes to break in on a meeting of the cartel dons. And it was even less likely for him to possess news worthy of doing so.

"Eldridge Raymore," Fuentes announced, "on behalf of the Federal Government of the United States of America, I am placing you under arrest for a succession of serious crimes including murder, conspiracy to commit murder, bribery of public officials, and other counts as detailed in a warrant for your arrest issued by the 9th Circuit Court of the United States and conferred upon the U.S. Marshal's office in San Francisco for execution. I am arresting you in the capacity of a formally deputized representative of that office."

Eldridge Raymore, who for all his bravado had been unable to shed a measure of unease from the recent turn of events, gaped in shock. Juan Calderon burst out laughing.

"You're going to make me pee my drawers, Marco, but you really shouldn't make jokes around a man like Mr. Raymore. It's not good for your health."

"This is no joke," Fuentes replied, his eyes steel, his posture firm. "Unfortunately, I do not have jurisdiction to deal with *you*, Mr. Calderon. But someone who does will be here shortly."

Calderon's smile vanished in an explosion of anger as

he launched out of his chair. "Listen to me, you mouthy little prick. I don't care who you're working for of what kind of game you're playing. You can be carved up and fed to the sharks like anyone else. And don't think for a minute Langley is going to play heavy with us if we happen to 'lose' you. They send a replacement, and life goes on. So how about you stow this bullshit and go sit in your quarters till we're done with our business? Leave the gun here. And by the time I come see you, you'd better have a brilliant explanation."

Fuentes, with both door guards' rifles trained on his head, slowly withdrew the Glock from his shoulder harness and laid it on a side table as told. He then unfastened two shirt buttons over his chest, revealing a trace of threadlike wire.

"I'm just delivering the message," Fuentes continued, not showing an ounce of give. "I'm not taking you down by myself. I'm well aware you could put a bullet through my ears right now. But I *am* wired, both video and sound, and I don't believe we have you for murder of a U.S. government agent, yet. Besides, killing me won't make a bit of difference in how this goes down."

His gaze shifted and a smile suddenly creased Fuentes's face; the look in his eyes made Calderon turn around. He stared out the window wearing an expression of shock and disbelief.

"This is the United States Navy," a stern voice boomed from a bullhorn mounted on the black helicopter hovering two hundred yards away. "We have you sealed in and we are taking charge of the island. Put your weapons down, come outside with your hands on your heads, and lie face down in plain sight on the airstrip. If you comply you will not be harmed. Anyone not clear of the buildings, face down on the airstrip with their hands on their heads when we deploy on the ground, *will be shot*. This is your only warning. There will be no exceptions." The message was repeated in Spanish.

The terns and cormorants circling above the shoals of

Isla Tesoro enjoyed an unprecedented show that day. Three small naval tactical groups, launched from Guantanamo before dawn, approached at equal distances from the east, west, and north. From their overhead vantage, the birds could also spy the dark silhouette of a submarine patrolling the channel between Tesoro and the Havana coast. Individual craft began breaking formation at three miles out, forming a ring of formidable speed and firepower that no rum-runner could hope to breach.

With this net cast and tightening, two Blackhawk helicopters, each bearing a Marine commando squad, swept in and hovered over the great house preparing to deploy. A pair of Apache Longbows bristling with ordnance wafted in behind them to discourage any ill-advised heroics.

Out filed the cartel soldiers, one after the other, their weapons left behind. It was an easy push. They had already been demoralized by the drudgery of erasing evidence, the weeks of aimless sitting, the interruption of their pay, their California daimyo exposed and exiled in disgrace. The end was almost a relief. The airstrip filled up with prostrate figures as first one Blackhawk, then the other, touched down, pouring out Marines.

Out marched Eldridge Raymore, Marco Fuentes at his elbow. He made a show of walking slowly, hands pressed firmly to his head. He was angry and unhappy, but he didn't want to die. Given what waited for him in the Afterlife, that was probably wise.

Only Calderon remained. He sat blank and motionless inside the great house, saying nothing and thinking less, consumed by a dull and disbelieving anger. *This couldn't be happening on* his *island.* He could almost pretend it wasn't. Only when Rear Admiral Ted McFadden, hastily reinstated to active duty to lead the operation, personally entered the salon at the head of an armored entourage was the God of Isla Tesoro finally dislodged from his wicker throne and shunted aboard the first chopper load out.

Generations of Tesoro sea birds had witnessed three

centuries of atrocities. Their descendants cawed approval as that legacy came crashing down for good.

EXACTLY *WHY* HE NEEDED TO see the DeLeons one last time, at first Michael couldn't really say. A subconscious reach for closure, he supposed. As painful as it was, at least this final look would wrap up the whole episode with Beth that had ended so differently than he had hoped.

It would be his last visit to Marblehead Neck, that was for sure. It might even be his last return to the mortal world. The pain would ebb in time, he hoped – how could it not when the future was eternal? And he had the merciful comfort of his Place to salve him until then. But now, here in this moment, peeking through the master bedroom door in the dead of night, the hurt was raw and deep.

And there they were. Rick DeLeon, snoring like a sawmill just as Beth had described, his peaceful look reminding Michael not so much of their high school days but of the grammar school pictures Beth had shown him in a scrapbook. Close by lay Beth herself, ravishing even in sleep, her smooth, full cleavage visible under her burgundy camisole evoking a recurring angst over whether his resistance that night in the bungalow had been admirable, or just plain stupid.

They were holding hands like newlyweds, and in a sense he supposed that's what they were. Between them lay their daughter, her slumbering countenance an affirming picture of cherubic bliss. And that, he realized, was what he had come to see. He needed to feel that his sacrifice hadn't been empty, that his anguish, if he had to endure it, was for a purpose.

And here was all the reassurance he would ever need. Elise was happy. She would grow to adulthood in a proper family, nurtured by her real mom and dad working lovingly together. Rick's detour into the drug trade would become a lost memory, a trivial blip on her road to happiness and prosperity. If they started putting up plastic fairy palaces in Manhattan, she would be there. If they didn't, well then, inheriting her mother's charms to complement fine qualities of her own, she would be just as successful at something else. She would make her way in the world, and she would marry a worthy suitor, a man of enduring substance and not just fleeting roguish appeal. He had no doubt Beth would see to that.

He descended the stairs and walked through the dark house surrounded by packing boxes, the walls and floors now bare in anticipation of the move. Michael had not looked into where the government was going to settle them, and he wouldn't. He didn't need to know the location or the new names under which they would be establishing their sheltered life. He didn't *want* to know. There would be some comfort in the knowledge that he couldn't trace them even if he wanted to. The futility would help stifle that urge should it ever arise to haunt him.

He passed through the front door without opening it and walked down the driveway in the crisp autumn night. The leaves had all turned now, the tree limbs almost bare. It would be Halloween soon, and he couldn't conceive of a more glorious setting for that holiday than New England. It warmed his heart to know that Elise DeLeon, whose family a month ago had looked irreparably broken, would be trick-or-treating with her beautiful mother on one side and her Papa Bear dad on the other. *Yes, Michael,* he congratulated himself, *you did good.*

He had not intended to stay for more than a few minutes. He never consciously decided to do otherwise. But it felt good walking down Harbor Avenue between the hoary elms, and when he reached the Ocean Avenue causeway, smelling the sea life and feeling the harbor wind on his cheeks, he kept walking.

His loneliness was soul-rending. He spent a full hour

of the walk, moving along the beaches and quays where he could and winding through sleeping neighborhoods when he couldn't, trying to figure out *why*.

He wasn't agonizing over the reuniting of the DeLeons per se. He had engineered that for purely noble purposes: Elise's welfare, freeing Beth to live her natural mortal life, even granting the contrite and penitent Rick a second chance. He knew that putting their family back together had been the right thing to do. But throughout his life, all kinds of relationships – romantic most of all – had failed to flourish. Everybody liked him, and he was grateful for that. Women dated him, and people wanted to be his friend. But over and over, time and again, this coworker or that cute girl would get so close to him, and then no closer. It was as if an invisible wall went up. And the pattern was so consistent that he could not escape the conclusion that the problem, whatever it was, was *him*.

He was full of excuses. For starters, it seemed understandable and obvious that his accursed empathy should take a mental toll. It was emotionally exhausting feeling compelled to give in a thousand little ways every waking hour. It barely left time, not to mention energy, to nurture personal bonds. Or he could tell himself it was because of Vicki, or Max; that losing a brother and a love so intimate under violent circumstances had scarred him. And so they had. But when he was fiercely honest about it – alone in the dark at 2:30 in the morning, or at the bottom of his third drink – he faced a less savory truth: that personal relationships *asked too much*. That passing up a parking space or tossing a fiver into a glass jar was once and done, whereas true friendship and pair bonding created a raft of strings. And the deeper things went the worse it got until your whole existence became a sea of obligations that were humanly impossible to fulfill. And *that* – the inability, or more accurately the unwillingness, to become so beholden – was what was wrong with Michael Chandler. His isolation and his failures at love were his own damned fault.

Except for Vicki. That love was *real*, and a contrary voice inside him denied vehemently that he should have accepted its loss in stride. His love for her had *defined* Michael. If she had lived, and they had married, it would have made him whole. From that adamantine foundation he would have been perfectly capable of sustaining deep friendships *and* his penchant for serial charity alongside their romance. The loss of Vicki had *broken him*. That was why normal relationships felt too much to bear. It was like stacking cordwood on a bridge of toothpicks – it wasn't the picks' fault that they couldn't handle the strain.

But Vicki *had* died. And unlike Michael, Vicki had moved on. Presented the majesty of the Afterlife, Vicki had adapted. She had sailed headlong into those gloried winds and they had carried her so high she was now beyond his sight. She had chosen not to gaze wistfully back but to rush forth and *embrace her Eternity*. Of course she had. It was so like her. And Michael, blind to that wonder and feeling sorry for himself, had instead chosen to stagnate, turning his back and fixating on the affairs of the mortal world. His folly was less than Sid Raymore's only in degree.

It made him think of a parakeet with a mirror. All its life the little thing pecked and chattered and preened and played peek-a-boo, believing its reflection was another bird. It had only to look behind the mirror to see that it had been alone the entire time. Michael had seen in his soul's mirror not himself, but Vicki. He had lived his whole life in vain around her memory, never looking beyond it. No wonder he had felt lonely. *He was alone.*

In the end, what it came down to was the simple fact that he was Michael Chandler. He was powerless to be otherwise. The realization did not comfort him at all.

Dawn rose pink and cold over the Atlantic. Michael took the Blue Line bus from the Wonderland station into Boston proper, then continued on foot all the way down to Brookline. Finally, on the sidewalk in front of a familiar Victorian home, he stopped.

He took a few steps onto the driveway to read the teasers at the top of the *Boston Herald* lying there waiting to be retrieved. SOX LEAD SERIES 2-0, it proclaimed. Michael smiled. He wondered how the Giants were doing. Were they even in the playoffs? It seemed so strange, how life here could just go on, intently concerned with baseball games and politics, completely oblivious to the wonders awaiting just beyond this life, unaware of the difference their every step was making in the world they would find there.

The door opened, and out stepped Dr. Dan Hendrick, whether to collect his newspaper or because he had noticed the stranger in his driveway.

"Can I help you?" Dan's voice was cordial, free from any menace or trepidation another man might have understandably displayed.

By now Michael had internalized that people who had known him in life would not recognize him. Still, he couldn't bite off the quip before it left his tongue.

"I think you did."

"How's that again?"

Michael smiled, and spoke from his heart. "Just have a great life, man. That's what you can do for me. Have a fantastic, wonderful life. Do what's important to you. Hug your wife every day. Don't let a single chance to put a smile on a stranger's face pass you by. Can you do that for me?"

Dan laughed, as much in surprise as amusement. "I'll try."

"Good." Michael waved, and Dan returned the gesture as he picked up the paper and started back toward the house. Michael resumed his stroll along the sidewalk, turned toward a small neighborhood park at the next corner, and was gone.

ON A SUNNY FALL SATURDAY morning, a government limousine pulled up to the curb in front of a modest house in a quiet neighborhood of San Mateo, California. A lone figure emerged from the passenger side adorned in the service dress blues of a rear admiral in the United States Navy.

George Chandler answered the door. When he saw the formal military attire, he was bewildered.

"Yes?" he queried apprehensively.

"George Chandler?"

"Yes."

"Ted McFadden, U.S. Navy," the visitor announced. "I believe your son knew my daughter in school."

"Oh, *McFadden*, sure." George smiled. "Beth McFadden, you're her father? How's she doing these days? What a lovely girl."

"She's well." Ted returned the smile and extended his hand for a brief shake. "Mr. Chandler, I'm here to talk about Michael. Do you have a few minutes?"

Before George could respond, his wife Cheryl appeared in her bathrobe from around a corner behind him.

"George?"

"It's all right, dear, I've got it," George said hastily. "Nothing you need to be concerned about."

"Oh, all right." Cheryl nodded absently through her Valium haze and headed into the kitchen to refill her coffee.

"Your wife really should hear," Ted said quietly.

"No. I'll handle that. She's not … well. I'll sit down with her on my own after you've gone."

"Fair enough." Ted nodded. "In that case, why don't we step out here so she doesn't hear something inadvertently."

Over the next fifteen minutes, Admiral McFadden delivered as compassionately as he could the news that George Chandler's son was dead and that it was likely the body would never be found. It had to do with that Raymore affair, but not in the way the media had portrayed. It had been proven beyond a shadow of doubt that Michael had played no role in Sid Raymore's death. On the contrary, the rumors that Ridge Raymore himself was to blame appeared to be true.

What Michael had done, the admiral told his father, was nothing less than pit himself knowingly and without hesitation against Raymore's international criminal empire. In fact, Michael was personally responsible for rescuing a number of young girls kidnapped by Raymore's outfit for the sex trade.

Many details he was not at liberty to reveal, and some, for national security reasons, would likely never come out. But the Navy and the United States wanted the Chandlers to know that their son had given his life nobly. McFadden himself had submitted Michael to the Secretary of the Navy as a candidate for its Superior Public Service Award, the highest honor his branch of the military could bestow on a civilian. There was no guarantee that it would come, but the referral alone should be considered a resounding commendation, and he handed George an envelope with a copy of his Letter of Recommendation inside.

"Your son was a hero, Mr. Chandler. If he had been in the Navy, I would have been proud to have him under my command. I know it doesn't bring him back, but don't ever forget that. I hope it gives you folks comfort someday."

George Chandler stood there, clutching the envelope, long after the limo had gone. They had longed desperately for news, even such as this just to know what had happened, but even so it was hard to have confirmed with finality that what they had feared and expected was true. He had thought he would be prepared to hear it. He wasn't.

He had no idea how he was going to break the news to Cheryl. But he was proud of Michael. *Fiercely* proud. And it *did* help to know that someone else gave a damn, that this Naval officer had thought enough of his son to recommend him for a national honor. And there was some solace in having his name cleared of Raymore Jr.'s death.

But no parent should ever have to bury a child, and facing it twice was unbearable. Tears sparkled in George's eyes.

CHAPTER 33
Lauria

IT WAS NEARING DUSK. MICHAEL and Charlie sat together on a granite outcrop under the majestic redwoods of Charlie's treehouse Place, watching the river swirl and dart by on its eternal journey. The sky's indigo was deepening and the first faint stars winked benignly above them through breaks in the trees. An eight-point buck, some peculiar deer species from before the last Ice Age it looked to Michael, browsed the grass along the river's edge a few feet away, paying them no mind.

Michael didn't *feel* like a hero. Michael was brooding. He knew it wasn't healthy or helpful; bitterness never was. But he felt possessed by an irresistible need to wear it.

That was one reason he had come to Charlie's: so he could spew forth freely to a sympathetic ear. Another was just to stay clear of his own Place, because he didn't want his anguish relieved. Deep down, he knew that this surrender to bitterness was beyond unhelpful: it was *dangerous*. No doubt a mood very like this had consumed Sid Raymore and made him easy prey for Darkened recruitment. He wasn't so far gone as to be cavalier about it, but he felt like he *needed* to stew. Here he was in Heaven – well, the foothills of Heaven anyway, going by his imperfect and quite possibly inaccurate understanding of what Charlie had told him so far – and something just seemed *wrong*.

It felt *unfair*. All his life, Michael had put others before himself, helped those he randomly encountered, made
little anonymous sacrifices for people he would never meet.
He had not *required* any reward for this, but in the back of
his mind he had always assumed there would be one, that
something like karma would ultimately come into play. Now
he was at the end of his road, having tied up all his mortal loose ends, and there was *nothing*. No, that wasn't true:
his grandfather and Charlie were something; his Place was
something; eternal life was *certainly* something. What he really meant was that the most important thing to him – maybe
the *only* important thing, when life was stripped bare – had
been denied him. And the Great Cosmic Order didn't even
have the decency to relieve his yearning for it.

Vicki Valentine was gone. Beth DeLeon he had voluntarily relinquished. That, he felt most of all, was deserving
of recompense. He had never doubted it was the right thing
to do, but no one had *forced* him. He had taken great pains to
repair a broken family, at considerable cost to himself, and
what had it gotten him? *Subsistence*. Lonely subsistence. A
forever life and a place to hide. *Everybody* got that.

"I did warn you," Charlie reminded him gently. "Getting too involved on the mortal side is like a Vegas gamble.
The little wins are intoxicating, but the odds are stacked in
the house's favor. The game cannot be won long term."

"Coming from you, that's horseshit," Michael chal-
lenged. "You spied on me and your mother for *ten years*.
Then you put together this elaborate scheme with Barbara
Jordan and spent a week personally escorting me to Boston."

"It wasn't 'spying,' and that part was meaningless. It
didn't affect you, you didn't even know about it. That sort of
thing is common, and harmless. In fact, it's precious; it lets
deceased parents see their children graduate or get married,
and it helps kids like me to know that their mom is still there.
As for the Boston thing, that wasn't our doing. Were we supposed to tell the angel no?"

"So if an angel says to do it, it's okay."

Charlie's face contorted with exasperation at having to confirm the patently obvious. "Um, yes!"

"So according to you, since I never had an angel, I shouldn't have gone back. I should have let those girls be sold."

Charlie frowned. "That's not for me to say. What I believe is that you were being used as an instrument for good. What I know is that you were hand-picked to fulfill some divine purpose. Angels don't just intercede in mortal affairs at random. Whether it was the girls, or taking the Raymore guy down, or if the whole thing was just the first step on a road to something bigger, I don't know. It could be any of those."

Michael sighed. "I don't know why I'm obsessing over this. It's a moot point. The fact is, Charlie … I've come to a decision. I'm never going back."

Charlie looked up sharply. "For real?"

"For real." Michael shook his head in self-disgust. "The girls had to be saved, I'm not sorry for that. But I understand now what you meant about mostly making things worse. The whole thing with Beth was a joke. What was I thinking? I wasn't thinking. I was just feeling. And look where it got me."

"So, you're *never* going back," Charlie pressed, with a touch more intensity than Michael would have expected. "What does that mean *exactly*? You won't get curious? You won't want to look in on your parents?"

"I'm sure I'd want to from time to time. But I can't let myself do it. There's nothing but pain for me there. I'd love to see my folks, but I know what would happen. My mom has got to be inside-out upset. She's probably in the hospital again. My dad takes care of her, but it wears him down. If I went back to see them, all it would do is remind me that I'm the cause of it. I can't handle that, Charlie. Knowing there's nothing I can do, rubbing my face in it would kill me."

"And there's no one else …?"

"Who else is there?" Michael spat. "Beth is dead to me. I mean … you know what I mean." He allowed himself a little smile at the faux pas. "There's only my Grandma, and maybe Carl Adams — my old buddy at Wal-Mart. No, not even Carl, as I think about it. Not anybody. Would I be curious? Yeah, I'm sure once in a while I would. But I can't go back there. Because no matter what, man, my parents or strangers, I'd see people sad or in trouble, and I'd want to help them. These little powers we have make it even worse for me. I'd want to help them all, and I can't. I know that now. And *that's* why I can never go back. I couldn't stand the helplessness. I can't see suffering and just walk away."

"No. I don't suppose you can." Charlie looked him in the eyes. "But are ... you ... *sure*?"

Michael propped himself up. "What are you on about, Charlie? You're acting all weird about this. What is it you're not telling me?"

"Nothing," Charlie reassured. "Just that if you're serious, if you're really through with going back, well ... there are a few things you should catch up on. There are a lot of folks who'd like to see you, for one. Like your Grandpa. You can understand that, can't you? If you'd been here for years and, let's say, your mother passed, wouldn't you want to see her as soon as you could?"

"Of course," Michael replied, and now that Charlie put it that way, it suddenly struck him how little consideration he had given to that simple truth. Of *course* his Grandpa would want to see him. His great aunt, too. In his wonder of discovery and his obsession with old mortal business, Michael Chandler, paragon of compassion, had neglected the very simple and obvious feelings of his own kin.

"I'll set it up if you want," Charlie offered. "We can have a little party. Get it out of the way, make sure they know you care. Then when that's over, if you want to go sailing with your Grandpa or bug hunting with your cat or whatever, you can do it at your leisure."

"Bug hunting with my cat?"

Charlie scowled. "Do you want to do it or not?"

Michael sighed. For a moment he felt resistant to any

impositions on his schedule, he was so tired of being on the
go for one thing or the other. But when he thought about it,
that schedule was blank. He didn't have any plans. He had
intended to look up Grandpa soon. And Charlie's suggestion
made sense: get it over with, make sure they know you care,
then turn yourself loose on the world.

"Yeah. That would be great, Charlie. Thanks for offering. And thanks for reminding me." He gave his friend a
smile. "This is my life now. I have to realize that. I need to
start acting like it."

"I'll get right on it." Charlie pushed himself to his feet.
"But before the whole crowd gets involved, there is one thing
I think you should do. Barbara Jordan has been real anxious
to welcome you, man, but she's been waiting, to be polite. I
think you should see her. We couldn't have done what we did
without her – you or me. I think she deserves better than to
be shunted into a cattle call with everyone else. Besides, you
might have noticed, she's kind of cute."

"Uh, sure, I guess," Michael answered, confused and a
bit uneasy. It seemed like an odd left turn from where Charlie had been heading. But there was no harm in it. If he really
was going to let go of the past and embrace his new reality,
well, this was a part of it. He might as well start now.

"Head back to your Place, that'll be best," Charlie encouraged, standing half in the tree trunk doorway on his way
upstairs. "I'll bring her there. It should only take me half an
hour or so, an hour at most. If for some reason I can't get her,
I'll let you know by then."

ON THE WALK BACK TO his Place, playing Charlie's
words over in his head, Michael found himself seized by
a sudden thought. It was a notion that in retrospect seemed
obvious to the point of unavoidable, yet it had never once

crossed his mind until then. Now, after chewing on it for twenty minutes, it had him pacing up and down the Pirate House entry like an expectant father.

When speaking of her with Charlie, Michael had mentally relegated Barbara Jordan to the role of a supporting player. Far from insignificant – she had, after all, obtained the car and credit cards that had been the staples of their drive east, to say nothing of the artful intercept at the airport. But still, in Michael's mind, a figure whose personal interaction with *him* was incidental. Except that it *hadn't* been, had it? What had occurred that night came rushing back to him now: how he had been stunned by her beauty, how the sight of her had resonated so powerfully with his memories of Vicki that for a few seconds he had been confused. At the time, of course, he had not known that Barbara was *dead*. He hadn't even met Charlie yet. And so, after she had ambushed him with that tearful kiss and sent him on his way, their exchange had been all but discarded. She had made it clear that she wasn't going with him, she had refused even to give him a telephone number, and he had spent the next week driving three thousand miles in the opposite direction and subsequently traveled farther from her still. After the airport, she'd had no relevance. She was nothing but the name on the cards.

But *now* ... now that *he* was dead, and he knew *she* was dead ... were there possibilities? Had God intervened that early on? Was Charlie's relationship with Barbara, and her consequent introduction to Michael, more than chance? Was *this* the woman he was meant to meet? Was this why Vicki had been cleared from the table and Beth had been denied to him? Was this the explanation for the odd kiss? Had the angel told Barbara something not even Charlie knew? Had she known what was coming, and been unable to keep her cover?

It was strained fantasy, and Michael knew it. *God plotting my love life!* He laughed at himself. *Well, if that's what's been going on, maybe it's time God got back to stockpil-*

ing for the Apocalypse or whatever he's about these days. I couldn't have worse luck.

It was a joke of course, but there was a serious residue. Why not Barbara Jordan? He supposed she might be spoken for. He had no idea how love worked in the Afterlife beyond what Charlie had said about married couples. Probably someone with Barbara's appeal *had* been married, but you never knew. It wasn't certain it had been a happy marriage even if she had. Charlie had allowed that couples sometimes drifted apart, and that seemed to indicate some flexibility. So why not Barbara? Now that he thought about it, for all intents and purposes, she was the only woman in this world he knew. Vicki had outgrown him and Beth wouldn't be here for decades. And she *had* kissed him. Surely she wouldn't have done that if she were romantically attached to someone else. So why not? What could happen? A guy had to start somewhere.

And then an epiphany hit him. *Barbara Jordan was Lauria!* It made perfect sense. She had expressly denied it when they had met at the airport, but Charlie had lied initially, too. Could that be what this whole crazy trip was about? Had it been Destiny's way of delivering Michael to the woman he was cosmically ordained to love?

There came the expected knock on his door, and by that time Michael had worked himself into an irrational frenzy. The worst part was that he knew he had, he saw his self-delusion for what it was. Yet he was powerless to stop it. Since Vicki had died, the hole in his heart had hounded him without mercy. When he tried to ignore it, it bit harder; when he tried to assuage it, it made him do ridiculous things. The incident with Beth was a prime example. It looked so *stupid* now. Had he really believed he could finesse a woman like Beth away from mortal suitors for a lifetime? Even if he could, had he ever considered how unfair it would be to *her*?

He forced himself to the door and turned the inside latch, his heart thumping madly, praying that he might appoint himself gracefully but fearing that fear itself would sabotage his efforts, would overcome even God's desire to hold him up straight.

The door opened and in they came, Charlie first, then from the fragrant jungle dark the sweet, demure form he had been obsessing about, not gliding into the room like some gossamer Cinderella, but just walking in, just smiling, just—

Vicki.

THE WHOLE WORLD STOPPED.

Seeing her now, Michael could not believe that he ever could have missed it. *Barbara Jordan* was just a made-up name. *Barbara Jordan was Vicki.* How could he not have seen?

But he *had* seen! He had recognized her from the start. It was only after, when his left brain kicked in with logic and his right brain became poisoned with fear, that he had let the illusion win. But she had been there all the time, pulling him by the hand, struggling for composure while she fished things out of her purse, looking at him with those intoxicating, desperate eyes. She had even *kissed* him, and it had launched him like a rocket. *How could he not have realized?*

And there was another truth here, an even more incredible one, hitting him between the eyes like his first glimpse of Charlie as the little boy in his mother's locked room. Looking into Vicki's eyes, and only there, he could see yet another face. Barbara Jordan was not the only guise Vicki had taken. She had returned to shepherd him later. In fact, if not for her steadfastness and presence of mind, the raw *courage* it must have taken, the price of Michael's destiny might have been paid in the blood of Beth DeLeon, Elise, and twelve kidnapped children. No wonder he couldn't sense her in the Afterlife. She hadn't been in the Afterlife. She had been in the mortal world, in a cage on Tesoro, a beacon of love enabling him to return.

Felicity.

"Oh, Michael!" Vicki could stand it no longer. "Oh, God, oh God, *Michael!*"

They were all over each other. The force of the hug might have crushed an ox. It may have gone on for eons. All Michael felt was a surge of warmth working its way through to his marrow like the splendor of a hearth fire at the end of a long, cold winter's day. And winter it must have been somewhere, for all around them, in every dimension, in every direction of time and space, the world lit up like Christmas.

NEITHER OF THEM WOULD EVER be able to say how long the embrace went on; for Michael and Vicki, it was time out of mind. Charlie had respectfully let himself out; he had matters to attend to, but more importantly, he wasn't taking any chances of disrupting the reunion. They didn't even hear him go.

Eventually, when they had absorbed each other to overflowing, the hug ended. The restored love lingered; people would say that for weeks afterward it left a visible dusting of joy anywhere the two of them went. It was just talk, of course, harmless romantic babble. Then again, love is a powerful thing.

But there was much to do.

"Vicki, I have so many questions."

"Let's go out front," she urged. "I *love* the view."

Michael started toward the door. She grabbed his arm.

"Not *that* front, silly."

"There's another one?"

Vicki began to laugh. Then she saw it: he wasn't being coy. *He really didn't know.*

Her expression went from amused to excited. "Come

with me."

She led him to the T hall and stopped in front of the Nivulum sculpture. "Draw the sword," she said.

Michael was perplexed. "It's solid rock."

"*Lift* it," Vicki insisted. "You're the only one who can. Just grab it by the hilt and pull."

"What am I, Wart the stable boy?" Michael joked.

Vicki scowled at his impertinence. "Trust me."

He did as told. Amazingly, the sword *did* pull free, the sculpture's hands and arms tracking with it. After four inches it would go no further. He turned to ask Vicki what it meant, but was immediately interrupted by a low rumbling, grating sound.

Incredibly, the section of wall behind the sculpture began to split at seams so fine they had been impossible to see. It slowly sank into the floor until the smooth, flat top of it melded gracefully in and its own seams vanished.

What it revealed was jaw-dropping.

THE PASSAGE BEHIND THE WALL revealed a spacious, fully-furnished room, nothing cavernous like the sea cave but at least the size of the 'great room' in the DeLeon house. The furniture was exquisite, artfully laid out, and suited to myriad purposes. The walls, illuminated with more tiki torches, were handsomely hung with what he took to be African art. The room extended out of sight around corners to the right and left, and there were other doors, four all told: his Place was obviously much, much larger than Michael had known. He would need to investigate it all soon.

But it would not be now; there were more immediate matters. Straight ahead, commanding all of his attention, was a vast wall of glass with a sliding door out onto a rock terrace, an overlook with an irregular limestone ceiling like the mouth of a cave. And the scene that terrace and those windows overlooked took his breath away.

It was a broad, circular saltwater bay, hundreds of feet below and several miles across, ringed with tropical cliffs broken only by a wide outlet to open ocean in the furthest distance. The entire cliff ring – all the way around, on both sides, right out to the outlet – was striped white with waterfalls. In some places they fell in thin rivulets, in others, braided forks. Three broad swaths crashed over the cliff edge in domineering torrents reminiscent of Niagara or Victoria Falls. But everywhere – *everywhere* – was water. And Michael Chandler – to his own utter astonishment after all those years of fear – *absolutely loved it.*

Up from the center of the bay thrust an island, the steep-sloped pinnacle of an ancient volcanic cinder cone, long since dormant and now clad in emerald finery laced with ribbons of waterfall and streaked here and there with red and pink floral flourish. At the top of the island spread a narrow plateau, where the pointed peak had exploded in a fire shower with the volcano's final eruption. The rounded alabaster structure perched like a watchtower scouting the entire bay, and from the center of this rose a thick column of light, a huge spotlight in reverse, casting its golden beam more than a hundred feet straight above the building before its intensity thinned gradually to nothing, a shifting finger of illumination whose brilliance glinted white off the polished stone walls and made sparkles in the hillside pools below.

On the island, the alabaster aerie stood alone. But among the outer cliffs, along the beachfronts and dotting the forested slopes between cascades, other structures could be seen. Shelters some may have been, others perhaps small inns or shops, human touch-points built of indigenous wood, thatch, and stone tucked unobtrusively into the majestic milieu.

To the right, as far in that direction as the view revealed, a dark pyramid mountain exhaling crimson wisps of smoke rose above the jungle hills, a living cousin of the brooding behemoth the bay-bound island must once have been. Vicki pointed Michael toward the dramatic scene.

"What do you think, did I get it right?"

"Huh?"

Vicki frowned. "The mural, downstairs. Was I close?"

And suddenly he saw it. His jaw dropped.

"You painted that?" He gasped. "On the wall in the sea cave?"

"From memory," she preened. "Well, I popped out to have a look once or twice. But pretty good, don't you think?"

Michael shook his head. He was so stunned he couldn't even begin to ask how the painting moved. All he could do was utter, "My God."

"And you haven't seen *this*," Vicki continued, turning his attention toward the volcanic island with the alabaster. "I thought Charlie would have shown you everything, but I guess there hasn't been time."

Michael was mesmerized. The island's beauty haunted him like a snatch of dream that can be recalled but not described. "What is it?"

"That's *my* Place."

He looked at her in wonder. Things had been happening so fast he hadn't given a single thought to what Vicki's Place might look like, or where it might be.

"You live there?"

"I live where I am from moment to moment," she lilted. "But that's where I go to rest. Pretty convenient being right inside yours. You know what causes that, right?"

"*Inside* mine?" Michael was getting lost. "My Place is that jungle."

"Oh my God, Michael, didn't Charlie tell you *anything*? That kid."

"I don't understand. You mean my ... *my* Place goes all the way out *there*?"

Vicki nodded and gave a sly grin. "Your Place is *famous*, Michael Chandler. People come vast distances to see it. You're thought of as sort of a celebrity for making it. And it has a name – not many Places do. I suppose Charlie neglected to mention that as well?"

"Yeah, I guess so."

"Its name," she told him, "is Lauria."

Michael was thunderstruck. All he could do was stare.

Lauria. He mouthed the word in amazement. *It's not a person. It's this Place. The apparition was sending me ... home.*

"It's from the Elder Tongue," Vicki went on. "The first language. What angels use among themselves. It means 'The Water Place'."

Michael laughed so hard he almost choked. All his life he had been afraid of the water, terrified by the thought of eternity in a universe consumed by it. Now, here was his personal paradise, not only inundated with the object of his former fear, but actually *named* for it. He would never again doubt that God had a sense of humor.

"How far does it go?" he asked, eyeing the tableau in this new light. "My Place?"

"Far?" Vicki laughed. "It's everything. Beyond what you see in all directions. More magical landscapes than I could ever describe. Mist-covered mountains you can get lost in, steaming rain forests filled with life, color-streaked deserts with lush, fruited oases. Lakes you can see right to the bottom of, linked by thrashing streams and quiet rivers that go on forever. Vast blue-green oceans with massive coral reefs, honest-to-God sea monsters, and islands of every description beyond count. Impossibly tall cliffs and dark hidden canyons – the tallest waterfall in the universe is here, or one of them. Little inns and villages here and there, to stop by or hang around for months, where you cross paths with fascinating people from every place and time. There's even a utopian version of San Francisco waiting for you to savor, a really amazing mix of past and future, if you need a break from the solitude.

"And that doesn't *begin* to tell it. You could explore for a thousand lifetimes and not see it all. In fact, you could walk in a straight line forever and never leave it. Because, you see, it has no border. It's the whole ball of wax – or maybe I should say the whole ball of water. This planet – Lauria – is *four times* the size of Earth, Michael. And *your Place is the entire thing.*"

WELL-WISHERS CAME LIKE PILGRIMS, IN numbers beyond count. Many Michael recognized, most he did not. Some came by to greet him, up on the bluff where he and Vicki sat near a quiet waterfall pool with a dazzling view of the bay, to give him a little hug, shake his hand, thank him for what he'd done: some forgotten word or gesture or other kindness that had made more difference to them than he could have dreamed. For most, it was enough just to be in the area, to share in the experience, to explore the storied terrain that circled the bay or picnic in their favorite spot knowing that Michael Chandler, the Water Man, had finally come home.

First that day came his grandfather, on the cliff before dawn with Charlie and some of his friends helping to set up a fire pit and a dispensary for drinks. Michael recognized him at once, but it was not the Ed Chandler he remembered. This was a strapping young man around Charlie's apparent age, arm and leg muscles bulging, a thick shock of dark black hair where ragged grey had been in Michael's time. The voice was thick and strong, the speech faster than he remembered. But the intonation was unchanged, and his manner of speaking, all business with an undercurrent of wit so dry it was never possible to be sure of humorous intent, was unmistakable.

He spoke remarkably little to Michael, given the effort he made to show up early and stay late helping to return the site to its natural state, not to mention the untold hours to build, set up, and furnish every inch of the Pirate House. For one thing, he did not seem particularly comfortable with Michael's profuse expressions of gratitude. But he talked a great deal about Michael, and he made no effort at all to shield his grandson's ears from the pride and boasting he freely dispensed to all who happened by.

One exchange between them did stick with Michael, as he was thanking his forebear for the lovely books. His grandfather had explained that, while there were alternatives, there were actually people who were *happy* to meticulously hand-letter and manually bind them, as an act of craft and pride, and that every volume in Michael's collection had been produced that way.

"If you like Heinlein, there's a ton of new Mark Twain you might want to try. I met him once. He does science fiction now, been writing like a madman ever since he died. Don't look for Sherlock Holmes, though." His Grandpa scowled. "That bastard Conan Doyle hasn't put out a single thing. Says he's working on 'the penultimate Holmes mystery' and won't rush it even if it takes a million years. At this rate, it might."

When he inquired about Max, his grandfather's face darkened. "I've seen him," he affirmed guardedly. "Stop by my Place in a day or two and we'll talk. Now is not the time." The response troubled Michael, but he was sure Grandpa was right; by his tone, this was a discussion to have in private.

All morning and into the afternoon, they paraded by. Michael was especially touched when Mano Tejada's son, the thirteen-year-old gunned down by a rival gangster, thanked him for giving Mano a second chance. He had been horribly worried, he said, about the Afterlife that awaited his father. Now he knew everything was going to be okay. Even a dog dropped by, a bounding Australian Shepherd that licked his hand even before Michael saw him. He thought he recognized it as an abandoned pet he and Vicki had dubbed "Calico" and surreptitiously fed through the bars at the shelter several times. Its presence raised a cornucopia of questions, and reminded Michael that his understanding of Afterlife was in its infancy.

Among the memories forged that day, none would be more poignant than the image of Rosemary Hart, the alcoholic from Kingman, whom Michael barely recognized. She was *scintillating*. It was her Afterlife look, he realized, but still. *What a promising life must have been scrapped in her,* he thought. She came in the company of a man named Peter, a social worker who had helped children with serious medical conditions reintegrate into the mainstream after treatment, a bright, gracious fellow who had died in his forties of leukemia but continued his work right up to the last. Obviously, they hadn't known each other long, but they seemed to be a natural match. It made Michael smile.

"I just wanted to thank you for what you did for me," she told him in a clear, intelligent voice, clutching one of his hands. "I know it must have been hard for you. I can imagine what you must have thought, how you must have wondered if it was the right thing. But Mr. Chandler, *you have no idea.* I wasn't going to accept treatment no matter what you did. And if I had died that night before you came, I would be in *hell* right now. I was totally lost, so full of pain and anger. You made me smile. You made me feel beautiful. I died *happy*. I'm … sorry for the way I acted, all that 'be my husband' nonsense. I'm just so glad you didn't walk away."

"Gee, Rosie, don't be embarrassed. I wasn't offended. That part was fun."

She flashed a glowing smile. "It was the right thing, I want you to know that. It made all the difference. *You saved my soul.*"

Michael had thought he was long past crying over Rosemary. He was wrong.

AS AFTERNOON LANGUISHED, GRADUALLY THE crowds began to thin and the stream of well-wishers fell to a trickle. Vicki, who had understood the necessity but was fairly bursting with pent-up desire to have Michael to herself, could contain it no longer.

"Let's go," she prodded in a low voice. "Everyone who really wants to has had plenty of time to say hi. If someone missed you, they'll have another chance. Eternity is a long time."

Michael, by now tiring of his own smile, was grateful for the intervention. "Where are we going? Back to the house?"

"No, my Place. I can't stand it any longer. I want to show you."

Michael gazed uncertainly across the water toward the green cinder cone with the alabaster spire, its light spike barely visible in the sun. "There appears to be a rather serious moat between us and there. What are we going to do, swim?"

He meant it as a joke, but to Vicki it wasn't. "That's what I usually do." She shrugged.

He was about to protest when a voice called sharply from nearby. Michael looked up to see his Grandpa, sampling somebody's homemade ice cream with some friends, grousing spiritedly just like they were back on the Colorado farm.

"*Swim*? For cryin' out loud. Haven't you kids got a lick of sense? *What do you think the boat is for?* Come with me, you knotheads! I'll show you how it works."

THE SUN MOVED LAZILY DOWNWARD. It sank into the horizon like a melting creamsicle, framing palm tree silhouettes along the tropical hillsides like a host of Zulus in feathered war garb. Flickering torches and amber lanterns began illuminating the inns and village cobblestones. Visitors began flocking to the pubs and cafes. A wandering theatrical troupe readied themselves in the pit of a shorefront amphitheater. All of Lauria would be festive this night.

No celebration would be more joyous than the one shared by two halves that had finally been rejoined. Alone, they felt like they had the universe at their feet.

Vicki stood at the rail to help navigate as Michael edged the little galleon noiselessly up to the one-boat dock. It maneuvered effortlessly. It was something in the craftsmanship, something in the wood, maybe even something in the water. It certainly wasn't his maritime skills. Probably, he thought as the two of them jumped off and tied the *Archangel* down, it was something in the love with which the beautiful craft had been made.

They climbed the trail of rock steps toward the island's summit, steps set so naturally into the lush terrain that they seemed more like a creek of stones than a work of artifice. Now and then where the trees broke, they caught a glimpse of the house and the pillar of light came into view, translucent now like an acetylene flame and dimming with the sunset.

"Is twilight really so bad?" he asked. As always, the dusk was elevating Michael's sense of romance, that is, if anything could elevate those feelings now that he had Vicki back.

"I never said it was," Vicki pronounced. "I just don't like soaking in it around the clock. Once in a while when the wind is wrong, some of that thin volcanic fume that hovers over your jungle to keep it dark all the time drifts out over the bay. If I'm not in the mood for it, I just turn on my sunbeam. Mostly I leave it off, but it's nice to have the option. I *love* having a courtyard full of sunshine when there's a raging storm outside." She paused briefly, closing her eyes, drinking in the sumptuous image. "Besides, as you well know, I need natural light to paint. This lets me have it whenever inspiration strikes."

The island felt like a world of its own as they ascended through thick forest and airy clearings, past quiet streams and gentle waterfalls, everywhere enchanted by a musky pine smell, a whispering breeze, and distant bird calls. As they neared the summit, the way narrowed and the slope softened until the steps gave way to a path of pavers. They walked through a natural pergola formed by rows of swirling-branched Manzanita trees draped in fuchsia and wisteria; where they emerged from this tunnel of blossoms, the path was flanked by quiet pools. Here the subtle sunbeam towered above in its full glory, casting shafts of warm light between the leaves and creating dancing reflections on the water. And there at last, beyond the pools, stood the door, a smooth stone arch rimmed with a filigree of glowing runes. A crescent symbol flickered as Vicki touched it, and the door swung open.

The inside was a model of simplicity exquisitely furnished. It was roughly donut-shaped, with a circular inner wall surrounding a traditional hedge garden that could be enjoyed from any vantage through the wall's missing upper half. The outer wall was lined with doors and hung with animated paintings whose style Michael recognized: seascapes and dreamscapes, intimate forests, animals and flowers caught in the act of life. Every scene flowed in elegant motion that preserved composition and emotional impact perfectly. And now he understood about the alabaster: its soft translucence made a perfect backdrop for the art.

Among the lush plantings and fragrant blossoms, at the courtyard's center stood a round reflecting pool, accented by a contemplative marble bench whose mottled colors shimmered on the water's surface. From this pool rose the light shaft they had seen from afar, gentle now, casting a subdued, romantic illumination against an evening sky not so different from that August night in San Mateo that had started it all.

"Wow," was all Michael could say. Vicki beamed.

FOR A LONG WHILE THEY lay together in the soft grass near a path of natural stone pavers at the foot of the light fountain. Michael thought he could actually feel tiny sparkles of sunlight, alighting on his cheeks like mist. They clung together lazily with barely a word, Michael on his back and Vicki draped over him with her head on his chest, content just to hold each other in peace after so long apart.

It was Michael who broke the reverie. "Things could have been so much easier," he started without preamble. "God, Vick, all you would have had to do was tell me. I mean, I know I couldn't recognize you while I was mortal. That part I get. But once I was *here* ..."

"I couldn't," Vicki rejoined, and there was a touch of hurt in her voice. "You hadn't made your choices, Michael. You were still obsessed with your old girlfriend. I couldn't show myself until you sorted out where that was going. Until you let go of the mortal world for good ... or bound yourself to it."

"What, *Beth?* Oh, no, Vicki, you've got that wrong. I was—"

"I *saw* it," Vicki pressed, her torment now bare. "You have no idea how hard it was for me to sit there, with those poor little girls in that horrible dungeon, and watch you with her. The way she looked at you. How you melted when she flashed that nauseating coquette routine."

Michael was caught totally off guard. "No, Vicki, she was ... I didn't ..." He propped himself up on one elbow, took both of her hands in his, and looked her earnestly in the eyes. "Vicki, I didn't know where you were. I tried to find you. I couldn't. I thought you'd left me behind. Gone on to the next level, or whatever, without me. If I had known for one instant — if you had just come to me—"

"*No*," she persisted, bristling with defiance, tears now shimmering in her eyes. "I *couldn't*, don't you see? Because what if I had? Would you have dropped her right then? Probably. And for the rest of our lives, for the rest of *Eternity*, I'd always wonder. I'd never know for sure whether you dropped that woman for me ... because you *preferred* me ... or if Michael Chandler, the sweetest, kindest, most empathetic man that ever lived, had left his dream girl for the same reason as he does everything ... just to stop my pain."

"Oh, Vicki." They were both crying now. Michael took her in his arms, feeling her warm tears soaking through the fabric on his shoulder.

"Beth wasn't my 'dream girl'. She may have seemed that to me in high school, but that was before I met you. Before I had any inkling of what true love is."

Slowly, with infinite tenderness, he touched his lips to hers. The electricity of the gentle kiss startled them both.

When the magical moment was over, Michael resumed. "Vicki, you must never forget this. When it came down to it, even when I believed you were beyond my reach, I chose to release Beth. I did that for good reasons, but here's the point: even under the exact same circumstances, I could never have let *you* go. No matter what the reasons. No matter what the consequences. Do you understand?"

Vicki nodded against his shoulder. And as he held her, he felt her anguish dissipate. It unhitched from her heart, wafted free from her body, and evaporated into the twilight wind, forever gone.

At length, the tears forgotten, their collars dry, the peaceful bliss restored, Vicki spoke to their future. "So ... what do you want to do?"

Michael shrugged. "I'm perfectly fine right here. Geez, Vick, if you're bored, you must have a million things to tell me. I want to hear all of it. I want to hear everything you've done, everything you've discovered, all the little things I need to know, being new to this. We could whip up some passion fruit daiquiris or whatever you've got, and I'll be happy to sit here listening all night long."

"I'm not a bit bored. I wouldn't let you up right now if you begged. I meant tomorrow. And the day after. There's *so* much to do. Or we could just stay on the island. We could go down to the village, you've *got* to see the Swan Inn. We could go swimming and look for plesiosaurs. You can breathe underwater now, did you know that? We could—"

"Anything you want, Vick. Really. I'm just happy to be with you."

Vicki's gaze narrowed. "You know, sometimes I wish you would be just a *pinch* more selfish. It would make you a lot easier to please." She kneeled beside his chair and took his hand in hers. "Now, here's what I want you to do. None of this 'anything you want, Vick' BS. I want you to pretend tomorrow's your birthday. If you think about it, it sort of is."

She was right. He did feel as though he had been reborn. He was an infant in this world, and he really knew very little of it. Until today, he hadn't even realized the extent of his own Place, and his experience outside of it was limited to Charlie's redwoods. He had seen almost nothing. There were more worlds out there than seconds in the lifetime of the universe, and they were all waiting to be explored. And who knew what lay beyond the event horizon? Did the true universe go on forever? If it did, they would *never* run out of things to explore.

"When the birthday's over, we can go back to 'whatever Vicki wants,' at least until you know what there is to choose from. On his birthday, though, Michael lets Vicki pamper him. It's just one day. Your first *real* day. Now, tell me, love, what would make you happy. *Really* happy. Even if it's sitting by yourself in the dark just so you can recharge. God knows you've earned it. I won't be upset. We'll get around to everything eventually. We have forever."

Michael smiled. God, she was beautiful.

"I don't want 'alone in the dark.' I can't get enough of you, Vick. I've been without you so long I didn't even realize how thirsty I was just to look." He eyed her earnestly, having decided to accept her offer with grace. "To tell you the truth, I am burned out. I didn't realize how badly until we sat down here. It's the first time I've had real breathing space in a long while."

"Then it's settled." Vicki smiled triumphantly. "We'll just camp here for a few days. Weeks, if you want. I'll show you my paintings, show you how the paint works. It's really amazing, Michael, it picks up your emotions. It's ... well, we'll get to that later. I want to show you the island, too. There must be a hundred kinds of parrots. There's a little bush down the eastern slope, the village side, down in a little hollow, it has the *best* huckleberries. You won't believe the flavor." She paused, marveling as if she had only just discovered these things for herself. "I guess I'd forgotten how many things there are to do *right here*. Being alone so long, I guess I took them for granted. It might take us a few weeks, at that."

"It all sounds *perfect*." Michael smiled. "Maybe we could even bring my cat out here. Do you think that would be okay?"

"Alex? Of course it would. He likes it here. He's part of the family. Although I have to tell you, I don't think he's a big fan of swimming. He prefers playing Lord of the Jungle, and he's a furry tadpole compared to some of the things that live in the bay."

Michael started to ask about Alex having been there, but the day was wearing on him and he lost the train of thought before it reached his lips. He stretched his back and sighed. Vicki turned him a compassionate look, seeming to understand what he was feeling completely.

"Let's just go to bed, love. I know *my* brain could use a little recharging, and you've got to be worse. In the morning, whenever you feel like getting up, I'll fix us something and we can just sit here and talk. Or *not* talk. And when you're up to it, I'll give you a nice massage you can just melt into like butter. Touch is different here, Michael: it conveys some of the other person's *essence*, like a charge of electricity flowing between souls. I've been waiting ten long years to know how a *real* touch feels here … how you feel."

She would have to wait no longer.

For a time they just held each other, lying there in the garden, watching the sky darken, then cuddling under the stars. Her caress seemed to revive him. When the time was right, she stood up wordlessly and tugged him by the hand, leading him back into the house.

They wouldn't sleep just yet.

IN THE MAGICAL AFTERGLOW OF that first deep, sweet intimacy after so long, the most immersive lovemaking they had ever shared, Vicki pulled the covers up under her chin and snuggled contentedly against his chest. It was just like old times, as familiar and comforting as a Sunday slipper, yet every bit as exciting as fresh love always is. It felt to both of them as though no time had passed, and that they had lost nothing, as if they'd never been apart at all.

Michael basked in bliss. He felt truly fulfilled, at one with the cosmos. For the first time in his existence he felt utterly, completely, whole.

He closed his eyes smiling. It was *only* the first time. There would be many, many more.

EPILOGUE
The Open Door

MICHAEL WOKE ABRUPTLY IN THE dead of the night with an odd feeling of urgency. He had the sense that there had been a light flash – in fact, he was sure of it, because his retinas still retained the afterglow. From the position of his head, he surmised that it must have come from the hall beyond the bedroom door. Even now, though his lack of familiarity with Vicki's Place made it impossible to be sure, he thought he could detect a faint light beyond the bedroom that hadn't been there before. As he sat up the subtle glow seemed to intensify, and with it, the mysterious sense of insistence. In fact, though his ears heard nothing but wind in the trees, within his mind he felt the undeniable sensation of a voice whispering his name.

Something was out there, calling him.

He reached over to rouse Vicki, then decided it would be best not to involve her until he knew what was going on. Moving catlike so as not to wake her, he climbed out of bed and followed the light, around the curved hall, through an archway, out into the garden courtyard.

There, in the center of the garden near the rock fountains, stood the most magnificent figure Michael had ever seen, surpassing even the Nivulum that had borne him on his cosmic tour.

The form was female, and the ferocity of her beauty

outshone anything even *possible* in a human being. She was so beautiful that beholding her seared the soul in the same way that staring at the sun could blind the eyes.

She was larger than human, but not grotesquely so, in no way disproportionate to him as the Nivulum had been. She shared one feature with the Nivulum: she wore no clothing in a human sense, but seemed to be adorned in an indescribable wrap of energy. She was not, however, transparent, her skin solid and smooth and radiant. The majestic white wings tucked behind her shoulders gave final confirmation that he was in the presence of an angel.

What Michael would forever recall first when thinking of her was the eyes. Her irises were *golden*. Not merely light brown or deep yellow but literally *golden*, shiny like metal and faceted like a finely cut diamond so that they sparkled in the shifting light.

"Welcome, Michael Chandler," she said in a tone both strong and gentle. "We are Desedaraya. We are to prepare you for what is to come."

As she spoke, Michael was dimly aware of an echo, a shadow voice speaking each word a fragment of a second before and after it left her lips. Even more vaguely, at the very edge of perception, he thought he saw ghost images of her: one mimicking her movements, another anticipating them. It was like watching a movie with the frames before and after the current one faintly visible in the background. Amazingly, Michael thought he knew what it was.

She's indefinite in time, he mused. *That's why she refers to herself in the plural. She perceives herself as the collection of her past, present, and future.*

"You're the one who guided Charlie?"

"And your companion. And your grandfather, and others. There is great love for you, Michael Chandler. And it fuels in you great power, which shall be revealed when the time to wield it has come. That is why you are bound to this Place."

Straining to make sense of her cryptic message, Michael was suddenly struck by similarities between the apparition on the stairs and the figure before him. Were they one and the same? No. The angel exuded none of the other's malevolence. The eyes had been different, the facial features different, there had been no wings, and it had been wearing some kind of garment. Yet it, too, had seemed tenuous in its connection to time and space. And it, too – though in a different, altogether terrible way – had worn supernatural beauty.

"When I was 'bound' to Lauria ... that thing in my townhouse, was it some other kind of angel? What did it mean when it said 'by the Timeless'?"

"The Timeless are two. The Creator, who exists beyond time, and the Enemy, called by some the Destroyer, whose origin *began* time. As for the one who uttered those words, that harbinger's nature will be revealed at the appointed time. For now, you may know that it is neither angel nor Nivulum, and that its power far exceeds that of either."

Michael pondered. He was having a hard time getting a full picture: so many details were missing. But he recalled what Charlie had said, that angels could not be negotiated with: they had their message, and that was that. If they weren't disposed to tell you something, you weren't going to get it out of them.

So he tried a different tack. "You said you had come to prepare me. For what? Does it have something to do with that ... thing?"

Desedaraya gazed completely away from him now, her full focus on matters distant in time and space.

"A great battle rages beyond the edge of existence. It is the War of Eons, waged between the Timeless since before the Dawn of Man. But things are changing. The Enemy grows bold. He seeks to force Judgment."

Michael gaped, unable to speak. He thought he grasped the outline, that she was talking about the struggle between good and evil, but she was going so fast and leaving out so many details that he could see no further into the fog.

"There exist universal laws which only the Timeless may trespass. Ever have they agreed not to do so. Now the Enemy breaches this pact. The Enemy stole your brother. Still you loved. He took your soul mate. Still you loved. He became desperate. And in his desperation, he sought to destroy you directly. But this stretched the laws too far. The universe tore, and what your friend calls your 'world line' tore with it. It spliced your past onto a mismatched future. This was conceived to cripple you, but instead it fused your Before and your After into the unified consciousness you were ordained to be. The splicing made you *stronger*."

Stronger. Yes, he did feel stronger, and not just because he had arrived in the Afterlife, assumed supernatural powers, and reclaimed Vicki. He understood what the angel was saying. There was something special about the combination, this welding of the younger Michael who had lost Max and Vicki to the later version of him that had been traumatized by Ridge Raymore and the creature on the townhouse stairs.

"But doesn't that mean ..." He didn't feel dualistic, but something still bothered him about the notion that he was the product of two realities unnaturally joined. "In some sense, am I not ... not the 'real' me?"

"On the contrary. Dan Hendrick does not know all truths. No mortal can. He is correct that earthly lives manifest in an infinite variety of possibilities. But he knows nothing of what takes place beyond.

"Only *one* soul crosses over in death. The true soul, the one closest to Grace. For most, this soul is one continuous strand of reality. In you, it is the joining of two strands. And thus, by the Enemy's own rashness, he has forged the very thing he sought to destroy."

The angel's revelation was comforting. But t its implication, that he personally held some profound significance worthy of interference by Cosmic Evil, shook Michael to the core.

"But ... why would this *Enemy* care so much about *me*?"

"He sees your destiny. He fears it."

"*What* destiny?"

Desedaraya took on the aura of a clarion. "At the appointed hour, you shall personally take up arms in this conflict, You will be set a task that you alone can perform, the you whose life created this Lauria. That is why you have been bound *now*."

As the import of her words sank in, Michael began to feel weak in his stomach. Each time he thought he had the world calibrated it seemed to get larger and more complicated.

"What kind of task?"

"We have revealed all that can be known."

It was exasperating. Michael was beginning to feel the same kind of frustration as he had felt at first with Charlie.

"Wouldn't it be easier for me to prepare if I knew what was going on?" he protested, with no real hope of prevailing. "Wouldn't it make it easier for me to do things right?"

"Ever has it been so. But in some things, easier is not *better*."

A look of forlorn helplessness spread across Michael's face. Desedaraya became sympathetic, turning to him a comforting gaze.

"Despair not. Your blindness to the future and powerlessness against the past are blessings. For without them, what would your choices mean?"

He heard her words, understood what they meant, but Michael was shaking his head slowly. It was just too much, too fast.

"Be at peace." The angel's voice soothed him in a way that transcended its melodious tone. She laid a hand gently on his shoulder, and it was like a shot of morphine. He was instantaneously serene. His thoughts clarified. He began, *just began*, to see.

And now, to his amazement, he found that he was able to face her, to absorb her glory, to endure her radiance without shying away. He felt like a flower opening in the sun.

And suddenly he possessed the courage to voice the question he had been too afraid to ask.

"Charlie said that you told him there could be no salvation for me," he said calmly. "Is it true? And if it is … what does that mean?"

"Do you *feel* saved?"

Michael thought for a moment, and then he nodded. "Yes."

The angel's eyes glowed brightly. "Follow your heart, young one. You have much to discover. Your love has waited patiently and faithfully: be with her. There will be time for the two of you before you are called."

"How *much* time?"

"Enough."

A thousand questions flooded his brain. He would waste no effort in pressing the angel with questions she had already deflected. But it occurred to him that there were other matters she might be willing to clarify, and the possibility made it worth asking. He had the feeling it might be a very long time before he would have another chance.

"What about Max? Will I ever see him again?"

"Your brother is in your future."

Michael absorbed this with encouragement. It was *something*, something tangible in all of this to hold on to.

"One more thing, if it's not too much. The Nivulum, as Charlie called it, the one that flew me here – why wasn't there just a light at the end of a tunnel like everyone else? Why did a Nivulum carry me?"

In her reply, Michael learned something that seemed to him profoundly significant. He learned that angels smile.

"That one too lies in your future." Desedaraya glowed. "He bears you a special affection. He simply desired to ease your way."

Somewhere in him frustration lingered, but it was fading. The angel had opened his eyes sufficiently to see the wisdom in her advice. He had Vicki again. He had eternal life. He had a huge world of his own to explore, and an infinity of worlds beyond.

"Undreamt horizons await you," Desedaraya affirmed as though reading his thoughts. "Seek them without fear."

"All right." He nodded and managed a little smile. "Thank you."

"Farewell, Michael Chandler. Be blessed. May you know happiness and love."

The angel shimmered. There was a flash of light, and she was gone.

About the Author

Once upon a time, Mark Tucker walked away from a perfectly good job in a Seattle law office and moved to a picturesque beach town to pursue his dreams. In addition to writing fantasy and science fiction with encouraging success, he is a musician, songwriter, audio producer, and developer of computer games. He fancies himself a low-grade amateur scientist, hunting fossils and keeping current with developments in physics and cosmology, and counts among his dearest moments the first time he found the Andromeda galaxy with his telescope. He enjoys travel, the less scripted the better, and collects representative coffee mugs and Hard Rock Café City Tee shirts from the locales he visits. A collection of African and Polynesian tribal masks adorns the walls of his den. He revels in the beauty and temperament of the Hawaiian islands, and plans to settle on Kauai when circumstances permit.

Mark considers The Lord of the Rings the most satisfying fiction he has ever read, and holds writers Philip K. Dick and Jonathan Carroll in awe.

Mark's incurable vices include a fanatical devotion to the band Genesis (to the point of sitting happily for two hours in shorts and sandals in the pouring rain for their reunion concert at the Hollywood Bowl) and an almost religious reverence for Batman. There may be therapy for this, but for Mark it is much too late.

THE BEYOND TRILOGY

The Just Beyond
The Far Beyond
Beyond All Else

Made in the USA
Charleston, SC
07 January 2014